BECCA DIVES IN

BECCA DIVES IN

KATE BREITFELLER

BRETHBOOKS
PUBLISHING

ISBN: 978-1-73530-48-2-3

EBOOK ISBN: 978-1-7353048-3-0

For my "Owens"

1

Becca sat in the shade, feet outstretched on the wooden steps of her cottage, petting the tabby cat that had taken up residence under her stairs. She had coaxed the feral cat indoors a few times with treats, but it had only been in the last few weeks that the cat had deigned to allow Becca to stroke its back. She lightly ran her nails down the cat's spine and was rewarded with a nudge of approval. Becca smiled as the cat bumped into her again with its head. She was slightly concerned that all the progress they had made would be lost while she was away. Amelia had promised to stop by and continue to give the cat treats, so Becca hoped the stray would stick around.

Almost as if conjured by Becca's thoughts, Amelia appeared around the corner of the little fence, swatting the wide sleeves of her caftan where they caught on the thorns of the bougainvillea that grew there.

"Don't be surprised if you see some serious pruning when you get home," Amelia said, glaring at the overgrown plant. Becca smiled, Amelia might grouse about the state of Becca's tiny front yard, but she loved the chance to play gardener. Other than a few pots of herbs on deck, Amelia couldn't indulge herself with a garden on her boat.

The previous spring Becca had panicked when she was notified the boat she lived on was to be sold and the new owners no longer needed someone to live aboard. It was sad to leave the boat behind, but all the months of living rent free in Key West, along with her savings, had allowed her to put away enough money to buy the tiny cottage.

Her new house and life were totally different from her previous suburban lifestyle, where bigger was always better. The cottage's compact size suited her perfectly. She adored the large windows that filled the front rooms with light, and gave a view of the wild tropical yard. Set apart from the prime tourist area, the street was peaceful; only the occasional tourist buzzing by on a scooter interrupted the quiet. Her favorite feature though was that it had the space she needed to pursue her art career. She loved that she could leave her easel up and paint whenever she wanted.

Much to Amelia's dismay, Becca's artistic bent didn't extend as far as landscape design. She was happy letting the native plants have their way, only whacking them back when necessary. However, Amelia had discovered a dormant passion and dove enthusiastically into fixing up Becca's tiny yard. One morning, Amelia appeared with a young man, various power equipment in tow, and began issuing orders, gesticulating energetically at one clump of green after another. Alerted by the noise, Becca stood on the covered porch with a bewildered smile. When Amelia noticed her, she simply flashed a mischievous look and turned back to continue her instructions.

Becca smiled fondly, remembering. If it made her friend happy, Becca didn't mind letting Amelia have her way with the yard. Watching her fuss at the bright pink flowers that had finally relinquished Amelia's sleeve, Becca felt a rush of affection. She didn't know what she would have done this past year without the older woman.

"I'm serious." Amelia continued up the path, wagging her finger at Becca. "You have to stay on top of all the green stuff here in the tropics, or it will be on top of you!" Startled by the interloper, the cat pulled back and hid under the stairs, glaring malevolently at Amelia. "Hey, Furball. I've got something here for ya." Amelia rooted in her macramé tote until she pulled out a Ziploc bag.

Becca recoiled as Amelia opened it, and the pungent smell wafted over the porch."Ugh! Are those sardines?"

Amelia blinked at Becca as she pulled one out and tossed it in the cat's direction. The tabby snatched the fish off the ground and retreated further down the porch to enjoy her treat.

"Of course! You said you wanted me to babysit your flea-ridden wild animal while you were away. How's it going to work if I can't train her to like me?" Amelia's tone made it obvious she thought Becca was insane to be concerned about a feral cat, but since moving in, the cat had become a type of pet. "Did you ever name it?"

"No. She's not really mine."

Amelia rolled her eyes and muttered under her breath.

"I heard that! Your hippie heart should love that I'm not taking ownership of another living thing." Becca did her best not to smile when Amelia hmphed.

"Well, I'm calling it, Furball."

Becca couldn't stop the laugh that slipped out and Amelia's lips twitched as well. "I'm sure the two of you will be best friends when I get home next month."

A month! It was a long time to be away... together. Something of her nervousness must have showed up on her face.

"Go on. Spit it out. What's bothering you?"

One of the things Becca loved most about Amelia was her frank honesty. Amelia didn't bother with the social niceties of small talk or beating around the bush. She may not have a filter, but Amelia was the least judgmental person on the planet. Becca could be honest about her misgivings without worry that she would be the target of gossip. Until she had moved to Key West, Becca had been used to a very different type of friendship. Amelia was the exact opposite of the women back in Sun Coast.

"It's nothing specific. It's just that it's a really long time to travel with someone. Things have been great between us... when Harry is in town... but we've never spent this much time together before!"

Amelia cocked her head to the side, considering. "It *is* a long time, and you can't spend the entire trip in bed."

Becca blushed and let out a frustrated breath. "You aren't helping."

"What do you want me to say? That this is the happily ever after you've been waiting for? That everything is destined to be perfect from now on? Suddenly your troubles disappear and... wait, is that a song?" Amelia frowned, hummed a few bars, and shook her head. "Nope, that's not it."

Becca bristled. "I'm not looking for a 'happily ever after'!"

"Hmm, that's good, because they don't exist."

Becca scowled at her. "Harry and I are far from knowing what the future holds for us. He's never brought it up."

Amelia peered at her closely. "Is that what's bothering you? You want a commitment? Are you waiting for him to decide for you?"

"No! I'm still trying to build a life for myself here, a career..." Becca stopped. It was true. She *did* want to succeed on her own, prove to herself that she was capable of it.

But, oh, wouldn't it be nice to trust that he would always be there beside me...

Becca cleared her throat. "What Harry and I have right now is perfect." She glared when Amelia raised her hand in objection. "Fine! Not *perfect,* but I'm happy the way things are between us.

It's just... I... I'm worried about what might happen over the next month!"

On paper, the trip sounded cinema-worthy romantic—a three-week cruise on her handsome boyfriend's yacht, stopping to check his island properties before spending a week at his private island resort—so why was she so nervous?

Amelia sat on the step and took Becca's hand. "What exactly do you imagine is going to happen that will be so significant? You're going to discover that Harry gets grouchy when he doesn't get enough sleep? You won't like how he drops his clothes on the floor? That he snores? I'd think by now you'd know all that."

Becca shrugged. She wished it was just the mundane relationship things that worried her. She and Harry had both kept secrets from each other, and that had contributed to a rocky start. She was pretty sure he hadn't even liked her when they first met and had simply assumed she was a flaky ex-suburban housewife who ran away to paradise.

"Don't create problems because you think it's too good to be true. Trust me, life has a way of creating its own ups and downs. You don't need to borrow trouble before it arrives. You have to enjoy all the parts. I'd think better than most, you'd know life rarely turns out how you plan. Stop planning, just let go. What are you afraid of? What is the worst that could happen?"

Becca knew Amelia was right. Her life had completely changed and she was happy... but she couldn't help that she worried about Harry. He was so different from anyone she had ever known, and she was concerned that he would get bored of her. Which in turn made her angry at herself for caring! The whole point in uprooting her life and moving to Key West had been to take control of her life and not to let other people's opinions dictate who she was or how she behaved!

They'd been seeing each other for most of the year, and at times it was so intense it took her breath away—but then he would leave on a 'business trip'—and regardless of how she phrased the question, he never wanted to give her details. In a book, mysterious handsome jet-setting men who disappear from time to time are exciting. In reality, it was far from it. It was too reminiscent of her ex-husband. Jake had refused to discuss what he did all day, as if she was too naïve to understand. That had ended with a mistress and divorce. She knew Harry wasn't seeing other women. Her body tingled as she remembered how enthusiastically he greeted her after he'd been away—but it still bothered her.

Amelia's voice interrupted her thoughts. "Look, you've worked so hard all year. Between the hours at the gallery and working on your own art, you haven't stopped in months! You deserve a break. Go. Relax! You've got nothing to worry about."

Amelia jerked her head toward the cat, who had crept closer, clearly hoping for another sardine. "I'll take care of Furball and your house."

Becca shook herself. She was overthinking; everything would be fine. "Thanks, I'm being silly. I mean, how often will I get the chance to sail around the Caribbean on a private yacht!"

2

Becca lifted her hand against the sun's glare and set her coffee cup down. The light breeze off the water, as the ship slipped through the surf, blew the curls off of her face. It was already hot on deck, and though the steaming beverage wouldn't help the situation, she would be useless without her coffee. The doors to the main cabin shushed open behind her, and Becca smiled even before the hand caressed her shoulder. She tipped her head and looked up into Harry's green eyes. "You're up early," she joked.

Harry leaned down and pressed a lingering kiss against her lips before taking his own seat at the breakfast table. He reached for the basket of croissants. "This *is* early for most people," Harry grumbled, as he slathered the bread with butter and took a large bite. Becca pressed her lips together and lifted her coffee mug to hide the smile threatening to break out. One thing she had learned these last couple of weeks was, though Harry might look like an Armani model when he rolled out of bed, he was extremely grouchy before two cups of coffee. Harry downed one cup of coffee quickly and promptly began on his second. The boat turned, and Becca relaxed back in her chair now that the sun was no longer doing its best to blind her.

"Thanks, Tasha," Becca said, as the young steward replaced the coffee with a fresh carafe and exited quietly to the interior of the boat. For the billionth time, Becca marveled at her surroundings. Amelia had been right. Not only had she needed a vacation, she had needed this time alone with Harry. The last three weeks had been amazing as they stopped off at Harry's properties to ensure each was in perfect order. She had seen a different side of him. Business Harry was impressive. He took incredible care of his projects, giving attention to every detail. What had she been so worried about?

At the second property they visited, a building contractor had met them, and when Harry suggested she walk down to the water while they talked, Becca asked if she could stay. She held her breath, waiting for the answer. Would he dismiss her? He looked puzzled, but shrugged his agreement. While Harry and the contractor discussed plans to upgrade the property for hurricane season and Harry's plan for the construction of another home on the island, Becca listened fascinated. She hadn't been aware just how big Harry's vision was.

As they walked to the tender that would carry them back to the yacht, Harry apologized. "This must be really boring for you, sorry. If you would rather stay on board next time, it's okay."

"It wasn't boring at all! You forget, you may have grown up in the Caribbean, but for me the idea that people rent islands for a vacation is brand new."

He had searched her face, and then visibly relaxed. "You're just saying that."

"I'm serious. You've never talked about what you do on your trips. I've asked you, but you always change the subject."

"You know what I do." He seemed taken aback. "I've told you all about Turtle Bay and my other properties."

"True," Becca said, slipping off her sandals to wade into the water where the tender was tied up. "But not specifics about what you do when you are gone. Who you are meeting, problems you are having... that kind of thing." She tossed her sandals into the small boat and moved to climb in, but Harry caught her hand and turned her to face him.

"Why would you want to hear about that?" He seemed genuinely confused.

Becca squirmed, and she considered making a joke, but she was tired of waiting for Harry to read her mind. She took a deep breath and said, "I want to learn everything about you. Everything. The boring, the mundane... *everything*."

Harry stared at her intently. "You mean that, don't you?" He took her face in both his hands and gently kissed her. "You are extraordinary."

It was Becca's turn to look confused. "Because I asked what you do at work? That's pretty basic relationship 101 stuff." She chuckled, but Harry's expression remained serious, his thumbs tracing her cheekbones.

"No, because you are truly interested. No one has ever cared about what I actually *do* or how my day was, beyond the most superficial. In most cases, they don't wait for the answer before asking if I got us on the VIP list for some club or pitching some new business they want me to consider."

"You are a lot more than what your money can give people, Harry."

Instead of answering, he had stared at her with uncomfortable intensity for another moment before helping her into the tender. She worried she had said too much, but there was a definite shift between them after that. At every stop, Harry included her, and he began to open up more with stories about his past.

SHE FELT FOOLISH WHEN SHE REMEMBERED HOW SHE HAD assumed he was keeping things from her. He wasn't being mysterious; it just hadn't occurred to him that she was interested! Becca's eyes took in the crystalline blue water around them before sliding over to look at the handsome man next to her. She sighed happily. Wasn't this the exact dream she had that night a year ago when she had walked away from her cruise ship?

"Becca?" Harry's voice startled her out of her reverie.

"Sorry, I was a million miles away. What did you say?"

Harry took another sip before answering. "I was just wondering how your latest series is coming along? You get up so early every morning; I know you must be excited about it. I'd like to think there is a *little* incentive to stay in bed." He waggled his eyebrows, and Becca laughed.

"Well, it's kinda hard to do a series of sunrise paintings if you don't actually witness them," she said.

Harry chuckled. The second cup of coffee was obviously doing its job. "Very true. So, *did* you have a good morning?"

It had only been this past year that Becca had tried to make a living as an artist. The support and praise Harry had shown for her work overwhelmed her a bit. This was the first time in her life she had experienced it from someone she cared about. It still blew her mind when she thought about the fact that, not only had she actually had a real art show, but that people wanted to purchase her work. After the first positive reception, she had taken some of the feedback and begun working in different mediums. Watercolors felt too intransigent for the vibrant land-scapes she was trying to capture, but she was decades out of practice with oil. She had just hit her stride when she agreed to accompany Harry on the cruise.

"How did your work turn out?"

"Pretty good. It was getting a little windy, so I packed up before some of my hair became a permanent part of the texture." She brushed back a loose curl that had come free from her bun. "Occupational hazard," she said wryly.

"I'm sorry. The conditions aren't optimal for what you are trying to do, but hopefully, while we are at Turtle Bay for the week, you'll feel more settled."

"I'm sure it will be perfect!" Becca was excited to see Harry's resort. It had been getting ready to open when they first met and was a large part of why, for many months, they weren't able to spend much time together. In truth, it may have been for the best. After being kidnapped and nearly murdered, Becca had been forced to pretend to Harry and the police that Katie, the woman who had attacked her, was still alive and on the run. It was the only way to keep Becca's family safe from the Olivera cartel run by Katie's father.

Becca's head ached just remembering those tense months last winter. It was just as well Harry had been so preoccupied with the various problems that arose when his resort opened. It would have been difficult to maintain her silence about what had really happened if she were with him every day. Becca frowned. That sounded terrible. She wasn't lying to him... exactly.

Harry's hand reached out and brushed her cheek. "Hey," he asked, "that's a weird look. You okay?"

She smiled into his eyes and reached up to cup his hand. "I'm fine. I was just thinking these weeks together have been some of the happiest of my life."

Harry's eyes darkened. He leaned closer, and his lips moved against hers as he spoke. "Me, too." Becca closed her eyes, anticipating the kiss, but the doors behind her shushed open again, and she sprang back, flushing. Too embarrassed to look up, she pretended to be absorbed in her coffee cup while the Captain and Harry discussed their entry into the Bahamas. She had gotten to know Grace a little over the last few weeks, but she still wasn't comfortable. She got the distinct impression Grace disapproved of her, or at least of her being on the ship. However, Harry and Grace's conversation caught Becca's interest enough that she forgot her embarrassment at making out over the break-fast table.

"We don't all go ashore for customs?" Becca had never sailed into the Bahamas and had just assumed it was like an airport.

"No," Grace explained. "We'll drop anchor, and put up our quarantine flag off Congo Town. Then, as the Captain, I'll go ashore with all the paperwork. A customs official will come back with me, give the boat a quick once over, and double check who's on board. After that, we are free to sail around the Bahamas."

"They just do a 'once over'? That seems pretty trusting. Amelia said you could..." Becca trailed off as Harry shot her a look. "I just meant, isn't that the cliché? Little boats going between islands, secret compartments..." Becca joked. She hoped Grace hadn't caught her slip-up about Amelia.

Becca still found it hard to reconcile her warm-hearted friend with the sensational stories Amelia had told Becca about her years as a smuggler. It had shocked Becca when she first learned about the smuggling culture in the Keys, and how widely the community accepted it. Amelia told Becca that the sudden influx of drugs and guns in the 1980s had changed the traditional Caribbean pastime. "It's not the same as trying to cheat the government," Amelia had explained. Even though Amelia's family had a long tradition of trading contraband, after her husband had died, Amelia left the business.

"Most people at sea aren't criminals." Grace's voice was distinctly frosty.

Ouch! I must have struck a nerve.

Grace cast a quick glance at Harry. She smoothed her face into a polite smile, but her chin was tilted up in defiance. "If they catch you with contraband on your boat, not only is the boat seized, but everyone on board goes to jail. It doesn't matter if only one person is responsible, everyone pays the price. It's a serious offense, and no one reputable would risk their license for it. I certainly wouldn't."

"Of course not," Becca murmured. She looked up through her lashes at Harry and saw that he was trying not to laugh at Grace's offended tone. His lips twitched giving him away.

"Just a question, Grace. She wasn't challenging your integrity," he said and then smiled widely. "Boat life in the islands isn't something everyone is familiar with—and the fact is, people *do* sometimes try to bring things ashore that they shouldn't."

Grace nodded curtly. "At any rate, we are getting ready to drop anchor in a few minutes. After lunch, we will complete the trip to Andros Island and keep our customs appointment. If it is all right with you, we will stay at anchor until morning before continuing on to Turtle Bay."

After the Captain left them alone again, Becca asked, "Is it just me, or did Grace take that whole smuggling thing a little too personally?"

Harry shrugged. "She is very serious about her job."

Becca rolled her eyes. "It's not like I accused *her* of smuggling."

Harry shifted in his seat and fiddled with the silverware. "She's not totally paranoid…"

"What does that mean?"

Harry leaned back, and thrust his hands through his hair before leaning forward again. "It's not a big deal… seriously. A couple of times… I had guests on board," he grimaced, "who were using drugs, and had a stash. Luckily, I found out before we reached land, but ever since then Grace has been a little… skeptical… of my guests."

"Hmm, I suppose if there were a parade of women coming on board with drugs, I'd be suspicious, too."

"Hardly a *parade*. There were two... no, three times."

Becca noticed he didn't correct her assumption that the guests had been female. She kept her smile light, but she felt a pang at the idea of him sharing the cabin with someone else. It was ridiculous. She wasn't naïve. Of course, there had been women before her—she'd been married herself—but there was no ignoring the tight knot that was taking up residence in the pit of her stomach, and she hated it.

"How many bimbos make up a parade?" *Damn!* She hadn't meant to say that out loud.

Harry tilted his head sideways; a grin stretched across his face. "Jealous?"

"Pfft! I'm sure you've had tons of women on this yacht. It would be pointless to be jealous." The words spilled out before she could stop them. "I mean, isn't that what single men with yachts do? Have lots of girls and parties? Did you have bubble parties? On TV, the guy with all the girls on the yacht always has a bubble party. DJs..."

Shut up, Becca! You are making this worse!

Harry rubbed his chin thoughtfully. "Now that you mention it..." Becca smacked his arm. "Just kidding. I'm not saying I've never had a party here, but I've never brought someone on a trip like this."

"Good."

Harry chuckled when Becca flushed.

"Whatever."

Harry laughed harder and leaned over to kiss her again. "You are so adorable when you turn red like that."

Becca scowled. "Ha, ha."

Harry took her hand in his. "Look, I don't have a spotless past. I've done things that I regret, bad things... If I had the chance, I would do them over—but I'm a different person now. You've shown me things don't have to stay the same—that my past doesn't have to define how I move forward. You started over, took a leap of faith, and thank god you did." He gave her a soft smile. "Mine may not be as drastic as walking away from a cruise ship in a strange city, but you and I—it's a new start for me. I want to keep being this better person that I feel like I am when I'm with you."

Becca swallowed hard. A crazy idea began to take shape. "Let's do it together."

"Do what?"

"Take a leap together. Go up to the top of the boat and jump in. C'mon it will be fun, not to mention symbolic."

Harry's tan face paled into an unhealthy green. "Nuh uh. No way. I am terrified of heights."

"Oh, I forgot. What if you close your eyes? I'll hold your hand," she teased.

Harry shook his head emphatically. "I want to jump with you, I really do. But…"

"It's okay. I get it. If you asked me to hold a snake…" Becca shuddered theatrically.

"You should still do it." He grinned. "I'm not quite as fearless as you yet, but I can be in the water below waiting to catch you."

"That works, too," she said, pressing a kiss against his lips.

When the boat had stopped and was fully anchored, they checked with the captain and verified that the water was safe. Becca hurried to change into her bikini bubbling with excitement. She climbed to the top of the second deck and looked down. The distance to the water below was farther than she had expected, and she hesitated with her foot up near the rail. Harry, floating below her on one of the inner tubes, waved and called out, "Do you want me to count to three?"

Becca laughed and twisted her hair up into a tight ponytail. She was going to do it. Part of her wished Harry was standing next to her, ready to jump, but then she heard Amelia's voice in her head. *'What are you afraid of? Just jump in.'*

"Back up. You're in the splash zone."

"Nope, I might have to rescue you. Ready?"

Becca stepped up onto the flat rail. "Three… two…" She didn't wait for "one." She raised her arms above her head and dove headfirst into the water below.

3

After dinner, Becca and Harry lingered on deck reclining on the sunbed and looking up at the stars. Becca, relaxed from the tangy rum drinks they had been served, said, "Tell me something I don't know about you?"

"Like what?"

"Anything." She shrugged. But there *was* one subject Becca was curious about, and Harry never spoke of it. "Tell me about your mom."

Every time she had probed on the subject, he had shut her down, turning the conversation back to her own odd family dynamic. Becca assumed there were terrible memories relating to his mother, as there were about so much of his childhood. But it troubled her that it was a blank spot between them. Over the last three weeks, they had shared so much about their histories. Becca had been open with him about her difficult childhood and her parents' death. While he had been more vulnerable than in the past, Harry was unwilling to share the subject of his mother with her. It may not have been justified, but it hurt that he kept parts of himself closed off.

Harry stilled next to her, and Becca instantly regretted asking. She was pushing too hard, too fast.

"I don't talk about her." He abruptly stood, paced to the railing, then turned to drop into one of the thickly cushioned sofas on deck. He leaned forward, clasping his hands on his knees. Unable to sit still in the long silence, Becca stood and walked to the railing.

"I've never told you how my mother died." She could barely make out his low words.

Becca tightened her hands on the railing before turning around slowly to face Harry. "No," she said simply, afraid to scare him off. The dim light made it hard to see his expression.

"My father killed her."

Becca inhaled sharply. "Do you mean that figuratively or literally?" She had heard stories about Harry's father, not just from Amelia but also from the police in Key West. Becca wasn't sure what was true and how much was rumor.

Harry scrubbed a hand down over his face. "He didn't shoot her or stab her, if that's what you mean. But he was just as responsible as if he had." Harry groaned and tipped his head back. As he stared up at the stars, he absently fingered the coin he wore around his neck.

Becca frowned at the telling movement. The coin was a talisman of a sort for him, a reminder of how he had been betrayed by a friend. She pushed away from the railing and sank onto the sofa next to him. He was attempting to escape behind his walls. What would their future look like if he never let her in?

"I shouldn't tell you this," Harry said on an exhale.

"I'm glad you are."

Harry's hand rose to cradle her cheek. "My life has had some ugly bits."

"Whose hasn't?" His hand fell away, and she instantly

regretted her flip answer. "From what you've told me, you've had some unique challenges." Harry raised an eyebrow. "Okay, that's not the best way of phrasing it, but you get what I mean." She let out an exasperated puff of air. "If you tell me, I'll stop babbling."

Harry chuckled and pressed his lips against hers. "But you're cute when you babble." Harry's hand came up again, this time to draw her closer.

Oh, no! He is not distracting me that easily!

She pressed a finger against his lips just before they closed on hers again. "I want to hear about the ugly bits."

Harry's eyes flicked to her lips and his arm came around her waist to pull her closer. "Later," he breathed, sliding his hands down. Becca's body was more than willing to agree, but her heart was telling her that this was an important moment.

"Harry." Something in her voice must have communicated that to him because his hands stilled. "Please." For a moment, she worried he was angry, but he released her and sat back, blowing out a long stream of air.

"Fine, but this would be more fun if you were naked."

Becca made a face, but took his hand and squeezed. She knew this wasn't easy for him.

Harry let out another heavy sigh. "My parents divorced when I was five. I have no idea what the issues really were... I only had my father's side of the story."

"You never asked your mother?"

"I never saw her again. She died two years later."

"You never saw her—not once? Over two years?" Becca was shocked. Harry shrugged one shoulder and closed his eyes, but not before she saw the pain in them.

"No. My father had custody and moved us to the Caribbean right away. He told me she was an addict... that she had chosen drugs and alcohol over me." His voice had pitched down, and

Becca held still, barely breathing, so that she wouldn't miss a word.

What kind of parent says that to their child?

"I didn't find out until much later, when I eventually met my grandfather, that it had only been partially true. My mother was an addict, but according to her father, it was losing me that pushed her over the edge. My grandfather claimed my father must have either bribed or blackmailed every judge within a hundred miles. There was nothing, despite their money, that she or her family could do. My grandfather said losing me killed her."

That explained the comment about his father killing her, but Becca was still puzzled. Harry had never mentioned any extended family. "How did you meet your grandfather?"

"On my twenty-first birthday, I received a certified letter from an attorney about a trust that had been left to me from my mother. I was completely blind-sided. Her family had never contacted me before. I tried to find information about them a few times over the years as more information became digitized, but never found much. Turned out they were right there. I had an entire family in England... the whole time I was alone at school... they were in the same country."

"Did you ever try to contact them after that?"

"Why? They obviously had the ability to find me. The letter reached me with no trouble, and they had never bothered to even reach out. Why should I want to know them?" His voice was bitter.

It hurt her heart to envision what a young Harry must have chalked up as another desertion. Had there ever been an adult that *didn't* let him down? "But you met your grandfather. What happened?"

Harry pulled back, stood, and strode away to look out over the water. "I didn't for a while. I was angry... and young. My attitude was very much 'they didn't want me' so..." He made a rude gesture, and she didn't blame him. "But," he paused.

Becca cocked her head to the side. "You can't stop there!"

"The next part isn't so nice."

"I haven't heard anything nice yet," she pointed out.

Harry turned away from her, and for a moment the only sound was the water lapping at the hull. But she was determined to wait him out.

"I've never pretended that I was a saint. Before I was aware of the extent of what my father had done in Key West, and the treasure salvage dive in Cuba..."

Becca held her breath. Was he going to admit he was the criminal people had repeatedly warned her about?

"I grew up watching my father look for ways to make money. The next deal to be made. He never held on to it. It flowed out of his hands just as fast as it came in. Until I was older, I didn't realize quite how different our life was from everyone else. My father was charming, and everyone loved him. At least that's what I believed before he sent me away."

Harry had strayed off course. Becca didn't *mean* to interrupt him but... "Your grandfather?"

One side of Harry's mouth tipped up in a grin. "So impatient. Okay, but remember you asked for it. Our lives have not been the same. Things I've had to do in business... *people* I've had to work with in order to get things done... deals... I haven't always been strictly on the right side of..."

"Legal?" Becca asked. She had always suspected it, but they had never openly discussed it. "Were you a smuggler? Like Amelia?"

"That's not what I'm talking about."

That's not a denial. Becca let it go. She was dying to hear his story. She'd delve into Harry's not-so-legal business practices later. The old Becca would have been astonished by that position, but—she trusted him. Whatever it was, it couldn't be that bad.

She gave him an encouraging smile. "Just tell me. It won't change anything."

Harry's eyes hooded, and he set his jaw. "You say that, but…"

Becca rose swiftly, joined him at the railing, and framed his face with her hands. "Unless you tell me you've murdered someone, or like to torture small animals, nothing will change," she joked, hoping to lessen his tense stance.

Harry's green eyes searched hers. He must have found what he was looking for because he relaxed, and his jaw rested heavily against her hands. Harry reached up and covered her hands before pulling them down gently, still caught in his. "I hope to god that's true."

"It is." It *was* true, and even though she wasn't ready to say anything yet… she realized that she had fallen in love with him. She struggled to imagine something that would impact how she felt.

"Okay." Harry's chin touched his chest before he took a deep breath and met her eyes. "In school, I was an outcast. No family to speak of. No one visited and there was nowhere to visit over the breaks. I certainly never had the polo ponies or pedigree that the rest of them had." His mouth curved into a devilish smile. "But I had something they didn't. I had a knack for making money and wasn't afraid of taking risks." His eyes took on a faraway look, lost in a memory. "I didn't have to worry about being sent down or daddy's disapproval. I always knew I would have to make my own way… so I did."

"What does that mean?"

"I started a gambling ring at school." There was no denying the pride in his voice. "I started small… just dice, but then I added card games, which led to betting on horses, etc. It's amazing really, how quick those lads were to jump at the chance. I had one good friend with all the right connections. He introduced me around, and it took off from there. They were happier if one of their 'own' was involved." His face darkened a little. "Except at University the bets got bigger, and I had difficulty handling it all on my own so I... outsourced the financing."

"You got an investor?" Becca was thoroughly confused.

Harry laughed. "A bookie. I found a bookie who agreed to bankroll me. And it worked really well for a while. Just before graduation, there were some," he paused, "unexpected losses."

"I'm having a hard time picturing you as some kind of inveterate gambler." Becca thought of how controlled Harry was, how methodical he was about his businesses.

"I wasn't a huge gambler to be honest." His lips flattened. "I was happy to handle the bets and take the money off those who had more family money than brains, but there was this *sure thing*." Harry's eyes grew dark. "I was an idiot, and I trusted someone. The wrong person, as it turned out. I was getting ready to graduate and was at loose ends. Adulthood loomed in front of me, and I had no idea what I was going to do. Someone I was close to owned a horse. A *guaranteed win* her father told me.

"It would be, 'just the windfall that would help a young couple get started,' he said." Harry grunted in disgust. "I should have known better... trusted my instincts. Her father had never acknowledged me up to that point. I was a mongrel who would never be good enough for his blue-blooded daughter. Suddenly he's cutting me in, sharing his inside information." He grimaced. "For lack of a better phrase, 'the fix was in' for a pretty important race. He dangled his daughter and his acceptance of me, us as a couple, in front of my face. It was everything I had ever wanted. I would be part of a family, in love, happy... her father was finally seeing me as worth his precious Sarah, so I ignored the red flags." He laughed, but there was no humor in it. "So, I borrowed... a lot... from people I knew better than to borrow from." The skin stretched taught across his cheekbones. "More than I could ever cover."

Becca's heart twisted at what she suspected was coming.

"The horse came up lame, or so they said. Pulled up about fifteen seconds into the race. The fix was in all right. Sarah's father renovated his stables after that." Harry dropped her hands and leaned against the chrome railing. "There was no way to pay my debt." His profile tightened. "Everything you see in movies? It's actually a lot worse. These were not people you failed to pay back. I was done for."

Becca's lips parted in dismay, but Harry gave her a sweet smile. "It's okay. We're standing here after all. It has a happy ending."

Becca shook herself. She was being silly. He was right. The story he was telling had taken place almost twenty years before.

"The friend I mentioned—the one who 'introduced me to all the right people'—I reached out to him hoping to borrow just enough to buy me some time, but he had a better solution. He put me on his family's plane that night and flew me to the Bahamas to hide at their resort until I figured out what to do. At the time, I had every intention of staying in the UK. It was home at that point, so I was going to need to pay back the money, somehow."

He looked down at Becca with a smile. "But back to where we started—I didn't have any options. I had no idea where my father was and no one else to turn to, so I reached out to the barrister about my trust fund and agreed to certain conditions. I had to agree to a meeting with my grandfather. He paid to fly me back, and we met at a restaurant."

Becca doubted there was going to be a pleasant conclusion to this story. Harry had never mentioned having a family, and the tone in his voice confirmed her suspicions.

He leaned an elbow onto the railing and absently toyed with her fingers, lost in thought. "I'm not sure what I was expecting, really. Maybe a part of me hoped he would greet me like a long-lost grandson, but…" He shrugged again. "The first thing he said to me was 'you look just like your father,' and that was who he saw when he spoke to me."

His knuckles whitened on the rail. "He told me just how awful my father was—as if I wasn't well aware—and how losing me broke my mother."

Becca stroked a hand down his arm. "That must have been awful."

His lip curled. "And then the meal was over. I realized he hadn't asked me anything about myself or what I was doing. He had no interest." Harry shifted, and for a moment she thought he would stop. "It was nothing new. I've pretty much always been on my own. When my father sent me to school, it devastated me. Cut off from everything. Dan, who always seemed more like a father, no longer answered phone calls or returned letters. I was completely left in the dark."

Harry took a deep breath, and she slipped her fingers into his. This was difficult for him, and she didn't want to say the wrong thing.

"I thought that, just like my father, Dan had forgotten about me, that I must have done something, even though I knew I hadn't… I tried to imagine why…" His voice caught, and Becca's heart clenched imagining the pain a young boy would have endured not knowing why he had been exiled, with no one to depend upon.

Harry cleared his throat to cover the emotion. "Now, of course, I understand why Dan acted the way he did. I've come to terms with it—but I'm not sure I'll ever be able to forgive him completely."

Becca nodded. She had watched the relationship improve over the last year, but there was still strain between the two men. Harry stopped, and for a minute or two they stood in silence, listening to the water.

What about your mother?

Just when her curiosity was about to explode inside of her, he continued. "My grandfather said that my mother tried to see me. But my father had taken me to the islands and wouldn't allow her any contact. He even told me she had shown up when we were living in Antigua, but my father whisked me away again and had her arrested for trespassing."

Becca was stunned. *How could a father be so cruel?*

Harry rolled his shoulders. She suspected it was a way to distance himself from the memory. His tone when he continued sounded as if he were talking about a stranger. "She drank herself to death or overdosed—I never got the complete story."

Becca's heart sank. Not just for him, but for his mother. How horrible it must have been for her, fighting her own demons while also cut off from her child.

"I'm so sorry, Harry."

He stared out at the dark expanse of water, his face impassive. "It was a long time ago. It doesn't normally bother me, but when I see how you feel about your son, I wonder what it would have been like if my mother had lived, how my life would have been different." He made a face. "Then again, she was an addict and nothing like you. Perhaps my father did me a favor." His tone made it clear he wasn't convinced. His hand tightened on her's. "I'm sorry. I shouldn't have dumped all that on you."

"No, I'm glad you did," she said hurriedly. "It explains some things."

Harry raised an eyebrow at her. "Like what?"

"I don't know, the fact that you always seem to be waiting for someone to let you down." She recalled his troubles with Dan. "Or that people only want to be with you for what you can give them."

Harry tried to pull his hand from hers, but she tightened her grip. "The first few months of our relationship, every time I didn't return a call, or if you came back into town and I was busy, you always assumed I was avoiding you or didn't want to see you." She squeezed his hand. "Trust me... I'm not going anywhere. I don't want anything from you." Harry's eyes burned into hers. She saw he was struggling to believe her. "Just you. I only want you."

Harry made a sound in his throat before pulling her roughly into his arms. His arms were tight around her, his breath harsh against her hair.

4

The resort was even more incredible in person than the pictures Harry had shown her. Turtle Bay was a tiny island, only thirty-five acres, and the resort Harry had built was the sole occupant. It was accessible only by boat, and guests were greeted at the dock by staff in golf carts and then transported to a small, one-story central building that contained the registration area. There were a few gathering rooms in the building as well, in case a larger group activity needed to be accommodated.

Twenty villa-style homes dotted the property, each outfitted with a full kitchen, bicycles, and a golf cart. Eduardo and Marta, Harry and Becca's friends from Key West, oversaw the staff, and Becca was excited to see them again. The young couple had moved with their young son to the private island, and Becca missed seeing them. They lived in the onsite staff housing, separated from the guest area by dense foliage, but still easily accessible by the paths that wound through the island.

In his quest for a semi-green resort, Harry had left most of the vegetation in place. He wanted to work with the environment rather than bend it to his plans. "I hate it when developers destroy the natural habitat just to accommodate more guests. It is pure greed."

Harry's dream was for the property to feel more like a second home than a hotel. Guests filled out extensive preference sheets, and the villas were generously stocked before they checked in. Although there were no restaurants or spas on the island, private chefs and massage therapists could be brought in. Most of Harry's clientele valued their privacy and rented the villas for weeks at a time. It was the next best thing to owning their own private island.

As the golf cart whisked them down the crushed-shell paths to Harry's personal villa, the beauty of the surroundings captivated her. Each villa had its own small pool and private beach access. You wouldn't have to see another soul unless you wanted to, she realized. It was the epitome of a private island getaway.

The next few days were as close to idyllic as Becca had ever experienced. She rose early—some habits are just too ingrained —and slipped out the French doors off their bedroom, past the plunge pool, down to the white sugar sand beyond. Before the sun was fully up, Becca had their beach to herself, and she loved the privacy to do her morning work-out. The breeze off the water kept the humidity to a tolerable level for August, and it was a relaxing way to start the day before joining Harry for coffee on the lanai.

Halfway through the week, Becca woke and stretched languorously under the soft white sheet. A smile stretched across her face. *Is this really my life right now?* Even from her prone position, she could see the cerulean blue ocean. She turned her head to look at a still-sleeping Harry. Gently, so as not to wake him, she brushed back a thick lock of black hair that had fallen across his forehead.

A rush of emotion filled her, and she allowed her hand to trace softly down across the heavy stubble on his jaw. A sudden fear spiked in her chest. She couldn't remember the last time she had been this happy, and she didn't want to lose it. She shouldn't let herself get carried away in case...

Stop it! Everything is going great! Stop overthinking.

Becca shifted irritably. What was wrong with her? Why couldn't she just accept how well things were going without imagining heartache around every turn? She was as bad as Harry!

She put a hand to her forehead. She was doing exactly what Amelia had warned her about! Her motion must have disturbed Harry because he murmured sleepily and started to move. Slowly, Becca lowered her hand and willed him to keep sleeping. *Way too much soul searching before coffee!*

Becca lifted the sheet back carefully and eased out of bed. Pulling on a pair of loose shorts and a tank top, she grabbed a bottle of water from the mini fridge next to the bed, and headed out for her morning ritual. She padded through the cool, loose sand until her toes curled into the packed sand at the water's edge. The crystal clear water was warm against her ankles, and after a few deep breaths, Becca took a several steps backward and began going through the yoga poses that made up her morning routine.

She concentrated on her air, and for those minutes, she simply existed with the sand and the waves. Her previous anxieties wafted away, and she felt at peace. *I guess Amelia's metaphysical stuff has rubbed off more than I thought.* No way I'm admitting that to her though, Becca vowed.

Becca had gone to yoga classes before when she lived in Sun Coast. It was a popular thing to say—*Oh, I just fit it in after dropping the kids in car line, but before I meet my friends for coffee. Self-care is so important!* However, practicing the forms next to the ocean, just out of bed, felt profoundly different than it had when she used to plan out the perfect Lululemon outfit and made sure her ponytail was just right. She may look rumpled this morning, but she felt more powerful.

When she finished, she unscrewed the top of the water bottle and took a drink. She was energized by the exercise and her thoughts strayed to her current painting. It was a large piece depicting the view from the door of the villa out to the sea. They were leaving in a few days, and other than some finishing touches, she wanted to complete it before they left.

She gazed wistfully at the turquoise water that expanded to the horizon. It would be hard to leave, but she loved her little house in Key West. She even missed the cat under the stairs. Back in the real world, with their competing schedules, would she and Harry be able to maintain what they had developed?

Distracted by her thoughts, she was startled when Harry's arms came around her waist, his stubble gently scratching as he nuzzled her neck. His hands crept upward as he murmured in her ear, "Come back to bed."

Becca turned in his arms and lifted her lips to his. "I'm sweaty."

His eyes darkened, and his arms tightened around her. "I don't care."

Just as Becca was about to drag him back inside the villa, the unmistakable sound of his alarm sounded from inside the open doors. She pulled her head back and grimaced.

"Your master is calling," she whispered, a little out of breath. Harry's eyes were hot, but with a quick kiss she gave him a gentle shove. "Go. You have work to do. Important people to see," she joked. "Besides, I want to work on my painting before the sun gets too fierce through the glass."

Harry pretended to scowl. "You know, I almost regret getting all that stuff."

Becca grinned and shooed him away. "No, you don't."

He smiled softly at her and tucked some of her wild curls behind her ear, making her heart turn over in her chest. "No, I don't."

How am I NOT supposed to get carried away? It's like a freaking romance novel!

Harry's phone rang from inside the room, breaking the intimacy of the moment. "Aargh! Does Eric keep an alarm for me on his phone, too? I can get myself up!"

Becca fought a smile. Harry might complain, but she was aware he had grown fond of his eager young assistant. "I guess I better hit the shower." He raised an eyebrow. "Care to join me?"

Becca laughed. "Then you really will be late for your meeting with the architects."

Harry pushed his lips out in a mock pout and started to walk away. After he took a few steps, he stopped. "I should be done by mid-afternoon. I believe the boat is scheduled to come get them by three. Do you want to meet up for a late lunch or will you still be busy?"

"I'll be ready for a break by then. Just call me when you are done."

It had taken awhile for Becca to get used to the fact that Harry was serious when he asked if she would be available. He understood how important this upcoming show was to her. She was comfortable that if she had said she wasn't available for lunch, he might have been disappointed, but he wouldn't sulk like her ex-husband Jake would have. He respected that her artwork was as important to her as his project meetings were to him.

Harry reached the doors and turned to wave. Feeling bold, Becca cast a quick look around to be sure they were alone, stripped off the tank top and shorts, and skipped into the ocean. Even across the distance, Becca heard Harry groan, "You are killing me!" She let out a carefree laugh and dove under the waves.

After a quick breakfast of fresh mango and yogurt, Becca settled with her coffee mug in front of the large painting. The sun was up, but the west-facing view prevented glare making it the perfect spot to work in the morning. Picking up her palette, Becca squeezed out the amounts she needed to blend. The water that stretched over most of the canvas required several layers of color. She had experimented over the last few days, but was satisfied that she had achieved just the right shades.

She and Harry had lingered over breakfast on their first morning in Turtle Bay, appreciating the privacy. The yacht was amazing, but Becca had been self-conscious, knowing there were always ears around. Besides Captain Grace, there were a handful of other essential employees. And then there was Eric—so eager to please but also so intimidated by his boss. He never seemed to be able to decide between hovering at inopportune times, and being completely petrified whenever Harry asked him to do something.

After breakfast, they had gone for a swim and when they returned to the villa, Becca was shocked to find a mini art studio set up in the main room. She had stood open-mouthed, while Harry gleefully pointed out all the supplies he had procured.

"Surprised?" he had asked.

"Stunned." And she had been. She had packed some supplies so she could work during their extended trip, but she hadn't wanted to presume too much by packing large canvasses.

"You said a couple of weeks ago that you wanted some larger pieces as an anchor for your next show. I got acrylics because that's what you had packed. You said that the oil wouldn't dry fast enough during this trip, right? I know you probably can't finish a whole painting in a week, but I thought you could at least make a start... Becca?" His voice was concerned. Becca's eyes, bright with unshed tears, stared at the large, blank canvas set on an easel in front of the windows and at the rows of acrylic tubes lying next to a new palette. A brand-new set of brushes in a variety of sizes covered the table. She wasn't even sure what some of them were for!

"Those are good tears, right?"

"Absolutely." She nodded. "This is the most thoughtful thing anyone has ever done for me." She couldn't believe he remembered about the acrylics!

Harry cleared his throat. "I felt bad that this was going to be in part a working vacation for me..." He tried to keep his tone light, but his boyish grin showed how pleased he was by her reaction.

BECCA BEGAN LAYING PAINT ONTO THE SEA. SHE WAS SURPRISED by how much progress she made without the daily distractions of her regular life and job. When she finally took a break a few hours later, she rolled her sore shoulders and took stock of the painting. A few more days and it would be complete!

Becca reached for her phone, complete with the satellite attachment Harry had gotten her because he knew she wanted to be able to contact Owen. Becca splayed her paint-spattered fingers in front of her. Better clean up first! She wanted to check in with Owen before he left for his father's wedding the next day. She paused. As happy as she was in her new life, it still felt odd that someone she had been married to for so long, and raised a child with, was going to be somebody else's husband.

She wasn't in love with Jake. Over time, she realized she hadn't been in love with him for a long time. It had become a marriage of convenience, but because they had grown up together and raised Owen, in some ways she would always care about Jake—even if he had turned out to be a cheating jerk!

Becca scrubbed her hands in the kitchen sink, surprised when she noticed the clock on the oven read it was past noon. Plenty of time for a nice long chat with Owen. *Ha! I'll be lucky if I get five minutes!* That gave her pause. For most of his life, she had been very close with her son. She had been barely out of childhood herself when he was born, and over the years, as Jake became more ambitious, they had been left on their own as a duo. The events last year had changed everything. After her escape from Katie, Becca had been more fearful than she had been in the past. The nightmares had lasted for months. Her fear made her over-protective of Owen, and for a twenty-year-old young man, there was nothing worse. Their problems came to a head when Becca had questioned Owen about how he afforded the luxury car he had purchased. Owen had exploded, insisting he was an adult, and could take care of himself. They hadn't spoken for two weeks. Thankfully, after they both cooled down, things had begun to get better.

Disturbed by the memories, she made herself a tall glass of ice water and took it to the shaded chaises by the pool to make her call. As she dialed, Becca admitted to herself she was jealous and resentful. Owen was tight with his father now, and Becca was left on the outside. When Owen answered after just two rings, she was delighted.

"Hey, Mom." The connection made Owen's voice sound more tinny than usual, but she quickly got used to the unfamiliar sound.

"Hi, honey! How have you been?"

"Good. Just getting everything ready for tomorrow. I didn't realize how much I'd be responsible for as Dad's best man." He stopped, and there was a brief silence. It was obvious he was worried about how she would take the reference to the wedding. It stung a little that he was part of his dad's wedding party, but she understood why he was.

"I can imagine!" Her voice was intentionally bright and unconcerned. "Do you have to keep track of outfits and stuff?"

Across the ocean, Becca heard a relieved sigh. "Yeah, he's

just doing a suit for both days though, so not too bad. It's the other stuff. Like I'm supposed to keep track of the binder that has all the travel arrangements for guests, and I had to mail all the welcome gifts to the hotel, and make sure they are in everyone's rooms. Can you imagine if I screw something up? You know how Nicole is... I mean... she's fine... nice... she's just..."

Yeah, I know exactly how the little home wrecker is—okay, that's not fair. Our marriage was done long before she came on the scene—but still...

"All brides are nervous before their weddings," Becca said through her teeth. "Nicole likes to have things done a certain way, so she might be more nervous than some."

Why in the world am I defending her? I deserve an Emmy for world's best ex-wife!

"I guess."

"So, what time do you leave tomorrow? They've chartered a boat, right?"

"No, it's Mr. Raybourn's boat. It's the one they take to meet their clients in the Caribbean. We are staying at a hotel in Ft. Lauderdale tonight and are supposed to be on the dock by six a.m.!" Owen was obviously excited about the trip.

"Wow, that's early."

"They want to get there before the afternoon thunderstorms build up."

"Hmm." In spite of herself, Becca couldn't help but compare Jake and Nicole's lavish destination wedding with the bare-bones ceremony in front of a judge that she and Jake had when they were eighteen. As she leaned her head back against the upholstered chaise, Becca admitted that her life looked different these days, too.

"Are you nervous about your first ocean crossing? I was. It's a little nerve-wracking to lose sight of land!"

"Nah," Owen scoffed. "Dad says it's a pretty big boat, so

there is nothing to worry about. It's just a couple of hours to the customs stop for the Bahamas and then another hour on to the resort."

"That sounds like fun." She was running out of small talk about her ex's wedding. She hesitated, "Everything else going well, though?" Becca bit her tongue. *Too far?*

Owen had gone through a rough patch when he'd been fired from his internship and experienced his first broken heart, resulting in him leaving school and returning home to Sun Coast. She had serious reservations about him moving in with Jake and Nicole in order to go to school nearby and work in their wealth management firm, particularly when she found out John Raybourn had left his job, at a much larger firm, to partner with them. It was John who had fired Owen the fall before, and Becca was concerned that working in such close contact with him would be difficult for Owen. But to hear Owen talk, it hadn't been hard at all. He loved working there.

"Work's good…"

Becca frowned. His tone sounded different than it normally did when he talked about his job. It was typically a safe subject for Becca to ask about.

"Actually, there are some things that have happened. I'm worried about…" There were muffled noises, as if Owen had covered the microphone. When he came back on, it didn't reassure her when he quickly changed the subject. "When you get back from this vacation, you are going to be in Key West for a while, right?"

Voices sounded in the background and she realized he had an audience. *What had he been going to say that he didn't want overheard? Nope! Stop it! Stupid overactive imagination!*

"That's the plan," she said. "I have a show in late October at the gallery I work at. My boss Dana set it up, so I'll be working to get ready for that."

"I'm proud of you, Mom."

She heard the sincerity in his voice and flushed with pleasure.

"I was thinking I'd come down and stay for a week for Fall Break?"

Becca's face broke into a wide grin. Owen hadn't come to visit except for a brief stay last spring. During the trip, she had nagged him, wanting him to stay by her side the whole time. She had missed him terribly, but her desire to be close had achieved the polar opposite result. By the time he left, there was a definite distance between them.

"I would love that!"

"Awesome! Okay, well I better get going."

Becca bit her lip. She hated to end the call, but now she had a week to look forward to. "Will you call or send me a text when you are safely on dry land?"

She could almost hear him rolling his eyes. "Sure."

"I love you, Owen."

"Love you, too."

5

"Hey," Becca said, looking up with a smile as Harry entered their villa. Putting his phone on the entry table, he crossed the room to stand behind her. He pressed a kiss to the top of her head before stepping back to take in what she had been working on.

"Does it have a name?"

She cocked her head, contemplating the turtle that took up almost a quarter of the canvas. "Petunia?" she deadpanned.

Harry nodded with mock seriousness. "Definitely a Petunia." He walked toward the small kitchen, and Becca heard the unmistakable pop of a cork. Standing, she stretched her arms over her head to relieve her stiff muscles before joining him. She happily accepted the glass of wine he extended.

"How was your day?" The familiar tingle that Becca always got when her art flowed well was still skittering through her body, and though she wanted to hear about Harry's day—she really did—she was eager to tell him that Owen had decided to come stay.

"It was fine. Sorry that I'm later than I thought I would be." He opened the refrigerator and pulled out the plate of fruit and cheese she'd been nibbling on earlier. He set it in front of him on the island.

Becca frowned. "Did your meeting not go well?"

"My meeting? Oh, with the architects. No, that was fine. The call with the solar company went longer than I expected. They think they may have a more efficient battery for storing the solar energy, but it has only had limited field testing." He lapsed into silence and then absently took a large sip of wine.

Okay...

"I talked to Owen today."

Harry fiddled with the plate in front of him. She had been so excited to share the news with him that she was a little nonplussed that he wasn't even paying attention! "Harry?" she prompted.

"Hmm? Oh, yes." He looked up from the plate apologetically. "Sorry, what were you saying?"

Becca's smile dimmed. "Nothing tremendously important"

Harry picked up an apple slice and took a bite. After a minute, he drained his glass and poured another almost to the brim. Becca bit her lip. That didn't seem like a good sign. Something was clearly bothering him.

"Actually, I got a call from an old schoolmate."

"That sounds nice." She said, even though Harry's voice had been devoid of enthusiasm.

"His family has owned a hotel and casino here in the Bahamas since the 1920s. They've just undergone a huge refurbishment, and when he heard I was nearby, he invited us over for a night as a catch-up." Harry's tone was flat.

So, not nice? Becca was grateful Harry was staring down at the counter and couldn't see her frown deepen as a troubling thought poked through. He had told her he had been an 'outcast' at school, so who was this friend?

"That could be fun," she said cautiously.

Harry nodded and drained the second glass. "Yeah, we

should go." Harry's obvious reticence made Becca uneasy, not to mention his uncharacteristic downing of pinot. "I'd like to see Sean."

"Did you meet him at University?"

"No, at boarding school. We must have been, what? Fourteen?" Harry stared blindly past her and then chuckled. "Sean was the friend I told you about—the one who helped me—the scruffy kid from America, and not even America proper. Most of my childhood was running wild in the Keys, completely unprepared for the posh British boarding school my father left me in. I wonder what stories he told them—for them to let me into their hallowed halls. Because I clearly didn't belong."

His throat worked. He had told her this story the week before, but his recitation seemed to be more for his benefit, as if he were reminding himself. "Sean had spent a lot of time in the Caribbean. Because his family, the Pintners, had the resort here in the Bahamas, he understood the culture shock." Harry let out a sound that was half laugh, half exhale. "And it *was* a shock. I went from the bright, color-saturated Caribbean, laid-back lifestyle to the overcast horizon of the UK, full of the most buttoned-up individuals ever created, all within a week's time." Harry splashed more wine into his empty glass and then topped off Becca's. "I thought I was in hell. Sean made it bearable. He taught me how to get along and stood with me against some of the more aggressive bullies."

"I'm glad you had a friend there."

"Yeah," Harry paused in the middle of raising his glass again. "I'm not sure what would have happened to me without his help, even before—huh, maybe I wouldn't have survived long enough to get myself in trouble at Uni." Harry set the glass back on the counter and seemed to shake off the mood. "I'll call him and let him know we will come over tomorrow, if that's okay? I saw a news report that there is a tropical storm south of us that is strengthening, but it's not projected to come this way. Still, I'd rather not be out on the water if the seas are rough."

"That works for me." Becca felt a slight pang at leaving in the middle of what had felt like genuine progress, but it was just for the night.

"I think the chef is dropping off food soon. Do you mind listening for him while I pop into the pool for a quick swim?"

Becca smiled her agreement, but it faded as Harry slipped out the door, shucking his shirt as he went. She was happy that Harry was continuing to open up to her, but he wasn't happy about seeing his 'old friend' no matter what he said aloud.

"I WONDER IF YOUR SON REALIZES HOW LUCKY HE IS?"

Becca lifted her head from his chest. She was so comfortable cuddled up by the fire pit she must have dozed off. "What do you mean?"

Harry stirred restlessly. "Everything you do… it's always about how it affects Owen."

Becca felt a stirring of unease. Was that a criticism? There had been plenty of times during her marriage that her ex-husband had resented her putting their son first. Owen might technically be an adult now, but he would always be her baby.

Harry's head listed to the side, and as Becca sat up, she realized he was drunk. He must have kept drinking after she had fallen asleep. She had seen him happily tipsy before, but for the first time, Harry seemed not to be fully present or aware of what he was saying.

"He's everything to you. I admit I'm jealous."

Becca tensed. Harry had been in an odd mood all evening, and she didn't want that mood to dissolve into an argument. Owen had always been her priority, and she wasn't ready for that to change yet. Maybe someday, but Owen was still young.

"I've never been number one to anyone," he said.

Becca frowned. What could she say? From what Harry had told her about his life, she didn't have any evidence to contradict him, and that was heartbreaking.

"My mother loved me."

Becca's heart seized. She lifted a hand to Harry's chest but stayed silent.

"She did. No matter what he said." Harry closed his eyes. "I don't remember what she looked like. I mean I've seen pictures, but I don't remember... her." Harry reached up with a hand and seized Becca's where it rested on him. His eyes flashed open and his expression was fierce. "My entire life has been a collection of secrets and half-truths. My father, Dan, women..." He shifted and looked her in the eyes. "You don't lie, Becca. You are honest and loving... it's why I love you so much."

Becca's heart stuttered and then stopped. He loved her because she was honest? She had to tell him. She would come clean about what happened last year, and he would understand. Her heart restarted at a full gallop. *It will be fine.* A soft snore stopped her. He was asleep.

She had missed her chance. But worse than that, he had just told her he loved her... and she wasn't sure he would remember in the morning.

6

Harry's friend Sean met them when they arrived. Having grown used to the seclusion of Turtle Bay, Sean's resort was a shock to the senses. It was on one of the larger islands, though still smaller than the major islands of Andros or Grand Bahama. After Grace dropped them in the marina, they were met by a car that drove them the few miles to the property. As they pulled up the long drive, she saw tennis courts and various buildings stretching wide from a large main building in a broad Y shape.

"For some reason, I assumed it would be ocean front."

"It is," Harry said, peering through the window. "The ocean is on the other side of all these buildings."

Becca strained to see, but the view was blocked by groupings of one-story bungalows that flanked the central building.

"This isn't what I was expecting."

Harry cocked his head. "What did you think it would look like?"

She shrugged. A large grass lawn stretched straight in front of them, the drive diverging on either side. The car veered to the right and pulled under the vast portico.

"I guess I was expecting something more... beachy? This place looks like an English estate with palm trees."

Harry laughed. "Well, the Bahamas were still a British colony when his family purchased the land. They designed it to be a private club for the British, so I guess they modeled it after the style in England. Though I have to admit, the only thing I recognize is this building. The rest looks like it's brand new."

The car came to a stop, and Harry shouldered her bag along with his large duffel. "I don't know how he did it. The last time I was here, it felt like a relic. I can't believe how much they've added. He's done a good job of making it feel new but keeping the sense of history." His tone was approving.

"Thanks, mate!" A tall, attractive man with sandy hair and bright blue eyes approached them and slapped Harry on the back.

Becca had been nervous about what to expect. Harry's mood had changed after the invitation from Sean yesterday, and combined with his revelations last night, she was still feeling off kilter. He had woken up complaining of a headache, but with no mention of what he had said. It was killing her not to ask if he remembered! Also, even though Harry had said he wanted to come, she wasn't sure he was telling the truth. At this point, she was a bundle of nerves.

Instead of the standard half-hug back slap she was used to, the men extended their hands to shake. Harry had been tense on the hour boat ride over, but now his face creased into a grin, and Becca felt her own muscles relax. Sean's smile was equally wide.

Maybe she should take it at face value. Harry said they were friends. Period. She needed to stop over dramatizing everything.

"You look good, old man," Sean said, before turning a speculative gaze her way.

I don't like him. He's too slick.

The errant thought surprised Becca. *You met him thirty seconds ago! Sheesh!*

"You must be Becca." With his hands on her shoulders, he air-kissed both of her cheeks, then cut his eyes mischievously to Harry. "I was eager to meet you when I heard you were staying at Harry's new place. I've never known this old dog to keep someone around long... and to bring you to his precious Turtle Bay."

Was Becca imagining the edge to Sean's flip comment?

Yeah, I don't like him.

"He's been drawing and dreaming of that place for as long as I can remember!" Harry stiffened next to her, and Sean suddenly laughed, holding his hands up. "Put away the knives, Harry. I'm just teasing. It's absolutely brilliant that you've finally done it! Who would have imagined the two of us pulling off our boyhood dreams?"

"The property looks incredible," Harry said, looking around the spacious lobby. They had entered through sliding doors and were immediately faced with a two-story bank of glass windows and doors on the opposite wall. A large, coquina fountain gurgled in the center, and three hallways radiated off to the right. A heavy, mahogany reception counter stood centered to their left, with a closed door behind it. On the left side of the desk was a wide, marble hallway and to the right, thickly carpeted stairs led to opaque glass doors and what was most likely the casino. Potted palms in brass pots were arranged in attractive groupings, breaking up the vast room.

Sean preened. "I wanted to keep all the old charm but bring it into this millennia. It took long enough, but it was worth it... oh, darling!"

They had moved closer to the reception desk when a tall, willowy brunette languidly strolled up to them. She was stunning, with long, straight hair that fell in a curtain almost to her waist. *How does she do that in this humidity?* Becca was suddenly very conscious of her curls, frizzy and windblown from the boat ride. The woman's chocolate eyes passed dismissively over Becca and landed on Harry.

The muscles in Becca's neck tightened. It's not that she wasn't used to people taking long looks at Harry, but this woman wasn't even trying to hide her interest.

Oh my god! Did she just lick her lips? Becca narrowed her eyes.

"Darling, this is my old school mate I was telling you about." From the tight corners of Sean's mouth and his clipped tone, Becca saw he had noticed where the woman's attention was focused, too. "Harry Brennan and his partner, Becca... I'm sorry. I don't know your last name."

Partner? The term startled Becca, but then she remembered it was the British version of significant other. *Partner, I like that!*

"Copeland," Harry answered for her, and reached for her hand. The other couple didn't miss the movement, and Sean's lips lifted on one side.

"This gorgeous creature is my wife, Celine."

Wife? Damn! And she's ogling Harry right in front of her husband?

"Enchanté," she said with a light French accent. Her gaze sharpened, and she looked from Sean to Harry. "Harry Brennan? Are you..." Whatever she was going to ask was lost because Sean caught her hand and squeezed—hard. With a tiny wince, Celine swallowed her words.

"The developer that just created the most talked about green resort? Yes," Sean said, as if he were answering her question.

Celine adopted a bored expression, though she not so subtly pulled her hand free. Becca stole a look at Harry to see if he had noticed his friend's action. His smile remained cool, but the flash in his eyes showed that he was equally bothered.

Celine turned her limpid eyes to Sean, her face blank. "I'm

going to Sebastian and Paul's tonight. I'll see you in the morning."

Sean's lips pressed together in a forced smile. "But, darling, they are only here for the night. We were going to have dinner and catch up."

"I have plans." Celine was unmoved.

Hoping to smooth over the awkward moment, Becca blurted out, "I'm sorry you won't be joining us, Celine. We were a last-minute arrival and you shouldn't cancel your plans."

Celine flicked her eyes at Becca as if to say, "Why are you speaking?"

"Well," Sean forced a chuckle. "Maybe tomorrow we can all have lunch before you leave."

"Great!" Becca's voice was too enthusiastic. She knew she sounded like an imbecile, and that knowledge wasn't helped when she saw Harry trying not to laugh. She smothered the urge to step on his foot.

"I just need to go over some items with my wife before she leaves, and then I'll give you a tour." Sean didn't wait for them to answer before taking his wife by the elbow and leading her away.

"That was weird," Harry said with a straight face.

Becca grimaced. "I thought it was just me... that it was a European thing or something."

"No, that was definitely strange."

"You've never met her before?"

Harry frowned. "I didn't even know he was married. He didn't mention it yesterday, even after I told him about you."

"Really?" Becca was dying to know what Harry had said about her!

He shrugged, and his face suddenly cleared. "That must be

why he was so insistent we come over and catch up. He wanted to show off his wife."

"Show her off as what?" Becca bit her lip. She hadn't meant to say that out loud.

Fortunately, Harry seemed to agree. "She was a little... anyway, it's actually a relief! I was concerned that he was going to ask me for money."

Becca looked dubiously at their luxurious surrounding. "He looks like he's doing okay."

"Hmm, it does, and I'm glad. There were rumors a couple of years ago that he was looking for funding. The Royal has been in his family for almost a hundred years, and his dream was always to bring it back to its previous glory." He smiled at her. "You love history so you'll be interested that its original name was the Royal Rod and Gun, and it was *the* place to stay in the Bahamas for the well-heeled set for a good portion of the 20th century. The exclusivity of it being a private club lost favor with the tourist crowd in the 1960s, and it no longer was the place to 'be seen'. By the time I was visiting in the 1990s, they were really struggling."

"Did you come a lot?"

"Most school holidays, if we didn't stay with his parents in England. But it looked nothing like this! Everything was at least thirty years out of date the last time I was here. It was just the main building then. He's really turned this place around."

Becca wanted to ask more questions about his and Sean's past. On one hand, there seemed to be a tense undercurrent, but on the other, Sean's family had taken him in, and Sean had saved Harry by flying him on a private plane to escape a loan shark. Was it like sibling rivalry? Why had Harry never mentioned Sean before? Before Becca could continue to puzzle it out, Sean returned and gave them a tour of the expansive resort.

First, he led them up and down the hallways of the principal building. She was astonished by the number of bars and restaurants they passed. One hall was dedicated to boutiques, offering everything from swimwear to evening wear. As luxurious as it was, it reminded Becca more of a Vegas hotel than a tropical resort.

"These used to be guest rooms, right?" Harry asked at one point.

Sean nodded. "Modern guests expect more than just a day at the beach. They want all the amenities of a city but on a tropical island."

From the number of people Becca saw walking around, Sean must be correct. The resort seemed full.

"Of course, one of the big draws is the casino." They had returned to the central lobby, and Sean gestured to the carpeted steps that led to the heavily smoked glass doors. "We have everything a gambler could want—slot machines and table games." His eyes sparkled as he pulled a few poker chips from his pockets emblazoned with the Royal logo. "Even stakes for the high rollers." He winked at Harry.

Sudden tension rolled off of Harry, and Becca slipped one of her hands into his. She didn't believe for one second that Sean's comment was a coincidence.

"I see that. A thousand-dollar chip? I'm surprised your guests gamble that much on a beach holiday."

Sean flipped the magenta chip Harry mentioned into the air. "You'd be surprised how much money rolls through here."

Harry gave him a tight smile. "I'm sure."

"We have a lot more to see, better get going." Sean winked again and led them to the bank of glass on the back wall. He pushed open one of the doors and gestured for Becca to precede him. She gasped at the unexpected beauty of the view. In front of her was a lush carpet of grass, a perfect match to the long entrance to the Royal. It stretched out appearing to dissolve into the ocean.

Sean put his hands on his hips and surveyed the area with

pride. "It's an amazing illusion. You can't see from here, but we are actually on a bit of natural elevation. When we get closer, you will see that between the grass and the water is actually the main resort pool. Of course, each of the bungalows has a private pool inside a walled courtyard." He raised his arm to point at what looked like a tiny neighborhood of individual buildings, separated by concrete walking paths. "There are three rows of buildings, and it curves back toward the parking lot on the south side."

"You've tripled the size," Harry said looking around. "It doesn't even look like the same place."

"We had to clear out a lot of the vegetation to make room, but it was worth it." Sean's tone was challenging.

Harry's jaw flexed, and Becca guessed the two men had this environmental argument before. Compared to the natural seclusion of Turtle Bay, Becca felt as if they were in a different country, not simply an hour's boat ride away. Sean smirked when Harry stayed silent and continued their tour down one of the wide walkways that bordered the long stretch of manicured grass.

Just as Sean described, after a couple of minutes Becca could see the grass stopped and a short set of stairs led them to a massive pool. The pool, surrounded by rows of Queen Anne palms, had several private cabanas as well as a busy snack bar. Past the pool was the sandy path to the beach, where umbrellas and sun chairs were laid out for the guests.

The property was overwhelming in its size, but as they walked back to the lobby and passed elegant sitting areas complete with fire pits, she was more impressed by Sean's passion for his family's legacy. He lost some of his smarminess when he regaled her with stories of the well-to-do and glamorous, who had once frequented the hotel. He was proud of his family and their legacy and it showed. "We were a favorite of the Americans, particularly during prohibition!" He winked.

When they returned to the lobby, Sean handed them their passkeys. "I put you in a suite on the second floor. It overlooks the back lawn, but you can see the water from the balcony. Let's meet, say around six? The casino is open all day, and of course, there are the pools and such. I'm sorry I have to abandon you, but we've got a big wedding here in a couple of days, and some VIPs are checking in this afternoon. I need to make sure everything is taken care of." Sean grinned suddenly and chucked Harry on the arm. His voice was full of sincerity when he said. "It really is good to see you." With a wave, Sean disappeared through the door behind the reception desk.

"Wow!" Harry said, turning to look at her.

A burble of laughter escaped Becca. "It's a lot!"

Harry shook his head disbelievingly. "I just can't get over how different it is. He must have poured ten million into this place. The hurricane upgrades alone in a place this size! Did you see the size of that generator? I can't even imagine how much power it takes to keep just the electronic locks going on this place... and emergency lighting..." He continued as they made their way to the bank of elevators.

Becca couldn't help but smile. She was fascinated by the history and the beautiful setting, but the developer in Harry was consumed with the building code. Suddenly, she pulled to a dead stop.

No way! You have got to be kidding me!

Becca dropped Harry's hand and dashed behind several potted palms nearby, turning her back to the lobby. "Psst." She jerked her head to indicate that Harry should join her. He stared at her as if she had lost her mind. *Have I?* Carefully turning her head to peek around the plant, she had her answer.

She hadn't lost her mind. Candice Davenport was standing in the hotel lobby, not twenty feet away, with her head thrown back in laughter. *What in the world is she doing here?*

"What are you doing?" Harry whispered, leaning over her

shoulder. He followed her gaze to see what had grabbed her attention. His forehead creased as he watched the woman. "I know her." Harry straightened, and his frown deepened as he clearly struggled to remember where he had seen the blonde before. Taking in Becca's scowl, his face cleared. "Ah, she's one of the jackals from your old town, right? She was at that party I went to with you at..." His voice trailed off as he remembered at whose home they had been.

Becca had recovered from her astonishment, and now anger grew inside of her. "That's the woman who had the affair with Evie's husband. She's the reason Evie came back to see me in Key West... and was murdered."

Harry looked at the woman and then down at Becca, before turning her shoulders so Becca's back was once again toward the lobby. "Are you okay?" She realized that she was breathing hard and immediately forced herself to stop. His concerned expression reminded her that people like Candice were her old life. She was happier now, and she needed to remember that. He rubbed his hands down her arms. "Why don't we go to the casino for a few minutes, and then we can go up to the room before we have to meet Sean for dinner."

Becca nodded. "That sounds like a great idea!" She refused to let Candice spoil her day. "But I've warned you about my poker face," she joked.

"Your non-existent one you mean? Oh no, wait, I forgot." He rubbed his chin in an obvious effort to make her laugh. "You have that magical, suburban woman mask." He pretended to shiver. "I better not play against you then."

Becca stuck her tongue out at him, but his antics had worked, and she was feeling much better. By silent agreement, they followed the edge of the lobby around to the steps that led to the casino. There was no use risking an unpleasant encounter by walking through the middle of the lobby, past the woman she once considered a friend. Becca's foot was on the first step when a familiar voice called out.

"Mom?"

Becca closed her eyes and moaned softly. Harry cursed. For the second time in a handful of minutes, Becca wondered at the universe. She had no other choice but to turn around. In front of her, standing wide-eyed, was her son, Owen. Only a few steps behind him stood the angry duo of her ex-husband Jake and his fiancée Nicole.

They are getting married... here? Seriously?

7

Harry slipped in the keycard and pushed the door open, revealing an elegant room filled with light teak furniture, accented with navy and white throw cushions on the upholstered chairs and couch. Large glass doors led to a small balcony, and she could see a bedroom through the door to her left. She set her purse on the coffee table, opened the doors, and stepped onto the balcony. Becca inhaled deep breaths, hoping the lush, green landscape below would help her control the anxiety rolling through her. She gazed blindly at the group of bungalows jutting out at a right angle to the building, and beyond them to the sea.

Neither she nor Harry had said a word after the scene in the lobby. She stayed stone-faced in the elevator, and Harry watched her warily. The Bahamas consists of hundreds of islands. What were the odds that not only would Jake's wedding be on this particular island but in the same hotel!

I'm a nice person. I recycle. I don't go out of my way to squish bugs… why is the universe doing this to me?

The image of Jake and Nicole's faces when she said she was staying in the hotel… a snort escaped, and once it slipped out, the horrible irony of the situation erupted as laughter. Harry looked alarmed, but when she continued, he smiled, too.

Poor guy. He's probably afraid that I've lost it.

"The look on their faces! They totally think I'm a stalker." Becca cackled harder at the absurdity. "And then," she gasped for air, "when you said 'see you around,' I expected fire to literally shoot out of her eyes!"

Nicole had been furious, but Jake had only stood in silent shock.

Harry laughed. "I didn't know *what* to say, but I figured a quick exit was our best option." He shoved a hand back through his hair. "Who else do you think is going to show up from our past?"

Becca's smile faded. Owen had looked so nervous, his eyes darting between the two groups. She leaned forward resting her forearms on the railing. "Hopefully, we don't run into them again before we leave tomorrow." Beneath her, Candice appeared and strode rapidly off toward the bungalows, entering one close by.

Becca swiveled back to Harry. She wasn't going to let this ruin their night. Harry was here to see his friend, and at the rate Sean seemed to be needling him, they appeared to have enough drama already.

I'll just pretend like they aren't here, and it won't be a problem. Yeah, right.

WHAT IS NICOLE DOING?

The sleek brunette, attired in a white, silk wrap-dress, a large diamond necklace, and heeled sandals, was standing at the last cashier in line. Even among the nicely dressed resort guests, Nicole stood out. But what caught Becca's attention was Nicole appeared to be pulling wrapped bundles of money out of her designer purse and passing them through the window. Becca squinted, convinced she must be seeing things. After a moment, the cashier pushed two stacks of magenta-colored chips through the opening in the plexiglass window.

Becca's jaw dropped as she recognized the thousand-dollar chips Sean had shown them earlier. Every time Becca had met Nicole, the woman always appeared completely controlled—to an almost clinical level. Even in her obvious anger at seeing Becca in the hotel this afternoon, Nicole had kept her tone of voice and facial expressions calm—for the most part anyway. She hadn't been able to hide the rage in her eyes. Becca had an extremely hard time imagining the woman as a gambler. Particularly one who risked so much!

I guess everyone has to blow off steam somehow, Becca reasoned. It had surprised her to learn Harry had been a gambler, so maybe this wasn't that out of the ordinary. *Still... that is a lot of money.* Nicole swept the stacks of chips into her bag. Becca noticed that several other casino customers had noticed and were watching with interest. *So, I'm not crazy.*

When Nicole was done with her transaction, she put the bag on her shoulder and leveled a cool look at her audience. It was enough that most looked away, embarrassed to have been caught gawking. Nicole paused when she made eye contact with Becca standing twenty feet away. Without even a nod of acknowledgement, Nicole turned on her heel and headed toward the tables.

For a split-second, Becca toyed with the idea of returning to the room and convincing Harry to return to the peace of Turtle Bay, but she knew it wouldn't be fair. Besides, it was almost time for dinner. She stroked her hand down the knee-length skirt of her green, halter-style, cocktail dress. She'd splurged when she saw it in a boutique in Key West, even though she hadn't imagined when she would have the opportunity to wear it. She threw it into her luggage for the trip on a whim, thinking she might dress up one night for dinner with Harry. Now, seeing how fancy the Royal was, she was glad she had.

Nicole settled in a seat at the blackjack table. After arranging several stacks of chips in front of her, she looked up. Raising one eyebrow high, she gave Becca a haughty look. Becca rolled her eyes.

Yes, Nicole. I'm totally here just to watch you.

Becca cursed, and her cheeks heated as she realized that was precisely what it looked like. *Aargh! I can't just stand here staring at her while waiting for Harry!* She tried to look nonchalant as she left the casino and descended the steps to the lobby.

"Becca! Oh my god! Is it really you?"

Crap! Her friends Anna Nelson and Michelle Caplan stood nearby gaping at her with expressions of shock. *Friends? Is that still the right word?* It was too late to pretend she hadn't seen them, so Becca pasted a smile on her face and closed the distance between them.

Becca hadn't seen or spoken to either woman since Evie's funeral. From their twin, highlighted hair styles and practically identical, body-skimming dresses, it was evident nothing had changed. After Evie's murder, Becca had wanted nothing more than to forget everything about her former life. She was getting seriously annoyed that every time she turned around today, she was being slapped in the face with it!

"It's been, like, *forever!*" Michelle cried. She took a step back and gave Becca a thorough once over. "You look amazing! Did you get something done?" She peered curiously at Becca's face, trying to figure out what was different.

Becca laughed. Michelle meant it as a compliment, but Becca didn't know how to answer. *Once I removed myself from your toxic world, I figured out how to be happy?* She settled for, "Nope! It's just the relaxed vacation vibe, I think."

Anna's face looked pinched. "Or, it's that hot guy you brought to the party last year. I heard you brought him along." She elbowed Michelle in the side, reminding her not to be too friendly. Michelle, however, took a step to the side to get out of range.

Becca's smile froze. They hadn't seen each other in almost a year, and now in a different country and after less than five minutes, gossip was still the first thing on their mind. How did they even know Harry was there?

"Are you here for the wedding?" Michelle asked cautiously.

Anna guffawed. "Don't be stupid, Michelle! Why would Nicole want her here?"

Becca ignored her. "No, the owner is an old friend of Harry's… the hot guy," she clarified for Anna. "We just came over for the night. We ran into Jake and Nicole in the lobby. Small world, huh!"

Just keep smiling, Becca.

"So, it was a surprise that they were having the wedding here? It's just a *coincidence*?" Anna's voice dripped with disbelief.

"Why would she want to crash the wedding, Anna? She's got a new, rich boyfriend!"

Becca resisted the urge to shake her head at the absurdity of Michelle's defense. Two minutes before, Michelle had assumed Becca was there for the nuptials.

"We are leaving right after lunch tomorrow, so way before the ceremony." Becca wished she didn't feel like she had to explain.

"See, Anna. It *is* just a coincidence."

Hmm, who is this new Michelle? In the decade that they had been friends, Becca had never known Michelle to take a stand against any of her friends.

"Whatever! Dang!" Anna reached to her eye and pressed at her fake eyelash that had abruptly come loose and crept down her eye like a fluffy black caterpillar. "Screw it!" Anna peeled the lash off, leaving her with an almost comical, lopsided look. "C'mon, Michelle. I have to go get the glue from my room."

Michelle shook her head. "I'll wait here."

Becca thought Anna was going stomp her foot in frustration at this latest defection. "Suit yourself!" She tossed her hair over her shoulder, before she stormed off.

"I'm sorry. She and Nicole have gotten close over the last year. What they have in common besides Candice, I have no idea!" Michelle gave a little laugh.

In that moment, the incongruity of Candice being at the wedding struck her. The last she had heard, Candice had been ostracized from their social circle because of her affair with Evie's husband, Adam. The fact that Adam had been Jake's best friend made it more bizarre.

"Candice and Nicole are friends?" Becca was incredulous.

Michelle had a peculiar look on her face. "Well, sort of. Candice and John Raybourn are together now."

Candice is dating Jake and Nicole's business partner? How did that happen?

Becca felt like she was spinning into the twilight zone but brought her focus back to Michelle, who was still talking.

"I actually wanted to talk to you alone."

Uh oh.

Michelle fidgeted and looked over Becca's shoulder. "When you moved last year... ya know... when you walked away from everything... like how did you decide? That it was the right thing to do, I mean. Weren't you scared?"

She wasn't sure what she had expected Michelle to say, but it certainly hadn't been that. It had been those last few days on the cruise ship with her former friends, and specifically the fight the night before she left—a fight that Michelle had factored hugely in—which led to the impulsive decision. She couldn't say that!

"I *was* scared, and for a long time I doubted whether I had made the right decision, but it came down to the simple fact that I needed a fresh start. Sun Coast held too many memories for me. I didn't belong there anymore."

Michelle nodded. "I know what you mean. This last year has been awful!" Her face scrunched and Becca thought Michelle might cry. Instead, she took a deep breath and gave a quick scan of the room to make sure no one was in earshot. "Brad got fired last year after Candice blabbed about Adam's prescription."

The previous summer, on a girls-only birthday cruise, Candice had revealed to their group of friends that Evie's husband was taking Viagra. She had learned the secret after Michelle's pharmacist husband, Brad, was indiscreet and let it slip. That disclosure led Evie to discover her husband's affair— with Candice.

"After Evie was... gone, Adam even filed a complaint with the State Licensing Board. Brad lost his license!" Michelle continued miserably. "It wasn't fair! Adam was the one screwing around on Evie! I don't see why Brad had to be punished."

Becca bit back the urge to remind her that HIPAA laws were around for a reason. "It's not like he spilled the beans on every-one! And then everything, like, fell apart and Brad got super depressed and fat! Jake got him into some real estate investing, and that's keeping us afloat but, like... people were really mad at Brad!"

Becca pressed her lips together... hard. How could Michelle fail to understand that people were upset that the neighborhood pharmacist was sharing their medical histories with his wife? Particularly when Michelle then shared that information with the most vindictive gossip in town. Michelle huffed an angry breath, her face suddenly clearing.

"Anyway, I was thinking things might be better for us if we moved, too. Brad's always so cranky these days. If we go some-where else where they don't know about... you know... I even thought I could be an artist like you!"

Becca poked her tongue into her cheek and blew out a long breath. Michelle didn't mean to be condescending, but Becca had worked extremely hard the last year to improve her skills and make the connections needed to get her paintings in gift stores back in Key West. She had spent plenty of hot weekends under a tent at art festivals throughout the region before she even considered approaching a gallery owner.

"I took one of those Master Classes online for photography, and I've been taking pictures of like, everything. You know, to get practice and stuff. I always have my camera with me," she said, her expression earnest. "Well, not right now, obviously cause we are going to dinner..." She giggled. "But like, usually. I never know when the muse will strike!"

"Hmm," *Is a response necessary?* Michelle stared at her with her wide enthusiastic eyes, and Becca unbent a little.

Anything's possible! Maybe Michelle is the next Ansel Adams? No one in Sun Coast was aware that I loved to paint. We were all too busy being the perfect, accessory wives.

"That's great, Michelle! I'm so glad you have something you are passionate about."

I should be supportive. Without Amelia's and Harry's encouragement, I may never have tried to make art my career.

She doubted Michelle would find encouragement from Anna. The pack didn't like it when one stepped out of line, as she well remembered. "I'd love to see them sometime."

Michelle's face lit up. "Oh, yay! I'll email you some." Michelle frowned, looking over Becca's shoulder. "Shoot! I guess they are waiting for me. It was great to see you, Becca!" Michelle gave her a quick hug. "Let's talk soon."

When Becca turned to watch her go, her mouth fell open in shock. If he hadn't been standing with Anna and her husband, Chris, Becca may not have recognized Brad. Michelle hadn't exaggerated. Brad had put on a substantial amount of weight, and his face no longer resembled the smiling man she remembered. Instead, there was bitterness and tension in every line of his body. Becca felt a moment of guilt for thinking so harshly of him before. He made a mistake in revealing Adam's secret, but he was clearly suffering because of it.

"What are you staring at like that?" Harry's warm arm slipped around her waist. Her mouth snapped shut. She saw to her dismay that, across the lobby, Brad had seen her gawking.

"Just some people I used to know."

DINNER TURNED OUT TO BE MORE FUN THAN BECCA HAD expected. Sean had apparently decided to stop trying to get a rise out of Harry, and both men were relaxed and laughing as they traded stories. Sean was charming, but his accent became thicker the more Scotch he put away, and it was a challenge to decipher some of his slang.

After their plates were cleared, they had gone to the piano lounge for a nightcap. Sean and Harry were halfway through a shared story about a prank played on an especially obnoxious head boy at their school, when Anna, Michelle, and their husbands entered and took a table in the center of the room. Becca couldn't help the resentment she felt when Candice and John soon joined them. Evie had been their friend. They were all just pretending like nothing had happened! Her legs felt restless, and she wanted to go over and ask if they had all just chosen to act like Candice *wasn't* a terrible person.

Sean's laughing question brought her back to the moment. "So, which of those blokes is it you're looking to off?"

Becca grimaced and pushed her half-full wine glass away from her. She'd clearly had enough if she was contemplating doing something so reckless.

"Sorry, I got distracted."

"Do you know them?" Sean asked, looking at the table of couples.

Becca sighed and gave Harry a quick look. He made a face

as if to say it was up to her. Becca decided it would be easier to just explain.

"I used to, very well. In fact, they are all here for my ex-husband's wedding."

Sean's face slacked. "You're joking?"

Becca shook her head ruefully. "I wish I were. It's the world's worst timing."

Sean continued to stare at her with an odd expression. "Copeland. Jake Copeland is your ex-husband?"

Why is he looking at me like that?

"Yep."

Harry's eyes narrowed with Sean's continued scrutiny of Becca. It seemed unusual that the owner of the resort would be familiar with the name of the groom at one of the onsite weddings. Sean placed his hands flat on the table in front of him and chuckled. "What a bizarre coincidence. His firm, Premier Properties Wealth, is the one that organized the group of investors that allowed us to remodel the Royal." He stared hard at Harry. "Did you know that?"

Why does Sean sound so suspicious?

Harry noticed the change in tone, too. He eyed Sean speculatively. "No, why? Does it matter?"

Sean glared thoughtfully at the table before leaning back in his chair. He lifted his cut crystal glass in front of his lips. "Sorry, I've gotten paranoid over the last few years," he said, before finishing the drink in one swallow.

Becca cut her eyes to Harry to see if he understood Sean's sudden mood swing. He shook his head slightly to show he was just as lost, but his eyebrows drew down until they almost met.

Sean spun the empty glass in his hand. "We had a hard time finding investors who would agree to the terms we wanted. Some groups walked away, but others," Sean grimaced, "used small investment firms as fronts, and we didn't find out they were actually large development groups until it was almost too late. They could have tied us up in legal disputes for years, and with deeper pockets, they would have simply out waited us. We needed the money, badly, but this hotel means everything to my family. We couldn't afford to lose the controlling share. Most of the developers would have preferred to pull it down and start over. Copeland and Raybourn's group..." Suddenly Sean smiled and saluted the table of Sun Coast residents with his empty glass.

Becca followed the movement and saw that they were also being observed. Sean lifted his hand in acknowledgement, and John inclined his head. He leaned close and said something to Candice, which caused her to turn and glare at Becca. The back of her neck prickled. It felt like the temperature in the room had fallen ten degrees, and Becca rubbed a hand over the goose-bumps that had risen on her arm.

"What was I saying?" Sean's eyes were unfocused. "Oh yes, their group was perfect. A bunch of American nouveau riche enthralled at the chance to own a piece of a historic property. I was more than happy to take their money." He chuckled like he had made a joke, but then sobered. "You really didn't know?"

Harry's voice was icy. "I met the man once, and frankly I couldn't care less about his business."

"No, I don't suppose you would," he said, casting a look at Becca. "Still, a hell of a coincidence."

"Jake and Nicole thought so, too."

Becca's dry tone made Sean let out a bark of laughter. He tapped his glass with a finger, signaling to the server he would like a refill. Becca widened her eyes at Harry and was relieved when he understood.

Standing, he said, "We're for bed, I'm afraid."

Sean had slumped in his seat. "You sure you can't stay for another? I'm sure Becca doesn't mind going ahead? I need to ask your advice about something."

"Not tonight. In the morning?"

Sean had no choice but to acquiesce, but his voice was morose. "In the morning then."

As Harry and Becca made their way to the entrance, they were forced to pass the table of couples. Becca kept her eyes straight ahead.

"What was that all about?" Becca asked, after Harry pushed the button to call the elevator.

Harry's face darkened. "It's almost as if he thought I was lying about knowing his investors. If I wanted to invest in his hotel, I would have come straight to him, but he knows that I never do business with friends."

Becca crinkled her nose. "Maybe it was just the Scotch."

"Hmm. Sean always had his moods, and alcohol makes them worse." He paused. "Isn't that your son?"

Sure enough, emerging from the elevator at the end of the bank was Owen—and Nicole. Owen stopped when he reached them, but Nicole tilted her chin in the air and kept walking. Owen watched her go up the steps to the casino before bringing his attention back to Becca. Her stomach clenched. She hated he was stuck in the middle.

"Hey, Mom," he said, giving her a kiss on the cheek. "Harry."

It bothered Becca that, even though Harry and Owen had met a couple of times the week Owen spent in Key West, he had never warmed to the idea of Harry. He was never openly rude, but he also asked zero questions about Harry. Owen had no problem working with his dad and Nicole, and if this rendezvous were any indication, they even hung out together. Harry made her happy. Why wasn't that enough for Owen?

"Big night at the casino?"

Oh my god! Is it possible for me to sound any lamer?

"Uh, yeah, I guess."

"Do you like the cards or table games?" Harry asked.

Owen's gaze had returned to the casino doors and he didn't

answer. Becca felt a spurt of anger. Owen could at least be polite! Just as she was about to say something, Owen's eyes snapped back to Harry's.

"I've never really gambled before. Nicole said she would teach me. Uh, she's waiting."

Becca grit her teeth and tried unsuccessfully to force her lips into a semblance of a smile. "You should go then. We're heading up, anyway."

"Okay. Thanks, Mom. Maybe I'll see you tomorrow?" But Owen didn't wait for an answer. Instead, he strode quickly away and into the casino.

Becca's throat was thick, and tears pricked at the back of her eyes. As they got in the elevator, she sniffed, determined that they not fall. "I'm sorry about that."

Harry shrugged. "Remember, he's still young. He's trying to do the right thing, but it's not always easy at that age to figure out what the right thing is."

"I taught him better manners than that. You'd think…"

"Hey." Harry put his arms around her and placed a soft kiss on her lips. "That was a one-off. He's normally fine. It is a complicated situation for him right now. His dad is getting married, and his mom is suddenly here to witness it. It would probably put anyone off their game."

"I wish I could just forget they were all here!"

Harry's lips curved in a mischievous smile before pulling her close. "Let me see if I can help you with that."

8

When Owen called her the next morning, Becca was caught off guard. She hoped Owen didn't feel he needed to check up on her. "What's up, honey? Did you have fun last night?"

"Yeah, it was okay. Um, are you busy? I need to talk to you about something."

Becca frowned. That didn't sound promising. "Sure, is something going on?"

Becca had learned early in her son's teenage years that the quickest way to make Owen clam up was to show concern of any kind. Unfortunately, she had also learned that she was not in fact the "cool mom" she always assumed she was when Owen burst into hysterical laughter at her misuse of current slang. It only made matters worse when she asked, "Isn't 'what's the dilly-o' still something you say?" *Whatever!* Getting her son to open up could be tricky. Therefore, she was taken aback when Owen responded with, "I'm not sure, but I'm worried."

That got Becca's attention, and she sat up straighter. "Do you want to get breakfast?"

"You haven't already eaten?"

Becca glanced at the remains of the meal on her plate and crossed her fingers. "Nope! Getting a late start this morning."

"Okay, great. That sounds good."

"Why don't you come by here, and I can order room service?"

"No!" Owen's response was quick and telling.

Becca peeked through the door at her and Harry's unmade bed. *Yeah. Here may not be the best spot.*

"How about we meet at the casual restaurant off the lobby? I think they do breakfast."

"Sounds good. Can you come now?"

Becca's mom antennae shot up. "On my way."

BECCA AND OWEN FOUND A SPOT ON THE OUTDOOR PATIO THAT had a bit of a breeze. The air had taken on the heavy, humid feeling it always did before a big storm. Clouds scudded in thick, gray ropes above them.

"Are those outer bands from that tropical storm?" Becca asked, looking up. Owen fidgeted with his fork, pushing his eggs around, ignoring her question. Becca waited as patiently as she could, but they had been making small talk—and very little even of that—for the last twenty minutes. "Spit it out," she wanted to say, but didn't. Her curiosity had always been a little out of control, and she couldn't hold her tongue any longer.

"It's funny you all ended up at this resort at the same time as me. Not ha-ha funny, but..." She bit her lip. The look Owen gave her made it clear he didn't find it amusing at all. In fact, his eyes had narrowed a bit. He didn't think she had planned this, did he? "What a weird coincidence," she finished lamely.

That finally spurred Owen to speak, his expression pinched. "It was just a coincidence, right? I mean, I never told you *where* the wedding would be... not specifically."

Becca's stomach twisted into a knot. "I didn't even know this place existed until a couple of days ago, Owen. We were on Harry's island when an old friend invited us over. He owns the place, or at least his family does."

"I knew it had to be something like that." Owen's face cleared. "I promised Dad and Nicole that I hadn't told you, but they thought maybe I had." He sighed, looking unhappy again. "Nicole is convinced you are here to ruin the wedding."

Becca stared at him in disbelief. She was there with her boyfriend. *My hot, rich boyfriend, thank you very much! That woman thinks everything is about her!*

Becca struggled to keep the scowl off her face. Her conscience stabbed at her and she had to concede Nicole had a teensy point. "I guess if I were in her shoes, I might be worried about the same thing," Becca said grudgingly, but then added hurriedly, "but I was here first!"

Owen gave her a little smile. "It's just they are so stressed out about what's going on at work. Nicole has been freaky paranoid for over a month, constantly double-checking things I normally do, and then insisting she's going to do it herself. Like filing is too complicated for me or something. She keeps making excuses about why I can just work from home now, running reports."

"Is that what you're worried about? That Nicole is checking up on you?" When he had been fired unexpectedly from John Raybourn's Atlanta firm last fall, his confidence had taken an enormous blow.

"No, not exactly," Owen exhaled a long breath. Then his words tumbled out so fast Becca had to concentrate on what he was saying. "Okay, look, you can't tell Dad I told you any of this! He told me not to talk about it with anyone, but I'm for real, kind of worried about him!"

Owen glanced around to make sure no one was close. Alarm

bells rang in Becca's head. Whatever it was, it wasn't good. She resolved not to react, no matter what Owen told her.

"It's okay, Owen. You can trust me." Inside, she was already seething. What the hell had Jake done that was stressing their son out this much?

Owen lowered his voice so much that Becca had to lean over the small table to hear him clearly. "Last week a bunch of people showed up at the office and started going through a lot of the files. They took Dad and Nicole into separate offices. When they came out, Dad looked really mad and told them he was calling his lawyer! Then he grabbed my arm and we just left them there with Nicole!"

"Are you serious?" Becca flapped her hand. "I know you're serious, but... I'm... just surprised." Owen stared at her expectantly while she tried to wrap her brain around what he had said. "What do you mean 'people'? Who were they? Clients?"

Owen shook his head. "No, I mean like police, but not police. When Dad and I were leaving, they were filling boxes with files."

Oh my god! This is bad! Police but not police?

It took every ounce of Becca's self-control to keep her voice calm. "But they were definitely law enforcement? Were they SEC agents?"

Owen was obviously describing the execution of a search warrant. But why? Jake was an unfaithful asshole and negligent father, but he was rigidly conservative. She couldn't picture him breaking the law!

"The guy that talked to me said they were FBI."

Becca's eyes widened and her stomach fell to her knees. "They questioned you, too?" Her voice cracked as her anger built.

I am going to kill him. I am going to literally disembowel Jake.

She needed to tread carefully. She had to get as much information as possible because Jake would never be honest with her. "I would have been terrified! Was it like on the shows we watch?" Becca kept her tone light and tried not to give away how upset she was.

Owen scoffed, his bravado coming back. "Nah, the guy was actually really cool. He said I had nothing to worry about because I hadn't been there long." Owen's forehead wrinkled. "He asked me how my classes were going and how did I like being home instead of in Atlanta."

Becca's stomach shot from her knees to her throat making it difficult to breathe. How had the FBI known Owen left school in Atlanta last year? That seemed like an in-depth look at someone who was just an intern.

I'll cut his head off, too.

"I'm sure they looked into who was going to be at the office —like a background check. I'm sure it's routine," she lied smoothly. Owen nodded, happy to be reassured. "What did your dad say about it?"

Owen shrugged. "He said it wasn't a big deal, that it didn't have anything to do with him or Nicole. They were looking into some SEC violations of one of the clients or something."

"Hmm." Becca gripped her coffee mug so tightly she was surprised it didn't shatter. If they were just looking into one person, they wouldn't have seized so many of PPW's files. And Jake wouldn't need a lawyer unless he was involved.

Sean's comment the night before when he referenced Copeland and Raybourn's firm, popped into her mind. "Was John there? Did they question him, too?"

"No, he's been on vacation for a couple of weeks. Some-where here in the Caribbean, actually. Dad said he was going to tell him about it, but that this kind of thing happens all the time."

"But you don't believe him?"

"Of course, I believe him!" Owen's tone was hostile, and it

reminded Becca of his rude behavior the night before. He was behaving completely out of character, and that, more than his words, convinced Becca that Owen was afraid of something. "It's just, I don't... I'm not sure Dad is aware of what's going on."

What does that mean?

Owen began rotating his mug around with enough force that the liquid was in danger of sloshing over the rim. Becca reached out and placed her hand on his to still the movement. He kept his eyes cast down.

"What *exactly* is worrying you?" she asked quietly.

Owen lifted his gaze to hers, and she could see how troubled he was. "The morning after the FBI was in the office, Nicole was on the phone with someone. She didn't realize I was there. I had gone for a run but came back to get a hat. She sounded really worried. She told whoever was on the phone that 'they didn't find anything' and 'we're covered.' I didn't hear everything." Owen gulped. "The only other thing was, 'I'm not going to jail for anyone.' That sounds serious, right?"

Becca's chest constricted, and she closed her eyes.

Jake! What have you gotten yourself involved in?

"She wasn't talking to Dad either because he was in the shower. I heard it running upstairs. Should I ask Dad what's going on? I mean, I work there and live with them. Shouldn't I know what's going on?"

Becca's thoughts raced, each fighting for her attention. *Yes! Of course, you should, because they've involved you, but also —No! Stay as far away as you can!* Owen had done nothing wrong and she didn't want him caught up in Jake's problems, or worse be forced to testify against his father if Owen found out what was going on.

"There's one more thing," Owen said.

Great! What now?

"You know how, when you get to the Bahamas, customs

comes out to the boat when you arrive and then you keep going to wherever you are staying?"

Becca nodded.

"Well, after they did the whole customs inspection thing, we met another boat on our way here. Dad insisted I stay inside but I was curious. I snuck up to the main salon and saw some guy hand two suitcases over onto our boat. When I asked Dad, he said Nicole had forgotten some of her wedding stuff, so they had this boat rendezvous with them… to get it to her." Owen's tone made it clear that he wanted to believe his father, but the story was absurd.

Becca's blood ran cold. After last year's experience with smugglers, she knew that, more than likely, something illegal had been passed after they cleared customs. A headache built behind her eyes.

Search warrants, FBI, lawyers, secret suitcases… that decided it for her. If she told Owen what she suspected, he would start asking questions. It might lead anywhere… or to anyone! It was too risky.

"Wow! I'm not sure." She hoped her voice didn't sound as fake as it felt. "This whole traveling by water thing is new to me. If Nicole left something behind for her wedding, it would be easier to get it here by boat, than to fly it. Florida is so close." Owen nodded, looking relieved. "I'm sure there is nothing to worry about. You aren't involved, so it's probably best to let your dad handle his business."

Becca didn't know exactly what Jake was up to, but everything Owen had described sounded like Jake was in way over his head. She had learned the hard way how dangerous things could be here in the Caribbean when someone had a secret to protect. She wanted her son as far away as possible!

BECCA WISHED HER OWN WORRIES WERE AS EASILY ASSUAGED AS Owen's. Harry had gone for a run on the beach, and she didn't feel like going back to the room by herself. Left to her own devices she might just follow through on some of the homicidal fantasies she was having about Jake. Becca reached the lobby and was startled to see a line of people at reception.

A harried voice said, "Yes, Ma'am, we were able to get your family on a flight. If you will just wait out front, the next shuttle will be arriving shortly, and we will have you on your way." The group standing at the front of the line didn't seem to be difficult. In fact, they were all smiling with relief. The desk attendant's tone seemed odd, until Becca heard more murmuring in the line, and suddenly the crowd at check-out made sense. The tropical storm had turned and was now expected to brush the island.

Becca had lived through plenty of tropical storms and didn't consider them something to cancel a vacation over. It would blow through in a few hours, and then they would experience gorgeous weather. However, she understood that not everyone was used to a tropical climate, and being on an island during a storm might make them nervous.

She left the crowd behind and pushed open the door to the casino looking for a distraction. She cashed in a few dollars and walked to a line of slot machines. *Mistake.*

"My, my, you never know who's going to turn up do you? Like a penny… how does the saying go? A bad penny?" Candice tapped one long-nailed finger against her lips. "But that fits, I guess. Your hair and all."

Becca resisted the urge to touch her reddish blonde curls. She hadn't bothered with doing her hair and makeup in her rush to meet Owen, and in spite of herself, she felt the twinges of self-consciousness. To combat it, Becca put on her social mask and ignored Candice. She itched to walk away but she was still just prideful enough not to give the irritating woman satisfaction. Becca sat on the stool in front of a machine and inserted a token.

"But Chris really wants to!" Becca heard Anna whine nearby. "He's been talking about it for weeks. We'll be back before the ceremony. He just wants to do a drive-by and take a picture he can show his parents."

"No, there isn't time. Tomorrow is my day!"

"We were going to go in the morning. Chris said we might never come back here. This is his only chance." Anna's voice had firmed. "Can you please just give him the address?"

"You think I keep addresses of all the properties in the portfolio on me? At my wedding?" Nicole's voice dripped with scorn. "Tell your husband to forget it. Can't you control him?"

"He said if he doesn't get an address he'll just drive around the area. He's pretty sure he can spot it. He's got directions to the area it's supposed to be in, plus he has the pictures you gave him at the initial investment meeting."

Becca wasn't thrilled to be trapped at the slots with Candice, but she decided, given the alternative of chancing an encounter with Nicole, she'd stay put. After the first barb, Candice had fallen silent. Sneaking a glance in her direction, Becca realized it was because Candice was listening to the conversation on the other side of the slots with rapt attention.

"If he has pictures, why does he need to drive by for a picture?" Nicole hissed.

Out of the corner of her eye, Becca saw Michelle approaching. Instead of stopping, she continued to where Nicole and Anna were arguing. Becca didn't know why she was listening. She wasn't supposed to care anymore, but... it was like revisiting a soap opera you used to watch religiously. It was interesting, but you were no longer deeply invested in the outcome.

"What are you guys talking about?" Michelle asked.

"Chris wants to ride out to see one of the properties we've invested in that's on this island. He wants to send a picture to his parents, so they can see what it looks like, but Nicole won't give us the address."

"Oh yeah," Michelle said. "Brad wants to go with him. Can't you get the address online?"

"We don't list the addresses online, Michelle," Nicole said. Her voice made it clear her patience was thin. "To prevent this exact scenario. The house is rented this week, and they don't want looky-loos driving by to gawk at them."

"We aren't *looky-loos!*" Anna practically shrieked in outrage. "We are *owners!*"

"You aren't going and that's final." Nicole's voice was raised as well.

Becca's brows rose. This was getting interesting.

"Do you all want to keep your voices down?" Candice asked. She had risen from her seat in front of the slot machine and taken a step sideways to observe the women on the other side. "You have an audience."

Three heads appeared around the corner.

"It's just Becca." Michelle sounded confused.

Nicole was shooting her daggers but was distracted when Candice asked, "What are you squabbling about?"

"They want to risk missing my wedding to go see one of the stupid properties." Nicole turned her back to Anna and Michelle, and as she brought her hands up to cover her face as if she were upset, she shot Candice a meaningful look.

"We aren't going to ruin your day." Anna rolled her eyes. "It isn't that big of an island. It shouldn't take more than a couple of hours. You'll be in hair and makeup."

Nicole let out a dramatic sniff. Right on cue, Candice said, "Oh my god! Why are you so selfish! You are making her cry."

Michelle looked remorseful. "It's not us. It's Brad and Chris. When they heard this was the island the wedding was on, they were excited to see one of the houses they own here."

"Chris doesn't care if she cries," Becca heard Anna mutter under her breath and smothered a laugh.

"What's so funny, Becca?" Candice's voice lashed out.

Damn! She must have been louder than she thought. She stuck another token in the machine and pulled the lever causing the machine's bells and alarms to ring as the tumblers whirled.

She held a hand to her ear. "What did you say? Sorry, I can't hear you."

Candice opened her mouth, her eyes narrowed into slits. Before she spoke, Anna piped up again. "Nicole, I'm not trying to be a bitch. I'm really not. But Chris is dead set on going to see the house."

Candice's gaze whipped back to Anna. She tossed her hair over her shoulder. "Well, you *are* being a bitch." Anna gasped. "This is Nicole's wedding trip, and you are making it all about yourself. What are you going to do? Rush around and get back too late to have your glam done?" She gave Anna a scathing once over. "It's not a fast process. You'll probably be all sunburned and gross… I mean more than the burn you've already got."

Michelle looked stricken as Anna involuntarily touched her pink collarbones.

"Didn't you just say you needed a peel to get rid of all those wrinkles on your chest—what's the point if you are just making it worse?"

Anna paled under her slightly burned skin while Nicole looked smugly on.

Damn! This is a full-frontal attack.

But it worked; it shut Anna up. "I'm just going to go upstairs for a minute," Anna said her eyes full of tears.

Becca's lips turned down. *Stay out of it. Stay out of…*

"She's not likely to get burned in a tropical storm. I think you look fabulous, Anna."

The evil smile that crossed Candice's face should have made Becca nervous. There was a tiny gleam of pleasure in Candice's eyes. I guess it's not fun for her if the prey never fights back, Becca sighed to herself.

Ding, ding, ding! The slot machine clanged and dumped out a handful of tokens. *Holy Cow! I won!*

Candice began a slow clap. "That's sooo great for you, Becca. I know you must need the money."

Ignore her. You are leaving in a few hours and don't have to see her again. Then again, Candice might be just the target my latent anger at Jake needs. Battle joined.

"Hmm, do I?" Becca asked silkily.

"Rumor has it you are living on some boat somewhere... like a homeless person."

"I'm not sure how much footage a boat needs, to be considered a yacht, but regardless, I don't live there anymore. I own a home."

"Sure you do."

Becca raised her eyebrows. Was that the best Candice had? Evie's face flashed in front of her eyes.

"Where are you living these days, Candice? I was told you were no longer in the same house in Sun Coast."

Anna and Michelle nervously looked at Candice. The reference to Candice's husband kicking her out was a bit of a low blow, but she had it coming.

"I live in a lovely home on the golf course... with John."

"Oh, so somebody else's house. I'm glad for you." Becca's tone made it clear that she was anything but. Becca scooped up her tokens, stood and purposely caught Nicole's eye. The conversation with Owen about the raid at the wealth management firm came back to her as did her anger. Her comment was directed at Candice but meant for Nicole. "I hope you have another back-up plan in case John's not around."

Becca didn't know if John was actually in legal trouble but it worked. Candice fumed, but best of all, Nicole turned a sickly shade of white.

"What's your back up plan, Becca? When that boyfriend of

yours gets sick of you, are you going to keep trying to sell your little Crayola art? Beg Jake for more money?"

"I have a job, Candice. I make my own money. I get that it's not something you are familiar with."

"Spreading your legs is hardly a job! I looked up that guy you're with. He's way out of your league." She gave Becca's casual look a derisive once over. "It's only a matter of time until you have to crawl back under the trash pile he found you in. How you kept him this long is a mystery. You can't be that good in bed."

"I've got it on good authority she's not," Nicole said sotto voce, and then laughed.

Red hot anger flooded Becca. It wasn't the childish taunts that bothered her, though they did touch on her insecurities with Harry. It was that these two women, these two wretched women, thought they were so much better than everyone else, destroying everyone in their path. First Evie and now her son.

"I pity you, Candice. You are only back with these women because of John. Do you think they would still be your friends… after what you did to Evie, if it weren't for him? Nicole wouldn't even look in your direction."

Candice's face hardened. "It must be terrible for you."

She stopped and even though Becca's brain screamed at her to keep her mouth shut, she was too hot to listen. "What Candice? What is it that you think is so awful?"

Becca was fully prepared for another dig about Harry or her looks, but Candice's riposte took her breath.

"It must be just awful… knowing that the two men you love most in your life prefer Nicole's company to yours."

Becca had to clench her fists to keep from striking her. "At least I still see my child. Last I heard, your children want nothing to do with you."

"Becca!" Anna cried.

Becca? I'm the one out of line? Please!

However, Anna's exclamation achieved what Becca needed. She felt the anger drain away from her. She should never have engaged. All she had accomplished was sinking to Candice and Nicole's level and it made her sick.

"You're right, Anna. That was a terrible thing to say." Her eyes were on Anna and Michelle. She refused to apologize to Candice... not after everything. "I need to go. We are leaving soon."

Without another word, she walked away ignoring the mocking laughter in her wake. It didn't matter that Candice laughed. Becca may have slipped up, but this wasn't who she was anymore.

9

She emerged from the cocoon of the casino and saw, through the large glass windows of the lobby, the palm trees bending in the wind. The casino was well insulated, so Becca hadn't been aware of the rapidly worsening weather. She hadn't been in the casino long, but it was obvious that the storm had advanced faster than expected. Becca's heart sank as she recognized her chances of getting off the island were quickly disappearing.

Becca scanned the full lobby, and finally spotted Harry, off to one side, in conversation with Sean. Her path to them took longer than she anticipated as she dodged clusters of tourists besieging various hotel employees.

"The hotel is perfectly safe. We are built to the latest storm codes and have generators and plenty of supplies on site," a woman in uniform assured the group in front of her in a calm voice. Her irritation only showed when she lifted a hand to smooth back some of her hairs that had come loose from her previously-slick, French twist. Becca gave her a commiserating smile as she edged past. The tense faces on the guests showed they didn't believe her.

Becca wasn't particularly concerned about a tropical storm especially in a new building. She'd been through a couple of minor hurricanes, and while it wasn't fun when the power went out, taking the air conditioning and refrigerator with it, in a modern building there wasn't a safety concern. Plus, Sean had bragged yesterday about all of the improvements the hotel had. This was just a small depression... piece of cake!

A low whoosh sounded as a gust whipped by the windows, and Becca saw the bushes outside flatten. "I thought the storm wasn't going to be here until tomorrow?" she asked, as she joined Harry. He jumped at the sound of her voice, and she was a little unnerved to see guilt flash in his face. Neither man had noticed her approach, too wrapped up in their conversation.

"What is it? What's wrong?"

Sean grinned and winked at her. "Nothing at all." He cuffed Harry on the arm. "I'll just pop over and make sure house-keeping knows you aren't checking out. Dinner tonight?" Harry nodded.

Becca's eyes flicked to the glass doors again and she swallowed back a groan. "I take it we aren't going to go back today?" The sinking feeling returned as Becca realized she was going to remain stuck in the same hotel as her ex and his soon-to-be bride as they prepared for their wedding. It was a cosmic bad joke. Almost as if in sympathy, the wind howled again. "They blew that forecast, huh?" Becca tried to make light of the awkward situation.

Harry didn't notice her attempt at levity. He stared sightlessly at the crowd in the lobby, his mind a million miles away.

Becca frowned. His unease seemed out of proportion to the situation. Her nerves could be explained by the ugly scene she'd just been part of, but he had spent many years during his youth in the Caribbean, so it was unlikely the weather worried him. Was he concerned she would have a meltdown over being marooned?

Becca laid a hand on his arm. "Hey? You okay? It's just a tropical storm." Maybe he *is* nervous about it, she thought, and instantly felt guilty.

Her comment seemed to snap him out of his reverie however, and he shrugged. "It's actually a Category 1 now. They upgraded it. Good news is it's picked up speed, so landfall will probably be early tomorrow morning." He grimaced. "We won't be able to leave until it has passed and it's safe to sail."

Becca made a face. "So not until tomorrow morning?"

"Probably not until late tomorrow." He paused when she laughed. "That's not the reaction I was expecting... but... good?"

"There's nothing we can do about it. We can't exactly take the boat now." She gestured at the windy conditions beyond the windows. "I mean, am I thrilled to be stuck in a hotel, waiting for a hurricane, during my ex's wedding to his mistress? No, but it could be worse." Becca didn't say it out loud but part of her— a teeny, tiny part of her, but still there—felt it was only fitting that the cheater's celebration got interrupted a bit. Aloud, she said, "I'll just eat room service and watch TV all day, unless the power goes out."

"It shouldn't. It's just a Category 1 and Sean has those fancy generators." He looked at her suspiciously. "Are you sure you are okay? You seem a little weirdly relaxed about this whole thing."

Becca arched an eyebrow at him. "I'm fine. Besides, even if I wasn't, it's not like you control the weather."

Harry laughed. "Good point!" His brow furrowed. "Actually, I should make some calls and ensure that Turtle Bay is all set for tomorrow, and confirm that Grace has the boat ready..."

"Of course..."

"Great! I just need to make sure..." Harry trailed off already absorbed in the next task. Becca smiled fondly as she watched him disappear down the marble hallway leading to the conference and ballrooms. Ostensibly, that was where the wedding would be held now that the outdoor area would most likely be out of commission.

Becca sighed. She had put a good face on it for Harry, but she was not happy. Her nerves were still jangled from her run-in with Candice, and now she had a front row seat to her ex-husband's wedding festivities... surrounded by a bunch of her old friends. It was as if she had stepped into an alternate universe.

Becca scanned the crowd for wedding guests, prepared to duck behind the plants again in case she needed to avoid anyone. She rolled her eyes at herself. *Real mature, Becca.*

A large man in a maintenance uniform crossing the lobby caught her eye. She angled her head. Something about him was familiar, but what drew her attention was his determined walk and the way his head was awkwardly turned so that he faced away from the gathered crowd. *How odd!* Suddenly, an over-wrought guest, clearly worried about the weather, threw up her hand, striking the man's bent head in the face.

"Ow!" the man exclaimed, as he turned to glare at the woman. Becca stared in disbelief.

It can't be! Rey?

Rey gave himself away when he looked over to where she was standing. He'd known she was there, she realized. That was why he had kept his back to her. Becca bit her lip. What was he doing there, she wondered? The last time she had seen him, he was working undercover with a drug cartel.

Oh god!

Becca's eyes must have communicated her fear even across the room because Rey gave a slight shake of his head and surreptitiously lifted his finger to his lips.

"What the..." she muttered. *Was he still undercover? Oh no! Harry!*

Becca's eyes flew to where she had last seen him, but the entrance to the hallway was empty. Her gaze flew back to Rey—

he was gone. Frantically, she visually searched the room. She had to find him! She had to remind him to stay out of sight, that Harry would recognize him! Harry only knew Rey as one of the masterminds behind a drug smuggling ring they had disrupted last summer. The ring had used Harry's friend Dan's treasure museum as their cover in Key West. Harry still believed Rey was Dr. Navarro, a marine archeologist, and that there was a warrant out for his arrest. What if Harry called the Bahamian Police? He would find out she had lied to him!

Becca had kept her promise to Rey and never told anyone, including Harry, the truth about what happened the day she was kidnapped! How would Harry react if he found out she had kept this hidden for so long? He had made it clear, when he told her about his mother, how much he valued honesty.

She moaned. He trusted her. All thoughts of the storm and being trapped at Jake and Nicole's wedding preparations were gone. She had to find Harry and make sure he didn't see Rey!

Just then, Becca saw Sean emerge from a door behind the reception desk. His face was lined with worry. Was the storm worse than they had been told? Unease flicked along her nerves as she watched Sean frown and exit the lobby along the same path Harry had taken. Becca followed him. *This might work out perfectly. Sean will talk to Harry away from the lobby, and then I'll get Harry to go back to the room. I'll convince him to order in, and keep him there until we leave tomorrow.* Becca's lips curled up. *I'm sure I can think of something to distract him.*

Feeling better now that she had a plan, Becca quickened her pace. Even though she had practically race walked, when she reached the entrance to the long hallway, there was no sign of either man. There were placards next to each door frame naming the large rooms beyond. She pulled on the first few doors assuming that Harry would have gone through one for privacy, but they were all locked. She resumed her search, only to let out a squeak when a tall man pushed abruptly out of the room at the end of the long hall and quickly exited, slamming an exterior door. He was too far away to make out clearly, but his actions made it obvious he was angry. Her steps slowed as she reached the last set of doors, and two, deep voices reverberated through the door.

Found 'em!

Had the man been in there talking to Harry and Sean? She started to pull the door open when Harry suddenly exploded, "Damn it, Sean! Are you out of your mind?"

Becca froze. She'd never heard Harry like that. He sounded angry but also... worried? She should walk away or make a noise. The last time she had listened in doorways, she'd gotten herself in trouble. But maybe it was because of that memory, she couldn't just walk away. It is only natural to be curious, she thought, trying to rationalize her eavesdropping.

"It's not ideal." Sean's voice sounded reasonable. "This is just business. It doesn't have to involve you more than this. I've tried to keep him away from you. I guess he just couldn't help himself." Sean's accent deepened. "If it weren't for this blasted storm, you never would have even known he was here!"

Seen who? Becca's stomach sank. Did he mean Rey? That didn't make sense. They had to be talking about the man who had just abruptly left the conference room. The man had been tall like Rey, but she was confident that the man was a stranger. Why was Harry so angry about his presence?

"So, now we're trapped here." Harry's voice was furious. "How am I going to explain this to Becca?"

What does this have to do with me?

"Why do you need to explain anything? It has nothing to do with her."

Becca glared at the door. The rebuttal she'd hoped to imme- diately hear from Harry didn't come. In the silence, her chest tightened. Sean must have read something into the silence, too, because he continued, "Hey mate, as long as you are here..."

"No."

"It would really help me out if you'd talk to him."

"You are pushing it, Sean." Harry's voice was gruff.

"He might listen to reason if it came from you."

Harry let out a harsh laugh, and Becca actually flinched at the sound.

Something is wrong. Really wrong.

She needed to interrupt whatever was happening, but as she depressed the handle, Sean's voice, came through low and urgent. "I'm in trouble, mate. If he doesn't help me, I'm done for. He's likely to just take off..."

Becca held her breath as a few beats of silence passed.

Then Sean gave an awkward laugh. "I mean, I don't want to say you owe me..."

His voice like ice, Harry answered, "I know. I'll see what I can do."

Becca swallowed hard, feeling her entire body tense up. They'd come so far these last weeks. She had begun to believe that she *had* found her happily ever after, after all... but this was entirely too reminiscent of what had happened before.

"I have another phone call to make. I'll think of something to tell Becca."

Either of the men could leave the room at any moment, so ignoring the pain in her chest, she looked around for some place to hide. If she tried to run to the end of the hallway, they would definitely see her. Spotting a bathroom sign nearby, Becca hurried to conceal herself but stood by the door listening. She raised a hand and pressed it hard against her heart as if that would make the ache stop.

What is wrong with you! Don't you dare cry!

Becca took a few deep breaths. Don't overreact, she scolded herself. It meant nothing. Like Sean had said, it had nothing to do with her; it was just... business? Except it didn't feel like that.

It had sounded exactly like Sean asking Harry to do something he didn't want to do, and to lie to her about it.

Buuuuut, Harry's first reaction was to worry about telling me, so that's a good sign, right?

A door closed, and Becca peeked out in time to watch Sean stride purposefully back to the lobby. She couldn't hide in the bathroom forever! Becca cracked the door open, slipped through and swiftly walked halfway up the hallway but then hesitated. What should she do? Should she admit she had eavesdropped? Or just pretend she believed Harry when he lied to her later? She cast a worried look back at the lobby.

Crap! She had forgotten her purpose in trying to find Harry, and felt a guilty twinge. Both she and Harry were keeping secrets. She sighed heavily. Maybe the reason she was so bothered by Harry's conversation with Sean was that she was also hiding something pretty big. Was she simply projecting her guilt, and that's why she was so on edge?

While she was lost in her own thoughts, the door opened and Harry emerged from the room, his face drawn. Becca's heart sank. She had a suspicion that Harry's mysterious past had finally caught up with him. His face cleared when he saw her, and he smiled. For a second, she felt as she had the day before, happy and secure.

"Hey! I was just looking for you!" she lied.

"Sorry, my calls took longer than I thought."

Becca didn't let her smile falter, even though she knew he wasn't being truthful. But then again, neither was she.

"Did you get everything taken care of?" Harry stared at her blankly. "Your phone calls?" She gestured to the room he had been in.

"Oh…yes. Grace is preparing the boat and Eduardo is following all the protocols we have in place for storms. I guess I should be grateful that the first time we have to use them it isn't a big storm. We'll be able to see where the weak spots are."

Despite his words, his eyes were worried, and he was clearly thinking of something else.

"That's good." Becca almost winced at how inane she sounded, but Harry didn't seem to notice. "Do you want to go back to the room?" She mentally crossed her fingers.

"Sure." But he didn't move. Instead, he stared at her so intensely she became uncomfortable.

Her stomach twisted. "Are you okay?" she asked, mimicking the words he had used so many times over the last twenty-four hours.

Good grief! We are a mess!

He nodded.

"I need to tell you some things—not now—when we get home. I need you to understand about things I've done...my life..." He trailed off, his eyes troubled.

Uh oh. This can't be good. Is this about his conversation with Sean?

Not sure how she could push the issue since he didn't know that she had overheard, she gave him a bewildered smile and turned to walk to the lobby. She had enough to worry about right now. At least he doesn't seem to mind going back to the room...

Suddenly, Becca felt herself pulled backward and caught in his arms. "Harry, what..." but her words were cut off as his mouth crashed into hers. At first Becca's brain objected. They were in the middle of an open hallway. Anyone could... Becca lost her train of thought as the kiss heated further, and Harry propelled her until her back was pressed against the wall. She could taste his urgency, and her heart pounded. He pulled back, his eyes hot, and then pressed his forehead almost painfully into hers. His hands rose to frame her face. Her heart contracted at his expression. "I love you." Becca opened her mouth to answer him, but he silenced her with a soft kiss. Harry seemed to regain his equilibrium. He flashed her a smile that belied the intensity of the past few seconds. "What were you saying about going to the room?"

Becca matched his smile, her body still thrumming. He said he loved her... and he wasn't drunk! She was giddy but it was tempered by a foreboding that they were teetering on the precipice of something. She knew what *she* had to hide, but what was it that Sean wanted from Harry?

10

I can't believe he cancelled dinner, Becca fumed! Now she was stuck eating with Celine alone. When the phone rang earlier, she could tell by the tone of Harry's voice that it was Sean, and this was the moment of truth. When he left the bed and took the call on the balcony, her heart hurt. He was going to lie to her. When he returned to bed, he hadn't met her eyes and his kiss had a feeling of desperation to it that troubled her. She was braced for him to lie, but she hadn't anticipated that he would cancel their dinner plans.

"Sean wants me to meet with one of his investors. As a fellow developer in the Bahamas, he thinks my opinion will calm this guy's nerves about hurricane season. But he said Celine is looking forward to dinner, so, you should still meet her."

She had let it go, but it rankled that this 'meeting' with Sean and the investor was the secret favor Sean wanted, and leaving her with Celine just made it worse. She wasn't sure what to do about it. Becca glanced out over the balcony where the trees were whipping around, trying to ignore the knot in the pit of her stomach. She felt like crying and that made her angry. The island was in between squalls ahead of the main storm, so despite the wind, the rain was gone for the moment. She checked the weather on her phone and saw the storm was still barely a Category 1 and moving quickly. That's good at least. Let it blow over, and then we can get out of here, she thought.

She only had an hour before meeting Celine, and Becca knew she should get ready. It would be good to get out of the room where all she was going to do was brood. Her mood wasn't helped by her limited wardrobe choices. She hadn't expected to be here this long, and her vanity wouldn't allow her to wear the same green dress as the night before. Becca looked at the skirt and top she had hung in the closet, her only other option, and scowled.

No way! Not when there was a high likelihood of running into all of her old frenemies, not to mention the beautiful Celine. Harry had ditched her, and Sean was encouraging Harry to deceive her. Her ears grew hot. That decided it. She was going shopping and putting it on the room!

The boutique Becca chose had several cute options, and Becca quickly picked out two casual dresses. They may not be dressy enough for whatever Celine had planned, but it would have to do. At the moment she couldn't care less! She had bigger things to worry about than the arrogant woman who had blatantly ogled Harry, and who, Becca hoped, she would never see again.

Twenty minutes later, as she was leaving the store, Becca looked down to check the time on her phone. "Oomph!" She slammed into a large man hurrying past, causing him to stumble. *Rey!* He did *not* look pleased to see her. Without making a sound, and with a look back over his shoulder, he grabbed her by her bicep. He dragged her toward a door leading to the maintenance room, swiping a card hanging from a lanyard around his neck in front of the security panel, and practically pushed her inside.

When the door clicked shut behind them, he crossed his arms and glared at her. "What the hell are you doing here, Becca?"

"What am I doing here? What are *you* doing here? Has Dr. Navarro had a career change? It's a big jump from marine archeologist to maintenance worker." She nodded at the uniform he wore.

Rey exhaled through his teeth. "Why do you *always* turn up at the worst times? It's like you have a freaking radar for how to screw things up!"

Becca's eyes flashed, and she crossed her own arms. "I'm *so* sorry that my life doesn't line up with your plans, *Dr. Navarro*," she drawled sarcastically.

"I'm not Dr. Navarro anymore, and don't say that out loud. Are you trying to get me killed?" He glared down at her. "After Katie's disappearance last year, and the smuggling route getting busted up, Olivera wasn't particularly trusting of anyone involved. It's a little suspicious to be the only one still standing when something goes pear-shaped like that. So, Navarro disappeared... just like Katie." He looked at her meaningfully.

"Did they believe your story about witness protection?"

After Rey killed Katie in order to save Becca, he had concocted a story that he hoped would allow him to remain undercover with the drug cartel. The FBI "leaked" information that Katie had gone into the witness protection program in order to avoid arrest like the rest of the smuggling ring. Rey had explained to Becca that if the cartel believed Katie was still alive and a witness against them, they would concentrate their efforts on eliminating the threat. They would have no reason to go after Becca. He had sworn her to secrecy, and Becca had kept the fact that Rey was actually an undercover FBI agent a secret from everyone.

Becca hadn't had any contact with him since he had dropped her off on the side of the road that night. For months, being kept in the dark about what was happening with the investigation had driven her crazy. She finally accepted that no news was good news, and that if the cartel was coming after her, then the FBI would have let her know.

"Yeah, we laid a pretty good trail for them. Last I heard they were chasing a phantom in Belize." A satisfied smile teased around his mouth, but quickly disappeared. "You didn't answer my question. What are you doing here?"

"You didn't answer mine either," she snapped back. However, odd bits and pieces from the last two days were starting to fit together. "You're here about Jake's company. Aren't you? You're the FBI agent who questioned my son, right?"

Rey's expression was unreadable.

"You know Owen had nothing to do with whatever it is you think Jake has done. You didn't have to interrogate him. He's just a kid!" Becca fumed thinking of the worry in her son's face.

"First of all, I didn't 'interrogate' him. They were routine questions. And second, he's twenty years old, *not* a kid." Becca opened her mouth to argue, but he held up a finger to stop her. "And for the record, I don't *know* that your son isn't involved. That's why we have investigations." He sounded as if he were explaining something basic to a child. Becca resisted the urge to punch him.

"Don't be obnoxious! If you were able to get a warrant then you've already investigated, and now you are just looking for proof!" She balled her hands at her sides.

"You're a legal expert now?" he taunted.

"I watch a lot of true crime." Becca winced. It had sounded different in her head. Embarrassed, she rushed to add, "Owen has only been working there for a few months. He's an intern, for goodness' sake!"

Rey angled his head and pursed his lips. "Wasn't he also an intern at Raybourn's old office while he was in Atlanta? That's when he ran away from school, right? After some kind of blowup at the office? Did he ever tell you what that was about? It must have been serious. He fled the city after all, and then the next semester he left for good and transferred to a school near his dad, right? Once again, he's working for a Raybourn financial firm. Why?"

Becca's eyes were saucers. "Are you kidding me? You think my twenty-year-old son transferred schools because he was involved in some kind of federal crime?" She scoffed, "Well, Mr. Investigator, if you had done your job well, you would have easily found out that Owen left that job *weeks* before he left school. And I hate to burst your bubble, but as is usually the case at that age, his problems stemmed from a relationship. And 'for the record,' you are way off base if you think Jake has committed a crime."

Nicole? That's entirely possible.

"What was that?" Rey watched her closely.

"What was what?"

"You just thought of something. I saw it in your face."

Becca met his eyes and made her face blank. A year of living her carefree Key West lifestyle had destroyed her default defense of dissembling. Rey's face blanked as well.

Dang it! He's even better at it than I am!

"If you know something you have to tell me," Rey said.

"I have nothing to do with my ex-husband's business. And even if I did, I wouldn't tell you." What was it about this man that irritated her so much, she wondered?

Rey took two steps closer and leaned in. "It's against the law to lie to a federal agent."

Becca refused to be intimidated. "Fascinating. Now if you'll excuse me, I have dinner plans."

"Ah, yes." Rey curled his lip. "Loverboy and more of his criminal friends. For someone who claims to be clueless, you are awfully cozy with all the key players."

"What is that supposed to mean? Key players in what?"

Rey exhaled exasperated. "God, you are a lousy judge of character!"

"I am not!"

"Yeah, you really are. You prance around, stumbling into trouble and befriending every shady character you come across. Brennan, Silverman, your friend Amelia, and that's before you count the people at this hotel!" He stabbed a finger at her. "You need to learn to keep your eyes open and stop trusting everyone, damn it!"

Becca gaped at his intensity. "I am not... I don't... I don't know anyone here. I mean I used to... but not anymore." She hated that he could fluster her. "I'm only here because of Harry."

Rey tapped his finger to the tip of his nose. "Exactly."

When he opened the door a crack to see if anyone was in the hallway, she moved to edge past him, more than ready to get out of the room. He blocked her with his arm and tilted his head, thinking.

"You *should* go to dinner with your new friends *but* keep your ears open. If you hear anything suspicious, make a note."

Under normal circumstances a request like that would have sounded ludicrous. It didn't. Her gut told her that it was a little *too* coincidental that Jake's firm, PPW, was under investigation by the FBI, and that everyone involved just happened to end up at a hotel they were invested in—a hotel that was also owned by Harry's friend, who now demanded Harry fulfill some favor. Not to mention that whatever the favor was, Harry clearly didn't want to do it. And he had felt it necessary to lie to her about it. Becca tried to follow all the crazy threads but they just ended up a big knot inside her head.

"I'll check back with you tomorrow."

"No!" Becca burst out. She couldn't risk him seeking her out. Harry might see him, and then it would come out that she had lied about what had happened last year!

With his hand still on the door, Rey pressed his face so close to hers that their noses were almost touching, and his eyes burned into hers.

"If you are convinced that your son and ex aren't involved, then it's in your best interest to help me clear them," he said, misunderstanding her objection.

Becca swallowed hard, but before she could answer Rey was gone, the door shutting behind him. Becca sucked in a shaky breath.

Listen for what? Clear them of what? You didn't even tell me what you think Jake's done!

It wasn't until she was alone in the elevator that her heart finally slowed enough for her to think clearly. Owen was worried his dad was being duped because of what he overheard Nicole say on the phone. If Owen had understood Nicole correctly, it sounded like she knew who was guilty... of whatever crime it was. Becca groaned.

It might have helped if you filled me in, Rey, she thought testily.

Becca chewed on her nail. Nicole had said, "I'm not going to jail for anyone." Did that mean she was okay if someone else took the fall? Unfaithful ass aside, Becca couldn't let Jake go to jail if he was being set up. It would destroy Owen.

But how am I supposed to help if I don't know what's going on?

On autopilot, Becca dressed for her dinner with Celine. Her thoughts were no longer on the most likely, unpleasant meal ahead of her, but on what Rey had said. Who was he talking about when he said 'criminal friends?' Did he mean Sean? She paused, the mascara wand half-way to her eye. She remembered Sean's strange mood the night before and his suspicion over Becca's connection to Jake. Then there was the favor he had asked Harry about. It couldn't be something good. Becca's stomach turned to ice. She set the eye makeup down, and braced her hands on the counter.

Three days ago, everything was practically perfect. She was in their beautiful villa making real progress on the painting. She and Harry were closer than ever... he said he loved her. Now, she felt like they had slid all the way back to the beginning when she was full of doubts about who he was. If she had been asked a few days ago if she trusted Harry, her answer would have instantly been, "yes." And now?

She shook her head to clear it. She was getting carried away. Maybe when he was done with his meeting, she would ask about what she overheard, and he would tell her the truth about what Sean wanted. It could be just a coincidence that Jake's firm invested in this hotel.

Right!

Becca blew her cheeks out. Owen *had* to be her priority. The FBI didn't get involved in small crimes, so whatever was going on, it had to be big! Becca nodded at herself in the mirror. *You can do this, Becca.* Resolved to see what she could find out from Celine, Becca dropped her phone in her purse and left to meet the French woman in the lobby.

11

The light was much dimmer than when she had gone up to her room just twenty minutes before. Another squall must be moving in, she thought. The chandeliers were lit but were little match for the dark, greenish light coming through the floor-to-ceiling glass windows. A burst of rain hit the glass sounding like machine gun fire, and Becca jumped as did most of the people around her. For a moment she felt a frisson of concern. A Category 1 hurricane wouldn't normally phase her, but with everything else going wrong…

The lobby was crowded with both guests preparing to go into the rehearsal cocktail party and a variety of tourists with children. Becca could well understand the desire to be around a crowd rather than riding out a hurricane alone in a hotel room.

She met one woman's worried glance with a reassuring smile. Just then a large gust threw another sheet of rainwater at the glass, and the woman squeaked with fear. Simultaneously, there was a flash of light as Michelle took the woman's picture.

"I'll call it… *Fear*." Michelle ignored the woman's embarrassed flush and moved off again, snapping pictures of everything around her.

"Don't worry," Becca told the woman. "These squalls will come and go until the back side of the storm has passed over. I just looked, and it won't be that bad. The eye wall is expected sometime after midnight; we'll probably all sleep through it."

The woman gave her a wan smile. Becca wished she could say something to comfort her, but she had her own battles to fight right now. Becca scanned the room for Celine as she dodged various groups clustered around the room. She finally spotted her talking to Nicole by the entrance to the long hallway to the left of the reception desk. Becca frowned.

"Will you put that away!" a voice hissed just behind her.

"It's my art, Brad! The class said I should take hundreds of photos because you never know when, like, it's the *one*!"

"You are embarrassing me."

"It's *art*!" Michelle's voice pitched up in a whine. "Right, Becca?"

Yikes! Becca tried to pretend she didn't hear her, but Michelle tugged her arm turning her.

"Tell him, Becca!" she commanded.

Becca took one look at Brad's expression and muttered, "Hmm? What?"

NOT getting involved!

"Tell him that we must sacrifice for our art." Michelle clutched her camera to her chest as if she were protecting a baby.

If she says 'art' one more time…

"Mom!" Owen appeared directly in front of her, eyes wild and panting. "It's him! The FBI guy! He's here! I've gotta find Dad!"

Becca licked her suddenly dry lips. Was there any chance Brad and Michelle *hadn't* heard him? The avid curiosity on their faces gave her the answer. "Mom! Look! He's right there! The guy by the elevator!" Brad and Michelle's heads swiveled in the direction Owen was pointing before Becca pushed his arm down.

"Who? The hottie in the jeans?" Michelle blushed bright red

and looked at her husband. Fortunately, he didn't seem to notice, too busy squinting in Rey's direction.

"He looks familiar," Brad said.

Becca tried to catch Owen's attention, but he, too, seemed transfixed by Rey's appearance. Unfortunately, Rey chose that moment to turn and look straight at them.

"That's not an FBI agent." Michelle lifted her camera in his direction. Rey turned away and Michelle lowered the camera with a sigh. "That's John's new investor. I saw them earlier. He wouldn't let me take his picture, which sucks because he has incredible cheekbones. He was really rude about it, too."

"That's our new investor?" Brad asked, still looking at Rey, who thankfully was getting on an elevator. "What made you think he was FBI?"

Shut up, Owen!

Owen failed to heed her telepathic plea. "He's the one I talked to at the office."

That's it!

Becca stepped hard on Owen's foot while simultaneously dropping her purse.

"Oh no!" she cried, in a voice that was completely disproportionate to the event. "I hope I didn't break my phone!" Her shrill voice had drawn the amused attention of several guests nearby.

Brad scowled at her. "Why do you women always have to make a scene! Come on, Michelle. Let's go to the bar to wait until they open the doors for the party." With one last look of disgust at Becca, he walked away never looking back to see if his wife had followed.

Becca grabbed Owen's hand and, not caring who saw them, dragged him into a corner.

"Ow! What's wrong with you?"

"What's wrong with me? Are you serious? You just blurted out to a room full of your dad's clients that he's under investigation by the FBI!"

Owen paled, but adopted a mulish expression. "He isn't though. He said it was a client."

"I understand that's what he told you, and I hope that is the case, but you were the one who told me you thought something more was going on. Until we find out what is happening and how we can help your dad, we need to keep this information to ourselves, okay?"

Two deep grooves formed between his eyebrows. "So, you *do* think something is going on. You lied to me earlier."

Let me get this straight. Your dad gets you questioned by the FBI, but I'm the bad guy.

Becca bit her tongue until she controlled her frustration. "I don't know what is going on, and since we *don't* know, we should probably play it safe. Besides, this is his wedding weekend, he doesn't need any problems."

How in the world did I end up in the position of making sure my ex-husband has a good wedding day? I better be earning some serious good karma for this!

"I guess you're right." Owen rubbed his neck, then stood up straight with his hands on his hips. "But I'm telling Dad about what Nicole said and that FBI guy being here, as soon as the wedding is over. He should know that they are spying on him. He needs to protect himself."

His words were full of bravado but Becca saw his chin tremble and she pulled him into a tight hug. His muscles were rigid. She squeezed harder and whispered in his ear, "It's going to be okay. I promise."

When she released him, he shrugged one shoulder as if he didn't care, but his face was still taut with worry. "I should get back."

Becca gave him a tight smile as he left and mentally added Rey to the growing list of people she wanted to murder. She closed her eyes and wondered, if I click my heels three times, will I poof back home? Becca felt an acute longing for the simplicity of her cottage in Key West, where her most stressful challenge was getting a feral cat to like her.

She mentally shook herself. *No time for self-pity, Becca,* she silently scolded herself. *You'll be home soon and then you can sit back with a bottle or two of wine and have a real pity party.* Right now, she needed to find Celine and see what she could discover.

CROSSING THE LOBBY TO WHERE SHE HAD LAST SEEN THE FRENCH beauty, she gave a little wave to Michelle as she took Becca's picture... again... and moved on to her next victim. Becca felt a moment of sympathy for Brad. Michelle was just as bad as paparazzi!

Unable to find Celine, Becca finally asked the front desk if they had seen her and was annoyed when she was told Celine had already gone to the bistro restaurant. *So much for meeting in the lobby,* Becca groused, but then realized in all fairness she was almost fifteen minutes late!

The restaurant was full of guests because it was impossible to leave the resort for dinner during the storm. But it wasn't difficult to spot Celine. She was seated alone at an enormous table, in the center of the room eating a salad.

I'm a little late, and she's already ordered and eating? It's not like she was pining away in here! I just saw her in the lobby dealing with Nicole.

Becca put her hostile thoughts aside and put on her best social smile. If she was going to get any information, she had to make sure the woman didn't pick up on how much she aggravated Becca. Her smile was wasted though because Celine barely glanced up from her phone when Becca approached. Celine held the phone in one hand while she speared something green with the other. Her dark eyes flicked up for a nanosecond and she gestured with her fork for Becca to sit. Becca clenched her teeth so hard she was worried she would crack a tooth.

"Sorry I'm late." She couldn't afford to antagonize the woman, no matter how tempting it was to tell her off.

"It's fine. With the storm and everything going on, I didn't have time to wait for you."

That's kind of an apology, I guess.

"It must be really hard trying to manage all your employees and guests while also trying to get your property ready. Sean said several of the guests are your main investors. It must be extra stressful to make sure they are happy. Hopefully, when Sean gets done with his meeting, he'll be able to help you."

As her first gambit, it was bold to bring up the investors but Becca didn't know how long Celine would even stay at the table, and she was a little desperate to find what the connection might be between everything going on. Bonus points if Celine let slip why Sean and Harry were missing dinner.

Celine shrugged and took another bite of her salad, but Becca noticed her fingers had clenched the fork tighter. A server came over and handed Becca a menu. "It's a shame they couldn't join us tonight," she persisted, "but I guess whatever it is they're doing must be important... all Harry said is that it's business?" She pitched the words to make them a question.

Celine slowly blinked at her. "Sean does what Sean does. I don't question him."

This was harder than she had thought it would be. Becca changed the subject hoping to bring it back around more naturally. "Harry was surprised to find out that Sean had gotten married. Have you been married long?"

Celine sighed, and set down the fork, apparently resigned to what she obviously considered an asinine conversation. "Almost a year."

"Wow, that's great. Harry mentioned that it had been a while since he had spoken to Sean..."

Celine picked up her fork again and listlessly pushed the vegetables around in her bowl. Becca waited, but it was rapidly becoming apparent that Celine had no intention of helping carry the conversation. "Where did the two of you meet?

The slow blink returned. "Nicosia."

Where the heck is that?

"Oh, is that Greece?"

It sounds Greek.

With a heavy sigh that fully translated her exhaustion at having to suffer Becca's company, Celine said, "Cyprus."

Becca had a vague idea of where that was, but she wasn't about to ask for clarification. "That's exciting!"

"I suppose to some... I was working. The clubs are terrible there." She scrunched her nose. "Just business men visiting the banks."

"What do you do?"

Celine looked at her as if she's stupid. "I'm a model."

Of course, she was.

"How did you and Sean meet?"

Celine took a sip of her wine, her eyes suddenly shrewd as she finally gave Becca her attention. "There is a man there, who has fabulous parties on his yacht. I was there to party and Sean was there to do business. *That's* how we met." Celine's eyes held Becca's. "I think the man is another of Harry's friends. Have you met James?"

Ice sluiced down Becca's spine. She wasn't sure what hidden message Celine was trying to get across, but Becca had a feeling she wouldn't like it

"No, I haven't." Becca arched a casual eyebrow, but Celine only made a noncommittal sound and didn't elaborate. The woman wanted her to ask about whomever James was, but Becca refused to. A glass of wine was placed in front of her, and Becca looked up, startled. She hadn't even ordered yet.

"Sean told me you like wine. I hope red is all right," Celine drawled.

"Red is my favorite." Becca lied sweetly. She indicated to the server that she would have the same salad as Celine. After he left, she took a slow sip of wine, observing the woman across from her over the rim. "I saw you talking to Nicole earlier?"

Celine's hand jerked on the table, but she maintained her customary limpid expression.

Now I know she's hiding something! Was the whole vapid model thing an act?

"Of course. She's the bride." Celine's lips parted. "Oh dear, I forgot. Sean mentioned you were at odds with the bridal party. That there might be some... bad feelings about the bride and groom."

Becca laughed through closed lips, afraid of what would come out if she opened them. "You mean because the groom is my ex-husband. Not at all. I'm thrilled for them. My son is even the best man."

Celine pursed her lips and made a sympathetic noise. "No, I meant because they had been lovers while you were married."

Becca felt like Celine had slapped her. Would Nicole have told her? It seemed an odd thing to admit, even if they were in business together. Not likely. Nicole wouldn't tarnish her image like that. Becca's heart pounded, and her brain struggled to make sense of it.

The woman has to be guessing, but why? Is she trying to embarrass me? What is her freaking deal? She has been border- line hostile ever since I sat down. Is she always like this, or is it because she's clearly lusting after Harry?

Becca's fingers tightened around the stem of her wineglass, and she saw Celine's eyes flare in satisfaction. Becca was saved when the server delivered her salad, allowing her a second to pull herself together.

Celine tapped her long fingernails against her glass and

looked at Becca speculatively. "Such an odd coincidence though that you and Harry just happen to show up on the same weekend as their wedding, no?"

"Extremely." Becca took a gamble. "It's also odd that Harry has been back and forth to his resort for over a year, but Sean only learned two days ago that he was in the area, and it was immediately imperative for Harry to come here."

Celine's lips twisted. "My husband never fails to take advantage of an opportunity."

Becca frowned. "What opportunity is that? Harry was worried Sean was going to ask for money." It was indiscreet, but she didn't care. She was still angry about the Jake and Nicole comment.

Celine's fingers stilled on the glass. "Why would he think Sean needs money?"

That surprised Becca. She would have thought the statement would have elicited either an automatic denial or, at the very least, outrage on behalf of her husband.

"For the remodel?" Becca guessed.

Celine's lips curved. "Ah, but we have investors for that. A real estate investment group headed by your ex-husband's firm to be specific."

"Sean told us last night. He seemed to think that our being here, particularly considering the connection, was odd, until we reminded him that he was the one who invited us."

Celine made a noise of disgust. "Sean isn't thinking clearly lately. He's short tempered and sees disaster in every shadow."

"But why? It looks like the hotel is a success?"

"Let's just say he isn't used to having to owe anyone. He's used to doing things his own way. But the Royal always comes first with him, no matter what it costs him." Celine began to flick her salad angrily.

Becca was lost. She couldn't see how having investors would

be a great cost to Sean. "Do they interfere with what he wants to do?"

Celine looked up scornfully, but seeing Becca's confusion her face cleared. "You really *aren't* here because of them, are you?"

"The investment group?"

Celine laughed, the sound abrasive. "It really was a coincidence!" She picked up her glass, drained the contents, and set it back down so hard it tipped over. "He always was a lucky bastard." Celine ignored the glass, pushed back her chair, and stood up. She shook her head at Becca with pity. "It's painfully clear now that you are exactly what you appear to be. I thought it was an act… no one could be that naïve… not arriving with Harry Brennan. But now…" She shook her head in disbelief again and walked away without another word.

Bitch.

Becca reached for her glass surprised to see that her hand trembled. She pressed her hands down onto the table and realized with horror that she could feel angry tears building behind her eyes. She wanted to pass off Celine's comments as just bitchy, but her last statements sounded sincere, as if Celine knew something about Harry that Becca didn't.

It seemed like her worst fears were being realized. Rey was right. There was definitely something going on here, something Celine thought Becca should've already known. Was Sean trying to involve Harry in it? What about Jake?

Celine seemed to accept that Harry and Becca's arrival at the same time as the group from Sun Coast was a coincidence. But then why had Sean wanted Harry here at that precise time? He could have asked him for advice or whatever it was that he needed at any time. Becca's gut told her the timing had to be significant. Sean had been surprised to find out Becca was once married to Jake, so that couldn't be it. It had to have something to do with the money and the investors. Celine's reaction alone seemed to prove that. Harry hadn't been wrong. Sean wanted something from him. Becca had an awful premonition that there was a connection to what Rey was investigating, and that it was happening tonight during Harry and Sean's secret meeting.

Becca drank the red wine automatically not truly tasting it. What should she do? Everything in her wanted to find Jake and shake the truth out of him. How was it, that even after all these years, he was still causing problems for her?

She took a deep breath and let it out slowly, trying to calm her nerves. Should she try to find Rey and tell him about the conversation with Celine? What was the point? She hadn't learned anything. Becca pulled her phone from her purse and thought about texting Harry. She wanted to ask him to come back to the room so they could talk. But she didn't especially want to do that either. She wanted him to tell her on his own. But did she have the time to wait for that to happen? Pride warred with practicality in her head.

Frustrated, she typed out a quick message to Harry, letting him know dinner was over and she was headed back to the room. The bubble with three dots appeared, a sign that he was typing something back. Relief washed over. If he were in the middle of some nefarious scheme, he wouldn't be texting her right back. Everything was fine. It's Harry, and she was just being dramatic. Her muscles unclenched a little, and she relaxed as she waited for the message to come through.

Ten minutes later, when the text bubble had disappeared, and he still hadn't texted back, the knots returned. That wasn't like him. Not sure what else she could do, she returned to the room and got ready for bed. The squall that had been lashing the hotel before dinner had blown over, but the wind was still fairly strong. When she stepped onto her balcony, she was hit by a wall of thick, wet air. She recognized the sensation. The outer bands had reached them, and she could expect stronger storms off and on for the rest of the night.

A burst of angry voices reached her from somewhere in the darkness below. Becca craned her neck trying to see, but a large palm obstructed her view and the rustling of the palm fronds in the steady breeze obscured their voices.

"Stop!" a female voice cried out.

Becca leaned dangerously over the balcony trying to see what was going on. *Is that Candice?* A few people stumbled into view. Two men struggled together. Becca's room was on the second floor but, between the moonless night and the blowing trees, it was hard to be sure what she was seeing.

"Brad! Do something!" Michelle's high-pitched whine carried up to Becca. Becca saw a large shape, that she assumed was Brad, try to get between the two fighting figures.

Their movements brought them closer under Becca's balcony, and Becca was shocked when one of the men stepped into a pool of light and her ex-husband's face became clear.

"You're drunk," he snarled to the other man. Becca willed the other man to walk closer. Jake's hair was disheveled, and his shirt was pulled from his pants.

That must be some party!

Jake stepped back, his hands up defensively in front of him as John Raybourn stumbled forward into the light. John wobbled, barely staying upright, as he pushed past Jake and headed for the bungalows. Brad put his arm around Jake's shoulders and pulled him back into the darkness and, presumably, to the party.

Becca's head throbbed. She wished she could blame it on a bad glass of red wine or the barometric pressure, but the drama she had just witnessed below had pushed her past her nerves' limit. She turned off her phone as she slipped into bed. Everything would look better in the morning, she assured herself.

Becca estimated it was about an hour later that the heavy rain came again. Soon after, Harry opened the door to the suite. She listened intently as he moved around in the outer room. Why wasn't he coming to bed? The wind accelerated with its tell-tale high pitch as the gusts strengthened and whipped past the building. An electrical thunk sounded, and the lights outside the window disappeared. There goes the power, she thought irritably, but was gratified when less than two minutes later a low hum started in the distance. *Blessed be the generators.* She smiled wryly at her own joke.

When the bedroom door finally opened, she pretended she was asleep. Harry crept around the room undressing. He pulled the curtains partially closed before the bed dipped as he climbed in. But instead of pulling her into his arms as he normally did, he rolled his back to her and fell asleep.

12

Becca didn't sleep well that night. The whooshing of the wind and rain as the hurricane hit didn't help, nor did her unsettled thoughts. Harry had tossed and turned more than normal, as well. When the eye-wall of the hurricane passed over them and the storm was at its worst, Harry got out of bed and pulled the curtain back to look out at the storm whipping across the island. When he came back to bed, he pulled her snugly against his chest and wrapped his arms around her, pulling the sheet up to cocoon them. Becca wished they could stay safe and hidden not just from the storm outside but from all the trouble she feared was waiting for them.

Groggy and with a mouth like a desert, Becca rolled out of bed in the morning and was in the shower before Harry was even up. By the time she came out of the bathroom, Harry was sitting on the side of the bed.

"Good morning."

"Good morning," she returned. It was awkward, and she hated it. *Why is he being so formal?* He didn't know she had learned about his lie to her. To avoid making eye contact, Becca busied herself pretending to pick an outfit out of her limited choices.

Harry scrubbed a hand down his face. "A lot of the staff live on site, but I doubt they'll have room service for coffee this morning."

"That's okay. I can just make it here. The power is back on." Becca began fiddling with the coffeepot on the shelf. She inserted one of the pods, trying to ignore Harry watching her warily. "How was your meeting?" she asked with her back still turned.

There was a heavy sigh. "Becca, I'm sorry I wasn't able to text you back last night and that I got in so late. We got caught up making plans for Sean's business and realigning his deal with his investors."

The ubiquitous investors again!

"Oh, is that what he needed your help with? A realignment with the nervous investor?" It was possible Harry was telling the truth about what the meeting was about, but what about that needed to be a secret?

"He's definitely having trouble with an investor," Harry said carefully.

Becca frowned. "Jake?"

"No, but someone connected to that group." Harry walked into the bathroom and turned the shower on before sticking his head back out, and asking a little too casually, "Is this real estate investment thing, organizing investors to form a REIT, is that something Jake specialized in?"

Thankfully, Becca was still facing the coffee pot so he couldn't see her expression. Harry had never asked her about Jake's business before, and she didn't like that he was doing it now.

"Not that I'm aware of. Owen and I always thought he traded stocks or something."

"Huh."

The door closed, and Harry disappeared into the shower. *Okay, there's no denying that something is off. It's not just me. He's not acting like himself either.*

Becca took the first cup of coffee for herself and popped in another pod to make a mug for Harry. She took a sip and promptly made a face. She'd gotten spoiled over the last few weeks. Becca took another sip of the poorly flavored brew. *How am I going to trick him into telling me?*

That stopped her in her tracks. *Trick him?* That wasn't the relationship she wanted. Becca had thought Harry's finally opening up to her about his business and his past had been a turning point for them, that the relationship was no longer one-sided with her telling him everything and him telling her nothing. But you haven't been completely honest either, a voice whispered.

She was worried that if she asked him directly what specifically was wrong between Jake's investment group and the resort, he wouldn't tell her. It was scary, but how else was she going to figure out if Jake was involved? And how did Nicole fit into it? Was Raybourn also part of it? What about Anna and Michelle, not to mention their husbands and the other guests here who were clients?

Was figuring out what was going on with Jake important enough to risk what she had with Harry? Becca bit her lip.

But not asking him is also putting our future at risk because I will know that he is keeping something from me.

She set the mug down. And then there was Rey lurking about, his whole existence threatening their relationship. She thought about what Rey had said about her helping to clear Owen. She wouldn't risk Harry for Jake's sake, but there was *nothing* she wouldn't do to protect her son.

Ugh, I thought I'd left the drama behind when I moved to Key West. Maybe it's me?

Her lack of sleep wasn't helping her fuzzy brain. Becca

opened the doors and took her coffee on to the balcony, surveying the damage below. For the most part, the resort looked as it had the first day they had arrived, just wetter. There were some palm fronds strewn about the grass, but it looked like no major damage was done.

Becca had just settled into the outdoor chair with her coffee when a scream ripped through the air. Becca shot to her feet. *What the hell?* The scream repeated, sharp and staccato. People flooded out of the bungalows below, stopping in shock when Candice stumbled out of her bungalow. One hand was pressed to her mouth; the other hand pointed back into the bungalow. Her shrieks were barely muffled by her hand. "Help me! Oh my god! Oh my god! I need somebody to help me!"

Becca raced back into the room, grabbing the shirt and skirt hanging in the closet. She opened the bathroom door a crack, stuck her head into the steam filled room, and called, "I'm just going to the lobby, back in a minute." Becca didn't want to advertise why she was going. Her morbid curiosity wasn't necessarily her most admirable quality.

The elevator whisked her down, and in under three minutes, she was downstairs, following the crowd of people that flowed out of the hotel and onto the grassy area beneath her room. She hadn't been the only one drawn by the screaming. Michelle and Anna were already there, but there was no sign of Jake or Nicole.

Becca cut through the crowd to reach her former friend. Candice shook uncontrollably, her hands held straight out in front of her as if she were trying to ward off an invisible threat. There were a few blood smears on the front of her white robe, but as Becca scanned her, she couldn't discern any injuries.

"Candice are you alright?"

Sound rose around them as the crowd asked questions, speculating on what the trouble was. Right on Becca's heels, three security guards rushed up.

Candice's eyes, when they met Becca's, were glassy. "He's dead."

"Who is? John?" Becca asked, instinctively reaching for the distraught woman.

But Candice reared back like a frightened animal. "He... he's out there... by the pool." She pointed back toward her bungalow.

Becca watched as a security guard emerged, grim faced, and closed the door behind him. "Ma'am," he said to Candice. "Is this your room?"

"Yes." Candice's lips trembled.

"I need you to come with me, please." To the other two guards, he said. "I want someone at the door and another to get the guests back inside the hotel."

The guards nodded and began the standard, "there's nothing to see here, go back inside." One guard began herding the guests, waving his hands in front of him in a shooing motion as the other positioned himself in front of the closed bungalow door. The crowd shifted backward but kept their inquisitive eyes glued to the action, tracking as the third guard led Candice away.

Becca followed slowly behind the group that disappeared into the lobby. She had the sudden irreverent thought that this might be Candice's worst nightmare. Her friends staring as she walked by—dressed in a frumpy robe, make-up smeared, her hair straggled over her face.

What is wrong with me! She just found a dead body, and I'm what? Happy she looks terrible? That makes me as bad as her!

Chastened, Becca watched as they led Candice into the office, behind the front desk, and shut the door. Becca shifted from one foot to the other. She wanted to know what was going on, and by the amount of other people lingering in the lobby talking in small huddles, she wasn't the only one! Had John had a heart attack? No, that made little sense. There wouldn't be blood. But there wasn't *a lot* of blood. Becca's mind raced through all the possibilities. He'd been super drunk last night, she thought, remembering how John could barely walk upright. Had he had an accident? Becca felt a hand on her elbow.

"What's going on?" Harry asked, looking around at the crowded lobby.

"I think John Raybourn is dead." The phrase felt strange coming out of her mouth, but not as strange as it should have. "When you were in the shower, I heard screaming. When I looked out the window, I saw Candice come out of her bunga-low... she had blood on her robe." Becca's face flushed and her scalp tingled. She felt as if she were having an out-of-body expe-rience. She suspected the initial adrenaline was leaving her and the reality of what she was saying was setting in. "Hotel security took Candice into the office. To hold her until the police get here, I guess."

When Harry didn't respond right away, Becca looked up. The expression on Harry's face wasn't as shocked as she'd expected. He didn't even look surprised. In fact, though it wasn't a look she had seen more than once on his face, she recognized that the sudden lines bracketing his mouth and the ridge that had formed between his eyebrows meant he was worried. She rubbed her arms as goosebumps rose. Harry glanced down at her movement.

"Let's get back to the room. Us standing here isn't doing anything." Harry said. He was right, and though it was completely against her naturally nosy instincts, Becca nodded.

Once they were back in the room, Becca paced back and forth restlessly. "I don't know what we should do."

Harry looked at her strangely. "What are you talking about? What *can* we do? It has nothing to do with us."

"I knew him." Becca stopped her circuit of the room.

"You *used* to know him. You don't *anymore*." Harry's voice was unusually firm. He must have sensed her surprise because he placed his hands lightly on her shoulders and turned her to face him fully. "I'm sorry. I just... I just don't want us to get involved. His death has nothing to do with us," he repeated. "It's going to take a bit for them to get the police here. They'll be stretched thin after the storm, and you know me and law enforcement..." Harry gave a half-smile and tried to pass the comment off as a joke.

Harry began throwing clothes into his bag. "We should get ready to go."

"Do you think they're going to let us leave?"

Harry spun around. "Who's to tell us we can't?"

"Somebody is dead," she said patiently. "Won't the police want to question everyone in the hotel?" That's what they did on TV, she thought.

"I'm sure it's nothing. He was an older man, right?"

Becca shook her head. Harry hadn't known John, but his complete lack of interest seemed strange.

"Candice had blood on her."

A couple of smears on her robe anyway.

Harry shrugged and gathered items from the top of the dresser. "An accident then. Unfortunate for sure, but they happen."

Becca thought about how John had stumbled drunk to the bungalow the night before. "I guess that's possible."

Harry let out a heavy sigh. "Becca, it doesn't always have to be some sort of plot. Sometimes people just die and it's not a mystery. If we've learned one thing over the last year, it's not to go looking for trouble."

That stung. He was the second man to say that to her in twenty-four hours! She hadn't *looked for trouble* last year. It had found her! An unwelcome thought nudged her. "Why do you want to rush out of here so fast?"

"I'm not rushing." Red spread across his cheekbones, and he shoved a frustrated hand into his hair. "I can tell by the look on your face that you want to get involved. I know you. You aren't going to be happy until you've put yourself right in the middle of it."

"I think wanting to know what happened when someone suddenly dies is the *normal* response!"

"We need to get back to Turtle Bay, now."

"Why?"

Harry's mouth tightened, but he didn't answer. Instead, he continued to stare at her with an enigmatic expression. Alarm raced along her nerve endings, but she kept her tone flat. "What's going on Harry?"

"I need you to trust me. We have to go." He pulled his phone from his pocket. "I'll call Owen and tell him to meet us in the lobby. There won't be a wedding now."

Becca put a hand over her chest as if it would calm her racing heart. "You are going to call Owen?" To her knowledge, Harry didn't even have Owen's phone number. An unnatural calm descended on her, and she felt as if the world was moving slower than usual. "Why would Owen come with us?"

Harry didn't look up from his phone, and Becca snapped. She reached out, snatching the phone out of his hand. "Harry! You need to tell me what is going on... *right now!*"

"There is nothing going on." He held out his hand for his phone. "This is exactly what I was talking about, Becca. You are being overly dramatic and imagining a conspiracy where there isn't one."

Becca wavered.

Am I reading too much into this? Harry is probably right. There won't be a wedding now, and Owen shouldn't have to deal with the aftermath of John's death. Nicole and Jake had been good friends with John. Owen had worked with John, too, and is probably upset. Should I get him off the island?

But she couldn't ignore the red flags her brain was sending. Her voice sounded like it was coming from a distance. She wasn't conscious of forming the intention until the question was out. "Does your rush to leave have anything to do with your meeting last night with Sean? The favor he needed from you?"

Harry's eyes widened fractionally, but it was all Becca needed to confirm that she was on the right track. "I overheard what he said yesterday... and your answer."

Harry's expression didn't change, but his shoulders bunched. "I don't know what you think you overheard..."

"You asked him how you would it explain it to me, and he told you it was none of my business." Despite her best effort, Becca hated that he could hear the hurt in her voice. "Last night at dinner, Celine made it clear that you being in the area was an opportunity Sean couldn't let pass—and that was why we were invited here." Harry's jaw flexed, but Becca didn't let up. "You said yourself you were worried he was going to ask you for money—but that wasn't it, was it? So, what did he want? Why would you need to hide it from me?"

"I don't have to explain every business deal to you."

Becca's mouth fell open at his haughty tone. "Are you serious right now? You've told me all about your business over the last three weeks! You said that you *loved* that I was interested, and now it's 'Becca stay in your lane'? You are being ridiculous!"

Harry's eyes slid sideways. "This is different. You are just going to have to trust me."

Before she could respond, there was a sharp knock on the suite door. Exasperated at the interruption, Harry strode to the door but, at the last second, stopped to look out the peephole. Becca couldn't read the look he shot her over his shoulder.

"It's the police."

13

"Mr. Brennan?" the woman in the doorway asked. She was young, with thick braids tucked up under her police cap. She looked past him into the room until her eyes fell on Becca. "Ms. Copeland?" She gave them both a polite smile. "I am Constable Rolle with the Royal Bahamas Police. We are questioning all of the hotel guests about an incident this morning. You heard?" Becca nodded. Harry opened the door wider to allow the police woman to enter the room, but instead of stepping forward, she continued, "If you could accompany me, please, there are only a few questions."

"Why can't you ask them here?" Harry asked.

"I am sorry." The friendly lilt in her voice didn't hide the firmness. "My instructions are to bring you to the room where they are conducting the interviews. It shouldn't take long." Her smile softened. "They are questioning everyone."

Worry gnawed in Becca's stomach. Jake's offices had been raided only a few weeks ago, and now his business partner was dead. Not to mention she still hadn't discovered what Harry was keeping from her.

"Please," the police officer stepped back into the hall, indicating they should follow. Despite her choice of words, it was not a request.

"Fine. Let's get it over with." Harry's tone was curt.

They followed her to the elevator, and it surprised Becca when the woman pushed the button to go up. "They've taken over a suite as an incident room," she explained.

Becca could feel Harry's tension next to her, and by her curious looks, it was obvious the young officer could as well. Was this just his normal aversion to the police, or something else?

Why am I so nervous? I didn't kill anyone!

Becca slipped her hand into Harry's, and when he looked down at her, his face eased. He squeezed her hand and leaned so that the side of his body was pressed against her. Relief coursed through her. Everything was going to be okay. She absolutely had to get her imagination under control.

The doors dinged open, and they followed the young officer down the long hallway until they reached a set of double doors at the end. She knocked twice before opening the door slightly to stick her head in. The woman gave their names to someone inside, and then, with a smile, she gestured them forward.

Through the door, they found themselves in the main living area of a spacious suite. A bank of windows was covered by dark drapes, fully drawn. Every surface in the room was covered in masses of paper, and cardboard document boxes were stacked high. Becca frowned. The room had obviously been in use longer than just the few minutes that had passed since Candice's scream and the arrival of the police.

A woman with her dark hair pulled into a messy ponytail and bags under her eyes stepped forward. "I'm Agent Warrick." Despite the fact she had extended her hand to Becca, the woman's eyes were trained on Harry. "This is my partner, Agent Foster."

Becca's whole body seized in apprehension, and she began

silently begging the universe for a reprieve. The growl from Harry next to her signaled she wasn't going to get it.

"You bastard!" Harry roared, charging forward. Agent Warrick braced her feet, and with a hand on her holster, she blocked his path.

"Step back!" She barked.

Harry's fists clenched open and shut several times, and Becca could see a vein beating in his throat. His furious eyes traveled from Becca to Rey, and then back to Becca's guilt stricken face.

"I guess now we know why the police never found the missing marine archeologist," he spat. "Is Katie hiding in here somewhere, too?"

Becca froze, unable to pry her eyes off the floor.

When his outburst was met with silence, Harry turned and stalked back to where Becca stood. He stood close enough that she felt the angry heat of his body. Becca finally lifted her gaze, and the flash of raw pain she saw in his eyes almost brought her to her knees. Harry quickly shuttered his expression and Becca wanted to throw up. He had retreated behind his walls, drawbridge up. She wanted to grab him, to explain why she had needed to keep the truth of Rey's identity from him. But when she opened her mouth to explain, Rey's voice cut her off, reminding her they had an audience.

"Ms. Copeland, if you will go with my partner into the bedroom, she has a few questions. Mr. Brennan?" Rey appeared completely unmoved by the hostility radiating off Harry, but Becca absorbed every ounce.

Harry rolled his shoulders, and his whole demeanor changed. Suddenly he was the languid, cold man she had first met at the Tiki Bar a year ago. He strolled to the chair, arranging himself in it as if he didn't have a care in the world.

No! Don't go!

"Ms. Copeland?" Becca tore her eyes from Harry. Agent Warrick was waiting next to her with a humorless smile. Becca turned pleading eyes to Rey, willing him to explain what had happened. He gave her an almost imperceptible nod that allowed her to breathe again. Harry's shoulders stiffened, and Becca realized he had noticed their silent communication.

Agent Warrick moved closer, and while she didn't touch her, Becca took the hint and went into the bedroom, seating herself at the small table while the woman shut the door. Becca tried to concentrate on the woman in front of her, but her ears strained to make out the words in the room beyond. She had to know what they were saying!

"Ahem." The agent cleared her throat. Becca came back to the moment.

"Sorry." Becca wanted to ask the agent if she had been told about what had happened last year. She was Rey's partner, so Becca assumed she had.

Agent Warrick adjusted the pad of paper in front of her and picked up her pen. "Let's just start with some basic timeline stuff. Can you give me a rough estimate of where you were from late yesterday afternoon until this morning?"

The questions were so reminiscent of the questions the police had asked her in Key West that a thought occurred to her. Why weren't the Bahamian police conducting the questioning? It had been a Bahamian officer who had escorted them here after all.

"You're FBI, right? Why are you investigating John's death? Just because he is a US citizen?" Becca didn't think that sounded right.

"Correct. I am an FBI agent. Now, the quicker we knock this out, the quicker you can get back to…" She angled her head toward the other room.

As a distraction, it was perfect.

"I had dinner with Celine. She and her husband own the Royal—or at least they are part owners. Her husband is an old friend of Harry's from school. After that I went to bed." Becca shrugged. "I woke up, and while I was having my coffee, Candice screamed."

The woman's pen scratched across her pad. "About what time did you go up to your room?"

"It was about 8:30, 8:45ish? I can check because I sent a text..." She reached for her nonexistent pocket. "Oh! I must have left my phone in my room."

"It's all right. We can get it later if we need it. Was Mr. Brennan at the dinner with you?" Agent Warrick tucked a hair that had come loose behind her ear, and Becca noticed that while the woman's mannerisms and voice were casual, her eyes were sharp.

"No, he had dinner with his friend Sean."

The agent made a note. "When you went to bed? You two were together, I assume?" Her smile didn't reach her eyes.

Becca's stomach knotted. "No, I had a headache, and I turned in as soon as I got back. He came in an hour later."

Agent Warrick consulted her notes. "So, he was in the room with you by 9:30?"

Becca swallowed hard and ignored the hammering in her chest. "Something like that. I didn't check the time, but I was only dozing so it couldn't have been long."

"But you aren't sure?"

"No."

"Mm." More notes. "And when you woke, he was still there with you?"

"Yes, he was there all night."

"You're sure?" Becca nodded. "Did you hear anything during the night? Anything that seemed out of the ordinary?"

Becca stared at her for a second. "You mean besides the storm?"

A reluctant smile broke across Agent Warrick face. "Good point. So, nothing besides that?"

The fight between Jake and John flashed before her, but Becca shook her head and kept her face blank.

"You were acquainted with the deceased for a long time?" Agent Warrick adopted a sympathetic look.

Becca wasn't fooled, she was a *Dateline* junkie. She recognized the ploy. "Yes."

"Your ex-husband worked for him, is that correct? And your son as well, I believe? You are all pretty close then... this must be hard for you?"

Becca stayed silent. The woman cocked her head and, after observing Becca for a minute, her tone became more clipped.

"Your ex-husband and son worked with the deceased?"

"Yes."

"Does your ex-husband talk with you about his relationship with Mr. Raybourn?" Becca snorted and Agent Warrick's mouth flattened. "Your son, then. Does he talk to you about what it's like to work with Mr. Raybourn?"

Becca's antenna went up. "Sometimes."

"Does he enjoy working there?"

Why was she so interested in Owen? Was this just her way of trying to see how much Owen may have revealed about the investigation the firm was obviously under? Becca had already confronted Rey about the FBI search warrant and the interrogation of her son. Was Agent Warrick trying to see if she would lie? What was the point of that?

"Most of the time," Becca hedged.

"Recently, then. Has he mentioned any problems at work?"

Becca gave the agent a pointed look. "That's kind of a dumb question."

Agent Warrick's eyes narrowed, and Becca saw her clench her jaw. "Why is that?"

Was it possible Rey hadn't told his partner that he had filled Becca in? What should she do? "He mentioned the FBI had been there with a search warrant."

The agent's expression didn't change, but she was writing furiously. "Did he tell you what the warrant was for?" Her eyes watched Becca keenly.

"No, he didn't..." The sound of a slamming door interrupted her.

She sprang to her feet. "I need to go."

"Ms. Copeland, I only have a few more questions." The interior door opened, and Rey shook his head at his partner.

"It's okay. She can go." He looked at Becca with hooded eyes. "We'll follow up later."

It had been intended more for her than Agent Warrick, but she would worry about that another time. Right now, she had to find Harry and explain.

Becca didn't wait for the elevator and instead sprinted down the stairs to their floor. Her muscles were tight, and she missed the slot for the key twice. She swung the door open too hard, almost hitting Harry who was standing just inside.

"Harry." She reached out to touch his shoulder, relieved when he didn't flinch away.

"It looks like our problem has taken an interesting turn?" a gravelly voice said.

Harry's broad shoulders blocked her view into the room, so Becca was forced to move to the side, in order to see around Harry. An older man stood in front of the balcony doors with a coffee cup in hand.

What the hell?

He was striking, with dark hair and a chiseled jaw. Even across the distance of the room, she could make out his gleaming, green eyes. Her eyes flew to Harry's face, so similar to the stranger's. Harry eyes were shadowed, his face stricken. "Becca, I'm sorry..."

Her brow furrowed. *Why is he sorry? I'm the one who needs to explain about Rey.*

She felt as if her brain were full of fog. She looked again at the man, casually sipping coffee in her room. Like a lightning bolt, it clicked.

"Aren't you going to introduce me?" the man asked.

"How did you get in here?" Harry's voice was devoid of emotion.

"That's the least of our problems, I'd say?" The man tilted his head and gave a small smile. "Why don't you introduce me to your friend?"

Harry's chest expanded with a sharp inhale. "No."

The man extended his hand toward Becca. "I'm James Brennan... Harry's father. Lovely to meet you."

Becca's breath caught. The upheaval James caused clearly delighted him. Out of habit, Becca reached automatically to take his hand, but Harry knocked his father's hand away which only seemed to amuse the man further.

His father is supposed to be dead!

Becca tugged at Harry's arm, to catch his attention, but Harry refused to look in her direction. His face was like granite. Becca's head buzzed.

"You need to leave... *now!*"

"I don't think that's such a good idea. We have things we need to discuss, things to get in order... plans to make." James' voice was slick, and he tilted his head towards Becca. "I don't think your little lady friend needs to be a part of this conversation."

"Get. Out," Harry snarled.

The buzzing grew louder, and Becca pressed a hand to her chest as if would ease the constriction there.

Great! I'm having a heart attack, though to be fair it might be the least dramatic thing to happen today.

Becca struggled to keep a hysterical bubble of laughter

behind her lips. She ignored the two men glaring at each other, walked between them, and sank onto the sofa. Her action broke their stand-off.

"I will find you later," Harry bit out.

Harry's father appeared mollified by that. "Suit yourself, but there is a degree of urgency to this, and we need to get our ducks in a row, as they say."

When he was gone, Harry rested his hand against the closed door while Becca stared down at the coffee table. There was her phone... she had forgotten it; she absently catalogued the items in front of her. If she could just concentrate on the mundane details around her, the world wouldn't spin apart.

Harry sat on the edge of the chair facing her. The planes on his face were pronounced as if he'd had a shock, and for a split-second Becca felt sorry for him. "So that was... *is* the illustrious 'Brennan' whom I've heard so much about." Her voice sounded like it came from far away. "You said your father was dead."

She felt the bite of her nails into her palms. Becca strove to keep her voice as even as possible. She was afraid that if she relinquished even the tiniest bit of the rigid control she was exerting over her emotions, she would shatter into a million pieces.

Which catastrophe am I supposed to think about first?

Harry bowed his head and exhaled. Becca waited. After a few harsh exhalations, Harry's head lifted. "He was dead to me."

Becca pressed her hands onto her knees. "That's not exactly the same thing, is it?"

"I never once said he was dead."

That made her pause. Was that true? Becca struggled to remember what people had told her about Harry's notorious father.

"You let me believe it, though. You always referred to him in the past tense..." Her forehead wrinkled. "Everyone did...

Amelia, Dan, Detective Ryan." She shook her head. "Why are they all lying?"

Harry gripped his hair. "They aren't. They believe, as does most of the world, that he died in a boat explosion years ago."

Becca's frown deepened. This was all a little too James Bond for her. "So, what? He faked his death?"

Harry shrugged. "I guess so... I don't... it may have been his intention, or he might have taken advantage of a situation... I'll never know for sure. The first time I saw him was yesterday."

Becca's eyes widened with disbelief. "You seem awfully calm for someone whose parent was just resurrected from the dead?"

A muscle ticked in Harry's jaw. "I heard rumors a year ago that he might still be alive, but nothing concrete. I didn't pursue it because he was out of my life, and I was happier for it."

"It doesn't sound like he is 'out of your life.' It sounds as if you are doing a project with him... ohhh." She exhaled a startled breath. "He's what Sean wanted your help with." The skin over Harry's cheekbones tightened, but he didn't deny it. "Why are you helping him? After all the stories you told me, how he hurt the people you cared most about," her voice cracked. "Why would you still help him? You said yourself he was a criminal!"

"I'm not helping him. I'm helping Sean. My father, in his classic fashion, overreached and got himself into trouble. Only this time he involved Sean, and Sean will be the one who suffers the consequences. He could lose everything, and I owe him."

"You owe him." Something was dancing at the edge of Becca's brain, and she remembered where she had heard the phrase before. "That's what he said yesterday to make you help him. I overheard you talking. You didn't want to get involved, but Sean said that you owed him."

Harry stiffened. "It's the truth. If he hadn't been there to protect me all those years ago... he shared his family with me. You can't possibly understand."

"I understand why you would want to help Sean... that's what you do... but your father? Why didn't you tell me what was going on?"

Harry's jaw worked. "I couldn't."

"Why not?"

Harry shook his head bitterly and walked out onto the balcony.

Oh no! You can't just walk away to avoid the issue!

Becca stood and followed him. Below them they could see the bungalow taped off with crime scene tape and a police guard.

"I was trying to protect you," Harry said in a low voice.

"What does any of this have to do with me? When you asked Sean what you were supposed to tell me—I'm assuming that was about your father's sudden miraculous appearance—he even said, 'Why tell her anything? It has nothing to do with her.' I don't understand."

Harry slammed a hand against the wall, and Becca jumped at the sharp noise. "That's because at that point I didn't know how involved you were!"

"But... I'm... I'm not." She hated that her voice shook. Becca followed Harry's glance to the police guard now watching them from below.

Harry smiled for the guard's benefit and indicated that they should go back inside. By the time the door closed, he had regained his composure.

"Becca, you just have to trust me that the less information you have the better. I'm trying to figure out the best way out of this for all of us."

Becca threw her hands up. "I don't need protection; I haven't done anything wrong! I don't have any idea what is going on with your father, or Sean, and I definitely know nothing about..." She flung her arm back at the balcony. She froze, an ugly thought suddenly occurring to her.

Harry suddenly stepped forward, shaking his head. Had he read her mind? "How can you think that?"

"They were all in business together, weren't they?"

"There was no reason to kill John."

"So, they *were* in business together. Was John the trouble that Sean needed help with?"

"Leave it alone, Becca. You have no clue how messy this could get."

"Messy? John was *murdered*! Rey and his *FBI* partner just questioned us? I think we are well past messy!"

Harry's face was suddenly terrifyingly blank, and he looked like a stranger. "For a few minutes, I'd forgotten about Rey, *Agent Foster.*"

Becca swallowed hard.

"You are accusing me of lying to you about my father—when it wasn't even a sure thing—and yet you chose to lie to me a year ago and maintained the lie throughout our entire relationship."

Becca's heart plunged. "It wasn't like that."

Harry's smile was grim. "Wasn't it? I was terrified the night you disappeared. Trapped in the police station unable to find you. For weeks afterward, as you recovered, you pretended to be afraid. Amelia and I checked on you every day. It broke my heart to see you like that." He cleared his throat roughly. "You're quite the actress, Becca."

"I *was* afraid! You don't know the entire story! I didn't have a choice! Rey said that if the cartel found out the truth about what happened, then they would come after me and everyone I loved"

"Cartel?" Harry's eyes flickered, but then he crossed his arms over his chest. "So, tell me the entire story."

"I… I don't know if I'm allowed."

"Because it would upset *Rey*? Should I be expecting Katie to show up with a badge next?"

Becca blanched. "It was cartel drugs that were being smuggled through the museum, Rey said if they discovered my involvement..."

Harry cocked his head to one side. "You could have told me. I'm not one of your Sun Coast, milk toast, golf junkies. I could have kept you safe. The truth is, Becca, you wanted to handle it yourself. To prove your independence—because that has, and always will be, what is most important to you! Proving that you don't need to rely on anyone the way you did your ex-husband!"

"That's not true! I was trying to protect everyone!"

Harry made a slashing movement with his hand. "You didn't care enough or trust me enough to tell me what was really going on with you. You *lied*. You lied about what happened last year—about what happened to you, what the danger was to me, to Dan... " He swallowed. "To Amelia." He closed his eyes and exhaled. "*You* decided. You decided what was best for all of us." The lines by his eyes twitched and his mouth twisted. "It's your damn insecurity. You are so determined to prove that you can do it on your own, you don't care about hurting anybody else."

Becca felt a wave of anger. *This wasn't fair!*

"What I lied about was a life-or-death situation! Yes, I did what I thought was best... what I thought I needed to, in order to keep the people I cared about safe... including you!" Her voice broke. How could she explain that the terror she felt in the months following her escape had been greater than she'd ever let on? "I *couldn't* tell you! It would have put all of us in danger! Unlike you, I'm not used to hanging out with criminals, lying and covering up."

Hot tears slipped down her cheeks, but she didn't bother to wipe them away. "I didn't tell you what happened because it would have put you at risk... my family." She shook her head, feeling the last year slip away. "You lied about your father, about helping Sean... because you didn't trust *me*."

Becca watched as Harry turned to stone in front of her, and she felt her heart break. "Harry?" Her voice cracked, and she thought she saw him flinch a little before he gathered himself. Becca gasped as hurt hit her like a physical blow.

How is this happening?

Becca stared at him, willing him to understand that she had done what she thought was best... that nothing she had done was intended to hurt him. She had done it to *protect* him! Wasn't that *his* excuse for lying about his father and Sean? *What is he trying to protect me from?*

"You've been lying this whole time. I thought you were different."

"I thought the same thing about you," Becca cried.

She felt terrible that he was hurt, but he was being unreasonable! "You haven't told the whole truth yet either, have you?" She saw her words hit home.

Harry smiled sadly. "Isn't it amazing the lengths we will go to protect the people we love?"

"What does that mean?"

Harry closed the distance between them and kissed her on the forehead. Her throat clogged with tears.

That feels like a goodbye.

Harry pressed his forehead against hers and whispered, "Becca, I just..." He abruptly pulled back, and in two strides he had yanked the door open and was gone.

Becca began to shake. What was happening! She stared at the closed door in shock. *That didn't just happen. I am dreaming. It is just the storm. Wake up, Becca!*

Part of her wanted to run after him, but part of her was still angry. He hadn't even tried to understand—and his father! Becca's head was spinning. She took a shuddery breath.

Okay, don't freak out. Take a breath and figure out what's going on.

A broken heart would have to wait. Her first step had to be talking to Owen. The police were questioning everyone, that meant Owen. If they hadn't gotten to him yet and she could talk to him first, then she could... she could what? Tell him to lie to the police? No, of course not, she assured herself. But if he were prepared for the questions, he wouldn't say anything about his father's business. She paused. What was she worrying about? Owen didn't have anything to do with John's murder. Would Rey question Owen and Jake, or would it be the Bahamian Police? Could Owen incriminate himself somehow? What if while he was working at PPW, he saw something and didn't know it was illegal? Becca dialed Owen's number, relieved when he picked up right away.

"Mom, where are you?" Owen whispered.

"I'm in my room. Are you alright? Why are you whispering? Are you in danger?" It suddenly became very real to Becca that there might be a murderer in the hotel. "Where are you?"

Becca heard muffled noises, and Becca realized that Owen had covered the phone with his hand.

"Are you alone?" he asked.

"Yes." Owen's questions were heightening her anxiety.

"Okay, I'll see you in a few minutes." Owen ended the call, and Becca had no choice but to sit and wait. He must have been close by because only a few minutes later there was a sharp knock at her door. When she opened it, she was dismayed to find not just Owen, but her ex-husband Jake as well. Becca pulled Owen into the room and gave her ex-husband a fierce glare. She wasn't sure exactly how or why, but she blamed him!

"What's going on, Jake?" Her voice was harsh, but she had zero patience for her ex-husband at the moment.

"I don't know what happened to John. I swear!"

Becca's eyes bored into his. "I'm talking about what the hell have you done, and why is the FBI questioning my son? We can get to your dead business partner in a minute."

Did I really just say that? What happened to my life?
Jake blanched and darted a look at Owen.

"I'm sorry, Dad. I had to tell somebody. I was worried about you, and Nicole was acting…"

Jake puffed his chest out. "There's nothing to worry about. I'm fine. I have everything under control; it's not a big deal. Nicole was just stressed about the wedding."

"Not a big deal? Are you kidding me?" Becca cried. "The FBI—the actual Federal Bureau of Investigation came to your office with a search warrant! They interrogated our son! And you think it's not a big deal!" She threw her hands in the air.

"Keep your voice down!"

Becca struggled to keep her composure. She gestured at the sofa and chairs indicating they should sit. "Jake, the time for denial is over. John's dead! Do you think it's a coincidence that the FBI is in the hotel and then your friend is murdered?"

"They… they… have nothing to do with each other." Jake's voice was shaky.

Becca exchanged a look with Owen. "Hey Owen, can you go into the bedroom for a minute? I want to talk to your dad alone."

Owen's expression settled into stubborn lines. "No. I'm an adult. I'm a part of this, too."

Becca silently groaned. This wasn't the time for male machismo. "Look to be honest, it's best if you don't know what's going on, then you won't have to decide to lie if necessary." Owen scowled. "I'm just trying to protect you!" It wasn't lost on Becca that she was using Harry's own words to her son.

Owen looked at his father, and Jake shrugged before slumping forward, his elbows on his knees. A flash of contempt crossed Owen's face as he looked at his dad.

"Mom, I have to tell you something, and you need to stay calm."

Oh god!

"I am calm," she shrilled.

"It's not just Dad—or Nicole. I'm involved too."

Jake moaned, and he buried his head in his hands. Becca's face tingled. She was having a hard time drawing a full breath.

"Involved in what?"

Owen looked at his father again, but Jake, still hunched in his chair, clearly wasn't going to help him. Owen drew himself up to his full height and took a deep breath. "I'm the charter member of the REIT that Dad, Nicole, and John manage, the one that has invested in this hotel and a variety of properties around the Caribbean."

Becca shook her head, confused. "What are you talking about? What is a REIT?" That was what Harry had asked her about.

"It's a real estate investment trust. A group of people get together and invest their money together in real estate."

Becca squinted; her mouth opened but nothing came out. Owen sounded as if he were giving a book report.

"But you don't have any money!" Becca exclaimed. "How can you be a major shareholder in an investment group? You're twenty years old!"

Owen tried to smile, but his lips trembled, and for the first time she noticed his eyes were damp. "It's definitely not my money, and I never signed anything. I only found out about it, last night." Owen swallowed hard and then flopped into the chair.

"The investment group is what the FBI is looking into." Jake lifted his head, but couldn't meet her eyes. "Somehow, they've discovered that it's not totally legit, and according to your boyfriend, it's only a matter of time before they figure out that Owen is involved."

Becca's jaw fell open. Her ears rang, and for a moment she thought she might pass out. "That's impossible." She breathed deeply, and then the magnitude of what he said hit her. She turned on Jake, her fists clenched. "What did you do? How could you do this to our son? What is wrong with you?" Becca shouted, too furious to care who heard.

Jake's eyes were anguished. "I didn't know about Owen! I swear, I didn't... not til last night. When I tried to talk to John about it..."

Becca held up her hand. If Jake was about to implicate himself, she didn't want to hear it—not now, anyway. Right now, she only cared about Owen.

"You didn't know what? Exactly? What did you do that the FBI is involved and what precisely does this mean for Owen?"

"Becca! I would never put Owen in danger."

Becca snorted.

"I didn't know what they had set up, I promise. Not initially."

Was he telling the truth? Could Nicole and John have set Jake up without his knowledge? No, Jake was too smart. He had to have known about the investment group.

"Jake, you better start explaining this to me in very simple terms before I literally murder you." The second the words passed her lips, fear struck her again. "Oh my god! Does John's death have something to do with this—with whatever it is you've gotten Owen wrapped up in?"

"I have nothing to do with John's murder." Jake's eyes were earnest and Becca wanted to believe he was telling the truth, but he had lied successfully to her so many times before.

"Tell me about the investment group. What is wrong with it?" Becca struggled to keep her voice calm. Her head had begun to pound, and she wanted to run away, but she couldn't. She needed to have all the information so that she could figure out how to fix this mess for her son.

Jake scrubbed his hands over his face. "John came to Nicole with a great investment idea. He had a line on several properties in the Bahamas that were ripe for investment. The prices were all priced really low because of the back to back hurricanes—no one wanted them anymore. His old firm wasn't interested, and that's why he came to us. Our firm, Nicole, and me, had plenty of people looking for ways to diversify their portfolio. The stock market is volatile and real estate is a good option. Plus, people can understand the concept better than market trends. It was perfect. John identified luxury properties, multi-million dollar properties, that needed money. We had plenty of clients with money to invest who were excited at the prospect of owning properties all over the Caribbean. We would buy the properties at a discount and rent them out as exclusive vacation spots. People will pay top dollar to stay at a home on the ocean."

"I don't understand what the problem is?" The memory of a conversation flashed in her mind. Anna had asked Nicole for the address of a vacation home they had invested in through PPW because Chris and Brad wanted to go see it. Nicole and Candice did everything they could to dissuade them from going. "The vacation rentals, what's wrong with them?"

Jake looked startled and then over at Owen, who shrugged. "You only told me about it last night." Owen said.

"The properties John was supposed to buy were premium condos and villas—places that could be rented out to high-end clientele, or flipped when the market recovered. It could have been a phenomenal investment. Investors could get income, not just from the potential future sale of the property when it increased in value, but from the rental fees continually charged." Jake's face lit up. "You wouldn't believe the returns Nicole showed me on paper. Our clients *have* been getting regular payments. Everyone has been so happy."

"Then why is the FBI investigating?"

Jake's body deflated. "Because there weren't any luxury properties. Some aren't even actual buildings at all. Just vacant land."

Becca rubbed her temples. "I don't get it. How are you getting great return income from your rentals if it's vacant land?"

"Because it's only profit on paper. They told the investors

that they were buying properties for millions, when actually the properties they bought were worth much less. They've been using the investors' own money to pay them the returns. The rest is coming from somewhere else." Owen said. "They're laundering money."

Becca felt as if the floor had opened up beneath her as the pounding in her head increased. The floor shifted, and if she hadn't been seated, she was positive she would have fallen.

"Laundering money? But... but... how? For whom?" Becca thought of the trendy TV shows she'd seen. "But I thought they used places like laundromats, car washes," she referenced her favorite one, "casinos... oh my god! You're invested in this hotel!"

"It's not all fake!" Jake said defensively. "I came here before the renovations. This place needed millions. The owners were very grateful, and it turned out beautifully!"

Sean! That's why he was so surprised to find out she had been married to Jake and why he was suspicious of... Harry! What had Jake said, *"Your* boyfriend said it was only a matter of time before they found out Owen was involved?"

Becca had been so stunned by the news that Owen was implicated that she hadn't registered the reference to Harry. "Since apparently you were just this poor unwitting victim of your fiancée and old friend, how did you find out about Owen?"

Please don't be Harry.

Owen and Jake shared another look, and Jake's mouth curled. He was enjoying this part, and in that moment, Becca hated him.

"Brennan told Owen last night. I can only guess why he has that information."

Becca felt a hand on her arm.

"I don't think Harry knew before, Mom. He didn't say how he got it, just that he had been informed that my name was on some incriminating paperwork, and he wanted to see if I knew about it."

Becca nodded, but didn't trust herself to speak. Tears clogged her throat, and the pain clenching her chest was almost unbearable. She couldn't cry in front of Jake. She took a deep breath, forcing air into her lungs. Harry knew her son was in trouble and he hadn't told her.

He found Owen, though. He warned Owen. The little voice in her head pointed those facts out, but the betrayal was too great. Becca didn't have time for a broken heart.

"You got our son involved with money launderers. Do you know who needs to launder money, Jake? Terrible people!" Her nerves had reached their limit, and a rage, fueled by fear and pain, built inside of her. Her hands flexed open and shut, and she was concerned she might actually launch herself at Jake. She wanted to wrap her hands around Jake's throat and…

"He didn't know, Mom," Owen said hurriedly.

Becca tried to regain control.

"This was all Nicole and John."

Riiiight.

Becca glared at Jake. Owen might choose to believe his father, but it was obvious that he was lying.

"Nicole didn't understand what John was up to—at least not right away," Jake insisted. "She said by the time she found out it was too late. And she wouldn't have done that to Owen. She really cares about him."

"I'm sure Owen was at the top of her mind," Becca rejoined, sarcastically.

"That FBI agent in charge of the investigation is here, Becca," Jake said. "We have to figure out what to do."

Becca wanted to snap back at him that she wasn't interested in helping him or Nicole, but she couldn't, and Jake knew it. He recognized that there was nothing she wouldn't do to protect her son.

Wait! Why is Rey here at the wedding? Is he trying to catch them? Is he looking for the properties?

"You've been questioned already about John's murder?" she asked. They both nodded. "What did you tell them?"

Owen shrugged. "I didn't have anything *to* tell them. I saw Mr. Raybourn last night and he was really drunk. Everything was normal other than him and Mrs. Davenport being more wasted than usual." His eyes shifted to his dad. "I told them about the argument that he and Dad had, but not why. When they asked, I said Mr. Raybourn was too drunk and I couldn't understand what they were saying."

"Why would you tell them that?" Jake was outraged. "When they asked about the fight, I said there wasn't one. Jesus, Owen!"

"What did you want me to do? Lie to the police? Everybody saw it, Dad. Besides, you all were back at the party after that—so what's the big deal?" Owen looked to Becca for reassurance.

"Even I heard the argument, Jake. It was below my window. You made it worse for yourself by lying."

"They are going to think I killed him!" Jake moaned.

Owen looked stricken. "I'm sorry! They already knew! But I didn't tell them what it was about. I only told them Mr. Raybourn was drunk."

"What *was* the fight about?" Becca looked from Jake to Owen.

Jake sighed heavily. "After Brennan told me what he had found out, I confronted John. I wanted to know why he'd used my kid, but he was too drunk to make any sense."

"What about Nicole? What did Nicole say when you confronted her?"

Jake shifted uncomfortably in his seat, and Becca narrowed her eyes. "I haven't had a chance yet... not to completely get into it anyway."

"I'm sorry?" Becca was incredulous. "You haven't had a chance? What are you waiting for? I swear to god if you try to tell me again that woman cares about my son, I'm going to strangle you. If she cared about my son, she wouldn't have involved him!"

"Nicole said it was only because they needed a clean credit report and she thought it would help build a portfolio for him."

Becca gave him a withering look. "Where is Nicole? She could turn Owen over to save herself."

Jake looked horrified. "She would never do that!"

Becca held up a hand. "Whatever! We'll get to that in a minute. What exactly does Rey know?"

"Rey?" Jake asked suspiciously.

Becca squirmed. She hadn't meant to give away that she was on a first name basis with the FBI agent. "They questioned me today, too, remember?"

Jake seemed mollified. "All we told the FBI is that John came to work with us at PPW about six months ago and now we run the firm together. I have no idea what could have happened to him."

"What did you tell him about the investment group?"

Owen shrugged. "They never asked about that?"

Becca looked at Jake for confirmation, and he nodded. "They didn't ask about it. They only asked if John was having any problems lately."

"And you didn't think they were referring to the investigation?" Becca was incredulous.

"Maybe they meant something else?" Jake sounded hopeful.

Has he always been this stupid?

"Of course, they know about it. They served a search warrant at your office! They were obviously fishing for what you were willing to give up! They were probably hoping you were spooked by the murder!"

Owen shook his head. "They asked basic stuff, like where I was, when, and who was there—that kind of thing. I don't have an alibi, though—and neither does Dad. That guy pointed it out to me." Owen's face scrunched, and Becca stood, pulling him into a hug. It was frustrating that Owen seemed to have a better grasp of the disaster they were in than Jake.

"It's going to be okay, honey. You couldn't have known what was going to happen." She pulled back and turned to Jake. "Why don't you have an alibi? Weren't you with Nicole?"

Jake opened his mouth to answer and then closed it again before responding, "Yeah... yeah... we were together." His eyes shifted.

"No, you weren't Dad—not the whole time they were asking about! You were in my room when I got back from walking," Owen said flatly. "I saw Nicole crossing the grass, remember? I even asked you this morning, first thing, why she was out in the storm. So, you weren't with her all night."

"Oh... I, uh, don't remember it clearly." He looked up at Becca with sheepish eyes. She recognized the tactic. He'd screwed up, and he thought the expression made him look adorable. Becca stared at him hard, and he looked away mumbling about having too much to drink.

"Okay, so what's our next move?" she asked

"Harry said we should keep our mouths shut," Owen said.

I need to talk to Harry and find out what he found out and how... and why he had told Owen and Jake and not her! And what about Rey? She needed to find a way to.... Ahhhhh!

Becca's forehead tightened. If she could just get a minute to figure it out... she could do this... she had to.

14

After Owen and Jake left, Becca stood in the middle of the room staring bleakly into space. She felt like she needed to do something but wasn't sure what it was. It was frightening to feel so helpless. She walked to the door and rested her forehead against the glass. Below her, she could see police moving in and out of the bungalow.

They must have freed up more officers from the storm recovery because now there were several of them milling about. Sean stepped into view directly below her, folded his arms, and watched the proceedings. The sight of him spurred her back into action. She needed help to make sense of what was happening.

Becca dialed Amelia's number, not sure if she actually wanted her friend to answer or not. She was torn. On one hand, she needed to talk to someone, but on the other, Harry and Amelia had a much longer history than she did with either one of them. Would Amelia be able to give her good advice, or would she tell Harry all that Becca had said?

"Hey, honey!" Amelia's voice chirped over the line, and Becca instantly felt calmer. Calling Amelia was the right choice.

"How did you guys survive the storm? I saw a weather report that said you all took a more direct hit than expected."

"The storm wasn't too bad, just a couple palm fronds down, from what I can see... but the rest of the world has fallen apart" Becca said.

"What's going on?"

Becca felt tears prick her eyes, and she struggled to keep them out of her voice. "Oh, Amelia, where do I even begin?"

Her voice must have given away her turmoil because when she answered, Amelia's voice was serious. "Are you okay? Harry?"

"Physically we're fine." No reason to mention that her heart felt shredded. "Neither one of us is very happy with the other right now though."

"Oh no! Did something happen at the ex's wedding?" When Becca realized they were stuck on the island, she had texted Amelia asking her to check on the cottage and Furball in case the storm veered west. She had filled Amelia in about Jake and Nicole's wedding, but not on her suspicions about Sean and the mysterious favor.

"You could say that. One of the wedding guests was killed last night... murdered."

"*Murdered?* In the middle of a hurricane?"

"They are pretty sure it was murder, yeah." Becca thought for a minute. Had anyone other than Jake said it was a murder? She had just assumed by the questions the police were asking... and Candice's bloody robe. "It's been a nightmare!"

"Wow! That's... crazy!" Amelia's voice was confused. "But what does that have to do with you and Harry? You didn't kill him, did you?"

Her off-hand question made Becca laugh, but her laughter swiftly became tears. "You're the only person I know who wouldn't think that was a bizarre question. But, no. The problem is... is... I think my son is in trouble. My ex got him involved in something... everything is so messed up!"

"Honey, you've got to take a deep breath. I can't understand what you are saying."

Becca inhaled deeply and held her breath for a second before letting it out. It helped. In a moment of clarity, she realized it was time to come clean with her friend.

"Amelia, I have to confess something to you about what happened last year."

In a rush, the story came pouring out—Rey's undercover job and Katie's death. She also told Amelia about the investigation into Jake's investment group and Owens's involvement.

"I haven't told Harry the whole story yet. I should have made him listen, but I was so hurt..."

"Well dang, honey, that's a lot."

It was slightly gratifying that even Amelia, her unflappable friend, sounded overwhelmed. "I wish you had told me last year because it certainly explains a lot. I had a feeling you had left out some of the interesting bits, but I figured you'd tell me when you were ready. For the record, I think you did the right thing. Those cartels don't mess around, and they have long memories. Now you've gotten mixed up with money laundering? What happened to that cute, suburban mom I met last August?"

Becca sniffed and then cleared her throat. "Actually, Amelia, there's one more thing." Becca hesitated to tell Amelia that James Brennan was still alive. It wasn't her secret to share, but it felt significant that he had turned up. Amelia had known the man, and she was the only person Becca knew who could help her figure out how James fit in and why Harry would have kept it from her. "Did you know Harry's dad is still alive?"

Becca heard glass breaking, and Amelia cursed.

"James is dead." Amelia said sharply. "It's impossible. I have it on good authority he was on that boat when it exploded. He has been dead for five years." Becca heard some angry huffing noises. "Does Harry know? Pfft, of course he knows if you do."

"He knows. He said he heard rumors last year. Why would he lie about that, Amelia? He always spoke of his father as this evil monster, and only now that he was dead could Harry move on."

To be fair, he never said the words "my father is dead." I just assumed that was what he meant when he said his father was gone. But he said nothing to contradict it!

"And how could he not tell me last night that Owen was being used by these money launderers?"

"Well, if James has turned up then it makes more sense," Amelia said dryly. "It's a small world. Money launderers and James Brennan—that's not a gigantic leap." She paused, and it was clear what her friend was implying. Becca had been so shocked to learn about Harry's dad, she hadn't put together how he might be involved with the investment group trouble.

"I don't know that he is connected," she said slowly. *But Harry implied that he was.* "Jake said that the real estate group used the funds to buy fraudulent vacation properties and a share of this hotel. What would that have to do with James?"

James. Why was that name sticking out to her?

Amelia let out a humorless little laugh. "My guess is he was the one who introduced all the parties."

Oh my god! Introductions! Celine said that she and Sean were introduced by their friend James. "He's Harry's friend, too."

Celine was aware of exactly what she was saying and was testing Becca to see if she knew about Harry's father.

"Oh." Her voice sounded weak but she was having trouble stringing together a sentence in her head.

"I shouldn't be surprised that he's turned himself into a criminal matchmaker. Ha! Sounds like something up James' alley. Lord knows he has connections to plenty of characters, but he's allergic to doing the work himself. Makes sense he set up one of his connections with another for a cut of the profit. I wonder how he met your ex though?"

Pieces in her memory clicked together and Becca groaned. "I'm such an idiot! I saw Nicole! She was gambling with a huge amount of money. She and Jake make good money, but not enough to be risking that much." Another piece fell into place. "Owen told me that after they were cleared through customs another boat intercepted them, and they transferred a couple suitcases over. Jake told him it was stuff Nicole had forgotten."

Jake is lying. He's known what was going on this whole time! I'm going to kill him!

"That would be the money. Trick's older than I am," Amelia said.

"I can't believe Jake did this with our son on the boat! He had to know what Nicole was doing. Unless he's a complete moron. Which contrary to his current actions hasn't always been the case."

"He lost you, didn't he?"

That brought a small smile to Becca's face. "Thanks, Amelia, but I think we're past the pep talk portion of this adventure. What do I do? I'm really concerned that the police are going to think that Owen had something to do with the murder."

"Why would they think that?" Amelia reasoned. "Just because he's in business with somebody doesn't mean he has a reason to kill him."

That is a good point. Why should they suspect Owen, or even Jake and Nicole? On the surface, they are all making money together. Harry said "there was no reason to kill John." Oh god! How involved is he in this?

"But then again," Amelia continued, "it's a little odd that he would suddenly die with all of his criminal conspirators waiting in the wings."

Becca's heart dropped. Amelia was right. It was too coincidental. "The fact the FBI was already here concerns me a lot. Makes me think they knew something was about to go down."

"Me, too. But what? And does it put Owen in danger?"

Becca heard Amelia tapping her fingernails.

"Unless the FBI already had people embedded in the casino, they had no way of catching any laundering. They would have to compare the pattern of receipts."

Becca was lost, but trusted that her friend knew what she was talking about. Over the last year, Becca had stopped asking how the older woman had so much information about breaking the law. She trusted that Amelia grasped the situation.

"What's that FBI guy telling you? Rey?"

"He hasn't said anything, just the normal questions. He's never going to tell me anything. He asked for my help but didn't even tell me what I was supposed to be helping with!"

"You're gonna have to find a way, honey, to make him tell you what he knows and why he's there."

"How am I supposed to do that?"

"Like I said, you'll figure something out. You're pretty resourceful. I wish I could get over there to help you out, but that storm is still out there, and even though it's going to go north of us, I can't sail for at least another couple of days."

"I know and I appreciate you wanting to be here," Becca hesitated. "I hate to ask you this, but... could you hold off talking to Harry about what I've told you. From what he's said, I think he might have more information about the money laundering than I do, but I want him to hear about Rey from me. He's so angry with me right now I'm not sure how much it matters anymore."

"It's that bad?" Amelia asked somberly.

"I think it might be. After he found out about Rey, he said he couldn't trust me anymore and... you know how he is..."

There was a deep sigh and then a quiet, "Yeah." Becca's stomach hurt. She'd been hoping that Amelia would contradict her. That if Amelia, familiar with Harry's history the way she was, thought it would be okay, then Becca could hope. That sigh confirmed her worst fears.

"I can't believe he kept it from me that James is alive! I won't say anything to him until after this is over, but you better believe I'm gonna let that boy have it when I do. You stay safe, honey. Call me when you need me."

Becca stubbornly pushed her concerns about Harry to the side. I don't have time to worry about him. There will be time in the future, *after* I'm sure Owen is safe. She had to believe that, because she was terrified if she thought too much about losing Harry, she would fall apart. Their relationship aside, she had to find out everything Harry had discovered about the situation. Then, she needed to figure out how she could use it to get Rey to tell her what information *he* had—hopefully helping Owen along the way.

She slipped her phone into her pocket and hurried to the elevators. She wasn't sure where she should start her search for Harry, but the lobby was as good a spot to start as any. However, after a quick scan of the lobby, the closest shops, and restaurants, there was no sign of him. Becca chewed on her nail, opened her phone, and sent him a text.

We need to talk. Where are you?

She stared at the phone, willing the bubble with three dots to appear that would show he was responding to her message, but the screen remained blank.

On her way back to the elevator, she saw Nicole walking away from the reception desk. Becca swallowed the rage the sight of the woman caused. Harry wasn't the only person she could get information from. Nicole's eyes were swollen and red, her face drawn with stress. Becca couldn't drum up an ounce of sympathy for her.

"Nicole!" Becca's voice was harsh.

Nicole looked up, startled, and even a little afraid.

She should be afraid now that I know what she's done, Becca thought angrily!

"You and I need to have a conversation." Her tone made it clear that she would not take no for an answer.

Nicole glanced around hoping for an escape route, but finally realizing there wasn't one, nodded. "We can go to my room."

The easy capitulation was unexpected, but so was Nicole's demeanor. The normally self-possessed and arrogant Nicole had been replaced with the unhappy woman in front of her. After a tense elevator ride, Becca was astonished to see the mess strewn about the hotel room. She'd never seen Nicole with a hair out of place; she assumed the woman's room would be the same.

The suite was identical to the one Becca and Harry were staying in. The only difference was that the throw pillows were striped in teal instead of navy. Nicole waved an arm for Becca to be seated on the small sofa, but Nicole remained standing, her arms tightly pressed to her sides. Nicole watched her coolly as Becca's eyes roved the room, taking in the clothes strewn about and the suitcase upended on the floor. Her attention returning to Nicole, Becca noticed for the first time the fresh scratches on Nicole's neck and bruising up her forearm.

In spite of herself, she asked, "Are you all right?"

"I'm fine," Nicole said coldly. "What do you want?"

Any concern that she had for Nicole vanished in an instant. "I think you know *exactly* what I want to talk about."

Nicole made a face. "Do I?"

"Does the FBI have the information about Owen being the charter member in your investment group?"

Nicole's eyes narrowed. "Who our clients are and how they make money is none of your business."

"Don't pull that crap with me, Nicole. I am aware of what's going on." She didn't completely, but Nicole didn't need to know that.

Nicole smirked, but the way her eyes flitted around let Becca know the woman was nervous.

"Jake told me all about it, already. What I need from you is how much does the FBI know? Jake's misguided allegiance to you allows him to believe that you're planning on protecting Owen. But Owen heard you on the phone saying that you weren't going to go to jail for anybody—so, who is anybody?" Becca challenged. "Did you always intend on letting Owen take the blame?"

Becca's rapid-fire questions had rattled Nicole. "I... I... didn't intend for *anyone* to take the blame. It's not like I planned on getting caught," she hissed. "There's no criminal implication for Owen. He is simply an investor. If for some reason the REIT were to be found guilty of fraud... not that I'm saying there has been fraud... but if there were, and the assets were seized by the government, then he would just lose the money he had invested in it. And since he never *actually* invested any money, he has nothing to lose, does he?" Nicole's smug tone made it clear she felt she was back on firm footing.

Becca thought for a second. "That may be true, except for one thing you said... Owen never invested any money with the REIT. Therefore, any papers that have his signature on them detailing his investment would be fraudulent, right?"

Nicole lifted an eyebrow but didn't answer.

"What were you thinking? It's bad enough that you are using this REIT to launder money and risking your legitimate clients, people who trusted you! But Owen? What is wrong with you that you exposed my son to money launderers?" Becca tried to keep her anger under control, but it was beginning to overtake her.

Nicole blanched. "It wasn't like that."

"It wasn't like what? It wasn't like my son could go to jail for fraud? You've risked his entire future!"

Nicole flipped her hair back and ignored the question. "I

don't see what you're so worried about. There's nothing with Owen's name on it that the FBI is going to find."

"Stop lying to me! I know there are documents. Owen and Jake learned about them last night!"

Nicole averted her eyes. "They're gone now. John said he destroyed the USB. He had the only copies."

Becca wasn't sure how, but she knew Nicole was lying. "There was only one USB... and John got rid of it?"

"Yes." Nicole didn't meet her eyes.

"Why would he do that? Better question: *when* did he do that?" What Nicole was saying didn't make sense.

"After the FBI raid. He told me he got rid of it."

Becca stared at her. She wanted to believe it was true, but why was Harry convinced enough that the USB existed that he told Owen about it? Something wasn't adding up.

"Do you know what happened to John? Did it have anything to do with this?"

She expected an immediate denial, but as Becca watched, the muscles under Nicole's eyes jumped and it was a long moment before she answered. "No, how would I? I was with Jake last night."

"No, you weren't. Not for the whole night anyway. You were seen outside during the storm." There was no need to tell Nicole that Owen was the one who had seen her.

Nicole's eyes flashed. "When?" she asked, her voice full of panic.

For the first time during the conversation, Becca was uneasy. Up until that moment, she hadn't actually suspected Nicole of having anything to do with John's murder, only that she might have an inkling *why* he was killed. Her reaction quickly changed Becca's mind. Becca's gaze zeroed in on the scratches vivid on Nicole's neck. Nicole reached up to cover them self-consciously, and Becca noticed that several of Nicole's French manicure tips had snapped off.

Time to go!

Nicole noticed where Becca's attention had gone, and she dropped her hand back to her side, tucking her fingers into a fist to hide the damaged fingertips.

"I didn't have anything to do with his death." Nicole sounded desperate.

"Okay," Becca said slowly. Nicole looked so fearful at that moment that Becca almost believed her. "But you were laundering money through the casino, weren't you?"

Nicole took a step back. "How did you know that?"

"Once I heard that the investment group was laundering money, and that they heavily invested in this hotel, it wasn't hard to put together. I saw you with all those chips at the table the other night, remember?" Becca was thankful her bluff paid off.

Nicole moaned. "You don't understand! This has gotten so out of control... It was supposed to be a way to make some easy money. No one was supposed to get hurt. Just turn a good profit. How could I have known who these people were? Where their money was coming from."

Becca felt her nerves dance along her skin. "What people? Where are they getting the money they are pretending to invest with you?"

Nicole leveled frightened eyes at her. "You don't want to know. You have no idea in your protected little world what real bad guys there are out there."

You might be surprised.

"Why are you so afraid, Nicole? What happened to your hand, and your neck? Why is the FBI here for your wedding?"

Nicole's eyes darted around and landed on the overturned suitcase. Becca looked closer and saw that the lining had been ripped. "Is that the suitcase the boat you rendezvoused with handed over... your missing bridal attire?"

Nicole paled. "How? Oh my god... Owen. I truly never meant for him to get as involved as he is. It wasn't my idea to put him on the paperwork. It was John's." She gave a little laugh. "All of this was John's idea. And once we were in trouble, he was the first rat to abandon the ship."

"What are you talking about?"

Nicole clasped her hands together tightly in front of her. "Never mind. It's not important anymore. You've got to go. I'm not talking about this. I have a wedding to prepare for."

Becca was dumbfounded. "You don't actually think you are having a wedding today, do you?"

Nicole reclaimed her hauteur as if the previous minutes had never happened. "Why not?"

Becca shook her head, but Nicole's delusions were the least of her problems. Now that Nicole had retreated behind her armor, she wasn't going to get any more information out of the woman. She opened the door, but turned back before leaving.

"If you didn't kill John, and I think we can agree that Jake and Owen didn't kill him, who do you think did? And why?"

The terror that crossed Nicole's face was all the confirmation she needed. Nicole believed that John's murder was connected to the PPW investment, and she knew more about it than she was saying.

15

Becca was at loose ends following her encounter with Nicole. Should she find Rey? Tell him her suspicions about Nicole? She had hoped to find Harry, but he still wasn't responding to her text messages. She wandered aimlessly down past the outdoor patio until she reached the pool. Some of the seating had already been replaced by hotel staff, and Becca sank wearily into one of the chairs. The temperature was climbing, and steam seemed to rise from the water-soaked grass and foliage around her. A man skimming the downed palm fronds and frangipani petals out of the pool nodded and smiled. The simple every day interaction boggled her mind. How could life be moving on when everything she cared about was at risk?

She was so lost in her thoughts she almost didn't notice Michelle walking around listlessly taking pictures. I have to hand it to her, Becca thought, regardless of everything going on, she really seems dedicated to her photography. When Michelle got closer, she lowered the camera, and Becca could clearly see the strain on her face.

"Hey, Michelle," Becca said. "How are you holding up?"

Michelle jumped, almost dropping her camera. "Oh! Hi,

Becca. I didn't see you there. I was so wrapped up in..." She waved her hand at the soggy plant she had been taking a picture of.

"It's been a rough day," Becca commiserated. "How is Candice doing?"

"Not great. I only saw her for a few minutes after they questioned her. I can't imagine how awful she must feel." She looked queasy. "Candice found him by their little pool... didn't even realize he was dead at first. It wasn't until she reached to help him up that she saw blood. She thought he'd had a heart attack and fallen or something. Or passed out and hit his head. We all saw how drunk he was last night."

Becca nodded. As much as she disliked Candice, it must have been terrible to stumble upon John like that.

"Did you hear they are saying they think he was beaten with a rock?" Michelle asked, with fascinated horror. "That's what Candice said."

Becca willed herself not to react, but her brain was whirling. "No, I hadn't heard that." Michelle was close to Candice, and Candice might have revealed to her more of what she saw and what the police were saying. Michelle would be a lot easier to get information out of than Rey.

"Do they have any idea who did it?"

"Brad says they'll think Candice did it. It makes sense, I guess... I don't know." Michelle looked miserably off over Becca's shoulder as if she didn't want to confront the reality that a close friend might have killed her boyfriend.

"I can see why the police would think that. She was the only one in the room, after all, and those bungalow pools are surrounded by walls. But why would Candice kill John? They seemed happy enough?" Becca let her voice trail upwards, hoping that Michelle would fill in the blanks.

"They were! I'm so glad you see that! Brad thinks I'm just being loyal to Candice, but there's no way Candice would kill him. He was going to take her on a surprise destination trip. Candice thought he might even propose. Besides, she says she can't even remember what happened last night." Michelle gave a little laugh. "I didn't think she drank that much, but she was pretty wasted when she went back to their room."

"Candice doesn't remember? Could John have tripped and fallen on their way back to the room?"

"Oh no, Brad, well Brad and I... we took them back because Candice could barely walk and John was no help. It had to have happened after we left. She said John was still dressed, so I guess he could have gone back outside."

"In the storm? I was in bed early, but it had definitely picked up well before the party was over. I'm not sure why somebody would go outside, even in just the outer bands, without a good reason."

Michelle looked around to make sure no one was nearby and whispered conspiratorially. "The party didn't go that late. John was so drunk he couldn't even form full sentences, and then he did something to piss off Jake. He left and Candice got drunk. They were so *embarrassing...*" Michelle was clearly enjoying sharing the gossip. "He came back and was practically yelling at Candice. I thought Nicole was going to kill him right there..." She stopped, realizing what she said. "I mean, not really."

Becca took pity on Michelle's anguished expression. "It's all right. I know what you mean."

Michelle smiled. "As soon as there was a break between the storm bands, everyone made a run for it."

"It was nice of you and Brad to take them back. Did he say anything before you left? You and Brad may have been the last ones to see him alive?"

Michelle stopped and stared suspiciously at Becca. "No. It was totally normal. Why are you asking me? Just because we helped them doesn't mean we had anything to do with it!" Michelle's voice rose an octave.

"Of course not. I'm sorry. I didn't mean to imply you did. I didn't realize you were all friends like that." Michelle and Candice were friends, but Becca found it hard to picture the grouchy Brad helping one of Michelle's friends out of the goodness in his heart, particularly during a hurricane.

"Brad liked him okay. He mainly knew him from golf. Jake invited John to join them after they started working together. He and Candice don't really come to parties, you know, because..."

Michelle didn't need to explain. The unspoken truth was that Candice's affair with Evie's husband and Evie's subsequent murder had fractured the Sun Coast social scene.

Michelle fiddled with her camera. "It's weird, ya know."

Becca didn't.

"I was looking through some pictures I took last night, and it's just so crazy to think they are, like, the last moments of his life," Michelle finished sadly.

Becca shivered in spite of the heat. Her phone buzzed in her pocket, and when she saw it was Harry who had texted her, she let out of whoosh of air. *Finally!*

In the room.

Becca had no idea what she said to Michelle before walking as quickly as she could back to the suite she shared with Harry. How should she handle it? She needed to tell him the whole story about what happened last year. Then he would understand. *And he can explain to me why he didn't think it necessary to tell me what he'd learned about Owen.*

When she opened the door, she was stunned to see that Harry had his duffel bag already packed and on the floor by the door.

"Hey," she said. Harry turned from where he was standing in the middle of the room. Her heart sank. Harry's face was completely closed, and his walls were clearly still up—this was going to be harder than she had thought.

"I'm heading back to Turtle Bay."

"You can't!"

Harry folded his arms tightly across his chest and stared at her. Becca's eyes frantically raked his face, but his expression was so aloof he bore no resemblance to the man she had shared so much with over the last year—he was Harry, the enigma, again. Desperation tightened her throat. He wasn't going to give her a chance to explain.

"Even if you want to ignore the fact that there was a murder here last night, there is no way the police are going to just let you leave. There's still a hurricane out there! Surely the water is too rough for you to go back!"

"Grace says it will be fine. The marina has some damage, but she can get the boat close enough to send the tender."

"But... but what about the murder?"

Harry's eyes shifted to the window, but he didn't answer. Instead, he looked at his watch. Her mouth fell open. He was acting like a stranger.

"What about your father?" The words burst out of her wanting to get a response. "I thought the two of you had unfinished business?"

A muscle ticked in Harry's jaw.

Good! At least it's a reaction.

"That's none of your business."

Becca drew back as if he had struck her. "The police and the FBI aren't going to just let you go." She sounded pathetic and she hated it.

Harry's eyes flashed, and his face took on an odd expression. "I wasn't planning on asking them, so unless you are planning on cluing in your FBI friend..."

"He's not my friend."

Harry shrugged and walked over to pick up his bag. "I've answered their questions, and they know where to find me."

"Harry. Please! Just wait a minute. I... I need to ask you something." It was a lame attempt to buy time, and they both knew it, but Harry paused with a hand on the doorknob.

His shoulders lifted as he took a deep breath, then turned back to face her, his eyes flat. "What?"

"It's not just a question. I... I also wanted to explain... about last year... about Rey and why I couldn't tell you..."

Harry's lip curled a little. "I don't care why. You lied. You didn't trust me, and so you deceived me for almost a year." His voice was like ice, but Becca saw his knuckles were white on the handle of his bag.

"I had a good reason!" she sputtered.

He shook his head, and the mask slipped for a second. Her heart clenched at the pain she could see in his eyes, and then the mask was back hiding him from her.

"Your reason doesn't matter, not to me. You..." He stopped and cleared his throat. "You've been lying the whole time. I don't know who you are."

His black and white attitude sparked her temper. She wasn't about to let him play the martyr role. "You lied to me about Owen!"

Nothing on his face moved, but she could tell she had surprised him. "I know about Owen being on the charter documents for that REIT John created. Jake and Owen told me all about it this morning."

Harry took a breath in through his nose and seemed to hold it. "Well then, now that you have all the facts, I'm sure you'll be able to handle it."

"It doesn't explain how you knew, though. Harry, I need your help. I need you!" Conflicting emotions warred on his face, before his face became blank again. "You should get your son out of here as fast as possible, Becca. They are going to need someone to take the blame, and Owen is a great candidate for it."

"That's crazy, he didn't have a reason to kill John!"

Harry stared at her dumbfounded. "Owen found out last night that John implicated him in a massive multi-million dollar fraud. That's a pretty good motive. So, unless he has an airtight alibi…"

She shook her head and Harry's mouth turned down.

"What do I do? How do I fix this?"

"You don't. Do you remember what happened the last time you inserted yourself into someone else's crime? It didn't end well."

"What choice do I have? It's Owen! I can't stand by and do nothing." Why couldn't he understand that she couldn't abandon her son?

"Becca, you need to keep in mind John's death may be just the tip of the iceberg. People who can go to banks don't need to launder money. John was killed for a reason. We don't know what that reason was, so we can't be sure more people won't die."

Harry's hand opened and shut on the handle of his bag. He closed his eyes, and in an unnatural voice, he said "I'm going back to Turtle Bay, Becca. I can't get caught up in this… this… I've been trying to distance myself from this kind of thing. You seem to be a magnet for it, and I can't have that in my life." He sounded like he was reading from a script.

Becca felt as if she had been punched in the stomach. "So, you're just going to leave me here?"

Something in his face shifted, and for a second she saw longing, but then it was gone. "I've already contacted Eduardo and Marta. They're going to pack up your things and ship them back to your cottage today. Contact Eduardo when you decide you are ready to return to the States, and he will arrange for a plane ticket."

Becca gaped at him. They'd had a fight. He couldn't seriously be breaking up with her for that! "You said you loved me?" He pulled the door open. "It's not enough." The door shut with a sickening click.

Is this a prank? He's going to stick his head back in and say just kidding? Right?

Becca concentrated on breathing in and out, staring stupefied at the door. It didn't feel like a prank, and the more seconds that ticked by confirmed it. It was insane. Yes, they obviously had some very real issues between them but to just throw it away... her mind flew through the memories of the past year: Harry helping her move, how he looked when she had woken up in the hospital, the art supplies he had so thoughtfully brought to their villa. She never told him that she loved him...

Why didn't I tell him?

Her breath caught on a sob. *He told Marta and Eduardo to pack my things? As if he truly never wants to see me again!*

Through her tears, she fumbled for her phone. "Amelia? He left!"

Becca managed to get the story out. On Amelia's advice, Becca instantly sent Harry a text. But no matter how many times she checked, he never even opened it.

He is done.

Amelia tried to console her, telling her that he would come around, but she wasn't very convincing. Because of how he grew up, Harry never let people in, never let his guard down... until her... he'd been open with her. And in his mind, she'd betrayed him.

She felt like she was going to throw up. How could she have screwed this up so badly? Why hadn't she just told him what had happened last year with Rey?

"I know it hurts, honey, but you have bigger fish to fry," Amelia said. Becca sniffed back her tears. "He'll calm down. He loves you. I'm positive he does."

He said it wasn't enough.

After she got off the phone, Becca went into the bathroom and stared at her reflection. Amelia was right. No matter how much Becca wanted to chase Harry back to Turtle Bay and fix things, she had to stay here and protect Owen.

16

"You look rough," Rey said, raising his glass in a toast to her.

"Shut up." Becca knew she looked terrible. Her eyes were puffy and her hair was a frizzy mess. She had stayed in her hotel room for the rest of the afternoon until hunger had driven her out a few minutes ago. She had tried calling Owen several times, but he sent her a text saying he needed space. Emotionally exhausted, Becca pulled the curtains shut against the bright sun and crawled under her covers.

Rey gestured with his glass of tea. "Buffet's not bad."

"Humph." Becca was hungry but her stomach rolled uncomfortably at the thought of eating. Maybe food was a bad idea. She propped her elbow on the table between them. She didn't have a burning desire to spend time with him, but the fact was, she didn't want to sit alone. She wasn't in the mood for one of her old 'friends' to join her and try to make small talk about the murder, or Jake, or… anything. She fiddled with the preset table setting, rearranging the silverware and pushing the empty glass around.

She was aware of Rey's searching expression.

"Not hungry?"

She hoped her fierce glare was answer enough.

"Okay." He put his hands up in surrender. After a few moments, he lifted his glass again to take a sip. "What's the matter? Trouble in paradise? Where's lover boy?"

Becca sniffed, unable to control the involuntary tears that welled in her eyes.

"Oh shit, sorry." Rey looked appalled and immediately started scanning the room for an exit.

Becca pressed at the corner of her eyes angrily to keep the tears from falling. "Stupid," she muttered to herself, and then louder, "So, what? You're just out in the open now?"

"It's a tactic. What's the problem? Why the tears?"

Becca cleared her throat determined not to be emotional. "Harry wasn't thrilled to find out I'd been lying to him for the past year."

Rey grimaced. "He's not in any position to throw stones. He's not exactly an open book."

Things had ended badly earlier that day with Harry, but it felt disloyal to discuss it with Rey.

"Look, you did what you had to do... and it kept all of us alive." He frowned. "It couldn't have been easy for you dealing with it alone... what happened on the boat..."

Becca met his gaze. They were both remembering the awful day when Rey saved Becca's life.

He cleared his throat. "But you seemed to have rallied. Your last show was really good. It was more than I expected."

"How do you know about my show?"

Rey shifted in his seat and picked at his green beans with a fork. "I heard about it."

Becca cocked her head in disbelief. "Yes, all those write ups I had in the newspaper from the Marathon art festival," she said sarcastically.

He scowled at her. "Mutual friends..."

For the first time in over twenty-four hours, Becca was amused. "Are you keeping tabs on me?" she teased.

Rey's scowl darkened. "Of course, we are. We have to make sure you don't blow it for all of us."

Rude!

It was disconcerting to realize that she had been the target of government babysitting this last year. However, if she were honest, it was comforting that she hadn't been totally on her own. Becca poured herself a tea from the pitcher on the table. "Good."

Rey raised his eyebrows. "Huh." And then he extended his glass to her for a refill.

Becca tipped the pitcher to pour, then met his eyes again. "What's the deal?" she asked. "Why are you here? You couldn't have known John was going to be murdered."

Rey took a sip and set his drink down. Becca waited, determined that she could out wait his silence.

Rey looked around the restaurant, and satisfied that no one could hear them, said, "Remember how I said I was going to try to 'pivot' my target? Well, it wasn't as easy as I thought. I got a tip off on what Olivera's new venture was, but I was too compromised to transition."

Becca winced.

"Before I had to get out, I uncovered enough that I figured out they were laundering money through the Caribbean. Unfortunately, I had to come in before I learned how." He gestured to himself. "So here I am."

"The cartel is here in the Bahamas?" After her conversation with Jake and Owen, she didn't like where this was heading.

Please tell me Jake isn't stupid enough to do business with a drug cartel.

"Was John connected to them? Did they kill John?"

How much had Rey found out?

Rey's eyes drooped, the expression reminiscent of when his

old undercover persona had terrified Becca. Not put off anymore, she raised a challenging eyebrow back at him. He grunted when he saw she wasn't going to be intimidated. But then his face relaxed, and she even thought she saw his lips turn up.

"I honestly don't know. From the wire taps we have, some of the more legitimate investors were getting concerned." He looked at her pointedly. "A lot of questions were being asked of PPW, and no one was getting straight answers. A few tried to get their original investment back but couldn't. People are suspicious, but from what we can tell, they think it's embezzlement not laundering."

Rey set his tea down and placed his hands on the table. He threw a glance over his shoulder confirming their privacy again. The last family had left, and they now sat alone in the restaurant. "I'm still trying to take down Olivera, and he has the same problem that all cartels have. They can never branch out into legitimate businesses with their dirty money. Banks want to know where sizeable sums come from when they're deposited. And even though the banking laws in the Caribbean have generally been lax, over the last ten years they've actually gotten stricter."

We are confident that PPW is laundering money for the cartel, I just can't prove it yet. Somehow, they are taking cartel money and disguising it as legitimate investments, and then using the return on those investments to funnel clean money back to Olivera. A lot of times the only way we can bring down an organization is to cut off their money supply. Do you understand what I'm saying?"

Becca rolled her eyes at him. "I have a television, Rey… and what you are describing is basically the plot to a lot of really popular shows right now. What I don't understand is why you are telling *me* about it."

"I don't normally give out information in an open investigation, but I think you can help me with this. You've got a vested

interest in wanting to keep your son safe... and out of prison."
He stared at her, and she inclined her head in agreement. "It's not
just your ex that is involved. Your son works there, too. He could
help me identify which of the investments are legitimate and
which are funded by the cartel."

"Can't you put someone else in with them?"

"We thought about it, but unfortunately, after what went
down in Key West last year, we couldn't get a new person in with
them in time."

"In time for what?"

"In time for it to make a difference," he said, exasperated. "It
takes years and years to gain these people's trust."

"Sean's one of them? That's why you wanted me to 'keep my
ears open at dinner.' Were you hoping to catch Sean doing
something?"

"Who said I was trying to catch him doing anything?"

"Why else would you be here?" Becca was annoyed by his
cat-and-mouse game. "You were seen talking to John."

Rey grimaced. "The ditz with the camera?"

"Her name is Michelle... and she told everybody."

Rey's gaze sharpened, and suddenly he was very alert. "What
do you mean she told everybody?"

"Well, not everybody," Becca admitted, "but when Owen
came up and told me he recognized you..." Rey groaned again.
"What did you think was going to happen? You were walking
around the lobby in front of the people you were investigating?
Didn't you think one of those people would recognize you?"

Rey growled but Becca ignored him.

"Anyway, Owen pointed you out and said you were an FBI
agent. Michelle said no that you were a new investor, that she
met you when you were talking to John." She paused. "Michelle
said John introduced you to her." Becca started tapping her
fingers on the table as she tried to fit the pieces together. "But
John wouldn't have done that... introduced you by name, that is

if he had something to hide from you... so that means..." Rey lifted a finger warningly at her. "That means John was working with you!"

"You are guessing." Rey's glare was scalding, but Becca didn't care.

She was happy things were finally making sense. "So, if he was working with you—what was he doing?"

"I never said he was." Rey growled again.

"Pfft. You asked for my help. I'm trying to give it to you, but I can't help you if you don't tell me what it is that I'm helping with."

Rey appeared to think about that for a minute, and when he finally nodded, she was pleased. She had expected him to just dismiss her.

"Fine! We executed a warrant at your ex's firm a couple weeks ago."

Becca nodded.

"We seized a lot of files, but it was just the beginning of their paper trail. There were obviously files missing. Company names and investors were referenced in the paperwork we had, but there were no other records of them. No client files. They are most likely shell companies. We need more than what we have. We need corroborating testimony, someone who can tell us who exactly is behind the shell companies and where the money is ending up. We also need proof that PPW had definite knowledge that the money they were taking was being funneled back to a criminal enterprise."

"John was going to testify?"

Rey frowned, and she thought he would stop talking. "Let's just say we were coming to an agreement."

"Was he going to go into witness protection like Katie did?"

"Not *exactly* like Katie did."

Becca winced at his sarcastic tone. "Does that mean the cartel killed him? To keep him quiet?"

Rey sat back and scrubbed a hand along his jaw. "I shouldn't be telling you any of this. I don't know why I am. Let's just say we are exploring all kinds of options."

"Rumor is he was hit with a rock?"

Rey's face turned thunderous. "What the hell? Can no one keep quiet?"

Becca smiled. "With this group of people? Absolutely not! Candice told Michelle what she had seen."

"These are your friends?" His expression didn't leave any doubt what he thought of them.

"They used to be. I haven't spoken to any of them in a year."

"Why?"

"I blame Candice for my friend Evie's death last year. Trust me, I have no loyalty to her or any of them."

"Do you think she's capable of killing her boyfriend?"

Becca thought for a minute. She didn't want to say yes, just because she hated Candice, but it would send Rey's investigation even further from Owen if he thought it was a crime of passion. It could buy her time to figure out if Nicole was telling the truth about the USB implicating Owen being destroyed.

"Possibly," she hedged. "Isn't the person who finds the body always a suspect?"

The corner of Rey's mouth tipped up. "You really do watch a lot of crime television, don't you?"

"So?"

"So, not everything is the way they make it look on TV."

Fair enough, Becca thought. "But she *was* the one who found the body, not to mention she was the only one there with him overnight."

"I don't know how the info leaked, but the current theory *is* that a rock was used. The police found one of the large landscape rocks next to his body, the ones that make up the border of the flowers. None of the others were disturbed, so it's unlikely that it was moved by the wind. Preliminary analysis looks as if it could be the murder weapon, but because it was exposed to the elements, the Bahamian Police can't get any fingerprints off of it. The storm washed away all the evidence."

"What about blood? Candice said she saw blood on his body."

"She's lying—or in shock. There was blood underneath. His body protected the evidence from the rain. She touched the body. That's probably how she transferred it to her robe."

Becca's brow furrowed. "How did Candice get that wrong? Was she just confused and upset, or was she trying to hide something?"

The skin at the corner of Rey's eyes twitched. "Do you think you're trying to solve this? You need to stay out of it, Nancy Drew."

Becca sighed, "Not a cartel assassination then?"

Rey shook his head. "No, but that was a good try."

"What's that supposed to mean?"

"I'm just saying you aren't as subtle as you think you are. I get it. You are familiar with a lot of the major players, and you're obviously worried about something. Are you worried your ex killed him? Do you still have feelings for him?"

Becca laughed. "What I'm feeling about Jake doesn't even come close to love right now." Becca propped her elbows on the table, laced her fingers and decided to be honest with him. "I am concerned that my son is going to get caught up in this. And like you told me yesterday, the sooner you make your case, the sooner you leave him alone."

Rey held his palms up. "That's true. You've obviously spent a lot of time thinking about it, and you know these people better than I do. Okay, detective, what's your take on it? Revenge? Crime of passion?"

He was mocking her, but she took his words seriously. "If he was hit with a rock, that seems spontaneous to me. Maybe there was an argument, and it got out of control?" Becca could definitely see Candice hitting John over the head in a drunken fight. "They were both really drunk last night. I saw John from my balcony stumbling around, and I was told they had to be helped back to their bungalow."

Rey nodded. "I saw that in the report. I'm not sure your friend Candice, in the state she was in, would have the strength to take down Raybourn. Plus, I'm not sure how she could have reached up to his head. We won't know for sure until an autopsy, but to me it looked like most of the blows were struck from above, and your friend is short."

Damn, he's right! Without heels, Candice is at most 5'3 and John had several inches on her! I so want Candice to be the villain.

"She's not my friend."

"Who's next, Nancy Drew? Who else might want to see this guy dead? I heard your ex-husband and son fought with him?"

This was going in exactly the direction she didn't want it to. "Stop calling me that," she snapped. "I saw part of Jake's... discussion with John... and it was a little heated. That's true. But I wouldn't call it a fight, and I couldn't make out what they were talking about. I never saw Owen even talk to John." She thought she should be nervous at how easy she was finding it to lie.

Rey tapped a finger against his lips. "It's definitely a missing piece. No one seems to understand why your ex-husband was so angry at the victim."

"Maybe it's because John was wasted at the party? Apparently, he and Candice made a scene."

"Possibly," Rey said thoughtfully. "From all accounts, Raybourn was practically falling down and spilling drinks on people. I guess at a hoity toity event that would be frowned on."

He pinched his lips together, and she got the distinct impression he was laughing at her because she had once been part of that world.

When she didn't rise to the bait, he continued, "The funny

thing is, nobody remembers seeing either of them with multiple drinks."

"They got it from somewhere. Maybe the bartenders don't want to admit they over served him and he ended up dead?"

"They don't really care about that kind of stuff in a place like this. Still, I'm not sure John's intoxication was the reason they were *fighting*." He used the word deliberately. "Your son was there, too. A witness says not only did Owen shove John Raybourn, but he may have threatened him. Why would your son be so upset with his boss?"

Becca paled. Owen had left that part out of his story. She licked her lips.

"I have no idea. I'm sure he was just being protective of his dad and... and... frustrated. He's the best man, after all. He might have taken his role too seriously. He's young. I'm sure it didn't mean anything. Besides," Becca was babbling, "there are other people who didn't like John. What about the other investment properties? Have you looked at those? A couple of days ago I heard Anna trying to get an address of one of the investment rental properties out of Nicole. Her husband, Chris, and Brad Caplan were insisting they go see it. Nicole and Candice were doing everything they could to keep them from driving out to look at it. There are a lot of people in the hotel who invested money with PPW."

Her voice became animated, as she warmed to her idea. "You said yourself the wiretaps indicated some of the investors were suspicious that someone was embezzling. One of them might have thought John was stealing their money, got mad, and killed him!"

Rey cocked his head to one side. "That's actually not an awful line of inquiry."

Becca blew out a satisfied breath. But it was short-lived.

"But none of these people thought their money had been stolen. There was suspicion by a few who tried to withdraw their funds, but from what we can tell of the paperwork we have seized already, it appears they were actually all making a tidy profit. That's how these schemes work. You get legitimate money to mix in with the investment in order to clean the money. That way it looks more legit to the banks."

"Not everybody was happy," Becca muttered. "Somebody killed him."

"Anybody else I should look into... besides your family, I mean?" he drawled.

An image of Nicole's broken nails and the scratches on her neck flashed in Becca's mind. The words hovered on her lips, but she kept them tightly closed. If she offered up Nicole's injuries and Rey challenged Nicole on them, Becca didn't trust that Nicole wouldn't reveal Owen's involvement to save herself, and that would just make things worse. Becca gave him what she hoped looked like an innocent smile. "Nope, but I'll keep my eyes open."

"You do that." Rey reached out and picked up her phone where it sat on the table. "No passcode? That's a mistake. I'm adding my number to your contacts, so you know how to reach me if you suddenly remember something," he drawled with a wink.

Becca struggled to keep her expression bland at his audacity. She refused to let him know he could bother her, and she suspected that was exactly what he was attempting to do with his sarcasm and the phone stunt. Rey gestured to something over her shoulder and rose. Becca turned and saw that Agent Warrick had entered the restaurant and was beckoning to him.

Once they were gone, Becca splayed her hands on the table in front of her, surprised to see that they were shaking a little. She wasn't sure how much longer she could keep this up!

17

Anna stood alone by the front doors dressed in a floor length silk dress. The unexpected sight caused Becca to stumble to a stop as she made her way through the lobby.

"Hey, Anna. What's going on?" Becca asked when she reached her. Anna yelped, clearly lost in thought. Even though her makeup was flawless, it didn't hide the lines of stress around her eyes.

"Oh! Hi, Becca." Anna's eyes darted frantically around, anywhere to not look at Becca. "Um… nothing… I mean… argh! Jake and Nicole are going ahead with their wedding tonight after all."

Even though she had an inkling the moment she had seen Anna in her dress, Becca was still shocked. "Are you serious?"

"We all got a phone call about an hour ago. It's going to be scaled down, obviously, out of respect for John, but Nicole insists she's getting married today." Anna's lip curled slightly.

"Wow!" Becca fumbled for words. What could she say? Even she hadn't thought Nicole and Jake would be this callous. Did Rey know? Is that why Agent Warrick came to get him? "Is Candice going?"

Anna's mouth turned down, and she shook her head. "She's still a mess but she's got her Valium. It's not doing much, but they won't give her anything stronger. I don't get why they are being so mean?"

Even though Rey said it was unlikely Candice could have physically carried out the murder, Becca wasn't quite ready to let her off the hook.

"It must have been horrifying for her to find him like that," Becca probed.

Anna nodded. "The worst of it is she said that she remembers nothing. She feels guilty, like maybe she should have helped him or something."

"Hmm." It was what Michelle had said, too, but it seemed awfully convenient. Becca had seen Candice drunk several times over the years, but she couldn't remember the last time she had heard of Candice getting to the blackout stage. Then again, she hadn't hung out with Candice in a very long time. Could she really have drunk so much that she missed her boyfriend being killed just yards away? "Candice had that much?"

Anna lifted a shoulder. "She claims she only had two glasses of champagne, and one of those she spilled all over her dress when John knocked into her. She had ordered a glass of wine at the start of the party, but John drank most of it. She was so mad!" Anna grinned and Becca remembered that Michelle had also been happy to gossip about her *friend*. She didn't miss that toxic environment *at all*!

"Candice's face got all red, and she was crying about how he always ruined everything…" Anna stopped abruptly and turned white under her make-up. "I mean she was mad but not like mad, mad. She was just embarrassed because he was drunk."

It appeared to have finally dawned on Anna that saying her friend was furious with her boyfriend just before he was killed wasn't the most loyal thing. Becca let it go. She wanted Anna's version of the night's events.

"That's funny. I heard he actually didn't have that much to drink?" Thank goodness for the ubiquitous *I heard*. In Sun Coast, unsubstantiated rumor was just as valid as proof.

"Hmm, I don't know where you heard that. He was definitely drunk. Maybe he hadn't eaten or something. He was falling all over the place and could barely talk. He was a little better when he came back, but poor Brad and Michelle had to help get them back to their room. There was no way Candice was going to be able to keep him upright. She was really wobbly, too." Anna pursed her lips, but then shrugged as if it didn't matter. "She must have found another glass of wine somewhere."

"Hey, Becca!" Michelle appeared next to them along with her husband Brad and Anna's husband Chris. It must be close to time for the ceremony.

"What do you mean…?" Before Becca could ask what Anna meant when she said John 'came back', Brad interrupted her.

"We better go in," Brad said, nudging Michelle's arm. Anna grimaced, and Chris kept his eyes on the door as if something outside was fascinating. None of them could look at her.

It *was* a little surreal. Even if the wedding wasn't taking place hours after one of the wedding party was murdered, the fact was, her friends were about to go to her ex-husband's wedding. Becca wasn't sure what to say. They all stood awkwardly in an incongruous clump until Becca gave a little wave. "Have fun."

I'm in the Twilight Zone. It's the only explanation.

The headache that had threatened all day now fully gripped her. Her head was pounding with bright little lights starting at the edge of her vision by the time she reached her room. The sight of the empty bedroom with only her bag on the ground caused a fresh stab of pain behind one eye. Becca pulled out her phone. No message. Becca crawled into bed wishing she were back in Key West.

BECCA ATE ALONE IN HER ROOM THE NEXT MORNING FEELING SAD and more than a little vulnerable. Despite putting her phone on silent while she slept away her headache, she was disappointed that there were no calls from Harry... or Owen. Her pride wouldn't let her keep calling Harry, but she wasn't sure what she should do. Had he been right? Should she have taken Owen and left?

When she finally emerged from her room looking for a distraction—unable to take her own thoughts any longer—she ran into several of the wedding party on their way back from breakfast. As soon as she stepped off the elevator, a few couples she recognized walked past with noncommittal polite smiles, averting their eyes. *The ex-wife at the wedding.*

Anna and Michelle both stopped when they passed. Anna held a Styrofoam box in front of her and looked annoyed, but Michelle was all smiles.

"Hey, Becca!"

Anna seemed to understand the awkwardness of the entire situation, but Michelle continued to act as if nothing had happened. Was Becca supposed to ask how her ex's wedding was the night before? "So, um..."

Becca needn't have worried because Michelle volunteered the information. "You didn't miss anything last night... not exactly the wedding Nicole was hoping for, huh?" She nudged Anna as if to elicit her agreement.

Did Michelle think they had to make her feel better about the wedding? The nerves and knots in Becca's stomach had *nothing* to do with how glamorous Nicole's wedding had been.

Anna glared at Michelle. Either Michelle didn't notice or didn't care because her words continued to pour out. "I mean, Jake looked miserable and Nicole was in a bad mood. Nobody felt like partying."

"Well, you can't really blame her, can you," Anna said. "She planned this wedding for a year! The caterer didn't come, and she didn't have any flowers except what they scavenged off bushes." Anna's tone made it clear that this was a horror of untold proportions.

Becca bit her tongue. A man was dead, not to mention the natural disaster the island endured. *How terrible that the florist and caterer didn't arrive!*

"Yeah, it was sad. But I took a ton of pictures for her, so at least she will have an amazing wedding album!"

Anna didn't bother to hide her eye-roll. "Come on, Michelle." She jiggled the Styrofoam container. "Let's get this food to Candice before it gets completely cold." She gave Becca a cool smile and stepped around her to push the call button for the elevator.

"She's still hasn't left her room," Michelle whispered.

The elevator dinged, and the doors slid open.

"Michelle!" Anna's voice was sharp.

"Bye, Becca. I'll try and see you later. Brad thought we'd be able to go home today, but Chris told us they had a bunch of damage at the marina, so our boat can't get out."

Becca started. She had forgotten all about finding transportation home. Before she could respond to Michelle, the doors had slid shut, and Becca was standing by herself gaping at her reflection in the mirrored doors.

Becca retreated to one of the sitting areas in a far corner where she could make a phone call. It took a few tries… the system must still have been overloaded from the storm. Maybe Harry had tried to call and couldn't get through, she thought hopefully, even though she knew it was unlikely. The phone continued to ring, and when Amelia didn't answer, Becca left a message for her to call. Becca didn't know how long this would all take, and she might need Amelia to feed the cat for a few more days. It was just as well she hadn't answered. Becca wasn't sure if she would have been able to stop herself from asking if she'd heard from Harry.

Becca approached the front desk and inquired if she could keep her room for another night. She wasn't sure how she was going to get home yet, but Becca imagined that some reservations would have been canceled in the storm's aftermath, and the hotel would have space.

"Of course, Ma'am," the young woman behind the desk said. "Your room is available for as long as you wish. It's reserved for special guests of the family." Becca wasn't a special guest, and she certainly wasn't Celine and Sean's friend. How much did this room cost? When she finally found the words to ask, the young woman explained that Sean had instructed that she was not to be billed for anything in the hotel.

"I can't possibly accept that!" Becca was shocked. "Is he in his office?"

"I'm sorry, Ma'am," the woman continued in her serene voice, "Mr. Pintner left the island yesterday."

The same as Harry. Had they gone together? It seemed a bizarre time to leave his resort—a hurricane and a murder! How had he gotten off the island? Just then, Becca saw Celine emerge from the doorway behind the desk. Becca would have loved to avoid her, but it was impossible. Celine handed the papers she was holding to the desk clerk and looked at Becca without expression.

"Good morning," Becca said.

"Is it?" Celine countered. Becca glanced at the clerk, who busied herself trying not to appear as if she were eavesdropping. "Why don't you take a break, Samara."

"Of course, Madam."

Becca gestured to the departing clerk. "She told me you and Sean are taking care of my expenses while I'm here. You are too generous. I'd hoped to talk with Sean again... to thank him for letting me stay… as well as yourself of course, but Samara said he left yesterday."

"You are quite welcome to stay, even though you weren't the intended guest." Without another word, Celine moved to walk away.

I guess that tells me where I rank.

"I was surprised Sean could leave the island after the storm or that he wanted to. He seemed so passionate about his family's property, and with the murder and all…"

"Whatever it is you are trying to say, just say it. I don't have time to waste with you." Celine looked bored.

"Did Sean leave with Harry?" Becca bit her tongue. That wasn't what she meant to say!

"I think you should mind your own business." She gave Becca a once over glance. "Brennan has clearly left you and your desperation is pathetic. He clearly couldn't get away from you fast enough. I knew he'd grow tired of your sweet, little dumb act. I just didn't think it would be that fast. Did he figure out that you were working with your ex-husband?"

"What are you talking about?"

Like a flash, Celine came around the desk and grabbed Becca's arm. Stunned, Becca didn't resist when Celine pulled her into the back office shutting the door behind them.

"I know who you are—who your husband and son are—and that you've been sent to spy on us. We will have your money soon!" Celine's accent grew thicker as she gripped Becca's arm tightly. "Sean made a mistake, but it's being fixed. The money will be back in the account by tomorrow."

The woman's nails dug into her. Becca shook her arm hard, pushing Celine away.

"I don't know what you are talking about." Becca tried to keep her voice calm even though Celine's behavior alarmed her.

Celine was panting, her eyes were wild. "I knew it! As soon

as Sean said they were having the wedding here, I understood what it meant—but it's done. Finis!"

Becca stood frozen. This might be her chance to find out what was going on.

"I admit, when you first arrived, you had me fooled. Your wide-eyed, dumb American act—but then I saw them go in your room earlier today, and it all came together!" She gave a harsh laugh. "Did Brennan find out? Is that why he left you here?"

Becca clenched her teeth to avoid lashing out. The reminder of Harry stung. Celine appeared to gather her composure.

"But we are all trapped in this together, ne c'est pas? Sean told me that he used those files to get Brennan's help. I admit I was a little surprised. I didn't think you had it in you, that you were capable of deceiving Harry Brennan like that. I was worried he was in on it, too, because of his father. It would have made more sense." She gave a Gallic shrug and brushed her hair back from where it had fallen over her eyes.

She gave Becca another appraising look. "Mais non, all Sean had to do was tell Brennan that your son's signature was all over the charter documents, and Brennan was more than happy to give Sean and James the money they needed." She wiped her hands as if wiping away her problem. "Now the money will be replaced."

Becca felt sick. "Harry gave you money?" She didn't understand why Sean had needed money, but the message that Harry had been blackmailed over Owen's involvement came through loud and clear. Harry's eagerness to get away from her made total sense now.

Celine's smile was cruel, and she let out a low chuckle. "Perhaps you didn't know after all." Celine sounded gleeful, as if she could tell the anguish that Becca was enduring and couldn't wait to add to it. "It was quite lucky that Brennan showed up when he did with his simple, little American girlfriend. Sean thought he could convince Harry to give him the money for old time's sake, but alas, his dear old friend had changed his ways. He wasn't interested in making money with us.

"Imagine our delight when we realized the connection between PPW and you. Sean approached the American, Raybourn," she clarified. "Sean admitted that he had borrowed some of the *client's* money, and that if Raybourn could help him replace it, Sean would pay him a larger portion of the next transfer. Raybourn was more than happy to share the information about your son, so that it could be used as leverage. Sean thought he would have to threaten to implicate Brennan, too, but apparently just the threat to your son was enough. He was *so* concerned about the young man's future." Her lips curved. "Normally, I'm not a fan of blackmail. It rarely works and always comes back to bite you—but in this case we were out of time, and you know full well what would have happened if we couldn't put the money back quickly."

Through her misery, Becca put together what Celine was saying. "Sean stole cartel money and got caught," Becca said. "That is profoundly stupid."

Celine huffed agreement. "He didn't steal the money—or didn't intend to, anyway." Her face twisted in derision. "That almost would have been preferable. If he showed some initiative. But no, he and James had an amazing, too good to be true, get rich quick scheme. The fools thought they would take the money out and get it back before anyone was the wiser, but they're both idiots, and they lost the money. There was no way to replace it on the deadline we were given."

"Why didn't Sean just borrow money from John? Why did you have to involve Harry?"

"Raybourn claimed he didn't have enough to cover it, and James didn't either. Fortunately for us, Harry was nearby. For a while we thought James was holding out on us, that if Harry talked to him then James would help us. But it turned out he really didn't have the cash. Sean offered to let Harry join in the operation to make money, but as I said, Harry has apparently changed his ways. It was Raybourn's idea when he saw you here with Brennan. He had a way of getting the money in exchange for getting part of our cut. I hated to do it, but it was better than the alternative. Raybourn getting killed was quite the bonus. Sean actually came out of it with a profit after all, now that he doesn't have to give Raybourn his cut."

Nicole claimed that John had the only set of files on a USB that implicated Owen, and that he had destroyed them. Had Nicole lied to her, or did John lie to Nicole? Becca's head was swimming. Did that mean the files were still out there somewhere?

"Did you give Harry the USB?"

Celine made a face. "Sean told him that it was being stored off site, and that they would do the exchange once the money was transferred." She gave a theatrical shudder. "I'm not sure how Sean plans on getting away from him when Brennan realizes we never had it in our possession. Harry Brennan isn't an enemy you want."

Becca didn't know what Celine meant, but Becca didn't have time to think about it or figure out what Celine was implying.

"Why did you trust that John wouldn't sell you out to the cartel the first time he was in trouble? Did you kill him to make sure that didn't happen?"

Celine's nostrils flared, and her face contorted into an ugly expression. "If we had killed him, you wouldn't have found the body."

Chilled, Becca stared at the woman.

Then, as if a switch had been flipped, Celine's attitude changed, and she adopted a smile and a saccharine tone. "I imagine it'll be hard getting a flight out for a day or two, but I hope you enjoy your stay while you are here."

She's insane, Becca thought. There was no other explanation.

She wanted to find Rey and tell him what she learned, but she couldn't do that without implicating Owen.

Oh god! Harry! He must hate me.

Everything he'd done to distance himself from his father's reputation... and because of his association with her, he was sucked back in. Becca hadn't thought it was possible to feel worse than she already did.

Becca pasted on her best society smile. "Thank you so much, Celine. I plan on doing just that."

18

She knocked quietly on the door of Candice's room. Anna wouldn't give her the room number, but Michelle had offered it up as soon as Becca asked. Anna was understandably suspicious. The scene between the two women in the casino had been ugly.

When the door opened, Becca wasn't positive what she had expected, but other than a slightly unfocused look to her reddened eyes, Candice looked much as she always did.

"What?"

"I just wanted to check and see how you were doing. I'm so sorry about John."

Pain flickered on Candice's face, but she shrugged.

"Can I talk to you? It won't take long," Becca asked, as Candice continued to block the door.

"Might as well. They don't like it when I leave the room. And I'm bored."

"Who doesn't like it? The Bahamian police?" That sounded like they considered Candice a suspect, despite Rey's opinion.

Candice waved her hand airily. "You know... people."

Becca squinted at Candice, wondering just how many

Valiums she had taken. The empty wine bottle on the dresser wasn't a good sign.

"I'm a suspect. I'm the one who found the body." Candice's tone was casual, at complete odds with her words.

"That doesn't bother you?"

She waved her hand again. "It's a bit rude I think because I'm grieving." Candice nodded seriously. She didn't sound as if she were grieving.

Candice was probably enjoying the attention, Becca thought.

"But I don't mind, I didn't do anything wrong." A slow, sleepy smile stretched across her face. "The doctor they brought in said I might have been drugged, because I don't remember anything."

Becca was dubious. "Why would someone drug you?" This sounded a lot like Candice's delusions of grandeur.

"Who knows?" She waved her hand, accidentally batting herself in the chest. She stopped and stared at her hand suspended in the air like she had forgotten how it got there.

"Candice, let's sit down." Becca guided her to the sofa. She didn't want to have to catch the blonde if her Valium and wine cocktail overtook her balance. Once Candice was settled, Becca asked her again about being drugged.

"They must have wanted to have their way with me." She pushed her lips out in an unsuccessful attempt to make a sexy pout as her bleary eyes struggled to focus. "That's what they do, Becca. They drug you because they'd never have a chance without it."

Becca closed her eyes. Being roofied wasn't a compliment, but Candice was beyond coherent conversation. Should she call someone? While Becca was trying to decide what to do, Candice whispered, "Or they wanted to get me out of the way so they could get to John."

"I'm glad to see you're not too broken up about it," Becca snarked.

In an instant, Candice's face changed, and Becca wondered if Candice was more affected than she let on. Becca felt a little guilty. It was possible Candice hadn't truly processed what had happened.

"I'm sorry. Had you been together long?" Becca asked, repentant.

"Not really." Candice's fingers picked at the fabric of the sofa next to her leg. Was this just Candice's normal self-preservation, pretend-she-didn't care attitude?

"Michelle mentioned you were getting ready to go away together." Candice's eyes flashed up to Becca's, and she seemed more lucid than she had been the minute before.

"Yes, John liked to spoil me. We just came back from cruising around the Caribbean. John had business at the banks. We were going on a trip." Her face fell.

Becca inhaled. *Banks?* "A trip to where?" Was John running away or was he obliquely referring to witness protection? Would he have taken Candice with him? Had John told her he was leaving her behind, and that sparked an argument?

Candice had helped Nicole dissuade Anna about going to the rental property. That implied Candice knew it was something that needed to stay hidden. Candice swayed a little on the sofa. This might be her only chance to get an unguarded reaction out of Candice.

"I know what's going on, Candice," Becca said, moving her head to catch Candice's eyes. "About the fraud… what you and John were doing."

"I have no clue what you're talking about." Candice's natural default was apparently deception even in her impaired state. With someone else, she might have gotten away with it. Becca was all too familiar with what a good liar Candice was, and looking down, she saw Candice's fingers gripping the seat beneath her.

"I'm talking about the fact that you were using Jake and

John's firm to launder money through bogus real estate." Candice made a choking sound. "There's no point in denying it. Jake has already told me everything." She left Owen's name out of it on the thin hope that Candice had never seen the missing documents. Could she get Candice to confess? That would clear Owen.

"I-I-I don't have any part of that." Her eyes were wide and flicked fearfully to the door. Becca realized Candice was afraid.

Of what? Does she know about the cartel, or did she see something when her boyfriend was being murdered only steps away? If she had, why won't she tell the police?

"Was John killed because of it?" It was a long shot, but Becca had to try.

"Of course not! I mean... what happened to John... I..." The rush of emotion seemed to sober Candice, and her fear turned to anger. "Why are you butting in? This has nothing to do with you. You are always so nosey! Can't you just mind your own business like everybody else?"

Becca narrowed her eyes. "I would love to mind my own business, Candice, but this is my family we're talking about."

"Jake's not your family anymore." Candice sneered.

"Owen is!" Becca snapped, and then bit her lip. She needed to get control of herself.

Candice jerked in her seat. She hadn't expected that. "Is Owen worried about his dad? Did *Jake* kill John?" Candice leaned forward suddenly intent. "It makes sense."

Becca took a risk. "The same FBI agents who are investigating PPW back in Sun Coast are here."

Candice paled, but was it because it surprised her that Becca knew about it, or because she didn't know herself?

"John was seen talking to them, here in the Bahamas. Were you aware of that?"

Candice couldn't hide her shock and her mouth fell open. "That's impossible! He would have told me."

"Well, obviously he didn't. So, what else didn't he tell you? Something that could have gotten him killed? Is it possible the people he was laundering money for found out he was talking to the FBI? Did you see someone that night?"

Candice was clearly terrified, but she was holding on to her bravado. "What? I'm supposed to take your word for it? How in the world do you know any this?"

Becca didn't want to give away that she had been talking to the FBI as well. "It's pretty obvious, isn't it? Michelle said she saw the same FBI agent who's questioning people, talking to John. In fact, after the raid at his office, John introduced him to her as a potential investor. Why would he say that, unless John was trying to hide something? He could have said the agent was anybody. John had to figure that eventually it would get out. Owen met him and so did Jake and Nicole."

Candice clutched her hands tightly in her lap. "He wouldn't do that. He wouldn't."

"Why?" Becca asked sarcastically. "The two of you were hardly a great love story. You said yourself you hadn't been together long."

If looks could kill, Becca would be laid out on the floor. "Do you always have to be such a know it all? It's survival of the fittest out there, Becca. Not all of us got a juicy settlement from our ex-husbands."

"Not all of us cheated on our husbands with our best friend's husband!" Becca shot back.

"You aren't so much better than me though, are you?" Candice sneered. "You fell into bed with the first rich guy that came along, too. Who are you to judge me?"

"I did not 'fall into bed' with Harry. I made a new life for myself!"

"So did I," Candice said coldly. Becca realized that in Candice's mind she had done nothing wrong. Candice had a lifestyle she wanted to maintain, and she wanted a man to provide it for her. "I'll always survive, Becca."

"I hope so, Candice. I hope that whoever killed John doesn't assume, like I did, that you know more than you do." Becca should have been ashamed of herself for scaring the woman, but she wasn't.

Candice paled. "Get out."

"Who is it?"

"I want you to leave."

"We've known each other a long time, Candice. Our kids grew up together. Even after what you did to Evie, I wouldn't want to see you dead. If you have information, you need to tell the police."

"I don't remember anything! Now, Get Out!"

Becca made her way back to her room, her thoughts whirling. She tried to put together all she had found out over the last several hours. Her phone rang, and for one second, she allowed herself to hope that it might be Harry. But when she picked it up, she recognized the number on the screen. Jake's voice was frantic on the other end.

"They just came and took him away! Owen!"

Becca's heart stopped and then began thudding painfully. "What are you talking about? Who arrested him? The FBI?"

Why didn't Rey give her a head's up?

"The Bahamian police. They think he killed John."

Becca swallowed against the acid taste in her mouth. "That's ridiculous. Why would they think that? They don't have any evidence." When Jake didn't answer right away, she leaned one hand on the wall to brace herself.

"Somehow they got the files, Becca." Jake's voice was so faint she could barely hear him.

Becca's body turned hot as anger rushed through her. "Files? The files you swore Nicole had kept safe, and she said had been destroyed? Those files?"

"It wasn't her fault. She said someone stole it out of her suitcase."

Becca remembered the torn lining of Nicole's suitcase and the disarray of her room. "How could she be so stupid? The two of you are under investigation, and she carries the incriminating evidence on her?"

"She thought it was safer to keep it with her instead of leaving it someplace where they could find it... with a search warrant. We worried they might search the house and storage units while we were out of the country."

Becca gnashed her teeth. He was defending Nicole. The woman had gotten their son arrested, and he was defending her!

"You're going to have to tell them the truth, Jake. There's no way around it."

"How would that help? They'll just say I'm covering for my son. If the files are supposed to be why Owen killed John, it won't matter if they aren't real."

Becca wanted to howl, but he had a point. "The police couldn't have been the ones that searched her room. They would need a warrant, right?"

"I don't know how the police got them. But they have them now," Jake snapped.

"But those alone can't be enough for them to arrest him! They won't realize what they mean or why they are important!" *Unless Rey told them.*

She didn't have a right to be hurt; he was doing his job. He had no loyalty to her. *Still.*

"I don't know! They just came and took him away."

"Stop saying you don't *know!*" Becca yelled into the phone. "You caused this. *You!* I have been trying to figure out what happened for two days, and you were too busy off getting married to care about fixing this!"

"I *don't* know, Becca!" Jake countered. "They suddenly showed up and said that they were detaining him under suspicion of murder."

"Did they take him to the Police Department?" Did they even have a police department building on this island? She wasn't sure how it worked with all the islands.

"No, I asked." Becca closed her eyes at his self-congratulatory tone and exhaled so she wouldn't say something that would make the situation worse. "They are keeping him on the property."

"Why?" Becca felt a little spurt of hope. If they were serious about him as a murder suspect, they'd take him to a jail... wouldn't they? "Where are you right now?"

"I'm in the lobby by the boutiques. We were shopping..."

Becca took another deep breath. Under investigation by the FBI, a hurricane, their criminal partner is murdered, and they were shopping.

Almost as if he read her thoughts, Jake continued defensively. "We don't have the right clothes in case we..."

"In case what? You decide to make a run for it? You're probably right, Jake, resort casual doesn't exactly blend when you are a fugitive. Know where you won't need new clothes, Jake? Jail. They provide the jumpsuit." Becca wasn't sure she had ever been this angry in her entire life. What was wrong with him?

"We shouldn't be talking on the phone. Just get down here."

Becca glared at the phone in her hand. If she killed him before he cleared Owen, it wouldn't help the situation.

19

Thankfully, Nicole was nowhere in sight when Becca found Jake. Given his attitude on the phone, she had assumed he wasn't worried, but one look at his haggard face proved her wrong and her anger dissolved. Some of it anyway.

"Did they tell you where in the hotel he is being held?" she asked without preamble. Jake shook his head. "I know someone who might be able to help."

"Your FBI friend?" His tone was accusing, and Becca spun around.

"Let's be clear. This problem is all you. I was happy! I made a life for myself, and once again you have *ruined* it."

Jake looked shocked by her vehemence, and then deflated in front of her. His shoulders drooped, and he stared at the ground. "I'm sorry. I never meant for Owen to be involved."

"You had him working in your firm while you were running a criminal fraud. What did you think would happen?"

Jake raised his eyes from the floor, and she could see his regret. "It was stupid. I see that now. It just never occurred to me. Nicole said…"

Becca held up a hand to stop him. "I don't care. Right now,

we have to concentrate on Owen." Without waiting to see if he was following, Becca stalked to the reception desk where she was happy to see Samara still on duty.

The young woman's smile was slightly more tentative than the last time Becca had seen her. Was that because of the argument Becca had with Celine, or because Becca was sure she looked like a crazy person? She certainly felt like one.

"Good afternoon, Ma'am. How can I help you?" Samara's eyes flicked to something over Becca's shoulder, and Becca assumed that meant Jake had followed her.

With a wide smile on her face, Becca asked, "Can you tell me where the police are? I mean, where they have set up? I need to ask them a question."

"I don't have that information, Ma'am. I'm not sure they are still here."

Becca didn't allow her smile to waver. "Is Celine in her office?" Becca didn't wait for the answer and rounded the counter, heading for the door. Her expression must have made it clear she would not be stopped because Samara jumped back, eyes wide. Becca didn't bother to knock, simply swung the door open. Celine was sitting at her desk and, at the sight of Becca, immediately ended the call she was on.

"There is a reason the rest of the world thinks Americans are so rude," she drawled.

Becca didn't waste time defending her country. "Where are the police detaining my son?" Jake came up beside her.

"Yet another handsome man by your side..." Celine shook her head in mock surprise. "I don't see your appeal, but then again you don't seem to keep any of them for long."

"Where?"

Celine sighed dramatically. "I have no idea where your son is."

"You're lying. The police are holding him on property so you have given them some place to do that." Becca was practically growling. "Where?"

Celine wrinkled her face and picked up her phone as if to make another call. "They've taken over the last bungalow by the parking lot... 1141."

Becca turned, pushing Jake out of the way as she left. Jake stumbled, and Celine chuckled. Becca was seconds away from having a complete meltdown.

"Becca!" Jake caught up to her as she was passing the fountain, heading for the walkway that led to the outer ring of bungalows "Wait!"

Becca stopped. "What? Do you want to tell me again that you didn't mean for this to happen?"

Jake's eyes were sad. "He's my son, too, Bex. You love to think you are the only one who can make things right... you don't have to fix this by yourself. Whether or not you like it, we are in this together." He reached for her hand. "I'm just as worried as you are. You have to let me help. I love Owen, too. We'll figure it out."

Becca closed her eyes and for a minute let herself pretend that the warm hand holding hers was someone she could rely on. Someone who could actually help. Jake was right. He loved Owen, but the question was did he love their son more than his own freedom? Becca pulled her hand free.

"I told you how you could help. You are choosing not to. I wouldn't think I had to fix everything if history hadn't shown me that it's true."

Jake's face hardened. "You tell yourself that, Becca, but it's not true. You never let anyone help because you are convinced you are the only one you can count on. If for one minute you could just admit that it's okay to lean on someone, you'd be a lot easier to live with!"

It was an old argument, one guaranteed to make her see red, not that it took much in her current mental condition.

"Really?" Becca exploded, not caring if the other guests in the lobby could hear her. "I could count on you? How about my parents? My friends? Harry?" Becca bit her lip hard as her voice broke. She hadn't meant to say that.

"Becca..."

"Mr. Copeland, I've been looking for you." Agent Warrick's voice cut him off, leaving whatever Jake planned to say a mystery.

Becca didn't wait to see how Jake answered the FBI agent, and the agent didn't stop Becca as she walked away. When she approached the correct bungalow, she saw Rey standing outside speaking to a uniformed man. Rey patted the man on the shoulder, and the police officer entered the unit.

All reason flew from her mind as she stormed across the space between them, determined to talk to the officer. Rey must have caught her out of the corner of his eye, because he turned to intercept her.

"What the hell, Rey? You know my son didn't kill anybody!"

Rey glanced from Becca, to the bungalow door, and back again. "Do you want to keep it down a little? You aren't helping by shrieking."

"It doesn't make any sense. They think Owen had an argument with John—which he didn't by the way, but that's hardly enough evidence to arrest someone!"

Rey stared at her for a moment before grabbing her by the hand. "Come on. We need to talk." Becca didn't resist as he tugged her toward the patio area by the pool and around the corner to where cushions were still stacked, waiting to be replaced on the lounge chairs. "Sit down." When she didn't move, Rey put his hands on her shoulders, and gently pushed. "Please."

With a frustrated huff, Becca sank into the chair. They were in a far corner, away from the other guests. Apparently satisfied with their privacy, Rey reached for a seat. Becca winced as the scraping of the chair Rey drew forward jangled her nerves. She was holding on for dear life and wasn't sure how much more she could take before completely falling apart, but there wasn't another choice. She had to get her son out of police custody and off the island!

Rey leaned forward, resting his forearms on his knees. His face was close enough that she could see the tired lines by his eyes and mouth. For some reason, that defused some of her panic... as if she wasn't alone in her concern. "You forgot to mention that your son was involved in the real estate group—in fact, you insisted he wasn't, that he was just a general intern."

"He wasn't involved."

"Then why is his name all over the papers of incorporation? He's not only a part of it, he's a charter stakeholder and principal member!" Rey's eyes burned angrily into hers. "Do you understand what that means?"

Becca's heart thudded painfully in her chest, and she clasped her trembling hands in front of her to hide her nerves.

Rey's voice was hard. "It means that your son could face federal charges, not only for money laundering but for defrauding investors. If he's *not* guilty and someone framed him... than that's motive for murder."

Becca's jaw dropped, and a cry escaped her. "But you know he didn't do it! They used him, but he wouldn't kill over it!"

"Look, I actually agree with you." Rey's shoulders relaxed. "I think the Bahamian police have made a mistake, but I don't have clear jurisdiction over this murder. He's an American citizen, and that's why they are looping us in, but there isn't much I can do."

Becca's face felt hot. "Why do they think it's him and not any of the other people John fought with? It can't just be the paperwork and an argument. How did they even get the documents?"

"Anonymous. A USB was found in an envelope on top of a trash can by the front doors—just out of sight of the cameras, with a big, obvious label, 'FOR THE POLICE', written across the front." Rey rolled his eyes. "Whoever it was wanted to be sure it was found, but didn't want to be associated."

Becca scowled. Nicole claimed she was the only one who had possession of the USB, even though she later said it had been stolen. Would she implicate Owen? Why, unless she killed John and needed a scapegoat?

Oblivious of her thoughts, Rey began ticking off the facts the Bahamian police were relying on. "One, John was about to turn on everyone and testify against them regarding the money laundering. Two, Owen knew I was an FBI agent, and there are plenty of witnesses who will testify that he was very agitated when he learned I was here. Three, Owen is implicated in the crime John was going to testify about, meaning he and his father were most likely facing jail time. Four, he was seen threatening John, both during the fight with your ex-husband and later outside. A witness heard Owen say, 'I'll kill you for this'."

Becca blanched. Said out loud it sounded bad. "Not to mention the fact that your son is a tall, strong, young man, and it's not a stretch to believe that he lost his temper in a fit of rage and beat the victim with a rock. It doesn't matter that I think it's flimsy, he's in a lot of trouble, Becca."

"Who said Owen threatened John? That didn't happen!" She braced herself for the answer. Had Owen lied to her?

Rey exhaled heavily and rubbed his jaw. "I don't know who the witness is or how reliable the information is. I didn't ask. I don't think that the police are convinced your son is responsible either, or they would have arrested him. He fits nicely with their theory so far, but as of right now, they don't have any hard evidence to connect him. Just a lot of theories. Hell, I don't think he was even on their radar until that paperwork came to light."

"What about fingerprints on the envelope?"

"They dusted it but there wasn't anything clear, mostly smudges. A couple of partials they could match, but they aren't concerned with *who* revealed the evidence. They are much more interested in who it implicates."

Becca leaned back into the cushions and put her hands over her face. "I can't just sit here and do nothing. What if someone were to confess to the money laundering? Confess that Owen had nothing to do with it." She would make Jake confess even if it required violence!

Rey's jaw firmed. "That would definitely help my case, but it won't help your son. His anger would have been even greater if they stole his identity. Also, your son's lifestyle will take a massive hit if his dad is convicted and loses all his money."

Becca's brow furrowed. "Why would Jake lose all his money?"

"I don't have time to get into the intricacies of this," Rey said as he stood up. "The best thing you can do is get your son a lawyer."

"Humor me." She could see the hesitation on Rey's face. "Please?"

"Fine. Basically, if an individual is arrested for money laundering, or really any financial crime, typically all their assets are frozen and then seized after conviction. That includes the business that was used as the vehicle for criminal activity. If Copeland has all of his money tied up in investments with his firm—which I think is a fair assumption—then his assets would be forfeited."

"That doesn't seem fair!" Becca thought of the innocent people who were going to be affected because they had invested their money with Jake. "What if the clients didn't know what their money was being used for? He manages a lot of people's funds. They can't all have been invested in this fake REIT."

"It doesn't matter. Frequently, the majority of the company isn't aware of the criminal enterprise. If the principals are found guilty, the courts will assess fines based on the extent of the crime. Any profits that were made, that would have been used as payouts to the investors, would have to go toward the fines. There's almost never anything left. Everyone who invested in this group is going to have lost everything they trusted PPW with. Either that or they are going to lose it in legal fees trying to prove their innocence."

"That could be a motive for someone else though, right? They can't blame Owen if there are tons of other people here that also would be upset at John." Hope sparked in her. If John testified against PPW, then everyone would lose their savings. She would bet most of the wedding guests were clients.

"That's true, but they would have to know that John was working with us."

"You said it yourself! Owen outed you and John in a lobby full of people!"

Rey grimaced, and inclined his head in acknowledgement of the point. Sensing that she was making headway, she blurted out, "Did you notice that Nicole, my ex's new wife, has scratches on her neck and broken nails. I noticed the morning after the murder." That definitely got his attention, and he took a few steps toward her. "She has just as much reason as Owen, more even, because she works there." Nicole wouldn't be able to prove that she didn't know what was going on, whereas Owen might be able to show that he never signed those documents. The more she thought about it, the more Becca realized that Nicole really might have done it. "I think she's the one who had the USB," Becca said.

Rey's eyes bored into hers. Without dropping her gaze, he leaned forward until he was only inches from her. Becca held her ground refusing to shrink back. His voice was too calm when he asked, "You gave me a list of people who you thought could be responsible. Why didn't you mention her? Injuries after a murder would have jumped her to the top of the list." He leaned back again. "Dammit, the police never mentioned them. How could they have missed that?" He paused. "What did you mean you think she's the one who had the USB?" His eyes widened; his face slacked. "You knew about the files before I told you. Didn't you?"

Becca took a deep breath. "Yes."

Rey surged to his feet and paced angrily back and forth in front of her. "How long have you known? Why the hell didn't you say anything?"

"I didn't, not until after John was killed. I couldn't tell you about Nicole or the money laundering! If I had, I would have incriminated Owen."

He stabbed a finger in her direction furiously. "You could have saved us a lot of time! We could have helped him."

Becca felt a moment of uncertainty, but she shook her head. "No, you wouldn't have. You still would have arrested him. You would have told the Bahamian police, and that would have made them even more convinced."

Rey threw his hands up and stalked back over to where she was sitting. He stared down at her with a stony expression before sitting again.

"The conversation we had at dinner, when I was explaining what we had figured out about PPW... son of a bitch, you played me. You already knew all about it!" Rey let out a harsh laugh. "I didn't think you had it in you, Nancy Drew. But I'll tell you this, if you want to keep your son out of jail, you need to tell me what you know. You won't be able to do much from your own cell."

"What?"

Rey pressed his lips together. "If you're helping them—do you realize you've made yourself an accessory after the fact?"

"I'm not!"

Maybe he was right. If she gave him all the information she had now, then maybe he could help figure out who really killed John. The only reason she had been protecting Jake and Nicole was to keep Owen out of trouble, but the police had found out about Owen's involvement anyway.

"Okay, fine. I'll tell you what I know, but it isn't much. From what Jake said, PPW told their clients that there was this great investment opportunity in the Bahamas. They said they could buy properties at crazy cheap prices because the properties had been damaged by all the hurricanes over the last few years, and no one wanted to live here anymore because of the threat of more storms."

Rey shot her a disbelieving look. "Did people believe them? That's the stupidest thing I've ever heard."

"I agree. I'm just telling you what he told me. In reality they were just buying cheap, vacant land. People buy land as an investment, but PPW had told their clients that these were luxury homes all through the Caribbean. What they bought didn't cost nearly as much as they claimed it did. I'm assuming that is why Nicole was hell bent on preventing Chris from driving by one of them. He would see the address had nothing on it." Becca shrugged. "Jake said the extra money they had from the investors was being given back to their clients. PPW pretended like it was the money they had made on their investment, but actually, it was their own money plus…" Becca made a pained face, "the money they were being asked to launder. But not everything they invested in was a lie. They've also invested in this hotel by financing a massive renovation."

Rey's brows grew together, and he began to pace again. Finally, he stopped in front of her. "They must be creating a paper trail for the dirty cash, so that it looks like there are rents coming in. That money, now that it's clean, could be deposited in a bank. The people in Sun Coast think their checks are from rents or home sales, when what's really happening is they are just comingling the investors' clean money with the cartel's dirty money, and by the time it is paid out as the investment return, all the money is clean. This way none of their investors know what's going on, and it looks like they are actually showing income. If a bank ever asks where a deposit is coming from, they can point at the REIT, and it looks totally legit. It's a pretty good trick."

"Okay, I get how they are cleaning the cartel money, sort of, but what I don't get is how does PPW make money? Why would Nicole and John do this?"

"Criminals who need their money laundered accept that they are going to lose as much as twenty-five percent to pay whoever is laundering it for them. Drugs are a cash business. They can't just walk into a bank with bags of cash or gold and deposit it. Too many questions and red flags. It's necessary for the cartels to clean *all* the money just so they can keep the seventy-five percent. They can take that seventy-five percent and put it in a bank and invest in legitimate businesses. Losing twenty-five percent is worth it to them. That's how PPW is making all their money. The paperwork has Owen as the principal shareholder. Somehow, I doubt they ever gave him that much money. Most likely it's being split between John, Nicole, Jake, and possibly the Pintners. We are talking millions of dollars, so even twenty-five percent is a lot of money."

"That's what she meant," Becca breathed.

Rey's face was hard. "Who? Don't hold out on me now."

Becca sighed. "Celine, Sean's wife. She said something to me about giving John a larger part of their portion." She didn't want to tell Rey what Harry had done for her. The least she could do was keep him out of it.

"She must be talking about returns out of the casino. It's a pretty classic move. PPW invests money by buying a portion of the hotel, and in return, the hotel will launder huge amounts of money through the casino. We suspected that was happening, but her telling you confirms it. PPW may have given them money for the renovation, but my guess is part of the deal was that the Pintners had to agree to let PPW use their casino. I'm sure they are getting a fee, too."

Becca was thankful he hadn't asked the follow-up question about *why* John would get part of Sean's portion.

"If you know they are doing it, why don't you arrest them? I thought that was the information you were trying to find?"

"It is, but there is more to it than just this property. We need *all* the ways PPW is helping Olivera. It doesn't do us any good to shut off only one of his income streams. We need to take them all, or he will just shift his operations again."

Becca nodded. That made sense.

"Becca." He hesitated, and she braced herself for whatever he was going to say next. "The evidence against Owen for Raybourn's death is flimsy. It seems out of character for your son, but I've been doing this long enough that I'm rarely surprised anymore. You need to ask yourself some hard questions. Are you absolutely positive that you fully understand just how involved your son is? I'm not saying he intended to kill John, but he might have lost his temper if he thought John was about to ruin his life, particularly if he thought John had framed him."

He held up his palm when she started to object. "Wait a second—you're his mom and you said that you are close but—" Becca's eyes narrowed at him. "Okay, maybe not the murder. What about the fraud? Let's be real, it's easy to have your head turned around at that age—people make a lot of bad decisions. Not to mention, it may not have seemed that bad if his father told Owen it was okay. The fact that he's in that office, working with his father, who I am positive…"

Rey held up his hand again, and his voice was hard when it continued. "Are you telling me you don't think it's even possible that your son could have been lured by the idea of easy money?"

Tears gathered in her throat. She thought of the new car Owen had bought, but even if it was expensive, it wasn't *that* expensive. From the things Owen said, Jake had convinced their son that this was a victimless crime. Could he… she shook her head to get rid of the thoughts. Rey misinterpreted the movement however and sat back in his chair. "I think you are lying to yourself, and in the long run, it's going to hurt your son."

"I'm not saying Owen couldn't be involved in *some* way, though I don't think he is," she hurriedly added. "But there is no way he killed John Raybourn. I'm *positive*." She saw he recognized his own words thrown back at him.

Rey cocked his head. "Like I said before, it does seem out of character for Owen. I haven't seen anything that indicates your son would be capable of this, and they've been under surveillance for a while."

Becca winced. How could all of this have been going on and she had no idea? Had she become so wrapped up in her own world that she had forgotten about everyone else?

"If your son has information about his father's operation, he could really help himself out by agreeing to talk to me."

"Wouldn't that incriminate him?" Becca asked warily.

"I'm sure there's a deal that could be worked out. We need somebody who will testify."

Rey stood and put his hands on his hips. "There *is* evidence against your son and his involvement in the money laundering scheme. It's going to be very difficult for him to prove he wasn't aware of what was going on under his nose, particularly now that these documents have surfaced. And now that I have a good idea how they are moving the money, I'll know where to look for more evidence. His only way out may be to testify."

"Is that a threat?" she asked incredulously. Becca wanted to kick herself. She had allowed herself to imagine that, based on what had happened before, they might be on the same side. She reminded herself that Rey was going to do whatever he needed to do to solve his case. She had just given him what he needed to finally build the case against Owen.

"I'm just stating the facts. I'm not the only one in possession of this information. There is a whole task force on it." Something like regret crossed his face. "Owen needs to get in front of this. He may not have the information we need, but he could point us in the right direction. There are only a few people left standing... but I only need one." His face was grim as he held her gaze before walking away.

Becca froze staring vacantly out toward the ocean. Jake wouldn't put his own son in jail... would he? No, even Jake wouldn't do that. Nicole... Rey means Nicole. *"I'm not going to jail for anyone."*

Becca remembered Nicole's agitated state when Becca last spoke to her—and the broken nails. If she had broken those nails in a struggle with John, surely there would have been evidence left behind! Would the rain have destroyed it? There was no way the Bahamian police were going to tell her about John's body, and at this point, she wasn't sure Rey would either.

Becca scowled at the bright blue sky and palm trees above her head. Now that the storm had passed, the island was beautiful again, and it felt almost a personal insult. How could the weather be so perfect when she was so unhappy? She chewed on her nail. What could she do? No matter what Rey said, she couldn't just sit around waiting for the police to realize their mistake.

Candice! Becca suddenly stood. Candice found John's body. She would remember if there had been scratches on him.

20

It took Becca over an hour to find Candice. She finally spotted her former friend ensconced by herself in a chair by the ocean, wrapped in a hotel robe. Several empty glasses on the cabana table made it clear that she had been there for a while. Apparently things had taken a turn for the worse for Candice after Becca had left her a few hours before.

When Becca's shadow fell over her, Candice tipped her head back to peer at Becca from underneath the broad-brimmed hat shading her face. The incongruous sight of Candice in a puffy, white robe and large, pink sun hat struck Becca as sad. When was the last time Candice had allowed herself to be seen looking like this? Her aggressive perfection was nowhere in sight.

"What do you want?" Candice slurred. This was either going to be easier than Becca expected or harder—depending on how confrontational and inebriated Candice was feeling.

"I need to ask you a question," Becca said.

Candice blew out a huffy breath before taking another sip of her drink. The straw slurped on the empty bottom, and she looked at it angrily. "You know you'd think at a fancy place like this, they could at least have people coming out to refill my glass and take away the empties."

"There *was* a hurricane," Becca said dryly.

Candice pulled her glasses down and glared at Becca, but her obviously red eyes blunted her desired effect.

Becca softened. "I need to ask you something about John."

Candice pushed her glasses back up and turned her head away from Becca. "You already asked me about John. Go away. I don't want to talk to you."

Becca squatted in the sand next to Candice and reached for her hand, resting over the tie of her robe. Candice jerked her hand away, but Becca couldn't be discouraged.

"Candice, this is important. The police have taken Owen in for more questioning." The woman turned her face back to Becca, but with her glasses on Becca couldn't read her eyes.

"So?"

"Candice, you know Owen! You were at his seventh birthday party—he didn't kill John!"

Candice's shoulders barely moved in a shrug, and Becca grit her teeth against the bitter words threatening to spill out. She needed Candice's help. She had seen the body. "Despite everything that has happened, and as hurt as you are right now, you don't want to see an innocent young man go to jail."

Candice sniffed, "Fine. What do you want?"

"When you found John that morning…" How could she ask this nicely—and then realized there wasn't a way. "Did he have a lot of scratches on him or… or… like open wounds?"

Candice's face crumbled. "You're disgusting, Becca. I can't believe you just asked me that. What is wrong with you? You always pretend like you are so much better than everyone else, Miss Holier-than-thou… but you are just a nosy, heartless bitch!"

"It's important, Candice."

For a minute Becca didn't think Candice would answer, and just as she was preparing to stand, Candice huffed again. "I don't know. I don't think so... I really thought..." Tears began sliding down her face from behind the sunglasses as she began to cry in earnest. "He was just lying there... lying all... all... by himself... out there in the rain... all night." Candice hiccupped. "He looked so normal at first, except he was on the ground. Then when I was closer, I could see his head..."

"Oh, Candice. I'm so sorry, I really am..." Becca leaned over to put her arms around Candice, but Candice angrily waved her away. She reached up furiously, swiping at the tears on her cheeks.

"Can you just go away now? Go away! I hate you... god... I hate you!" Candice's voice was low and bitter, and Becca knew there was nothing else she could say. As she walked away, Becca thought about what Candice had said. "He looked normal." That had to mean she hadn't seen any obvious wounds, scratches, etc. So, Nicole's broken nails probably weren't from an altercation with John.

But then again, Candice had been upset. She told Michelle there had been blood, but Rey said he didn't remember there being any visible. Did Candice just miss the scratches? Becca grimaced. This was so hard! It couldn't be a coincidence that Nicole had scratches, bruises on her wrist, and broken fingernails the morning after John was murdered. Why would Nicole fight with John? Was she upset that Jake found out about them using Owen's name, or had she somehow figured out John was going to testify against her?

Owen and Michelle had both seen Rey in the hotel. Nicole could have seen John and Rey together, or someone could have mentioned what Owen let slip in the lobby before the cocktail party. Nicole wasn't stupid. She would have realized the significance. Becca overheard the argument between Jake and John from her hotel room. Even at that distance it was obvious how drunk John had been. It stood to reason that Nicole had probably been drinking, too... did they fight? Besides, who else would have had the incriminating information to turn over to the police with Owen's name on it. Nicole claimed it was stolen, but she could be lying. Nicole might already be setting herself up as the next witness! Becca's body heated with anger. Nicole would never voluntarily admit that Owen wasn't responsible for the fraud. Becca would have to force the issue.

Fury surged at the sight of Nicole and Jake having lunch peacefully by the pool. Not far away, their son was being detained by police because of something they had done, and they were enjoying a club sandwich! Her blood boiling, Becca dropped into the chair opposite them, happy her sunglasses protected her at least a little. She wasn't sure she could bluff Jake if he could see her eyes.

"Are you having a nice lunch?" she asked sarcastically.

Jake had the grace to squirm, but Nicole simply raised an eyebrow. "Can we help you with something?" she drawled.

"Actually, you can," Becca said, reaching across to take a french fry off of Jake's plate. Nicole's lip curled in disgust when Becca took a bite of the fry and then double dipped in Jake's ketchup. She was deliberately provoking them and it felt wonderful!

"The three of us know that Owen had nothing to do with John's crimes, even though both of you listed him as a principal in your fake property investment scheme. You risked my son's entire future by getting him involved."

Damn! She hated that her voice shook. She couldn't afford to get carried away by emotion. She inhaled through her nose, ignoring an urge to leap across the table and throttle Nicole. "We also know that he didn't kill John, but someone in this hotel did —and odds are it was someone who had uncovered what he was up to." Becca was proud that this time she kept the emotion out of her voice. She angled her head toward Nicole, so that there was no doubt who she was addressing. "What I'd like you to explain is how you got those bruises on your wrist and the broken nails?"

Jake's eyes widened, and his throat moved as he swallowed nervously. A serpentine smile spread across Nicole's face as she deliberately reached for her glass, taking care to make sure that the backs of both hands were clearly visible as they wrapped around the sweating glass—displaying a fresh manicure of short nails. "I've always heard how dramatic you were, but really." Nicole's laugh was derisive.

Becca's temper sparked anew at the blasé attitude. "You can hide broken nails, but you can't hide your bruises as easily."

She had noticed Nicole's wrist when she lifted her glass. At first glance, the bruises also appeared to have disappeared, but as Nicole rotated her hand, the bright sun illuminated the splotches of slightly darker color on Nicole's wrist. She had obviously applied makeup to cover them. Involuntarily, Nicole covered her wrist with the opposite hand before regaining herself. She flashed her hands up before placing them on her lap beneath the table.

"I don't have any bruises."

"I can't see them now, but you thought I could—that's why you covered your wrist just now." Becca eyed the color difference between Nicole's exposed collar bones and slightly lighter neck. "You really should have used your foundation on your chest, too. I can see the line. Blending... it's important." Becca dipped her fry again. "Didn't anyone teach you that in high school? I can lend you a makeup sponge if you need it." Nicole's eyelid twitched. "I wonder if I were to point them out to my friend Rey..."

"Ah yes, your friend," Nicole snarled. "However could we forget that the FBI agent, who is suddenly so involved in our business and fabricating evidence to ruin our lives, is your *friend.*" Nicole's tone made it clear what type of friend she thought Rey was. "What a coincidence."

Becca couldn't help the laugh that escaped her. "Are you seriously suggesting that somehow I'm so irresistible, that I not only seduced an FBI agent into forming an entire task force against my ex-husband and his girlfriend, but the rest of the agents involved as well? It couldn't possibly be the fact that the two of you are actually breaking the law? I'm sure that has *nothing* to do with it!"

Jake straightened in his chair. "You're upset... so am I... it's a mess with Owen, but it's only a matter of time... they'll realize he isn't guilty."

Becca's lips parted in shock. "And you're willing to let him sit in that room—alone, frightened, and worried they think he murdered someone?" She seethed at his selfishness. She had to shock him out of this complacency! "This isn't going away, Jake. The FBI already knows everything."

She watched, satisfied, as the blood drained from both of their faces. Rey might do anything to solve his case, but she was just as determined to save her son. "They know," she repeated. "John was going into witness protection. He was going to testify against you."

"What did you do, Becca?" Jake's eyes were flat, but his tone had changed. His head jutted forward but she didn't flinch.

"I didn't tell them," she lied. "John did."

"John hadn't told them everything. If he had, they would have never let us come here." Jakes's voice was so cold that her suspicion suddenly shifted. Becca had always thought of Nicole as being the cut-throat half of the couple. She had believed Jake when he said Nicole tricked him. This coldness was something new. Becca had never entertained the thought that Jake might have been involved in John's death. She hadn't thought Jake had it in him.

But the look on his face now?

"Jake!" The word was little more than a breath. She pulled off her sunglasses so Jake was forced to look at her. "What did you do?" Becca was having a hard time reconciling the man she'd lived with for almost twenty years with the person sitting across from her. His face looked different, and it frightened her. "Did you and Nicole? Was it an accident? I can help you but you have to tell them! You can't just leave Owen to take the blame!" Jake's eyes turned to Nicole, and Becca saw that, despite Nicole's cool facial expression, her hands had shredded the napkin in front of her.

Abruptly, Jake's face relaxed, and he resembled his normal self again, but Becca still felt unsettled. She didn't know this man anymore.

"Honey, it's okay," Jake said, as he covered Nicole's hand. Becca held her breath. Was he going to admit what they had done? Her relief at Owen's exoneration warred with the disbelief that Jake had actually killed someone. Images of Jake as a scared teenager, holding her while she cried, after her parents had essentially disowned her when she told them she was pregnant, Jake holding Owen, their first home… the happy memories… before it had fallen apart. Even though Jake had turned out to be a massive disappointment as a husband, never in her wildest dreams would she have ever thought he was capable of this. Becca's throat burned, and she could taste acid in her mouth.

Her suspicion must have shown, because Nicole said quickly, "We didn't kill him." Nicole glanced at Jake and, when he nodded his encouragement, she continued. "John was acting… off… over the last couple of weeks, but we assumed it had to do with the search warrant. When Owen told his dad that the FBI agent was here, and Anna told me that Michelle had seen them talking, well… it wasn't hard to put it together." She hesitated and Jake squeezed her hand.

Becca tried to keep from gagging at his affectionate display.

"Jake tried to confront John about it, and about Owen's name in the files." She lifted her eyes from the table. "John didn't tell me he had done that... not until they raided the office. Then, John gave me the USB to hide. But... but I didn't know before that," she said earnestly, and Jake gave her a sympathetic smile.

Becca clenched her teeth. Nicole was obviously lying, but Jake would never see it.

"After the fight, I thought I could reason with him. Explain that it was better if we all stuck together." Nicole's tone implied that she viewed herself and Jake to be the victims. "The party broke up not long after; the storm was picking up. After Jake left, I went to John's bungalow to talk to him, but he was still drunk and belligerent. He was sitting in the rain by his front door, and he wouldn't go inside where we could talk like normal people!" Nicole lifted a hand as if this were evidence enough that he was crazy. "I thought if I could just get him to listen... I begged him not to do it. It would ruin us, possibly even get us all killed. I explained that if he testified, Owen would go to jail. He should have some sympathy for him at least, but he didn't." Nicole's mouth turned down at the memory.

"He laughed at me and said he'd think of me from his new home courtesy of the United States Government. I was so mad! I reached out to hit him, but he grabbed my wrist and threw me backward. I must have slipped on the wet stones because I fell into the landscaping." She turned her hands over for the first time, and Becca could see the abrasions on her palms.

"He was still laughing when I left. I came back to our room to tell Jake what happened..."

"But I had already gone to Owen's room."

"John was alive when I left him. I swear."

A tight knot formed in Becca's stomach. Nicole's explanation sounded plausible, but if not her or Jake, then who? Realization dawned on her. "If Nicole tells the police that John was alive after she left, and you were with Owen, then Owen has an alibi."

"He wasn't in the room, Bex," Jake said solemnly.

Damn it! She remembered that when they had spoken the morning after the murder, Owen told her he had seen Nicole out walking. That meant he still didn't have an alibi. Becca pushed down the panic rising in her throat. Owen couldn't have killed John—she knew it.

"He claims he was just wandering around the hotel. When the storm got worse, he figured he should come back to the room," Jake continued.

That made sense. Owen could have seen Nicole through one of the giant lobby windows, as she was coming back from her confrontation with John.

Jake exchanged a look with Nicole.

"What?" Becca snapped.

Jake let out a heavy sigh. "He said he'd been in the hotel, but... he was soaking wet. He lied."

21

Becca was at a loss. She didn't know how long she had been walking the grounds, trying to process what Jake and Nicole had told her. He hadn't said it, but Becca had the distinct impression Jake thought Owen might have murdered John. It was ridiculous, but also frustrating. Becca felt as if she had been questioning people for weeks, not just a few days, and had accomplished nothing.

She reached the sugar sand bordering the water. There was more debris than usual, greenery and chunks of wood washed up from the storm, but it was still breathtakingly beautiful. She wiggled her toes, staring at the horizon. How was it less than a week ago she was blissfully practicing yoga on a beach just like this? In that brief span, her new life had been entirely upended. Tears pricked at her eyes.

What is Harry doing right now? He tried to save Owen, but he has to have figured out by now that Sean tricked him. Sean never had the evidence. If Harry resented me for being caught in the situation with Owen and the money laundering, what must he think of me now, knowing it has been for nothing.

Becca pulled out her phone, her finger hovering over his

contact information. If she could just hear his voice… tears blurred her vision as she stared at his name on the screen before pushing the button to turn the phone off. If she called now, when she was in such a mess, it would just confirm his fears—that he was only ever wanted for what he could provide—then again, if he had told her what was going on…

She sighed. I'll call him after, she assured herself. *After I've figured all this out, I'll call him.*

"Becca!" She tamped down her irritation, the last thing she wanted right now was to make small talk with Michelle and Anna.

"Hey!" Becca said, as Michelle bounded up.

"I'm so glad we ran into you! How are you doing? We're sorry about Owen…"

Michelle looked to Anna but her friend just glared at her before addressing Becca.

"It's stupid, Becca. I don't know why they think Owen could be involved. None of us believe he had anything to do with it." Anna put her hand on Becca's arm.

"Thanks."

"Becca, we were just about to go to my room. Come with us! I'm dying to show you my pictures. I think because you're an artist, you'll appreciate them."

Anna rolled her eyes. How did Michelle not notice her friend's most common reaction to everything she said and did?

Becca wanted to say no, but she couldn't think of a decent excuse. It did sound preferable to wandering the resort alone, dwelling on what she couldn't control. Michelle's large hopeful eyes decided it. "Sure."

Michelle gave her a small smile. "It might take your mind off things, even if just for a bit."

Michelle was trying to be kind, but did she really think looking at photographs was going to help Becca forget the fact that her son was essentially being accused of murder? She forced her lips into a smile.

"We could find somewhere to sit, and you could show me on your phone."

Michelle practically hopped up and down with happiness. "Let's go to my room. I have my laptop and everything! I can show you on the bigger screen."

Anna sighed at Michelle's enthusiasm, but obligingly began walking after Michelle. They walked past the large pool area and followed a walkway that led them through a small courtyard to the second row of bungalows, behind the set where Candice and John had been staying.

"I didn't realize you were in a bungalow, too." Becca was a little surprised. Even though these bungalows didn't have a beach or pool view, they still had to be more expensive than the rooms in the main building. From what Michelle had said, Becca had assumed they would have been out of Michelle and Brad's price range.

Michelle looked back over her shoulder with a smile. "Yup, Brad said because it was a special occasion we should splurge." Her face clouded, and she looked to Anna, realizing the implication of what she had said and to whom. "I mean..."

"It's okay," Becca interrupted, hoping to ward off the pitying looks everyone cast her way at the mention of the wedding. If nothing else, these last few days had proven to Becca that her divorce from Jake had been a blessing.

Michelle's bungalow was at the end. When Michelle opened the door, Becca saw with dismay both Michelle's and Anna's husbands were sitting at a table with open beers in front of them. Becca wasn't up to making mindless chit chat. She could barely handle Anna and Michelle!

Brad's face was arranged in what Becca suspected was a permanent scowl—at least that was his expression every time she had seen him around his wife over the last couple of days.

Chris gave a half smile and wave, but he looked as if he wished he were somewhere else. They had been Jake's friends, not hers.

"Hey, ladies!" Chris gestured with his beer. "Do you want one of these? We're day drinking. Nothing else to do around here til the boat is ready," he guffawed, looking at Brad to back him up in that annoyingly perennial, frat-boy way.

Brad's lip stretched upward in a smile, even though it looked like it pained him, and he took a long pull of his beer. He looked balefully at Michelle, who seemed blissfully unaware of her husband's animosity. Anna noticed and shared a look with Chris.

Were Jake and I this obvious when our marriage was falling apart, Becca wondered?

"Heh, heh," Chris chuckled, a little nervously. "C'mon have a beer! This could be our last day of vacation."

Becca bit her tongue, hard. They were all so self-centered. Each of them seemed to ignore the fact that someone they knew had been murdered mere steps away from where they were guzzling beer.

"Chris," Anna hissed through smiling teeth. "Michelle wants to show us the photos she has taken on the trip. Why don't you guys go to the bar?"

"We just opened these!" Chris objected. "You girls, just go ahead, you won't bother us."

Brad's eyebrows drew down into an even deeper scowl. "Michelle, can't this wait till we get home? We are trying to salvage what we can from this vacation. Nobody wants to see your damn photos. It's not art just because you took a picture of an exit sign." He smirked at Chris who didn't hide his snort of laughter.

Michelle flushed red.

"Chris, go to the bar." Anna said with a meaningful look.

"Fine, fine. We're just joking around. We don't want to be here during all the girl talk. He said... then she said... then I said..." Chris mocked in a falsetto. The men erupted into laughter, and Brad slapped Chis on the arm.

Becca hid her disgust. It was hard to believe, but it appeared these men were actually getting worse with age! As much as she wanted to say something to him about his misogynistic comments, Becca kept her mouth shut. It wasn't worth the energy, and she definitely didn't have any extra bandwidth right now.

After they left, Anna threw an arm around Michelle's shoulders and squeezed. "Don't listen to them, babe. I think everyone's really thrown off by what's happened. Nobody's acting like themselves."

Michelle nodded. "I get it. I'm not a professional, but I really enjoy doing it. Sometimes, I just wish he would take me more seriously."

"You're *so* good!" Anna oozed excitement, but Becca recognized the tone. It was the same one Anna used with her children after they'd missed a soccer goal. Thankfully, Michelle didn't seem to notice. "Come on, get your computer."

Happily distracted, Michelle hurried to the bedroom to retrieve it.

"I feel so bad for her!" Anna said sotto voce, "Things haven't been great between them this past year, and most guys are self-absorbed jerks on their best day."

Becca gave her the appropriately commiserate smile, even while her thoughts strayed again to Harry. He wasn't self-absorbed at all, and she thought that Anna's excuse for the men's behavior was pathetic, but anything contradictory she said would *not* be appreciated.

"Here," Michelle began breathlessly as she returned and opened her laptop. "Let me show you," she began, quickly clicking through files until she found the ones she wanted. "These are the ones that I took when we first arrived."

Becca's eyes widened. She wasn't sure what she had been

expecting—the normal candid shots that everyone took on their phone. Even though Michelle must have taken pictures of every square inch of the resort, there were several that were truly composed beautifully.

"Michelle," she said. "These are fantastic!"

Michelle beamed, pleased. For the next several minutes Michelle talked about color perspective, Becca stopping her every so often to look at a picture more carefully. Anna lost interest after the first few and drifted back to the couch to do something on her phone.

As time passed, Becca fidgeted. She enjoyed the pictures but felt like she was wasting time! She wanted to see if they had released Owen yet! It seemed like Michelle wanted to show her every single one of the thousands of photos she took.

"Which ones are your favorites?" Becca asked. She didn't want to be rude, but she really needed to go.

Michelle looked a little shy, but then seeing Becca was really interested, she smiled. "I like the ones where I play with light. These." She opened a folder labeled "light perspective" and began clicking through images.

Once again, Becca was surprised by Michelle's talent. She could see why these were Michelle's favorites. They were all studies of contrasts—light and dark.

"This one in particular," Michelle said, "I like how the blue from the light glows down, but when it hits the window, it's still so dark that you can just see the thick, green palm frond pressed against the window from the rain."

Becca nodded. It was a striking image. "Where did you take this one?"

"In the lobby. It was after the generator lights had come on; it was a perfect opportunity to practice with low light." She gave a self-conscious laugh. "It wasn't like I had any other choice."

"No, they're wonderful. Particularly this one." It was another beautiful scene shot through the window. What had suddenly drawn Becca's attention was the image of a white-faced Nicole, her hair wet down her back, caught in the generator-powered, blue emergency lights. Becca's brain raced; this was proof Nicole was out in the storm. Becca didn't think Nicole had killed John, but if she had to throw another suspect to the police to save Owen, she would.

Who am I becoming?

"Would you mind sending me these folders?"

"You want copies? Really?"

"Yeah, I was thinking I could send them on to my boss, Dana, at the Gallery." Becca felt terrible for lying, particularly when Michelle's eyes lit up.

The door slammed open. "Bar's closed," Brad said, coming back in, Chris close behind. "Looks like we're drinking here. What do you ladies want?"

"I'll have some wine," Anna said.

Becca made a lame excuse and left. No one tried to stop her. The truth was her presence made the whole situation awkward, a reminder of better times.

22

It should have been a surprise to find Rey waiting for her by the elevators, but it wasn't. He leaned one shoulder against the wall by the bank of doors, completely oblivious to the hotel guests throwing him puzzled and nervous looks, as they waited for their elevator. A set of doors opened and the group jumped in.

Cowards.

When Rey saw her approach, he straightened and gave her a half-hearted smile. "Let's go up to your room," he said without preamble.

Becca scowled. "I don't really feel like talking to you anymore right now, Rey." The door slid open and Rey stepped in, staring at her expectantly. When she didn't immediately follow, he held his hand out to hold the doors open.

"No, really, you need to come with me."

"I don't want to," she gritted. She realized how foolish she sounded because why else was she going to the elevators if not to go to her room?

"Do you always have to argue about everything?" His beleaguered sigh only irritated her further.

"Fine."

He leaned forward, and said in a lower voice, "There's some-body waiting for you up there." He looked at her meaningfully.

Harry! He's back.

Becca hated the surge of happiness that coursed through her. She should have more pride, have confidence that she could handle this without his help, but she couldn't deny that she was comforted to have someone back on her side that she could trust. How was he feeling about her though? Becca put her hand to her head as she stepped onto the elevator. *Why can't anything ever just be simple?*

Becca refused to break the silence, although she was convinced Rey was trying to goad her with his self-satisfied smile. Why would Rey tell her that Harry was back? Rey couldn't stand Harry. What was going on? Even as anxiety swirled in her stomach, her heart thumped harder in anticipation. *He's back; that's all that matters.* However, the figure sitting on the couch in Becca's room wasn't Harry.

"Owen!" She rushed forward, engulfing him in a hug. "They let you go! Thank god! I knew they would realize you weren't involved!" She placed her hands on either side of his head and worriedly scanned his face. He appeared tired and drawn, but he seemed no worse after his detainment.

"I had a conversation with the Commandant," Rey said behind her. "I made it clear to him we thought Mr. Copeland here could be of more use to us out in the world—I also pointed out that as he is an American citizen, they would need something more substantial than just some questionable paperwork to continue holding him. Fortunately, they agreed with me, and released him into my custody while they continue to investigate."

"Of more use to you how?" Becca demanded suspiciously, catching Owen's hand, and squeezing. "Did you coerce him into cooperating? How did you get the key to my room?"

Rey shook his head. "You certainly have an interesting view

of me? Believe it or not, I don't make a habit out of bullying teenagers."

Owen was watching the interchange nervously. "Mom, it's okay. Agent Foster got them to release me and bring me to you. The French lady gave *me* the key. Agent Foster is going to help me." It was clear that Rey hadn't yet told Owen what the FBI was going to expect in return.

"Do they still think he had something to do with the murder?"

Rey shrugged. "Who knows. They are playing it close to the vest. They aren't exactly happy that I interfered, but even if they don't want to acknowledge it yet... what they have on him is pretty thin. He's going to have to stay with me though."

Becca nodded. She would rather have Owen with her, but if he had to stay with Rey, it was better than being in police custody.

"It's time though that we all had an honest conversation." Rey's eyes made it clear that he wasn't going to budge. Becca hesitated. After what Jake had said, she was a little worried that something Owen had done that night would incriminate him further, even though she was confident he was innocent. And then there was the mess he was in with the real-estate fraud. It had been surprisingly kind of Rey to get him out of police custody without Owen's agreement to help already in place. Despite the fact that she and Rey had forged a bond of a sort, he was still an FBI agent. She didn't doubt that if her son had broken the law, whatever nascent friendship she and Rey had developed, Rey would turn Owen in. She wouldn't let that happen, even if she had to get Amelia to smuggle him away.

Holy cow! Who am I?

Becca had always believed people should be held account-able for their mistakes, especially if it hurt others... but faced with the person in question being her son, some of the absolute certainties with which she had lived her life were falling by the wayside. Hadn't she told Jake and Nicole that she would help them if it meant saving Owen? Worse, she didn't even feel guilty about it.

"Let me talk to Owen first. Alone."

Rey looked at her speculatively. His expression made it clear he knew she was up to something. "If he says anything, regardless if you think I need to know it, you have to tell me." His expression hardened. "Remember what I said before. I am going to close this case, and while I'd like to do it with a cooperating witness, I'm going to do it, just the same. There's only one get-out-of-jail card available."

Becca didn't flinch. "I will tell you everything," she lied, "but I will not let my son say anything on the record that could possibly harm him without a lawyer present."

For a long moment Rey looked between her and Owen, who at this point looked terrified and confused. "Fine. Ten minutes." He pointed a finger at her. "Don't make me regret this."

Becca raised her eyebrows, refusing to be intimidated. Rey let out a soft growl of frustration. "I'm going to wait right outside the door."

"What are…" Owen began as soon as the door clicked shut.

Becca raised a finger to her lips, and then whispered, "Let's go into the bathroom." Becca didn't trust that Rey wouldn't try to eavesdrop. She turned on the shower to cover their conversation, no longer recognizing this version of herself. When had she become so suspicious?

"Okay, Owen, you and I need to have a serious conversation, and we don't have much time. Now is not the time to hold back or watch your words. You need to tell me everything." Owen cast a nervous look at the bathroom door, and Becca reached out to capture his hands. "I'm your mom. I will keep secret what I need to… but you can't leave things out because you think it is going to implicate your father or Nicole, or that I'll be upset. We are *way* past that now. Look at me!"

Owen raised his eyes from the floor.

"In case you haven't figured it out yet, the FBI has discovered everything your father, Nicole, and John were doing—about the laundered money, and they have a good idea who they are laundering it for. The FBI is looking for the proof that will help them make an arrest."

"But I don't know who the money's for—" Owen said hesitantly.

"The more immediate problem," Becca continued, "is that John was murdered... most likely because of what they were doing." Her heart ached at the fear that filled her son's face. For the billionth time in forty-eight hours, she cursed Jake silently for involving Owen. "You didn't kill John, but because they forged your name on the documents, and because of the fight, you make a convenient scapegoat. Rey knows you didn't kill anyone, but he wants something from you. Do you understand?"

"He wants me to testify against Dad, right?" Owen's voice was somber and sounded years older than he was. "That's what he meant by there only being 'one get-out-of-jail card.' They need another witness, me or someone else, now that Mr. Raybourn is dead. And the first one gets the best deal?"

Becca was startled. She hadn't expected Owen to put it together so fast. "Yes, you may not have enough information to help them, but I think if he sees you are trying, he will still help you."

Owen's mouth tightened.

"I understand you don't want to do that, but we only have two options. Either we figure out who actually killed John, or at least find something to point them in another direction for a while, or you're going to have to agree to become a witness against your father and Nicole. I've been trying to find another suspect for them, but I've hit a brick wall."

"No! No way, I'm not testifying against Dad." His defiant expression reminded her so much of her own. It was only the seriousness of the situation that kept her from smiling. "Besides, I don't know anything."

"But you are aware *now* that what they are doing is wrong. You know it's a crime. You didn't suspect anything? Where are you getting all your extra money from? Owen, most twenty-year-olds don't have enough money to buy a new BMW. You would just need to tell them what you saw." She was willing to do whatever she needed to protect him, but he needed to admit the truth.

"I earned that money! I told you that already." Owen scowled. He had been defensive about the new car ever since she had asked how he could afford it the previous spring. "It was a bonus, because they said I was doing such a good job. Nicole said it's how things work in the real world. Dad didn't seem to have a problem with it. I didn't tell you the whole truth about the money because you would just say Dad was trying to buy my love."

Sounds like it worked.

Becca ignored the jab. "Your father has been around long enough to realize that what they are doing is wrong. He isn't innocent in this, and he never should have gotten you involved."

Owen's bravado failed him, and his face crumbled. "He wouldn't have done this to me. It had to have been Mr. Raybourn! He must not have told Dad or Nicole what he had done. If Dad had known what he was doing, Dad would have stopped it. You're just still mad at Dad and Nicole. That's why you want to blame them!"

Becca wanted to howl. She was doing everything she could to help him, while Jake and Nicole ate a leisurely lunch, happy to let Owen take the blame because 'it'll work out.' And still Owen's loyalty was to them. It killed her.

"Someone filled out that paperwork with your name on it. That wasn't an accident. They intended to do it and didn't care if you had trouble because of it. Maybe it wasn't your dad—I don't think he realized at first how you were being used—but Jake's not stupid. At some point he became aware, and he did nothing to fix it! If the time comes, you *will* tell the FBI what they want to know."

Owen's eyes filled with tears, and Becca softened her tone. "Your dad doesn't want you to go to jail. He understands he is responsible for this. He wants you to be the one to make the deal." Or at least he would when Becca got through with him.

Through the bathroom door, Becca heard the door to the hotel room open and close. Becca stared hard at Owen. "You understand?" Owen nodded bleakly.

Rey began knocking on the bathroom door.

"This isn't a game. This is your life. Not a word to him about PPW business yet. Just talk about what happened the other night."

Becca jumped as the bathroom door swung towards her.

"Ten minutes, huh?" Her tone dripped with sarcasm.

Rey grunted and stepped back so she could exit the bathroom. "We need to speed this up. I just got word that the boat your friends have chartered back to the States is ready to go. The authorities won't let Owen leave, and he's going to be left holding the bag if they all get out of here. It's going to be hard to prove one of them murdered Raybourn—if they did—without them here to question."

Wide eyed, Becca stared him in horror. The clock had run out.

"My-my dad's staying though, right?" Owen asked.

"I don't know, kid. They have chartered a boat back to Miami, and most of that group is planning on being on it—including the victim's girlfriend, so we're out of time."

The knot in Becca's stomach tightened. "Okay." She looked over her shoulder at Owen. "He's ready to talk with you." She stared meaningfully at Owen, and he sighed.

"Yeah, I'll tell you what I saw."

They settled themselves into seats around the coffee table in the main sitting area. Becca sat next to Owen on the couch to offer him support, but when she reached for his hand, he jerked it away. Rey's eyes when they met hers were sympathetic, and that made her angry. It wasn't his fault, but he was the one in front of her.

Rey pulled out his phone and placed it between them on the table. The blinking microphone icon made it clear they were being recorded. "All right, so tell me how the operation worked."

Owen's eyes darted to Becca.

"Uh, uh," she said shaking her head. "First, he's going to help you with what happened to John, and once you work your magic with the Bahamian police, then you get to hear his story."

Rey scowled. She could see he was trying to come up with a way to thwart her, but finally he just nodded.

"Go ahead, honey," Becca said, with a reassuring smile.

"Well, I guess it all started during the cocktail party after the rehearsal," Owen said. "Mr. Raybourn was getting drunk... fast. They had done the champagne toast and the waiters were bringing the trays of hors d'oeuvres around. He was bumping into people and slurring a little. I could tell Nicole was mad because he was sloppy. One of the servers told me that someone wanted to talk to me. I thought it was you," He looked sideways at Becca. "I went out into the lobby." He looked again at Becca and hesitated.

Harry. Becca swallowed. She should be grateful that Harry had tipped off Owen, but somehow hearing it all play out hurt. She began going through the timeline in her head and realized that this would have been around the time she had texted him and he hadn't answered. Becca gave Owen a tight smile. "Tell him."

"It was my mom's boyfriend, Harry. He asked me all these questions about what I did for my dad, what I handled... that kind of thing. I couldn't understand why he was asking, but since he's, you know, my mom's boyfriend... I felt like I had to be polite. It was weird that he had pulled me out... I thought mom had sent him to ask questions as an excuse to find out how the party was going. They all used to be her friends..." He trailed off.

Becca grimaced. Why was it no one could believe she didn't care that her ex-husband was getting married?

"Then he said he needed to talk to my dad. I couldn't let him go into the ballroom. I didn't know what he was going to do, and I was worried he wanted to mess up my dad and Nicole's night... but..." Owen's eyes slid toward Becca. "He kind of insisted, so I went to get Dad. It took me a minute because my dad had some drinks, too, and he was hanging out with his friends, Mr. Nelson and Mr. Kaplan."

"I was friends with their wives, Anna and Michelle. Michelle is the one with the camera," Becca clarified. Rey frowned and shook his head. He clearly remembered the woman.

"When we got out to the hallway, it was pretty awkward because... well..."

"Did they argue?" Rey asked.

"No, not then. It was just... awkward. Anyway, Harry told us that there was a problem with the papers incorporating the REIT that my dad's firm runs, the one that invests here in the Bahamas. He said the documents had me listed as the principal charter member and as the major shareholder in a bunch of the smaller companies that were invested in the REIT. I had no idea what he was talking about. I thought maybe he was just trying to cause trouble, but he seemed super serious. Harry told my dad that he needed to take care of it because I could go to jail, which was bad enough, but then..." Owen fidgeted, clearly uncomfortable. "Harry was really mad, and my dad told him to mind his own business—I thought my dad was going to hit him. Dad said something like 'I bet you can't wait to tell Becca,' and Harry said that he would wait. That if Dad fixed it right away, he wouldn't tell her."

Becca ground her teeth so loudly she was surprised the others couldn't hear it. "So, the three of you decided I should be kept in the dark about something so important? This is your entire future, Owen!"

"I'm sorry, Mom! I didn't think it was that serious. Dad seemed cool about it after Harry left. He said Harry just wanted to make him look bad and not to worry about it. He would talk to John and take care of it." Owen paused again, and Becca could tell he was thinking about how to word what he said next to protect Jake.

"What happened next?" Rey beat her to it.

"When we got back to the ballroom, Mr. Raybourn was being really loud. He was laughing, waving around a cigar. It seemed to set Dad off. He went over and kind of grabbed Mr. Raybourn. Nicole came up and was pushing them toward the outside doors. By the time I got out there, they were already arguing. Nicole tried to keep them quiet, but it didn't work."

"That was the argument I heard from my room," Becca said.

Rey nodded. "The argument you told the police about, but, Owen, you claimed you didn't know why they were fighting."

"If I told the police why they were fighting, then I would have exposed what my dad and Nicole had done. I was freaked out, but I didn't lie… I just left some stuff out." Rey inclined his head, letting it go, and Owen continued, "Dad asked Mr. Raybourn why my name was on the paperwork, but Mr. Raybourn was too drunk for Dad to talk to. Some of their friends separated them, and Mr. Raybourn walked off."

"Yes, I saw him go to his room," Becca said.

"He came back though," Owen said. "It was about an hour later, I think. Dad had finally calmed down, and everyone was having a good time, but then Mr. Raybourn came back in." Owen shook his head in disbelief. "It was a miracle he was even standing upright. He was swaying back and forth. Somebody got Mrs. Davenport, and they left again. The party kind of broke up after that."

"So, Raybourn left with Candice Davenport. Did anyone follow them?" Rey asked.

Owen shrugged. "I don't know. I tried to find Dad but—"

"But what?"

"He and Nicole were arguing in the corner. I felt weird watching, so I left. I was still too worked up to go to bed, so I walked around a bit. I wanted to watch the storm through the giant windows in the lobby."

"Did you leave the building at any point?" Rey's voice was bland. He was trying to catch Owen in another lie.

"You said you were outside? For how long? Just for a minute?" Becca met Owen's eyes, hoping he understood he needed to tell the truth.

Owen glared at her. "Yeah. I've always loved hurricanes—before they get bad, I mean. It's just cool being out between the storm bands. It's like the hurricane isn't even happening until the next band hits!"

Becca gave a little smile, remembering the hurricanes when Owen was little and having to explain over and over why just because one band was gone that it didn't mean the hurricane was over. Becca shook herself, mentally refocusing on what Owen was saying.

"Despite what Dad said, I was a little worried about what Harry had told us—about me going to jail. I walked down to the ocean to watch the surf, but outside the building the wind was worse than I thought, so I came back. I got stuck in the rain for a few minutes because right as I got to the lobby door the power went out. I had to wait for the generator to come on again so the electronic key slot would work to let me back into the main building."

Becca blinked. The keycards. The hotel recorded when a

keycard is used. *So, if Owen used his to reenter the building, then he might have an alibi!* Lost in her own thoughts, Becca realized that Owen had stopped talking, and she looked back and forth between him and Rey.

"Won't the keycard prove Owen was where he said he was?" Becca asked. "What time was John killed?"

"It could," Rey said slowly. "They are still working on getting the data—the hurricane and lack of manpower has slowed everything down."

"Still! When they get it…"

"It will only show that a keycard was used to enter the building through that door. We've been told that the way their system works, once the generator is on, it no longer uses power to figure out which card is being used, just that a door is opening."

Becca made a frustrated noise.

"Besides, until the coroner has time to get to the body, we still don't have an accurate time of death. All we had to work with was the meat thermometer from the restaurant." Rey grimaced. "But no one present had the scientific experience to pinpoint a time with regard to the storm variable. So rough estimate using body temp, we are working on a window between 11:30 p.m. to 3:30 a.m. Unfortunately for you," he said, eyeing Owen, "you don't have an alibi for all of that time. The power failed just after midnight." He tapped his knee impatiently. "I'm going to need something else if I'm going to help you with the Bahamian authorities."

Owen's face pinched. "But I don't know anything! I didn't kill him, so how can I help you?"

"When you were walking around… did you see anybody? See anything out of the ordinary?" Rey's voice was calm, and it did the trick to refocus Owen.

"Kind of," he shrugged. "Yeah… I mean, there weren't many people wandering around. It was late, and because the storm had picked up and knocked out the power, the generator was on, but I saw Mrs. Kaplan taking pictures." He shook his head, bewildered. "She was all excited about the lights and how it did something to something." He shrugged again. "I wasn't really paying attention. Then she told me that me it wasn't safe to be outside. It was typical mom stuff."

Becca bit her tongue at his superior tone.

"Anything else?"

Owen licked his lips and averted his eyes. "I saw Nicole come back in right after me. She had been outside, too, but she didn't see me, I think she was trying to avoid Mrs. Kaplan."

Becca held her breath. Would he mention that Nicole was upset? This must have been right after her scuffle with John. Surely, Owen saw the marks on her arms and neck. If they gave the Bahamian police another suspect, they might leave Owen alone.

"Was Copeland with her?" Rey asked.

"No," Owen said quickly. His jaw tightened, and Becca waited. But as the seconds ticked by, she realized he wasn't going to say anything that would implicate Nicole.

"Owen! You need to tell him everything you saw. It's the only thing that's going to help you," Becca ground out. "It's too late to protect her."

Owen's eyes blazed angrily at her. "The lighting was pretty dim because they were just the ones the generator powers, but she looked upset. Happy?" he snapped at Becca. "I was soaked; I wanted to go to bed. My dad was already in the room waiting for me."

Becca let out an inward sigh of relief. It matched with what Jake had told her.

"You hadn't seen Copeland in the hotel or on the grounds when you were walking around?" Rey asked.

Owen shook his head. "And he was dry. We talked for a few minutes... he just wanted to make sure I wasn't worried about those files Harry had told us about. He promised he would get it all straightened out when we got home."

"Did you believe him?" Rey cocked his head, disbelievingly. "Did you believe that this was new information to Copeland, and that he could fix it?"

Owen's face froze and then flushed angrily. "Of course, I believed him! He's my dad! He would never do anything to hurt me. He treats me like an adult." Owen looked pointedly at Becca. "If there was going to be a problem, he would have told me!"

Rey continued. "But Raybourn obviously didn't respect your father, right? I mean, he drew up the paperwork, set the whole thing in motion without Copeland knowing what he was doing. Hell, he had so little respect for him, that he put the guy's twenty-year-old kid—you—on as primary member so that you were on the hook if they got caught." Rey snorted. "Sorry, kid. I just don't buy that any one of you thought that Jake Copeland could fix anything."

Becca narrowed her eyes at Rey's deliberate taunting.

Owen's face turned purple, and Becca could see veins bulge in his neck. His fists flexed, but he stayed in his seat.

"John Raybourn is nothing compared to my father! He must have been afraid of what my dad would do. That's why he hid it."

"Bullshit. I think Copeland knew about it and is lying to you."

"Rey! That's enough! This is his father, not *Copeland*," Becca hissed.

"He needs to stop thinking of him as his father. I'm calling him Copeland because they are very likely co-conspirators in a federal crime. Your son needs to understand that this has gone beyond being about *my dad*," Rey said, making air quotes. "If this deal is going to work, I have to know he is telling the truth. One lie and we're done. Is that clear?" His harsh tone was reminiscent of how he spoke when he was undercover last year, and she flinched.

"So, which is it, kid? Copeland wasn't strong enough to protect you, or he set it up ahead of time?"

Becca looked at Owen warily. But strangely, Owen seemed to have calmed down. His cheeks were still red, but he no longer looked like he was going to launch out of the chair and attack Rey.

"Neither." His voice was even though his eyes still burned. "I don't believe he knew, but he is smart enough to find a way out for me. I haven't done anything wrong, and my dad wouldn't let anything happen to me."

"You didn't ask him any more questions about the files? Not even if his girlfriend had been responsible for it? No lies, remember."

Becca blew out an exasperated breath.

"What?" Owen asked angrily.

Becca couldn't help herself. "You are so wrapped up in trying to protect him, you aren't considering the fact that, if Jake cared so much about keeping you safe, he never would have involved you in something illegal in the first place." Owen clamped his lips together. "If your dad is so *worried* about you, why did he figure out how to get himself off the island while you were still being detained? Is he the one here trying to help you? No! I am! Your dad is a *criminal*, and he made you one, too! I've found a way to get you out of this, but you have to tell Rey everything!"

"Whatever! You *want* dad to go to jail. Will that finally make you happy? Will it be enough punishment for him falling for Nicole?" Owen's voice was scathing, and Becca reared back, shocked.

Becca saw the hurt in his eyes, and her stomach plummeted, knowing that she and Jake were the ones who had put it there, but she steeled herself against it. There wasn't enough time to worry about his hurt feelings over their divorce, or how Jake had poisoned him over the previous year.

"If your father committed a crime, he should go to jail," she said coldly. "And unless you want to go, too, I suggest you tell Agent Foster what the two of you talked about."

Rey lifted his eyebrows with what she wanted to believe was respect.

"Fine." Owen turned his shoulder to Becca and looked at Rey. "I asked Dad what he planned to do. He said that Nicole told him she had the only remaining piece of evidence, and she was going to destroy it that night."

Becca couldn't stay quiet. "Well, that was obviously a lie."

Owen turned furiously toward her. "He didn't lie! She was planning on it. She just didn't have time!" He crossed his arms over his chest, but whether it was because he was angry with Becca or because he finally realized how improbable the story sounded, she didn't know. Owen swallowed. "The next morning, Nicole was really upset. She told Dad that somebody had trashed her room while she was at breakfast. It was before... Mr. Raybourn."

Becca asked, "Who else knew about it? Whomever it is had to be the person who left it for the police." Surprisingly, Rey didn't object to her taking over the questioning. After a moment's reflection, Becca made a face. "I saw Nicole's room. It was ransacked. She couldn't have predicted that anyone would come to her room, so there wouldn't have been any reason for her to stage it. They even ripped her suitcase lining open. It's possible that she faked it and turned the USB over so Jake wouldn't know it was her—but wouldn't its existence implicate her in what they had been doing?" Becca said grudgingly. She *really* hated giving Nicole an out.

Rey looked grim. "What about the girlfriend? Davenport, what's her name, Candice? Could she have discovered Nicole had the files?"

Becca shook her head. "I saw her right after she found John's body. She was in a robe and looked like she had just woken up. Her hair was messed up, and she still had her make-up on from the night before. I've known her a long time. She is deceitful and self-absorbed, but I don't think she could have pulled that off. She's not that good of a liar."

"Somebody else knew about the USB. Was anyone nearby when Nicole and your dad were fighting? Could they have overheard what they were saying?" Rey pressed.

"No, it was just them in the corner, and when my dad was arguing with Mr. Raybourn outside, they didn't mention it. My dad just kept saying, 'My family! How could you do this'? That's all he said."

Becca frowned. It wasn't just that she wanted to find out who was trying to frame her son. Whoever had stolen the USB and given it to the police could possibly be the killer. Why else would they bother deflecting the attention? Who else could have known?

It suddenly struck her that Rey wasn't asking about one of the most obvious facts. Harry had known. Owen had just told Rey, that it was Harry who informed them about the USB. Becca knew it couldn't have been Harry, because he was with her when Nicole's room was searched, and had made a deal with Sean to procure the files... but Rey didn't know that. It was puzzling, but Becca certainly wasn't going to bring it to his attention!

"Hang on. There is one other thing you need to know." She took a deep breath. Owen was going to be even more angry, but it was too late to care. "Nicole went to John's room that night, and they had a fight. He even pushed her down—she has bruises."

Owen's eyes rounded. "Mom! Don't!"

Becca ignored him and told Rey everything that Nicole had told her about the argument with John in front of the bungalow the night he died. "I don't think she killed him, but that's why she was coming back into the main hotel after being caught in the rain, like Owen. If they were fighting about John testifying against her and Jake, the REIT would have come up. I know I said I didn't think Candice had done it, but she had to have been in the room. Brad and Michelle walked them there. It's possible she heard what they were saying."

Rey closed his eyes, and muttered something that sounded like, "Lord, grant me patience," before asking more clearly, "Any other secrets you feel like sharing? Has someone confessed to you yet?"

"Not that I can think of." Her voice was sugary sweet in response to his sarcasm. Rey blew a long, frustrated breath to the ceiling. "What's next?" Becca asked. He rose to his feet and paced in front of her and Owen. Becca's hands curled into fists as she tried to wait patiently, but Rey's silent pacing was seriously irritating. "Well?"

He stopped and trained steely eyes on Owen. "You and I are going to have an in-depth conversation about your daily routine at PPW. It's hard to believe they've never slipped up in front of you. There may be something you don't even realize you know. If we do discover something together, you *will* testify about it. Is that clear? You need to sign documents committing yourself to that before I talk to the police on your behalf."

Becca held her breath.

"Yes." She wished Owen's voice didn't sound ashamed. She understood his loyalties were divided, but this was a catastrophe of Jake and Nicole's making, not his.

"Okay then. We will draw up a witness statement for you. You don't have to sign it yet. That can wait until we talk to the prosecutor. I'll talk to the Commandant." He turned to Becca. "There are no guarantees. He's a pretty convenient suspect, but they typically like to play nice with the FBI."

"What about a lawyer?" Becca asked.

"You are going to have to trust me. If it starts to go too far,

I'll stop him." Becca didn't like that answer but she didn't have many options. Rey grimaced and then scrubbed a hand down his face. "I can't believe I'm saying this…"

Becca tried not to smile at his aggrieved tone. She sensed what he was going to say.

"You need my help?" She was pretty sure she heard him growl.

"You know these people. If that Davenport woman knew about the USB, combined with the fact that Raybourn hadn't told her he was going into witness protection…"

"She might have thought he was leaving her." Becca felt a pang of sympathy for Candice. She couldn't stand the woman, but Becca remembered the raw panic on Candice's face when Becca asked her if she was aware John had been talking to Rey. Faced with the prospect of being left behind again… what would Candice have done?

"Exactly. And if she is responsible, then what better way to buy time to get off the island than to throw a suspect," he inclined his head toward Owen, "to the authorities."

Becca hesitated. What Rey said made sense, but Candice had seemed surprised when Becca told her they had taken Owen in for further questioning. Had she been wrong about her? Candice had fooled everyone she was closest to when she had the affair with Adam.

Is she a good enough liar to pull this off?

"I can talk to her."

"I'm not saying you should. You are not sanctioned."

"I get it. I'll just have a conversation with her and see what she says."

Rey shifted his weight on his feet. He clearly didn't want to ask for her help, and she loved that it was torturing him. "Normally, I would tell you to stay out of it, but the more information I have, the better my chances are to keep Owen out of custody."

"And testifying for you."

Rey's stare was flat, but he didn't contradict her. She didn't like the idea of Owen testifying against a cartel, even with his limited information, but she liked the idea of him being falsely convicted of murder even less. Owen's eyes had been tracking between the two of them.

"You want my *mom* to question Mrs. Davenport? How can she help?"

His question smarted a little, but before she could reply, Rey said, "You'd be surprised, kid." Owen's interruption seemed to be a catalyst, and Rey gestured for him to get up. "C'mon. I have the forms upstairs."

"Shouldn't he have a lawyer look them over before he signs?" Becca protested again.

Almost at the door, Rey turned with arched eyebrows. "We can wait while you get an attorney if that's what you want, but in the meantime the boat your friends have chartered will leave with all other potential suspects aboard. I imagine the Bahamian police want to close this case quickly, with the storm cleanup."

Becca scowled.

"It's fine," Owen said resignedly. "Let's just get this over with." He stood to follow Rey, and Becca took a quick step after him, placing her hand on his arm. He didn't shake her off, but he didn't face her either.

"I know this is hard, Owen," she said. "But it's the best way." Owen gave a slight shrug, but his misery was sketched all over his face. Rey opened the door and let Owen precede him through it. Rey's eyes were unsmiling, but he gave her a faint nod. Becca's lips trembled, and she raised her head slightly in response. Potentially, Owen was about to sign his life away—to agree to testify against a cartel, but as odd as it seemed, she was glad Rey was there with him. She trusted him, she realized. Not to protect Owen, but to treat him fairly, and in that there was some comfort. The door shut behind them and she was alone.

BECCA WALKED IN CIRCLES AROUND HER ROOM, TRYING TO THINK of a way to trick Candice into confessing. She didn't have any new information, no excuse to talk to her again. If she approached her for the third time that day, Candice would be on her guard.

Becca chewed the corner of her fingernail. *Think, Becca!* She had to have a concrete reason for the Bahamian police to turn their attention to Candice and away from Owen. Her conscience pricked her. *Do I even think Candice is guilty? Or am I just setting her up the way someone set up Owen... but... if Candice was responsible for the files getting out...*

That hardened her resolve. Who else could it be? As much as she would have liked Nicole to be the culprit, it was unlikely. The investment paperwork, while it condemned Owen, also revealed her involvement because she was a partner at PPW. It had to be Candice. She was the only other person who could have known about it and what it meant.

Lost in her thoughts, Becca was startled by her phone buzzing angrily on the coffee table. In the split second before she picked it up, her heart jumped into her throat. The screen displayed Amelia's smiling face, and Becca closed her eyes at the disappointment. She was acting like a teenager waiting for a boy to call. *Pathetic.* Becca swiped to answer, determined to ignore how her stomach ached.

More important things to worry about, Becca. Get it together!

"Hey, Amelia." Becca's voice sounded too loud in her effort to appear carefree.

"Hi, honey." Amelia's voice immediately cheered Becca up, a piece of normal in the crazy her world had become. "Just checking on you. How's it going there?"

"Not great," Becca admitted. "The police think my son killed John Raybourn."

"That's insane! Idiots." Amelia gasped. "Why in the world would they think that?"

Becca quickly filled her in on what had transpired since they had last spoken. Becca almost left out the part about Owen agreeing to testify, but Becca trusted Amelia, and frankly, she was tired of keeping secrets.

"Hopefully, the FBI will work it out with the police here."

Amelia let out a long breath. "That's dangerous stuff you're talking about, honey. Are you sure testifying against a cartel is a good idea? Better to take your chances with the police."

Her words echoed what Becca had thought before. It was dangerous to cross a cartel. Anyone who had seen a movie in the last thirty years knew that.

"Owen's not really testifying against them. His exposure to that side of it is limited. He would be able to tell them very little. He is just an intern." Becca crossed her fingers, hoping that was true. "Besides, Rey said he could give an anonymous witness statement. They may not need him to testify in court. They are just going to use his information to get more information out of Jake and Nicole." For the first time, it occurred to Becca that if Jake and Nicole did work with the FBI, their more extensive knowledge about how the cartel was laundering money would absolutely put their lives at risk.

"Hello? Are you still there?" Amelia's voice penetrated Becca's thoughts.

"I'm sorry. I was just thinking about what will happen to Jake."

"That's a lot for your son to shoulder. He's either putting his dad in prison... or losing him to the witness protection program." Amelia's voice was careful as she asked, "Owen is close to his dad—do you think he would go into the program with him?"

Becca felt as if she had been punched in the stomach. "No!" she exclaimed. "Of course, he wouldn't."

Would he?

Her blood boiled as she thought of all the ways Jake's greed had ruined her and Owen's life. No matter what happened now, Owen was going to be hurt. Her thoughts began ping ponging frantically around her head as she tried to think of a scenario where there was a good outcome for all of them, until she realized... there wasn't one. Owen would lose his father one way or the other. A tiny voice whispered, "unless he goes with them." But she ruthlessly silenced it.

"Are you okay?"

"Yeah." Becca tried to steady her breathing.

"No, you're not. But you will be." Amelia's voice was reassuringly firm. "Sort out what you need to then come home, honey."

Becca felt tears prick behind her eyes. Meeting Amelia in that tiki bar was one of the best things to ever happen to her.

"I can't wait to be home." She was embarrassed at how her voice quavered, and she cleared her throat to cover it.

"No time for that," Amelia said matter-of-factly. "Didn't you say you needed to go interrogate someone?"

Becca inhaled deeply through her nose and refocused. "Yes, Candice. She's the only other one that could have known about the USB. If she overheard the fight between John and Nicole, then she also would have learned that he was planning on abandoning her." Becca replayed in her head the conversation she had with Candice in the woman's hotel room. "I think she was in love with him. I mean, actually in love with him... not just pretending for what he could provide her."

"She wouldn't be the first woman to lose it when a man left her."

"The only problem is everyone keeps saying how drunk she was. That works with the theory of her doing something stupid in

the heat of the moment, but it doesn't work for her eavesdropping and understanding what Nicole and John were saying, and
then concocting a whole plan to steal the USB to frame Owen."

"You said she was a liar. She hid a long-term affair from the
people closest to her, didn't she? How do you know she was
actually as drunk as she said she was?"

Becca's eyes widened. "You're a genius! That must be
exactly what she did! But how do I prove it?"

"No idea." Amelia laughed.

Becca smiled. "Okay, I'll let you know how it goes."

After hanging up, Becca fiddled with her phone. How could
she prove that Candice wasn't as drunk as she claimed? Anna
and Michelle both said she hadn't had a lot to drink, but Michelle
said that she and Brad had to help the couple home. Becca
stilled. Michelle would have been the last one to see Candice
before the murder. She might have seen something that she
doesn't even realize. Becca frowned. She needed a reason to
seek her out again. They weren't that good of friends anymore.
Since Becca had spent the last year putting distance between
herself and her old Sun Coast friends, it might seem suspicious
that she suddenly wanted to hang out multiple times a day.

The photographs!

Michelle was truly passionate about her photography. Becca
would just pretend she wanted to ask her questions about the
photos Michelle had emailed. Becca opened up the file Michelle
had sent her on her phone. She didn't know that much about
photography, but surely there would be something she could use.
Using her thumb and forefinger, she enlarged a few of the
images, and searched for some element that she could use to start
a conversation with Michelle. She stopped on two of the photos.

In both, Owen stood just outside the glass doors of the lobby.
In the first, Owen's face was illuminated by the bright white
lights above him, as the rain soaked his clothes. In the second,
the rain still poured around him, and somehow Michelle had

manipulated the photograph so that the raindrops just around his head looked as if a blue aura surrounded him. Becca smiled. The look of frustration was clear on Owen's face, and combined with the ethereal blue lighting, he looked like an angry angel. That must have been when he was caught outside waiting for the generator to reactivate the keycard locks. Becca let out a breath. This would work perfectly.

MICHELLE LOOKED SURPRISED TO SEE HER WHEN SHE ANSWERED Becca's knock, making Becca doubly glad that she had her manufactured reason for the visit.

"I'm glad I caught you before you left!" Becca gushed. Michelle blinked in confusion at the enthusiastic greeting.

Dial it back, Becca.

"Oh. We aren't leaving until the morning. We are going to one of the local beaches to swim. Brad just left to tell everyone that we are meeting in an hour."

It was Becca's turn to be confused. Hadn't Rey said the boat taking this group back to the States was ready? Was it just a ploy to increase her sense of urgency so that she would push Owen to agree to testify? He was going on her 'to kill' list.

"Is something wrong? You look…"

Becca smoothed her face back into a friendly smile. "Nope, everything's great. I just remembered something I need to take care of later, that's all."

Michelle looked bewildered. "How's Owen doing?"

"Oh! Um, yes… they've released him… for the time being, but… actually that's why I came over. I wanted to talk to you about two of the photos you emailed me. I think they could make a great series." Becca smiled widely. "Can I come in?"

Michelle blinked again at Becca's rapid speech but stepped back so that Becca could enter the bungalow.

"Sorry, I don't have anything to offer you," Michelle began.

"I'm fine." A drink would have prolonged the visit. Becca still wasn't sure how she was going to turn the conversation from photography to Candice's behavior the night John died. "Um, do you have your computer? I left my phone in my room," Becca lied, hoping that Michelle didn't notice the obvious bulge in her pocket.

"It's out by the pool. I was working on some of the wedding shots…"

"Great! Let's go out there!" Becca arranged her face into what she hoped was a disarming expression. Michelle gave her an odd look. Once her back was turned to walk across the room to the French doors leading to the little courtyard pool, Becca grimaced. She was doing a terrible job!

They sat in the lounge chairs beside the pool; Michelle picked up her laptop while Becca scanned the pool area.

"Which ones?"

"What?" Becca had been distracted by the realization that this pool area was a replica of the one where John had died.

"Which pictures?" Michelle repeated.

"Oh! Sorry! This area is so beautiful. You're lucky to have had this room!"

Michelle relaxed. "It's been great. I love the privacy." She gestured at the solid walls surrounding the plunge pool. "We don't have to wear bathing suits."

"Mmm." Becca did not want to imagine Michelle and her surly husband in a romantic moment. Michelle's attention was back on her computer where she was opening the file she had sent Becca.

"It just occurred to me," Becca adopted a nonchalant air, "that this is just like the pool at Candice's." Michelle stiffened and her gaze fell to the narrow pool deck. "John would have been," Becca gestured at the ground.

"Yes." Michelle's voice was small. "It's morbid, but every time I come out here, I think about that." She shuddered.

"Candice is so lucky she slept through the whole thing." Michelle's eyes flew back to Becca. "She was passed out, right?"

Michelle licked her lips and nodded. "That's what she said. She didn't hear anything." Michelle looked nervous. *Did she also suspect Candice was guilty?*

Becca made a sympathetic face. "It must have been hard to get two people so drunk back to their room. It was really nice of you and Brad to do that. They could have hurt themselves. I understand they could barely walk."

Michelle frowned. "Not exactly. Candice definitely couldn't have made it back on her own. She could barely keep her feet under her. Brad practically carried her, and I was in charge of John."

"You kept John upright?" Michelle was tiny. There was no way she would have been able to hold John up.

"He was walking on his own. He just tended to…" She made a diagonal motion with her hand. "I kept redirecting him. He was being such a jerk, too—trying to grab my camera, saying he could take pictures, too. He was a mess! I've never seen him like that before."

Becca nodded absently, but thought about what Michelle had revealed. Was Candice *actually* too drunk to walk or was she pretending? But why would she pretend to be drunk… unless she had already figured out about John leaving her and wanted to create an alibi?

"That sounds awful. He could have damaged your camera."

Michelle nodded with an extremely serious expression. "I know. I'm so glad you understand. Brad totally didn't and got so mad because I was worried it was going to rain again and ruin my camera!"

Becca made a small sound of commiseration, but was thinking that it seemed to take very little for Brad to get angry at his wife, at least from what she had seen over the last couple of days.

"Was Candice throwing up yet when you left?" Becca asked again, trying to redirect the conversation. "I remember she always liked to make herself throw up before bed because she insisted it helped her hangover."

Michelle rolled her eyes. "It's so gross when she does that! I'm always the one rooming with her, too!"

"Was she though? Already being sick?"

Michelle closed her computer, the picture forgotten. "No, not yet. I got her settled... I hung up her dress, got her makeup off and stuff while Brad helped John."

"Got her settled? On the sofa? In bed?" If Candice had been sitting on the sofa, she could have easily heard the argument outside. Michelle looked at her strangely.

"Why are you so curious about the details, Becca?"

Damn! She'd pushed too hard.

"I'm just... curious, I guess. It's hard for me to imagine that Candice was so drunk that she slept through her boyfriend being murdered not that far away." Becca gestured toward the bunga-low. "It can't be more than twenty feet."

Michelle paled. "The doors were closed... the storm... what are you saying? You think Candice killed him?" Her voice was horrified.

"I'm not saying that." *Not yet, anyway.* "I'm trying to picture it in my head."

Michelle stood up. "Look Becca, you are worried about Owen but trying to blame an innocent person isn't going to help." Michelle's jaw firmed. "You don't like Candice, and I understand. I do. What she did to Evie was horrible, but she wouldn't kill anyone. She was drunk. I put her in bed while Brad undressed John. Period. End of story."

Becca opened her mouth. "But"

"I've got to get ready to go to the beach. Since we are leaving in the morning, I doubt I'll see you again."

Michelle walked briskly back into the bungalow and crossed to the front door, and opened it without looking at Becca. Becca had no choice but to follow. She'd blown it. However, something was bothering her about what Michelle said. Becca stepped through the door before saying, "Are you sure she was…"

Michelle closed the door on Becca before she could finish.

"Hello, Becca," Becca jumped at the greeting. Focused on Michelle she hadn't realized that Brad had walked up behind her.

"Hi. Going swimming?" Becca gestured at the stack of towels under his arm.

"We were thinking about it. I'm not sure it's actually happening though," he said, dropping the towels onto the decorative chair that sat by the front door. "People are packing and… uh, did you want to go?" His face was uneasy. Becca sighed.

You'd think I would be used to being a pariah at this point.

"I'm good, but thanks for the invite."

Brad's face flooded with relief. He looked at the door over her shoulder. "Were you here to see Michelle?" His face clouded again. "Is she bothering you about putting her snaps in a gallery again?"

What was his problem with his wife's hobby? Was he afraid she would finally have some independence? "Actually, I wanted to ask her about…" She stopped. Brad was even less likely to talk with her than Michelle. "Never mind, it wasn't important." With a brief wave, she said goodbye. As she walked away, she glimpsed the crime scene tape still up at Candice and John's bungalow. She'd gotten a little more information, but not enough. There was no way around it. She was going to have to confront Candice.

23

Finding a seat in the shade, Becca sat by the pool for a bit trying to figure out the best way to approach Candice. She waved off the server who approached her. Had she eaten today? She couldn't remember. Unable to come up with a viable plan, she decided her best course of action was to let Rey know her conversation with Michelle hadn't resulted in anything, and that she was on her way to Candice's room.

As she walked up the bungalow pathway to the hotel, Becca heard Agent Warrick's voice call someone's name. Becca hesitated but inevitably she gave in to her curiosity. She crept up the path as quietly as she could, ducking behind a giant bougainvillea when she was close enough to listen.

"Hey, Clarke," Agent Warrick said. "You got that data for me?"

"Ah, Agent, is that the only greeting I get?" the man asked.

Becca couldn't see what was happening, but Agent Warrick openly snarled at the man's flirtatious tone.

"Do you have the security report or not?"

"Yes, Ma'am. The deceased's room, 2021 was accessed by

the front door by the deceased's keycard at 11:50 p.m., and then again at 11:59 p.m."

"Twice? Why would he use his card twice? That's right before the power went out, why would he go back outside? The rain had to have been pretty heavy."

That must have been when Nicole encountered him—when he was sitting in front of his room in the rain, Becca realized. Why in the world would he leave his room to sit in the rain? She strained to hear what the police officer said next.

"The next keycard activity we have is from the rear door back to the interior at 12:10. The electronic locks were under generator power at that time, so we can't identify which guest's card registered to that room was used. We have to assume it was either the victim or the girlfriend."

"What time did power go out?"

"According to their computers, 12:08"

"Have you told your superior officer yet?"

"Yes, Ma'am. He asked that I inform you, as the official FBI liaison, you know." His voice was full of humor, but she was happy when Agent Warrick didn't respond in kind. Becca wasn't interested in witnessing any more of his awkward attempts to hit on the FBI agent.

"So, unless the perp scaled the wall around the pool in the middle of a hurricane, which is unlikely because the current theory of the crime is that he or she used an object of convenience— showing a lack of planning—the perp exited the pool area by 12:10. Last keycard entry into the room from the front was what time?"

"11:59"

"That narrows down the window for sure then. Sometime in those eleven minutes just before the power failed is when it must have happened. Pull all the key entries into the hotel from 12:10 until 1:00 for the bungalows as well as the rooms in the main building. One of those belongs to our killer."

Unless the killer was still in the room.

Becca hesitated, her mind racing. Something was wrong with what she had heard. Eleven minutes wasn't a long time to kill someone and to get away. The good news was if they had the keycard times, then they could pin down the time of the murder. That meant, if she could account for Owen's time... Jake had been in the room when Owen came back. He would be able to tell her what time Owen got to the room, and that would prove there hadn't been enough time for Owen to murder John!

Eleven minutes.

The keycard at the front door had to have been used when Brad and Michelle took Candice and John back to their room.

Eleven minutes.

Becca sifted through everything she had learned about what happened that night as she walked into the lobby and waited for an elevator. The first keycard entry had to have been Brad and Michelle entering the room with the drunken couple. Nicole had an argument with John when she found him sitting in the rain in front of his bungalow. So, the second entry was when John went back inside. At some point, John must have let someone in, and they both went out to the pool where John is killed.

Becca's phone buzzed in her hand signaling she had a text. She looked down swiping to unlock it. The text notification bar was highlighted across the picture she had been looking at before she left to talk to Michelle. The elevator doors dinged open, and Becca stepped absently into the car. She continued to stare down at the picture that Michelle had sent her of Owen trying to open the lobby door in the rain. Becca swiped back one picture to the photo of Owen under the white lights outside the door. She then flipped forward to him under the blue lights. Michelle must have taken them in rapid succession because Owen was standing in the same position. This must have been when Owen said the power was knocked out and he had to wait for the generator to kick on, so that the electronic locks worked again.

That's it! That's his alibi!

Becca wanted to shout with glee. The elevator door began to shut and Becca jabbed the button for the floor Rey's suite was on. She couldn't wait to show him! This proved Owen couldn't have killed John. Thank goodness for Michelle and her camera! Something tickled at the back of her brain. That's wrong. Michelle couldn't have already been in the lobby taking pictures when Owen came in. Could she have undressed Candice, gotten back to the hotel, and be in the middle of taking pictures in time?

Becca did a quick calculation. If the first key card was 11:50, the second at 11:59, and the power went out at 12:08, that left Michelle less than nine minutes to deal with Candice and be gone before Nicole arrived. Candice wouldn't have been easy to undress if she were that wasted... and Michelle said she hung up the dress and took Candice's make-up off. It was *possible* that she could have gotten Candice situated and left before the argument, if she really hustled...but not likely.

Was Michelle still inside during Nicole and John's argument? *Hang on, am I really considering Michelle as a suspect? No!* Michelle couldn't have done it either because her pictures captured when the power went out, and the killer used the keycard moments later. Michelle's pictures alibied not just Owen but the woman herself.

Brad!

Hadn't Michelle said they were together? Owen hadn't mentioned seeing Brad in the lobby with Michelle, and Becca had a hard time believing Brad waited for his wife to take pictures. Suddenly it hit her, and she knew Michelle had lied. Candice had complained about waking up in her clothes, but Michelle said she had undressed her, and Becca had seen the smeared make-up herself. Michelle had told Becca that Brad had undressed John, but John's body had still been fully clothed. Michelle had never been there, but someone had to have helped the couple inside. Brad must have been there alone. Why would

Michelle and Brad lie about both of them being there, unless they had something to hide?

Becca started down the hallway to Rey's room excited to tell him what she had discovered. But on a whim, she whirled around and pushed the call button for the elevator. She needed to confirm with Candice she had been dressed when she woke up. If Candice had exaggerated that, like she had about the blood on John's body, Rey wouldn't take her seriously.

BECCA KNOCKED ON CANDICE'S DOOR AGAIN, POSITIVE THAT SHE heard movement inside. Becca didn't care if Candice didn't want to see her. Candice was the only one who could confirm what Becca suspected

"I know you're in there, I can hear you." Becca pounded her fist against the door. "C'mon Candice open the door. I have to talk to you." Becca raised her hand to hit the door again, but it jerked open, revealing Candice with a dark scowl on her face.

"What do you want, now? Why can't you just leave me alone?" Becca shoved past her into the room.

"We need to have a conversation, and you need to be honest with me. It's about…" In Becca's rush, she had failed to notice Brad standing on the balcony. He strolled into the room.

"Hello again." His smile didn't reach his eyes. Alarm bells rang in Becca's head, and her body tensed.

What is he doing here?

"Sorry, Brad, I didn't know you were in here." Becca looked at Candice, who was inspecting her nails. "I'll come back."

"Don't feel like you have to," Candice smirked. "You are so obsessed with me." She flicked her hair over her shoulder. "But I guess you kind of always were."

Becca gaped at her for a second. *Obsessed with her?* Becca

decided it wasn't worth it to address the woman's narcissistic delusions.

Becca gave a weak laugh and moved toward the door. She hesitated, her anxiety spiking at leaving Candice with Brad. But in the few minutes it would take her to get Rey, Candice should be alright. Candice narrowed her eyes, and her face took on a pinched speculative expression. "Why *are* you suddenly so interested in me? Three days ago, you said you couldn't stand me, and now you are knocking on my door all day."

"I, uh, I just came up to check on you." Becca improvised. "You were in bad shape earlier, and I wanted to make sure you were still alive."

Candice winced at her choice of words. "I'm perfectly fine," she said coldly. "So, you can go." Candice turned her back in dismissal. Becca felt a retort building within her.

Not now, Becca. You need to find Rey and tell him what you suspect. He will get the answers.

"You said you wanted to talk to Candice about something," Brad said. "You banged on her door, so it must be important."

"Right." Becca's mouth was suddenly dry. Brad had moved closer to Candice, and by the look on his face, Becca realized he had already figured out why she was there. "Like I said, I was worried about her. When she didn't answer, I thought she might be unconscious."

"We were getting ready to go down to meet Michelle and go to the beach. You should join us."

Becca was thrown by the unexpected invitation. Was it possible that he didn't realize she suspected him? "Thanks, but I'm going to stick around here in case Owen needs me."

"I don't want to go to the beach," Candice whined. "I keep telling you that."

Brad's eyes bounced back and forth between Candice and Becca, before letting out a heavy sigh and squaring his shoulders. "Michelle said you had a lot of questions about what happened when we brought Candice home the night of the party. That's what you are here to ask her about, isn't it?"

A chill ran down Becca's spine. The expression on Brad's face had her instincts screaming for her to run! Becca reached blindly for the door handle, afraid to take her eyes off Brad. In disbelief, she watched as he pulled a small gun out of the waistband of his shorts and pointed it at her. "Get away from the door."

Becca's blood turned to ice. Her friend's husband, his features sharpened, stared intently at Candice who in turn gaped back at him.

"What are you doing? Where did you get a gun?" Candice screeched. Her eyes flew wildly to Becca's, but Becca was frozen.

He gestured at the sofa. "Both of you sit down."

Becca didn't take her eyes off Brad. Could she get the door open before Brad got a shot off? Probably not.

"I had really hoped it wouldn't come to this." He heaved a sigh.

Candice's mouth opened and closed.

"Knock it off, Brad, and put that gun away. You can't shoot us in the middle of a crowded hotel. Everyone would hear it." Becca was impressed with how calm her voice sounded because on the inside she was quaking.

"This isn't the way I had planned it," he said, with a nonchalant shrug. "But I can improvise. I've done it before. Now," he gestured again with the gun. "Get over here and sit down." Candice immediately sank onto the sofa, but Becca licked her lips and looked around the room, stalling for time.

Think of something!

"Now!" Brad barked, and then lowered the gun until it was only inches from Candice's face. Candice drew back and whimpered. Her eyes were wild as they met Becca's. "Sit down!"

Becca reluctantly let go of the door handle and walked

toward the sofa. Brad took a few steps back as she approached, putting a little distance between them. Should she try to get the gun? As if he read her mind, he trained the gun on her.

"I wouldn't. I've got nothing left to lose at this point."

If Becca could just keep him talking, she might calm him down. "Why did you kill, John?"

Before he could answer, Brad's phone rang, making everyone jerk. He glanced at it before tucking it away unanswered, but the flatness of his eyes wasn't reassuring. "I didn't mean to..." Before he could explain, his phone interrupted again. A spasm crossed his face at the sound.

Candice was panting softly next to her, and Becca worried the woman was bordering on hysteria. That wouldn't help anything.

"You killed John? *Why?*" Candice's voice was tiny and bewildered.

"It was self-defense. He attacked me!"

Becca kept her face blank and nodded. "You should explain it to the police. They'll understand."

Brad sneered at her. "Right, I'll just say he tried to kill me, and I accidentally took the two of you hostage. I'm sure they'll understand. I thought you were supposed to be the smart friend."

Becca swallowed back the hot words that sprang to her lips. "I think they would! They know John was a criminal. I think it is totally believable that he would try to kill you. It's not your fault. He made you do it." Becca adopted the cajoling tone she had heard Michelle use so many times with her husband. It made her want to gag, but she hoped it would get through to him. Instead, it only seemed to enrage him.

"He *was* a criminal! Were you part of it?" He swung the gun at Candice.

"I-I..." Candice stammered.

"She was duped like everyone else," Becca soothed. She wasn't sure if it was true, but she didn't think it would help for

Brad to have someone else to blame right in front of him. Her brows drew down. Why *was* Brad there, in Candice's room? With a gun? Had he planned on killing Candice?

Unaware of her thoughts, Brad scoffed, "I have a hard time believing that."

"No, really. I've been talking with one of the FBI agents. They believe only a couple of people at the top knew what was going on. I absolutely understand how upset you are about it. My son got caught up in it, too."

Brad frowned. "I am sorry about that. I never intended for Owen to get caught in this. Not as deep as it has gotten. That's why I'm here. To fix it." As surreal as it was, Brad actually sounded apologetic. "I thought when I left the USB for the police, they would see that obviously Owen had nothing to do with it... he's a kid, for heaven's sake! If they saw how ridiculous it was, then they would see that the rest of us were used, too!"

"I didn't know what they were doing either! I'm a victim too!" Candice had finally found her voice.

"You're lying," Brad shouted. "You had to have known. I heard him fighting with Nicole when I came back to get him from the chair by the door. I couldn't believe what I was hearing. The whole thing was a fake, and then when John told Nicole he was going to work with the cops, it was obvious what he meant. He would get away with it, leave the rest of us to deal with the consequences! Not again!"

Becca wondered if anyone in the adjoining rooms could hear him.

"You knew exactly what was happening, and you just didn't care. You were going to ruin me again!" he screamed at Candice.

"What are you talking about?" Candice cried. "I've never done anything to you. I'm your friend." Candice flipped her hair over her shoulder, and Becca gave a silent groan. She recognized the gesture. It was Candice's "how dare you talk to me like that" move. But this wasn't a disagreement over who was chairing the Little League fundraiser. This was a murderer… with a gun.

"Candice," Becca warned.

"Never done anything to me?" Brad threw his free hand up in the air, his eyes bulging. "You are the reason my pharmacist's license was taken away! If you hadn't run your mouth…" He shook his head.

"Technically, it was your fault, or maybe even Michelle's. You were the one who told your wife about Adam's Viagra prescription, and she told me." Becca wanted to slap a hand across Candice's mouth to shut her up.

Is she insane?

The garbled sounds coming out of Brad's throat sounded like he was choking. "Is anything ever your fault? You destroyed your family and Adam and Evie's with your affair. At least Adam had the decency to leave town. You stuck around as if nothing had happened." He was sputtering in his rage. "I lost *everything* because of what you did!"

Becca tensed as Brad advanced on them. His hand holding the gun shook.

"Brad!" A heavy banging on the door froze him in place.

"Thank god," Becca breathed. Brad narrowed his eyes at the door, and held a finger to his lips. The banging came again as almost simultaneously Brad's phone rang.

"Brad! I can see on my location finder that you are in there! Why aren't you answering your phone? Brad!" It was Michelle. Brad cursed but stayed still. "Brad!" The pounding came again.

Michelle showing up could help them so Becca kept her voice as calm as she could. "You better let her in before someone comes to investigate."

Brad considered for a moment, unsure. Then, as the pounding and Michelle's voice sounded even louder, his lips pressed into a tight line.

Becca took a chance. "Hang on, Michelle, we're coming!" she called out.

"Becca?" Michelle's muffled voice was surprised. Brad shot Becca a dirty look, then keeping his eyes on Becca and Candice, he lowered the gun and tucked it behind his back. Michelle rushed into the room the second the door opened.

"Why didn't you answer the door? What's taking so long?" Michelle drew up short at the sight of the two women sitting side by side on the sofa, and sent a puzzled look back to her husband. "What's going on?"

"Michelle! He's lost his mind," Candice cried, standing up.

"Sit down," Brad ordered. Michelle gasped as Brad brought the gun from behind his back, and pointed the gun at Candice, who promptly dropped back into her seat.

"Brad?" Michelle's jaw dropped.

"I'm sorry, Michelle. It wasn't supposed to happen like this." Michelle wrinkled her nose. "What wasn't?" Michelle's voice became shrill. "What is happening?"

Brad stared at her bleakly, but said nothing.

"Brad!" It was the firmest Becca had ever heard Michelle speak to her husband.

"It was self-defense. I swear!" His eyes pleaded with her and Michelle's face turned a pasty white. She swallowed hard.

"It was an accident, Michelle," Becca said calmly. If she could get through to her friend, Michelle might convince her husband to turn himself in. "But this," she gestured at the group of them, "is making it worse."

"John?" Michelle asked in a weak voice. Brad nodded. Michelle put her hands over her face and moaned. "I don't understand. This doesn't make any sense!" Her hands fell to her side. "Why? What happened?"

"He pulled a gun on me!" Brad wiggled the gun he was holding. "A gun! Can you believe that? I didn't have a choice. That's self-defense, right? I had to get this gun away from him."

"Absolutely, clear cut self-defense," Becca said agreeably.

Michelle's body stilled as she looked toward Becca and Candice seated on the sofa. "But holding them at gunpoint isn't."

Shut up, Michelle!

"No," Becca agreed. "But I think you could easily make an argument for extreme emotional distress."

Michelle shook her head and began pacing back and forth. Not a good sign, Becca thought.

"Why would John pull a gun on you? When I left the three of you, everything was fine. Ahh," Michelle looked up at the ceiling before her gaze narrowed on her husband. "That's why you volunteered to say you had been with me that night? The next morning, you reminded me I didn't have an alibi because I was taking pictures all over the hotel, but you didn't care about me. You needed an alibi for yourself." Michelle shook her head. "You don't care anything about me."

"That's not true!" Brad turned to face her.

This could be her chance! If she could just... but it was no use, Brad still stood between her and the door, not to mention he was holding the gun.

"Everything I did was because of you... because of our family."

"How can you say that?" Michelle asked through tears. "You've ruined us."

"*She* ruined us!" Brad roared, swinging the gun back to point at Candice. "I only wanted to get back at her!"

"Oh, Brad, what did you do?"

Brad's shoulders slumped. "It was just going to embarrass her. I swear that's all I meant to do." He let out a heavy sigh. "Before we came, I ordered some Rohypnol. I wanted her to look like she was wasted and for her to do something stupid. That's all. I couldn't know what was going to happen!"

"You roofied me? You jackass! I'm going to have you arrested."

Becca elbowed Candice... hard. "That's the least of his problems," Becca said under her breath, "so shut up before you get us shot."

Brad ignored Candice, lost in his ranting. "No, once again you slid right through. I had put it in your glass of wine... the one John took from you and drank. You drank just enough to make you a little loopy, but John... well, you saw what it did to him, and that dosage was for someone half his size. I had some leftover; it was a risk, but I couldn't let you get away again. I dumped what remained in your champagne when they were doing the toasts. It was too late though. John had taken center stage. Everyone was pointing and snickering. It was supposed to be you! Just once... just once! I wanted you to be the one to suffer." He jabbed the gun at her and advanced angrily.

"That's why John was so out of it," Becca said quickly, worried that if Brad wasn't diverted, he would hurt Candice in his rage. "You found out about the money laundering didn't you." She had to get his attention off his old grievance with Candice.

Brad's mouth fell open. "How do you know about that?" His eyes narrowed as he considered her. "Are you in on it, too?"

"Right!" Becca gave a half-hearted laugh. "Jake includes me in all his business dealings these days."

Brad frowned, but then nodded. "If you weren't aware of it, then you have nothing to worry about." She knew it wasn't true, but she hoped Brad wouldn't.

"Money laundering? You were laundering money?" Michelle cried.

"Of course not! The first time I learned about it was that night." Brad sighed.

"When? We were together the whole night? Why didn't you tell me?"

"You remember when we were struggling to get John and Candice back to their room?"

Michelle nodded.

"You wanted to take pictures, and it was taking so long,"

"I remember," Michelle snapped. "You were annoyed with me, as usual. You told me to 'go take the damned pictures' and I did."

Great! She wanted Michelle to calm him down, not start a fight, Becca thought.

"You took them back to the room alone," Becca said.

Brad spared a glance at her before turning back to Michelle. "When we got to the room, I couldn't manage them both. I put John in a chair by the door and used his key to take Candice inside. She was so out of it, I practically had to carry her. She was a disaster, flopping around, so I put her on the couch and returned to get John. When I got closer to the door, I could see him talking to Nicole through the window. I cracked the door open and heard everything they said."

"Nicole begging him not to testify," Becca clarified.

Michelle swung her eyes to Becca, and Becca shrugged. "Nicole told me what they talked about. I was trying to put the pieces together since the police thought my son had murdered John." She couldn't help the edge in her voice.

Michelle still looked confused. "Testify about what? I don't understand what this has to do with us, Brad."

"John was running away to the witness protection program," Candice said in an injured voice. "He was just going to leave me."

Becca closed her eyes. Were there no limits to the woman's narcissism?

Michelle must have thought along the same line because her face contorted in anger. "Yeah, Candice, you're the victim in all of this. Thanks for reminding us!"

Candice sniffed, "I'm just saying, oof..." Her breath exploded out of her as Becca's elbow found her again.

"She's saying nothing," Becca said sweetly. "Candice is a

self-obsessed idiot, and we all know it. She isn't worth getting upset over, and she certainly isn't worth getting in more trouble for." She glared meaningfully at Candice, who finally seemed to catch her meaning but couldn't resist crossing her arms across her chest.

"Well, he was…" Candice muttered.

Michelle stared balefully at Candice for another moment before shaking her head. "Witness protection, money laundering! Someone tell me what is going on!"

Brad continued, "That bastard, along with Jake, Nicole, and god knows who else, was using the money we all invested with them to launder money. I don't know exactly how… Nicole kept saying they all had to stick together, that if John testified, then they all would go to jail. She said she had the evidence in her room. There was a USB hidden there that showed how the real estate investment was structured, and that she could make a better deal than John because she had the proof."

Becca's brows drew together. Nicole had conveniently left that part out when she told the story.

"In that moment, I realized what they had done, how they had ruined my life."

"We were invested?" Michelle asked slowly. Becca didn't blame Michelle for being slow to follow what he was saying. It sounded completely insane. "John?" Michelle looked to Becca. "Jake and Nicole?" Becca nodded.

"Don't you see?" Brad said. "I sank everything we had left into that investment group. If John had testified against the group, we would have lost everything! After Nicole left that night, he seemed more sober. It could have been the argument, or the rain. It was really pouring then, but when I opened the door John was a lot more lucid. I asked him what was going on? He said we should go out by the pool, have a drink, and he'd tell me all about it. He was worried Candice would hear us, so he helped me move her to the bedroom." Brad's entire body drooped, and the gun dangled at his side.

Becca kept her eyes glued to it, waiting for her chance.

"I asked him if it was true... if the REIT was being used to launder money. He laughed." Brad, lost in the memory, sounded bewildered. "He just laughed and said he hoped I'd saved enough for a good lawyer because I probably would need to defend myself against a criminal charge. I didn't understand... he laughed harder." Brad raised his gaze to Michelle and then over his shoulder at where Becca and Candice were still seated. "He didn't care that he had put the final nail in our family's coffin... I put the boys' college fund in."

Michelle let out a whimper.

"I worked hard my whole life," he swallowed convulsively, "and because of her mouth," he gestured at Candice, "and my trust in a friend... my children's futures are ruined and I might go to jail."

For a brief second, Becca felt sorry for him, but then remembered he had been happy for Owen to take the blame. "What happened next?" Becca asked.

Brad squinted, as if he was trying to remember. "I'm not sure. It's kind of hazy. The wind suddenly gusted, and I think I said something about how I would tell, and he said it was too late... and then we were fighting and he pulled out the gun. But he was still feeling the effects of the drug and the alcohol so it wasn't hard to get the gun away from him. I couldn't let him testify. At least while the investment was still operating, I had a chance of getting my money out before it all went up in smoke. Those large landscape rocks were right there. I reached down... I just..."

He didn't complete the thought, but Becca could easily imagine what had happened.

Brad cleared his throat. "He was dead. I dropped the rock, I think, and tried to leave, but when I went to go back inside, the power had gone out and the electronic lock was frozen. I was trapped. It felt like forever. My heart was pounding, but the generator kicked on and the electric lock disengaged. I went back to our room in a fog, and when you came in later, I told you I had taken a shower to explain why my hair was so wet."

He glared at Candice again. "I lay awake all night because something was out of place, I'd missed something... and it wasn't until I saw you in the morning that I realized. The door to the bedroom was shut when I came back in. It wasn't closed when we went out to the pool. Candice must have gotten up while we were outside."

In a flash, Becca realized what he was saying. "You thought Candice heard you?"

Brad gave a curt nod and glared at Candice. "You pretended like you didn't remember anything, but I couldn't risk that your memories wouldn't eventually come back, and you would realize that I had been the one outside with John."

"Oh my god," Becca breathed. "That's why you're here, in her room I mean. You were going to kill her?"

"Why did you have to come, Becca?" His tone was almost regretful.

"I'm kind of wondering that myself right now," Becca muttered.

"I'm sorry. I really am, but I can't go to jail. My family needs me."

"My family needs me, too," Candice exclaimed.

A tic appeared in Brad's eyelid. "You only care about yourself."

"Brad," Becca interjected. "I think, if you tell your story, the police will understand. John was a horrible person, and no harm has been done here..."

"Right," he scoffed. "The second I let you go, you will tell them what happened. I'm not stupid. It would have been much easier to stage one accident at the beach, a rogue wave or a rip current, but I'll make it work." He looked around the room with a careful eye.

She and Candice were running out of time. It was obvious Brad felt he was backed into a corner. Surely Michelle could see the insanity of all this!

"Michelle," she began, but Becca's intent to win over Michelle must have been obvious because Brad caught both Michelle's hands in his one free one and turned her so that her back was to Becca.

"I never meant for it to go this far, but now we need to think of our boys, Michelle," Brad begged. "What will happen to them without me... if I go to jail? I was trying to protect our family. I love you. You know that you can't survive without me."

"I love you, too." Michelle's voice sounded as if she were speaking through tears.

No! No! No!

"Michelle," Becca said, and when the woman didn't acknowledge her, Becca called her name again, letting all of her desperation sound in her voice. "Please!" If Michelle would just turn around and look at her!

"What are you thinking?" Michelle asked Brad.

Becca's stomach dropped, and Candice began crying next to her. Michelle's voice had been resigned. This was ridiculous, Becca thought! She'd known this couple for over ten years, and now they were going to kill her?

Brad smiled down at his wife. "I knew you would see I was right." His lips twisted. "They both have to go. It's not like Candice doesn't deserve it. She's made people's lives miserable over the last decade. She deserves whatever happens."

"Am I supposed to feel better that you feel bad that you have to murder me?" Despite her fear, Becca's temper rose. "First you frame my kid, and now you are going to kill me... but keep telling yourself you don't have a choice if it makes you feel better!"

Brad ignored her and spoke to Michelle, "I think murder-suicide is the most believable."

Becca didn't wait to hear whether she was supposed to be the murderer or the victim. She lunged from the sofa with a cry. Caught off guard, Brad pushed Michelle out of the way to face her, but Michelle caught his arm and struggled to hold the gun down as Becca tackled him. The three of them hit the ground with a hard thud and the gun skittered away across the tile. Michelle lunged sideways, kicking at Brad's hands where they tried to grab her. Becca had landed partially on top of Brad and did her best to slow him down, using her body weight to pin him, but he was much stronger. He swept an arm up in an arc and threw her off. Her head cracked against the hard floor, and she immediately saw stars. Becca saw Michelle fast crawl toward the gun but was yanked backward when Brad's hand caught her ankle. "Bitch!" he roared. Becca struggled to rise, but her head was spinning. She had to help Michelle!

Michelle raised her free leg and kicked back hard, briefly breaking Brad's grip. It bought her the few precious seconds she needed. Michelle's fingers scrabbled on the gun, and she twisted until she was facing her husband.

"Brad, no! Stop!"

Brad froze where he was crouched on the ground and then sneered, "You aren't going to do anything. You're useless."

Becca had made it to her knees, and in the next second, the world exploded.

Michelle fired the gun wildly at the same time porcelain rained around them. Michelle and Becca looked at each other, coughing on the acrid smoke from the gun. Brad's body lay crumpled in front of them.

Over the ringing of her ears, Becca heard Michelle say in wonder, "Oh my god! I did it. I actually killed him!" She didn't sound remorseful.

"He's not dead, you idiot. Just unconscious." Candice's voice held no rancor as she took a step closer to look at her handiwork. The base of the heavy lamp she had hit Brad with was still intact in her hand. "At least I don't think he is. I can't believe he roofied me! Perv!"

Becca met Candice's eyes before looking at Michelle. A nervous giggle escaped. The three women stared at each other and then at Brad again.

"We should call the police," Becca finally said.

"I suppose we should." But none of them moved. The surrealness of the moment seemed to have paralyzed them.

Candice smiled wryly. "So, what do you think Anna is doing this afternoon?"

Becca couldn't help the incredulous laugh that escaped her. "Somehow I doubt whatever she's doing, that it's this exciting," Becca said dryly.

Brad moaned, and the women sobered as reality rushed back in.

"I'll call." Becca got to her feet, relieved that her head only felt a little woozy. She walked to where her phone had fallen in the struggle, and as she bent to pick it up, she heard Michelle say softly. "I'm going to be just fine without you." Then there was the unmistakable sound of a foot meeting soft flesh, followed by another moan. Becca didn't comment. She figured, after a lifetime of emotional abuse, Michelle was justified in getting a little retribution. Becca dialed Rey's number, and when she looked up, she was only mildly surprised to see Candice and Michelle hugging each other tightly.

The next few hours rushed by. Rey and Agent Warrick arrived within minutes, closely followed by two Bahamian police officers. The three women were separated and taken to different rooms to make their statements, while officers waited for emergency services to arrive to transport Brad, who was still only semi-conscious.

Agent Warrick accompanied Becca to her room. "You

certainly seem to constantly find yourself in the middle of things." The woman spoke without inflection.

Somewhere during the recitation of events, the adrenaline had left Becca, and she was swamped by exhaustion. "What can I say? I'm lucky?"

Her sarcasm wasn't lost on the agent, who flipped the legal pad closed and rose to leave. She gave Becca a brief nod and headed for the door, then stopped and turned. "It wasn't a criticism, just an observation." She tucked the folders and pads in her arms across her chest. "When we first saw you here at the Royal, I told Agent Foster there was no way you weren't involved. Too many coincidences. I know about what happened last summer, and I thought there is no way someone is either that unlucky or that stupid not to see what was going on around her."

Becca bristled, but the woman continued, "But Foster was right."

"Right about what?"

She met Becca's eyes with an unrelenting stare. "He said you were the unluckiest person he'd ever met."

"Gee, thanks," Becca said under her breath.

Agent Warrick continued as if she hadn't heard her. "He also said you couldn't be a part of it because you were too honest. If we needed help, you were going to be the best asset we could have here because you are like a dog with a bone."

Becca could have done without the dog analogy.

"While I don't approve of how you inserted yourself into the investigation," she said, as the corner of her lips twitched, "it was impressive how, once your son was in trouble, you didn't stop until you'd put it all together. However, if you had told us sooner what you had found out, we could have worked together, and you and your friends wouldn't have ended up in the position you were today." Agent Warrick stopped and pursed her lips. "I have to say I'm surprised how well the three of you worked together. Foster filled me in on some of the history, and I saw through our surveillance in the casino how you and the Davenport woman feel about each other. I'm surprised you all pulled together."

"Having a gun pointed at you makes it pretty easy." Becca could have cleared it up. She, Michelle, and Candice hadn't worked together. In fact, just before she jumped, Becca had been sure Michelle was going to support her husband.

However, the Agent was right. She should have told Rey what she discovered earlier. If she had, she wouldn't have gone to Candice's room. She could have told Rey that Michelle and Brad were lying about their alibis and let him handle it. Why didn't she? It had nothing to do with Owen, she suddenly realized. She felt a little sick. It was what Jake, and even Harry, had accused her of. She always felt she had to prove that she could do it on her own. She could have gotten them all killed.

"Mrs. Copeland? Are you alright?"

Becca removed her hands from her face. "I'm fine... just tired."

"I'll leave you to get some rest. Agent Foster is going to want to talk to you."

"Tomorrow. Tell him I'll talk to him tomorrow. I just want to go to sleep."

The woman nodded again, opening the door. "The EMTs don't think you have a concussion, so you should be fine. Be sure you check in with us before you leave the island."

Leave the island!

"Wait!" called Becca.

Agent Warrick caught the door before it shut.

"What about my son? Is he free to leave?"

"No, he's still in FBI custody. We will keep him protected until we have what we need, and then arrangements will be made."

"What arrangements?"

"Mrs. Copeland, your son is exchanging his potential testimony for immunity. It turned out, he had witnessed more than he realized. We need to have the proper documents drawn up by the federal prosecutor on the case, and then we will need to decide what his threat level is, and if he will need permanent protection."

Becca felt the blood drain out of her face and thought she might actually pass out. *I should have asked these questions before I pushed Owen, I should have...*

"You made the right decision." Agent Warrick's voice was firm. "You were out of options to help your son get clear of this, and you took the best one. We will look after him... I promise."

Becca made it to the bed before the trembling made walking impossible. She curled in a ball on top of the comforter. She had allowed herself to forget the mess Owen was still in because of Jake and Nicole. When Brad was taken away, she had been overwhelmed with relief that it was over... but it wasn't. Owen was still going to testify against a drug cartel, and despite Rey's assurances that Owen's low-level knowledge wouldn't put him in danger, she wasn't going to take the risk. Maybe she did have a savior complex, but she was the only parent Owen had that seemed to care about his future. Her mouth in a tight line, she reached for her phone.

24

"Interesting turn of events this morning." Rey was leaning against the wall opposite the elevator doors again, his thumbs in the belt loops of his jeans, when the elevator doors opened.

Becca didn't stop, but said over her shoulder as she passed him, "Oh?"

Rey smiled. "Yeah. Hey! Stop for a second." He tugged on the bag over her shoulder until she either had to let him take it or risk dislocating her shoulder. Catching her elbow, he steered her to the same grouping of potted plants that she had hidden behind with Harry.

Was that just five days ago?

"Are you leaving?" He gestured angrily at the bag now sitting on the ground between them.

"There's no reason not to."

Rey clenched his jaw. "Agent Warrick told you I wanted to talk to you."

"Yes, and I spoke with her again this morning, and she said if I didn't want to stay, I didn't have to. She said there was no specific reason, that she knew of, that required me to speak with you again. She also said that although Owen had to be transported back to the States with the FBI today, in light of the new witness, he could be released in a few days." She arched her brow. "Owen's lawyer told me the same thing."

Unable to sleep the night before, Becca had made a series of phone calls and spent most of the morning retaining an excellent lawyer for Owen, who in turn had already been in touch with the prosecutor.

"In light of the new witness," Rey mimicked her. His face relaxed and his lips spread into a wide smile.

Not for the first time, Becca was surprised at how handsome he was when he didn't have his stern FBI face on.

"How did you do it?" Rey asked.

Becca lifted her brows high and widened her eyes. "Do what?"

Rey let out a laugh. "I don't know how you did it, Nancy Drew, but... nice work. I can see the relation to your son. Apparently, in his attempt to over-achieve, he took the initiative to send out Fourth of July greeting cards to every client in the filing cabinet. When sixty companies came back as undeliverable from the addresses in the file, he asked Raybourn about it. After that, he was told explicitly to stay out of the files. We think those are the shell companies. He also told us his new step-mother and Raybourn took frequent boat trips to the Caribbean to help those same companies set up bank accounts." Rey's eyes twinkled. "We should be able to prove that easily enough with their calendars. Oh, and apparently they were sloppy enough to actually transfer suitcases of cash on their trip over, for Nicole to clean at the casino." He shook his head and laughed. "Arrogance gets them every time. With your ex-husband agreeing to testify, Owen most likely won't need to be a witness. No one will ever find out he was involved."

Becca gave him an answering grin. It hadn't been easy, but after filling Jake in on what had happened with Brad, and explaining that if it upset Brad enough to murder someone over the small amount of his investment, imagine how the cartel would feel, and what would they do to Owen, if he were to testify against them.

"Do you want your son to live his entire life in fear? Or go into witness protection and never see him again? You robbed him of the future he could have had. Only you can fix it."

Jake had eventually agreed, but when he knocked on her door two hours later with his suitcase, it was clear Nicole had not. Jake slept on her couch. In the morning, they called the lawyer Becca had found and then Agent Warrick.

Becca felt a wave of sadness. Jake wasn't an evil person. He was vain and greedy, not to mention tremendously self-centered... but in the end he had made the sacrifice he needed to for his son.

"How much time is Jake facing?"

Rey's eyes bounced between hers. "Do you care?"

"I probably shouldn't, but I do. We grew up together, and he's the father of my child." She shrugged.

"He is definitely going to do some serious time, but not as much as he would have if he hadn't agreed to cooperate. The wife will do more, unless she comes up with something your ex isn't privy to."

"She might. She was in it from the beginning, whereas Jake claims he only found out later." Her mouth twisted. "He could be lying."

Rey nodded. "I'll push her, see what I can get. It's pretty clear that none of the Sun Coast investors were involved, or that they had any idea how their money was being used. It's not a guarantee, and it could still cost these people a lot of time and money if they have to hire lawyers to defend themselves."

"How could they have done this to their friends?"

"Greed," Rey said.

"What about the hotel's involvement? Sean and Celine. Do you have enough evidence to arrest them?"

Rey's jaw hardened. "Not yet. I'm sure once we have Copeland's statement we will. In the meantime, I have agents watching the wife in case she tries to run. There's no sign of the other one. He left a couple days ago."

He had left with Harry, Becca remembered but said nothing. She owed it to Harry to keep him out of this if she could.

"What about Candice?" She asked instead. "Candice had to have known what John was up to, even if she didn't know he was about to betray her."

"There's no evidence. Nothing has ever come up on any wiretap or piece of paper that named her. So, unless something new turns up, it looks like she's in the clear, too."

Becca scowled, "It's not fair."

"I hate to be the one to burst your bubble, but life isn't fair."

Becca made a face, and he laughed. "Did you get a flight?"

"Yeah, to Nassau and then on to Miami. I'll have to rent a car and drive home from there, but I can't wait to get back."

"Will your son live with you there… when he's done with all of this?"

"I doubt it. He has school, and frankly, things haven't been fantastic between us this last year." She grimaced. "I was a little crazy overprotective—I'm working on it. Remembering how I felt when Katie told me she had kidnapped him really messed me up for a while. Even though it wasn't true, I couldn't shake the fear that something was going to happen to him." She snorted. "This experience kinda reinforces it."

"True," Rey said slowly. "He's been through something pretty traumatic, too. Being accused of murder couldn't have been easy for him. He's going to push you away, but hang in there. He is going to need his mom."

Becca forced a nonchalant smile. "You're right. Well, I guess this is goodbye." She extended her hand, but then dropped it and blew out a breath. If she didn't ask now, she would regret it. "Why didn't you ever ask me about Harry leaving the resort the day after the murder? You implied the evening of my dinner... when you said, "I should keep my ears open"... that you were lumping Harry in with the rest of them. If you thought Harry was involved why didn't you ask me where he had gone?"

Rey had a curious expression. "Brennan told me he was leaving, and at the time there was no way I could legally stop him."

Becca's mouth fell open.

What? Harry was furious about finding out Rey was an FBI agent. Why in the world would he volunteer to Rey that he was leaving? I'm missing something.

"When did he tell you that?"

This doesn't make any sense at all!

Rey's eyes hooded. "He came to me later that same morning, the morning we questioned both of you. He said he was leaving and asked me to keep an eye on you."

"What does that even mean? Why would he say that? If he was worried, he could have stayed and done it himself."

He should have told her what he was doing with Sean. But Harry hadn't wanted to. He wanted to get it over with and away from her as fast as he could. Becca ignored the stabbing pains in her chest.

"Who knows?" Something about Rey's demeanor made her think he was lying.

"Level with me." She had to ask, even if she was afraid of what he would say. The back-and-forth jibes and innuendos had become too much. She needed the truth.

Rey's body stilled, but he waited silently for her to find the words.

"Is Harry a criminal? You keep saying he is..." Her stomach clenched.

"Losing faith already?"

"Don't tease me, Rey. I helped you with this. I even got you a better witness! I deserve an answer! Do you have proof that

Harry was involved in any of his father's business schemes or any crimes of his own?"

Rey ran a hand over his mouth, and Becca felt her nails bite into her palm. "There's been no actual evidence that Harry Brennan was involved with any of his father's business enterprises, and there are no current investigations that I am aware of."

Becca sagged with relief.

"But," Rey obviously was unwilling to let Harry have a complete pass, "there's no proof that he isn't either. Your boyfriend associates with a lot of bad people, and typically the only people who do business with criminals are other criminals."

"So, you don't know then. It's just conjecture."

Rey searched her eyes. "Why are you looking for absolution from me, sweetheart? I'm not your father. You don't have to make excuses for the guy you're dating."

Becca flushed. "I'm not... we're not... I don't think... I just needed to know. Ever since I first met him, people have made comments. Things are a little up in the air with us right now."

Becca thought she had known Harry. But he hadn't told her his father was alive or about the threat to Owen. And there was still Celine's weird comment about, "Harry Brennan not being an enemy one wanted," to work out. Yet he had been upset with her that she hadn't told him the truth about Rey. Why couldn't he see the double standard? She could understand him being upset that Sean blackmailed him over Owen, but that hadn't been her fault or a result of anything she had done! Instead of talking to her about it, he had wiped his hands of her and left. He said that he loved her, but he hadn't been willing to fight for what they had.

"You're the one that said I'm a terrible judge of character," Becca finally said aloud.

"Look, I think Brennan walks right up to the line, but I don't know if he has crossed it; people like that, it's only a matter of time. It's in their nature."

"I don't believe that, but it doesn't matter anymore." Becca reached for her bag. "Bye, Rey."

"For now, but I imagine I'll be seeing you around. You can't seem to keep yourself out of trouble."

"You're hilarious," she said dryly. Sarcasm aside, it felt odd to be saying goodbye to Rey after everything they had been through in the last year. They weren't friends. Allies? She wasn't clear on what to call it, but they'd been through two life-changing experiences, and that brought a closeness she couldn't ignore. The thought that this was the last time she would see him made her a little teary.

What is wrong with me? The events of the last several days flashed lightning fast through her brain. *Oh yeah, I guess being a little emotional is understandable. My nerves are shot!*

"In all seriousness, I'm coming out of the field for a while. I've been under a long time, and I think I'm ready to get back to a regular nine to five life," Rey said.

"I have a hard time picturing that." She laughed, happy to break the weird mood.

"Me, too. I'll most likely be at the Miami Bureau. It might feel like a vacation compared to the last few years. Maybe I'll check in on you now and then."

"That would be nice." She stuck her hand out again, and said playfully, "In that case, I guess instead of goodbye, I'll say see ya!"

Rey looked from her hand to her face, and before she realized what was happening, he grasped her hand and pulled her hard against his chest, his mouth moving over hers.

Her brain caught up a few seconds, (okay, if she were honest, several seconds) after her lips. To her surprise, she found herself responding to the embrace. Her brain kicked in, and when she pulled back, Rey instantly released her. Becca pressed her fingers to her lips.

What the what?

"I've wanted to do that for a long time."

"I... I'm..." Her brain was reeling.

It was a nice kiss. Did she want Rey to kiss her? She didn't *not* want Rey to kiss her... I'm still in shock, that must be it she decided. *Coward.*

Rey picked up her bag and handed it to her. "See you around."

"Rey," she swallowed. "I'm not... a couple days ago... I don't even know if it's really over."

Shut your mouth, Becca.

"It's fine." He sounded like he meant it. "I probably should apologize for kissing you like that... but I'm not going to." He winked.

Not knowing what to say in response, Becca simply walked away to the front doors of the lobby where her shuttle was supposed to pick her up. She turned at the last second to see that Rey was still watching. He gave her a little wave, and Becca raised her hand in return.

"Ma'am?" Becca jumped at the man's voice close behind her. "Are you Mrs. Copeland?" the hotel shuttle driver asked.

Becca flushed. "Oh, yes. Sorry." She didn't look back again.

It's not disloyal, she assured herself. Harry had left her. He hadn't answered a single phone call or text message from her in several days, despite knowing he had left her in limbo with John recently murdered. Besides, who wouldn't feel something when a handsome man kissed her, she reasoned. Still, when she closed her eyes and leaned her head against the tiny window to look at the wisps of white on the ocean thousands of feet below, it was Harry that she thought of. Her chest ached as the memories flooded back. She was so angry at him and herself. She couldn't believe he had given up so easily. Becca shifted in her seat, trying to get comfortable.

He'll see reason eventually. He said he loved me. Harry isn't going to throw us away over this? Right?

Lights shone out of Becca's cottage when she finally got home. She set her bag down inside the door and sniffed the fragrant air, as she called out, "Hello?"

"I'm back here."

Becca followed the sound of Amelia's voice to the kitchen at the back of the house. To her surprise, she found Amelia sitting at Becca's tiny kitchen table, feeding bits of chicken to Furball, who sat regally next to her on top of the table.

"Wow! She's inside?"

"We couldn't wait any longer, we were starving," Amelia said, standing. She went to the oven and pulled out a platter full of roast chicken, potatoes, and carrots. "I had to do something to kill the time while I waited."

Becca was bemused. "I didn't expect you to be here, but I'm glad you are." She really was. On the long drive back from the Miami airport, she hadn't looked forward to returning to an empty house. "Chicken?"

Amelia folded her hands in front of her. "You've had a long week. I thought you might want some comfort food." Amelia's eyes flicked sideways toward the doors that led to the bedrooms.

"What is it?"

Amelia pursed her lips. "I didn't say anything before... you were already dealing with so much over there." Amelia threw her hands up. "Argh. I'm terrible at this!"

Becca's stomach sank. It was going to be something unpleasant. "I have to say I was shocked, I won't lie, when Eduardo called and told me to be here to accept the shipment." Amelia's eyes flashed with anger before swiftly turning sympathetic when they met Becca's. "For what it's worth, Eduardo sounded just as uncomfortable. He didn't say it, but I could tell."

Becca flushed red. Her luggage and painting supplies. That was what Amelia was referring to. *It's humiliating!* A wave of anger swamped her. Somehow until that moment, she hadn't really believed that Harry was serious when he said he would send her things home, that she wouldn't talk to him again, that she would never go back to the villa where they'd spent so many days and nights wrapped in each other's arms, happier than she thought she would ever be again. She would never get the chance to tell Harry that she loved him. She made an inarticulate sound that she tried to cover with a cough.

"I don't know what's gotten into him! I've never seen him the way he was with you—"

"Amelia, stop." She burned with embarrassment. It was bad enough that she had been dumped, but to hear how wonderful it had been was too much.

Amelia gave an exasperated huff and carried the platter to the table. "I'm just saying, I'm so—"

"Stop!" Becca's voice was louder than she intended. She took a deep breath. "I don't want to talk about it… right now," she said to appease the older woman, who crossed her arms over her chest. "Not tonight."

Becca retrieved a wine glass from the cabinet and poured from the open bottle on the table. She smiled. "This food looks delicious, and I'm starving, too." It was a lie. Becca wasn't sure how she was going to eat past the lump in her throat. Becca closed her eyes briefly against the pain in her chest. *I should have told him.*

When she opened them, Amelia patted her hand once and said brightly, "All right, then! Let me tell you about the idiots I have working for me at the Oar! You wouldn't believe these bartenders! If they aren't all over each other, they are hitting on all the tourists. Of course, I didn't hire such attractive people for nothing. It's packed in there every day."

Becca let Amelia's chatter wash over her as she sipped her wine. In the morning, she realized she hadn't heard a word.

25

While she waited for her coffee to brew, Becca forced herself to open the door to the tiny, guest room where Amelia had stored the things shipped from Turtle Bay. Becca stared at her luggage, boxes of art supplies, and the canvases all wrapped for shipping. Somehow, the careful deliberateness with which her things were packed stung her pride. She would have preferred to think that Harry had thrown it all together at the height of emotion, that he was as upset as she was. But it was Eduardo and Marta, she reminded herself. He hadn't even done that himself.

She had been wrong about what they shared. His rules for the people in his life were so rigid, there wasn't space for anything that didn't go according to plan or for anyone to make a mistake. He wanted a perfect person, and that didn't exist. She had been a fool to let herself get so carried away. Becca refused to think of how hopeful she had been when she left on the trip with Harry and now…

The cat suddenly jumped onto the boxes in front of her, letting out an insistent yowl. Becca chuckled. "Hey, Furball, you're a full-on pet now, huh? Okay, let's go see what we can give you for breakfast."

Becca was happy to see that, thanks to Amelia, the cat had recently acquired a food and water bowl. A few cat toys were scattered across the sitting room in front of the sofa. After the cat had eaten, she jumped up to join Becca on the sofa. "What magic did Amelia work on you? I guess I shouldn't be surprised. She did the same for me." Becca scratched the cat's ears, remembering all the ways Amelia had helped her start over. "Speaking of..." Becca pulled out her cell phone and called the owner of the gallery where she worked to let her know she was back from her extended vacation a couple of days earlier than expected. Dana sounded surprised, but thankfully had not asked any questions. Becca was sure Dana would try to worm the details out of her next time they were together. Since she hadn't been expected back and the shifts were covered, her boss encouraged her to keep working on the paintings she was hoping to exhibit in a few months.

Becca ended the call and made a face at the closed door of the guest bedroom. Not yet. She picked up her phone again, stalling the inevitable unpacking, by making phone calls to Owen and his lawyer to check on their progress with the case. It relieved her to hear Owen was safely in a hotel with his father, though he wasn't allowed to tell her where it was. She didn't like the implication when Owen mentioned their protection detail, but she was happy to hear Rey was with them.

"We are meeting with the prosecutor in a couple days to give my official witness statement, and then I'm done. Rey said they think they'll have enough after that meeting to get a warrant for Nicole's arrest." Owen sounded sad. "Dad's a wreck, but he's trying to pretend like he's not."

"This isn't your fault, Owen. She made the choices that put her in this position."

"Yeah, I know. Rey keeps saying that, too. It's just... that's not the person I..." he trailed off. "Do you think I could come down there to stay with you for a few days while I figure everything out? I don't want to go back to the house until Nicole's... gone. I can't face her."

"Of course! I'd love to have you here as long as you want."

"Not for too long. I have school. The semester is going to be starting in a few weeks," he said in a rush. "I can stay with a friend, until..."

Becca swallowed, not trusting her voice. What he said wasn't a surprise but it still hurt.

"You understand right, Mom? It's not that I don't want to see you, it's just... school is there and my friends."

Becca forced herself to sound cheerful. "Of course, I understand. I have some extra money this year from a few of the paintings I sold. If you don't ever want to go back to your dad's house... I could help you get an apartment."

"Thanks, Mom. Let's see how it goes over the next couple of weeks." He hesitated, and even though she couldn't see him, she sensed the tension on the other end. "You wouldn't ever consider moving back, would you? To Sun Coast?"

It broke her heart to disappoint him. Was she being a terrible mom? Should she move back to be there as a support for him? Becca chewed on her lip. She loved the life she had created in Key West, and going back to Sun Coast...

"No, I don't think so, sweetie. I'm sorry. I will always come the second you need me, but I can't make it my home again. I'm so sorry."

There was a pause, and then Owen said lightly, "It's okay, Mom. Really." He let out a little laugh. "Having my own place might be cool. Besides," she heard the smile in his voice, "you've got Harry down there. I haven't always been the nicest to him, but I can see how happy you are. I'm glad everything's going well for at least one member of our family," he joked.

Becca's throat closed. She couldn't tell him, not now that he had all these other things going on. "Yeah, Harry's great."

"I better go. Call you tomorrow! Love you."

"Love you, too." Becca slumped back into the couch with a groan. Her life had definitely not turned out the way she thought it would... again.

She frowned. The words echoed in her head, and she could almost hear Amelia's voice saying, "There's no such thing as a happily ever after. It's one adventure after another, and you accept that it's not always going to be sunshine."

Her show was coming up, and this would be her first opportunity to display her work to such a large audience. She wished... Becca took a gulp of her coffee. Nope, she was done with the what ifs. She had called and texted Harry enough—with no response. It was over, and she needed to move on. It wasn't as if this was the first time her heart had been broken.

Okay, Becca, time to get on with it!

Becca snatched her hand away from her chest realizing she had been unconsciously rubbing where it ached. Becca stood and squared her shoulders. This was *her* life, *her* adventure, and she wasn't about to let some stupid boy ruin it. Besides, she needed to clear the guest room for Owen.

Becca moved several of the boxes of art supplies Harry had purchased for the trip into the closet. Maybe I'll donate them to a school, she thought. The partially done paintings were a different story. She tore the plastic away from the largest canvas revealing Petunia, the giant sea turtle. Memories of the day flooded back, but she refused to give into them. She was proud of the work she had done, and she would not stop just because of memories.

Becca carried the large canvas to the easel she kept at the window in the front of the house. Her lips in a tight line, she mixed colors on her palette and picked up her brush. She breathed deeply through her nose. If she had learned nothing else over the last few years, it was that her future was hers to choose.

Owen's statement ended up taking longer than any of them had thought. It was almost two weeks later when Becca's phone rang as she walked home from picking up groceries.

"He's all done," Rey said. "He has completely fulfilled his obligations to the government, so he is free to move on. Owen shouldn't have any future problems with this."

"That is the best news I have heard in a long time."

"I have more. I thought I'd drive him down to your place tomorrow. Be there before dinner."

"Seriously? That is amazing! Thank you."

Becca approached the little gate to her garden, juggling the bags in her arms as she tried to navigate the latch and keep the phone to her ear. Amelia waved a glass of wine from the porch, and Becca smiled in return. Things were finally going to get back to normal.

"I'll put something together for us to eat." She paused, self-conscious under Amelia's curious gaze. "Call me tomorrow and let me know what time you'll be here. The gallery closes at five, or I could leave a key out?"

"Will do. See you soon, Nancy Drew."

"Bye." Becca almost squealed with excitement!

Amelia arched her brows in question.

"Owen's coming tomorrow."

"Yay! That's glorious news! Hope you don't mind." She lifted her glass. "Need help with those?"

"Yes, please! I'm about to drop these bags."

Amelia set her glass on the little porch table and came to take the bags from where they were precariously tucked in the crook of Becca's arm. "Oh good, you got more wine! Ice cream!" Amelia exclaimed, peering into the bags as she hurried into the house. Becca frowned as her phone pinged with an incoming text message. She didn't recognize the number. Her finger hovered for a second. Text spam ads had become so bad lately, but the attached image symbol intrigued her. She clicked on the image and froze. There, in the rectangle of her phone, was a picture of Harry, his arms around another woman. Becca's breath caught painfully in her chest. She jabbed at the phone to close the picture and looked again at the number. Who would send this to her?

"Do you want a glass?" Becca heard Amelia call from inside the house. Becca opened her mouth, but no sound came out. As she stared at the phone, it rang out with three more tones in rapid fire succession, showing that three more images came in.

Don't open them. Better not to know.

Becca wrapped an arm around her stomach as she opened the photos. Each showed Harry, in separate locations with different clothes on, indicating three distinct days. The one constant was that, in each, there was a different beautiful woman with him. At an outdoor dinner, in formal attire... kissing. Bile rose in her throat, but instead of throwing her phone across the porch like she wanted to, she closed the photos and tucked the phone into her pocket. Squaring her shoulders, she joined Amelia in her kitchen.

"What were you doing out there?" the older woman asked.

Through a fog, it registered that Amelia was holding out a wine glass to her.

"Sorry," Becca said, shaking her head to clear it.

"Are you all right? You're really pale." Amelia reached toward her, but Becca pulled back with a smile.

She wasn't sure she could hold it together if her friend touched her. She wanted to scream and cry, but she wouldn't. "I'm fine. I forgot to eat today is all. Let me put these away, and I'll make us something." Her voice sounded normal. *That's odd,* she thought, *because I'm pretty sure my heart is lying outside on the sidewalk where it fell out.* Becca braced her hands against the counter.

That's it then. It was a fun fling while it lasted, nothing more.

Becca remembered a conversation she had with Harry last

fall, when she told him that she wasn't interested in being one of the many women that he visited, depending on which port he was at. It really wasn't fair. She had done what everyone had advised—finally let go and dived in headfirst, only to find out she was right after all. Their relationship hadn't been different, or special. Within a couple of weeks he had moved on—repeatedly it would appear.

"How about a salad?" Becca heard herself ask, not waiting for Amelia to answer before she began throwing lettuce angrily into a bowl. She yanked open the refrigerator to get the dressing, making the items on the door rattle.

"Are you sure you're okay?"

"Hunky dory... Damn!" In her anger, she had poured too much dressing on to the greens. She heaved a heavy sigh and stared at the ruined salad.

Amelia peered over her shoulder at the salad soup Becca had made. "No offense, honey, but let's order something." Amelia patted her on the shoulder, and then turned Becca to face her. "You're trembling. What's going on? Is something wrong with Owen?"

Becca shook her head.

This is so embarrassing. Get it together!

"Oh, honey, something is definitely wrong! It's written all over your face! Tell me."

Becca swallowed hard, pulled out her phone, and opened the text thread with the pictures. She held it out so Amelia could see.

"Son of a..." Amelia's jaw dropped open. "Who sent you this?"

"I have no idea, but it doesn't matter."

"What on the ever-loving earth is that boy doing?"

"I think it's pretty clear." Becca couldn't keep the bitterness out of her voice.

Amelia scowled at the photos but used her fingers to enlarge them.

Becca turned away, not interested in seeing the details of the voluptuous blonde leaning over a dinner table, giving Harry an unobstructed view of her navel.

"They took this one without them knowing," Amelia murmured. "It's obviously from across the street, but the others look like shots of different society pages from Caribbean newspapers," Amelia squinted. "I recognize that hotel. It's in St. Barts."

Becca snatched the salad bowls and dumped the ruined food into the trash. "If you don't mind, I really don't want to talk about it."

"But there has to be a reason someone sent these to you!" Amelia shook the phone at her. "Whoever it is went to the trouble of finding the pictures in a newspaper or whatever. The one at dinner looks like someone was spying on him. That takes effort. Who would be so cruel to you?"

A catalogue of the faces of people who were unhappy with her flashed through Becca's mind—Nicole, Candice, Celine, Sean? Rey told her that after Jake's testimony a warrant had been issued for the couple, but even with an agent watching Celine, they had disappeared. The resort had been seized and was under a court-appointed administrator while Sean's family tried to prove their innocence in his scheme.

Becca shook her head. "It doesn't matter why someone sent them. What's in the pictures speaks for itself. Harry has moved on. It's fine." Becca forced her jaw to relax. The last thing she needed was a cracked tooth!

"But—"

"Amelia, he could have sent them himself. As a way of telling me to let go."

"That's ridiculous! Why would he do that?"

Becca would die before she admitted that she had called and texted Harry a few times over the last couple of weeks... without response. "Look, I don't know who sent them, and I probably never will. But it's obviously a message someone thought I needed, and frankly, it's for the best." Becca almost convinced herself she was telling the truth.

Amelia's face was thunderous. "This is nonsense! I don't know what this is, but... but... but this is nonsense! Even when Harry was young and wild, he never let his photo be taken. He hates publicity. We should call the number!"

Becca snatched the phone out of Amelia's hands. "Things change."

"No! He's different with you. He's never let anyone in the way he did with you," Amelia insisted, crossing her arms over her chest. "Something isn't right about this. It's not like you to not want answers!"

Becca was suddenly exhausted, and her shoulders sagged. "Maybe not, Amelia, but I'm done. I'm not chasing after a man who has made it clear he wants nothing to do with me." Becca softened her voice. "You love him, Amelia, and I never want what happened between him and me to affect that. I didn't come to Key West looking for a new man. I came to take control of my own life." Her mouth shaped into a wistful smile. "It was a lovely romantic adventure while it lasted, but the fact that it didn't work out doesn't mean it's the end of my life. Aren't you the one who told me I needed to embrace my new life—the good with the bad?"

Amelia scowled, but then she relaxed. "It's really annoying when you quote me."

"I bet." Becca smiled. "Now, do you want to order dinner and see what's on *Bravo* tonight?" Amelia hesitated, and for a brief second Becca worried her friend would not let the subject drop.

"Sounds good... but no salad."

Becca ordered the food and plopped on the couch with her wine and the remote.

"You're almost done. I like it."

Becca looked over to where Amelia was examining Petunia. Around the large canvas sat several smaller paintings, but Petunia still sat unfinished. There wasn't much left to do. Becca had struggled with completing the painting. Every time she began to make the final strokes, she found herself distracted by memories. Becca had put the painting to the side and created several smaller pictures for her show, but the large canvas had loomed, not just in the room, but in her mind. It felt as if when she was done with the painting, then she was done with...

"What did you get us? I'm starving."

"Chinese."

"Egg rolls?" Amelia asked as she joined Becca on the couch, stretching her legs across Becca's lap.

"Of course."

"I hope it's that cute delivery guy." Amelia wiggled into the soft cushions until she was comfortable. "Maybe I should get a house, too. I can't stretch out like this on the boat."

"You'd sell the boat?" Becca asked, surprised.

"Huh. Of course not." Amelia looked around Becca's cozy home. "I could get something like this, for when I feel like being landlocked."

Becca rolled her eyes. "Or you could just come here."

"Humph."

Later that evening, after Amelia had kissed her cheek goodnight, Becca stared at the painting of Petunia lit by moonlight streaming through the window. It was time.

She retrieved her phone and pulled up the awful pictures again. She swiped her finger across each image to delete them as well as the number that had texted her. Then, before she could change her mind, she deleted Harry's contact information as well.

Moonlight had given way to dawn by the time Becca set her brush down. Exhausted and bleary-eyed, she felt a sense of satisfaction she hadn't in weeks. Becca glanced at the clock and realized she had a couple of hours left before she had to get ready for work. She would need at least a little sleep before Owen and Rey arrived that evening.

Standing back, she took in the blue and green swirls that covered the painting. Becca had expanded the water in the painting so that it covered almost the whole canvas. Petunia's head peeked through the sea, coming up for air amid the waves, while gray and white clouds hovered on the horizon, signaling an approaching storm. Becca smiled. Petunia would keep swimming, and so would she.

Before you close the book—Please consider leaving me a review!

Reader reviews are powerful! They are the only thing many other readers will consider before picking up a book. A review from you would mean everything to me!

Would you like to recieve my quarterly newsletter? Newsletter recipients get the first look at covers, extra scenes, early access to chapters, and news about upcoming books.

If you would like to be included, go to: https://katebreit feller.com/contact/

Or follow my author page on Amazon: https://www. amazon.com/Kate-Breitfeller/e/B07R9XVR55

TURN THE PAGE FOR A SNEAK PEEK OF BECCA'S NEXT ADVENTURE!

Becca Swims On Available July 15, 2022

BECCA SWIMS ON

"So why are we here again?"

Becca lifted her champagne glass to hide her smile. "I told you. Dana has the flu, so I had to fill in tonight. It's an important fundraiser for *Art for Kids*. Dana has put so much work into it, and I'm hosting a workshop for the kids' next event. Besides," she tried not to giggle as Rey tugged at the collar of his tuxedo again, "you look nice and it's an open bar."

Rey grunted. "True. Not sure how you convinced me to put on this rig though." Becca's lip curled up.

"It's a good cause, and I told you black tie was required. You didn't have to come."

"Huh. You promised you'd make me wings for the game next weekend." Becca took another sip of her drink and rolled her eyes. Rey might complain, but there was no denying he looked impressive in the formal wear.

"So I did. C'mon, I need to make the rounds and represent the gallery. You can just smile and be my handsome date."

"Fine. I'm going to hit the bar first for something stronger."

Becca smiled. "Okay. I'm going to head down to the water and start with those groups. I'll come find you in a bit."

Rey nodded. "I'll come as soon as I get a drink. Do you want anything?"

"I'm good. I'm having a hard enough time staying upright as it is." She gestured with her half-empty flute at her high heels. "I'm out of practice."

"I like them." Rey grinned appreciatively. "See you in a few minutes."

Becca walked across the coquina patio of the mansion to the steps that led down to a large yard and an infinity pool that disappeared into Biscayne Bay. Carefully navigating the steps, she walked gingerly to a group of guests by the water's edge. Becca didn't know most of the guests but she recognized Barbara Ellison, "Bunny" to her friends on the charity circuit, as one of the women in the group.

"Becca!" The older woman greeted her warmly.

"I'm sorry to interrupt, Bunny, but I wanted to come say hi. Dana was so disappointed she wasn't able to make it tonight."

Bunny made a face. "I heard she was unwell. It's a shame because I really wanted to introduce her around. There are some heavy hitters here tonight." She winked conspiratorially at Becca. The three others in the group chuckled, clearly used to Bunny's forthrightness. "Let me introduce you to my friends. I'd love for you to tell them about the work you and Dana are doing for *Art for Kids*."

Becca put on her best social smile. She wanted to do a good job not just for Dana, but because Becca loved helping the at-risk kids and sharing her love of art with them. Bunny introduced her to the two young women and the older man that stood with her.

"Allison's date is around here somewhere, but Richard here is the one you want to talk to." Bunny bestowed an expectant smile at the man who gave a good-natured chuckle.

"It's why we are here after all." The man smiled. Becca was a little uncomfortable that both Richard and Bunny had dismissed the two young women, but she would just have to bite her tongue and play their social game tonight. "Tell me about this gallery of yours and what you do for the charity?"

Becca took a calming breath and then began explaining her role and why she felt that the *Art for Kids* charity benefitted their South Florida community. When her boss, Dana had told her she would need to attend the event, Becca had put together a succinct pitch, and she fully expected to repeat it several times over the evening.

She was just finishing up her speech when the young woman Bunny had introduced as Allison suddenly smiled, her face lighting up.

"Oh, thank god! I'm parched." Becca felt someone walk up behind her, close enough that he almost brushed her arm, as a glass of wine was extended past her. Becca's neck tingled, and she felt her breath freeze in her chest. Even before he spoke, she knew it was him.

"Sorry, there was a line at the bar." Harry's deep voice rumbled.

Sheer will kept Becca's smile in place, and she concentrated on not letting her legs buckle beneath her. She hadn't heard from Harry since the day he had walked away from her at the resort in the Bahamas—dumping her.

Becca forced herself to look at him with her social mask in place. He had moved so that he stood next to the gorgeous young woman, his arm around her tiny waist. The stab of pain in her chest took her by surprise, followed instantly by anger for caring. Harry was watching her, his green eyes unreadable and his face blank. Was he going to pretend like he didn't know her? Is he worried about his girlfriend she wondered, which only fueled her anger. She would be damned if he was going to pretend she didn't exist.

"Hello, Harry. It's been a long time. You look well."

Understatement of the century. He is just as sexy as ever, more so in a tux! Dang it!

If she hadn't been doing her own examination of him, she would have missed the way his eyes heated as they took in her tight black dress. When she'd first tried on the dress she'd borrowed from Dana, she had worried it was too tight. Dana had laughed. "You'll be fine, trust me. It's Miami. There will be much more revealing dresses there."

"Oh, you know each other?" Bunny asked, surprised.

Harry stayed silent, his eyes still on Becca.

"Yes, we've met," Becca finally said.

"Here you are! I've been looking for you." Rey's voice was loud, breaking the odd tension that had taken over the group. "Babe, I just got a call from the office. I need to go in. I'm sorry to tear you away so early."

Harry glanced down to where Rey had put a proprietary hand in the small of her back. "Agent Foster." Harry's voice was glacial.

"Brennan." Rey's voice was almost jovial in comparison to Harry's, and Becca guessed he did it on purpose to irritate Harry. "Who would have thought we would run in to you here. Sorry though, no time to play catch-up." He smiled at Becca and met her eyes. "I need to cut our evening short."

Becca caught his lifeline. "Bunny, I'm so sorry that I need to go, but when you're with the FBI…"

Bunny smiled. "I understand. And don't worry, I'll get Richard here to get his checkbook out before he leaves."

With a brief smile and a round of nice to meet yous, Becca turned and began to walk back to the mansion. Rey's hand on her back kept her moving, one foot in front of the other. When she stumbled on the first step, she was grateful when he caught her elbow and tucked her hand around his arm.

"You are shaking like a leaf." His voice was laced with concern but he kept it low so only she could hear.

"Was it obvious… back there?"

"No, I don't think so, but you'd have to be blind not to see there was something going on between the two of you."

"Good."

Rey steered her past the crowds and back through the house keeping hold of her hand until the valet brought his truck around. Becca clicked her seatbelt in place and closed her eyes.

"What the hell is he doing here?"

ACKNOWLEDGMENTS

Thank you so much to everyone who has been so supportive of this book! I foolishly thought writing the second book would be easier than the first... I was wrong!!!

I want to give special thanks to my niece and nephews Eric, David and Sky for being so encouraging and helpful and to my sisters who are always willing to take time out of their busy lives to help me.

Thank you to Mariella—for listening to my insanity even though you aren't biologically required to, and for helping me get through some seriously, sticky plot points.

To my supercalifragilisticexpialidocious awesome editors-proof, copy, concept and line—this book would literally not exist without you!

Thank you to my amazing beta readers for all of your helpful feedback. It helps more than you know!

Jason, Nick and Jack—thank you for always listening to me whine, complain, talk about murder and generally freak out at random times, as I try to keep my timelines and clues straight. You have always encouraged me and believed in me even when I didn't have faith in myself. I love you.

ABOUT THE AUTHOR

Kate Breitfeller writes character driven romantic mysteries, perfect for an escape from reality. *Becca Jumps Ship*, Book 1 of her Caribbean series was published in 2020. Kate has written nonfiction as well as several published articles dedicated to the antics of her family.

Kate currently lives on the Space Coast of Florida with her husband, two sons, and rescue dog, Charlie. Whenever she gets a chance, Kate escapes to the beach with a good book and a fruity cocktail.

Kate loves talking to her readers and you can find her at all of these places:

www.Katebreitfeller.com

 facebook.com/Katebreitfellerwrites

twitter.com/katebreit

 instagram.com/katebreit

 amazon.com/kate-breitfeller

ALSO BY KATE BREITFELLER

The Caribbean Series

Becca Jumps Ship

Becca Dives In

Becca Swims On

Made in the USA
Coppell, TX
25 August 2022

82086346R00177